Into A Heart of Darl
By Robert Mellott

Published by Robert M

Copyright 2014 (Robert Mellott)

Cover Design by Robert Mellott and Brad Robison
Cover Photo Illustration by Brad Robison

To Trisha, Miguel and Dawn

Chapter 1

"This is the last time." Grace told her mother.

"Ok, Grace."

"I mean it; I want out, I am telling Leopold I am done." Grace said forcefully.

"I know Grace, but you know it's not that easy. He will never let us out."

"I am tired of moving all the time; I just want to live a normal life. I want to go back home." Grace said with a sigh.

"You know we will never be able to do that."

"Maybe they forgot." Grace said in despair.

"I'm afraid not Grace, you'll have to wait at least another fifteen years for that."

With that they loaded up the car with the last of their belongings and headed to their new home.

Dawn woke up to the alarm going off again, and she pressed the snooze again. She had to count the times that she pressed snooze or she knew that she would be late, again. Just like her though she fell back asleep only to be awakened by her father pounding on her door and telling her to wake up or she would miss the bus, again. Dawn's father repeatedly hit the door and yelled out her name until he heard the signal.

"I'm getting up."

"I will believe that when you open this door." Her father replied.

Soon he heard the door unlock and opened to see Dawn's sleepy face.

"Good morning Sunshine."

"Yeah right"

"Get ready for school and don't go back to sleep."

"Ok, I won't."

"Have a good day; I have to get to work. I love you."

"I love you too." She replied as she entered the bathroom.

Mr. Sinclair would have liked to leave right then and there, but Dawn wasn't the most trust worthy in the morning and he wanted to make sure that she was going to get ready for school.

After waiting a few minutes Dawn was out again and heading to her bed room.

"Get ready for school, OK."

"I am.

As he went to leave he heard the alarm go off in his bedroom bringing his wife out of her sleep. Dawn heard it too and she knew that she better get her act together and get ready for school. Dawn wasn't always the most reliable in the morning; in fact she wasn't a morning person at all. She tried but it just seemed that she couldn't get up and running for about an hour. She tried to hurry to get ready and get her breakfast started before her mother came down stairs.

Dawn's mother tried to keep chaos in the house down to a minimum and chaos always seemed to reign in the Sinclair house in the morning. She set up a schedule for Dawn to keep, in order to keep her on time for the bus in the morning. Dawn knew that she had to be ready and finished before her mother came down if she was going to get to eat breakfast. She put on her clothes, combed her hair and rushed on some makeup.

"Oh crud." She thought to herself as she heard her mother's bedroom door open.

She finished what she was doing and rushed out to the kitchen. She hastily found a bowl and spoon and poured herself some cereal from the first box she could find. She added the milk and sat down.

"Dawn, don't eat that, it's stale." Her mother said just as she started to eat the first spoonful. A look of disgust came across Dawn's face as she tasted the old cereal. Her mother couldn't hold back her laughter as she looked at Dawn.

"Don't you dare spit that out, swallow it."

Dawn swallowed it very hesitantly.

"If you would get up in time and not just grab anything in the cupboard you might not eat stuff like that." Her mother scolded her.

At that remark Dawn knew that her mother was on to when she got up and that she was caught. Dawn never could seem to pull one over on her mother, even though she often tried. She often found it fun, like a cat and mouse game.

"Throw that out, it's almost time to go."

"But I didn't get anything to eat."

"Have a banana; it's not my fault that you don't get up when you should."

She finished the banana just in time to see that the bus was coming down the street.

"Dawn, you better get out there, hurry up!"

Dawn grabbed her book bag and ran for the door. Dawn's mother stopped her before she left.

"I love you, have a good day." Her mother told her as she gave her a hug.

"I love you too Mom, see you later."

With that Dawn ran out to catch the oncoming bus. Dawn found her seat next to Rebecca and the bus started back towards the high school. The excitement level on the bus was high and Rebecca could hardly contain herself. Dawn could see how excited she was but didn't want to start a conversation with her. Rebecca had the habit of talking and talking and talking until they actually arrived at school. She was really a nice girl but Dawn didn't need her morning babble about everything and everyone this morning. The bus ride was without incident as they headed the two miles to Saratoga Springs High School. Rebecca said very little realizing that Dawn was just not in the mood for conversation. As the bus stopped and they all exited the atmosphere was festive and everyone was counting the seconds until the last period bell would ring, like horses ready to leap out of the gate when the horn sounded. The last day of school was always a time of celebration. A three month hiatus from the prison called school. Everyone had great plans of doing something other than homework or hopes of a family vacation. Dawn on the other hand had some apprehensions about the day. Being out of school for the summer meant that she would be home during the day. That always meant some additional chore for her to perform and lately being home wasn't what Dawn wanted to do.

It wasn't that Dawn didn't like her life or home; it was just lately that her Mother and Father didn't seem to be doing so well. Their marriage seemed to be under more stress than usual. She was really concerned that her parents might end up getting a divorce. Even though her parents tried to shield her from their fighting and arguments she wasn't blind to the fact that their marriage was in trouble. It kept Dawn up at nights sometimes. She really didn't know what would happen if her parents got a divorce. She often thought that the reason that they stayed together was her and that they were waiting till she moved out in order to separate. She often prayed that they would work out their problems and find the love that brought them together in the first place. So while the rest of the school celebrated all Dawn did was worry and fret.

At the sound of the bell the school released its prisoners and the students ran to their buses or headed off down the streets to their houses. Well at least those who knew that they had passed.

Dawn headed to her bus; Rebecca was already there and had already started on her daily rant before she even had a chance to sit down.

"We're done with school and I passed!" Rebecca exclaimed.

"Did you?"

"Did I what?" Dawn replied.

"Did you pass?"

"Yes, I didn't want to die young, if I failed, my parents would kill me."

Rebecca started to ramble on and on like she always did, Dawn blocked out Rebecca and started to think about her life. She watched the houses roll past and within a few minutes they were at Dawn's house and the bus stopped to let her off.

"Have a good summer Rebecca."

"You too Dawn, see you around."

Dawn got her stuff and headed off the bus and up the side walk to the front door. She was glad to see that no one was home yet and that she would have a minute or two to herself. When Dawn was alone she often times would become overwhelmed with emotion and start to cry. It wasn't that she was sad all the time it was just a release of her emotions, a cleansing so to speak. With the cleansing there was often anger. Dawn was angry at her parents that they would do this to her. She still was just a kid, though she didn't want them to know that she still considered herself one. She wanted them to treat her like an adult. She still needed their love and care and wasn't ready to fly from the nest.

Dawn gained her composure when she heard the garage door open. She looked out the window to see who it was. She saw that her mother was home. She quickly wiped her tears and headed downstairs to meet her mother. She opened the door leading to the garage and asked her if she needed any help. Her mother nodded no and she went back into the house.

"Well, let's see it." Her mother said.

"Ok, it's not too bad."

Her mother looked at Dawn's report card. It showed that she had improved in math but stayed the same in English.

"Two A's, Three B's and a C, not bad, but I am sure you could do better. Don't you think?"

"In everything but English, I just can't get it. I do try Mom, really I do."

"Can you tell me that you did your best?"

"Yes, I did the best that I could."

"That's all that I ask. Should we go to McDonalds now and get you your free hamburger?"

"Mom, how old do you think I am, Twelve?" She retorted.

"I guess not, what do you want for dinner then?"

"I don't know, isn't Dad going to be here?"

"Not tonight, he called me before and told me not to worry about dinner and that he would be home around 8 p.m."

"Typical"

"What do you mean, little girl?"

"I don't know Mom, doesn't it make you mad at times. It seems that lately he loves his job more than us!"

"He's just trying to finish this book, things will calm down after he's done. You'll see."

"Yeah right"

"Excuse me?"

"Mom, get real, when he is done with the book and if it takes off, he'll go on another book tour and then there will be another book deal. So it won't get better, things will just stay the same."

"Ok, maybe that's right, but he still loves us. He just is busy right now."

"Stop treating me like a kid, I need to know something and I need to know it right now!"

"Hold on there Dawn, if you raise your voice to me again I will have to slap that pretty little mouth of yours, so calm down."

Dawn was taken back by her Mother's threat. Her Mother rarely ever slapped her, but when she did, it was memorable.

"What do you want to know?"

"Are you and Dad going to get a divorce?"

"Dawn, what would make you ask me something like that?"

"Mom, I can see and hear what is going on around here lately. Dad comes home late all the time. When he does come home, all you two do is fight any more. You both act like I am blind and deaf around here. I am old enough to know if you and dad are going to make it or not. So tell me, are you two going to get a divorce?

"No."

"Honestly?"

"Look Sweetheart, your Dad and I might be going through a rough spot right now, but that doesn't mean that we don't love each other or that we are going to give up on our marriage. It just means that we have to work twice as hard right now to get over this mountain. And as soon as we get over this one there will be another one, and another one. That is what marriage is all about."

"Well if this is what marriage is supposed to be like, I am not sure that I ever want to get married. You two used to be in love and it showed. Dad would come home and you both acted like teenagers around each other. What happened?"

"Life happened. Just because we haven't been getting along lately doesn't mean we're not in love, it just means that we have some issues to work out. Dawn, I don't want you to get the wrong idea about marriage. Marriage is a roller coaster and if you don't hold on it will throw you off, but if you hold on and work through it, it can be a fantastic ride. Don't get me wrong, it has its ups and downs, and at times you wonder will there ever be another up, but there will be. This is just another dip in the road. We'll be okay. Don't worry, we aren't getting a divorce. OK?"

"OK, Mom"

With that her mother reached out and hugged her.

"How did you become such a worry wart? You have to calm down or you're going to get an ulcer."

"Sorry mom thanks."

"Go get ready, let's get something to eat. If your dad won't be here, let's party."

With that Dawn mood changed. She wasn't worried any longer and she was happy to go to dinner.

Dawn's mother did her best to reassure her but to be totally honest with herself she had to admit that she wasn't sure where their marriage was heading. She was sure of one thing though, that they couldn't continue on the path they were going and stay together. She knew that things would have to change or the marriage would collapse. She was sorry that their fights and arguments had directly affected Dawn and that they acted like she was deaf. Trisha realized that time was flying by so fast. Within a year or two Dawn could be out of the house. She could now see how much her Dad had missed and that he was going to miss so much more if he didn't get his bearings.

Enough marriage problems for the day, let's have a good time. She thought to herself.

Dawn returned from her room ready to leave. They left the house and got into the car.

"Where should we go? How about Toni's?" her mother asked.

"We always go to Toni's. I am tired of Toni's."

"Well where then?"

"Let's go to Applebee's"

"Ok, What the heck."

The garage door opened and they went off to eat dinner.

About a mile a way Dad was sitting in his office with his hands on his head starring down at his desk. His young intern just sat there like a statue not knowing what to say or do.

"Dr. Sinclair, are you OK?" The intern asked.

"Dr. Sinclair, are you OK?" He repeated.

With the second question Dad came out of his trance and looked up. He seamed bewildered at first, like he had forgotten where he was.

"I am sorry for that Jim, where were we?"

Dr. Sinclair always had a good relationship with his interns. He always called them by their first name and they always called him Dr. Sinclair. Jim had just started two weeks before so he wasn't sure how to act around the Dr.

After seeming to lose his focus again he looked at Jim.

"Are you married Jim?"

"No sir?"

"Do you have any children?"

"No sir?" Jim replied with some shock in his voice.

"Where are you from?"

"Tampa, Florida."

"What brings you all the way to Saratoga Springs New York?"

"You did sir."

"Pardon me?"

"I read your first book when I was in Tenth grade. It inspired me to want to become an anthropologist. I decided that I wanted to learn from the master, and here I am."

"I am a master of nothing, but I am glad to see that my work has inspired at least one person in the world. I started to wonder if anyone was really awake in my class or not."

"I find it fascinating Dr."

"Ok, Jim, I get your point. Enjoy your weekend and I will see you on Monday."

"Good Night Dr. Sinclair."

Jim left and the Dr. gathered his things and put them in his briefcase. His mind was racing and he was bothered by the events of the day. It really bothered him to have to tell Trisha that he wouldn't be home for dinner. There was just so much to do. He was sure that she would understand. He had to wonder though what he was working so hard for. He wasn't blind or stupid to the fact of where their marriage was heading. He stilled loved Trisha and didn't want it to fall apart. He was just hoping that she could be strong just for a little while longer. He knew that he was straining the family to its limit, but he just had to finish this book.

"It will all work out, it always had. I will make it up to her. I really will this time." He thought to himself.

"Look at the time, I better get home."

He left his office and locked the door and headed for the exit. The building was quiet and the only sound to be heard was his footsteps, even though he wasn't alone. He was beside himself and made no thought that someone else was in the building with him, or that he was being followed down the hallway. He stepped out of the doorway and into the fresh air. There was a cool breeze and the temperature was just right as he took a few relaxing deep breaths and headed for the car.

He was temporarily blinded when the campus security car pulled up to him and the driver rolled down his window.

"You OK, Dr. Sinclair? Is there anyone else in the building?"

"Yes, I am fine and I was the last one out?"

"I would have sworn that someone was walking behind you as drove up to you."

"Maybe it was my shadow." Dr. Sinclair said with a smile.

"After all who would be there to hurt him in the first place." he thought.

"How are you tonight Jerry?"

"Swell, Dr. Sinclair, just swell. My oldest daughter is about to make me a grandfather here in a few hours."

"Congratulations, that's really nice."

"You have a good night Dr. Drive safe now."

"I will and you take it easy."

Their conversation was over almost as soon as it started but it did make him think. He realized in that moment what he was missing. He started to think about Dawn and how old she was. It seemed just yesterday that she was learning to walk and now she was going into the Twelfth grade. In a few years he would be telling someone that he was about to become a grandfather. That last thought was too much for him to bear with all of the other thoughts that he had swirling around in his head. He opened the car door and got in.

"God, what am I going to do? I hope she knows I love her. I will always love her. She's my little girl."

Being the man that he was he regained his composure before he was about to lose control of his emotions. He realized that he would have to change, and change quick. That he had already lost so much time and he would never be able to make it up. His professor side took over and he started the car and headed home. It was only a mile to the house so he was home in a matter of minutes. When he opened the garage door he realized that Dawn and Trisha were not there. He parked the car and grabbed his briefcase and headed inside.

He hadn't eaten anything since twelve o'clock but his last thoughts killed his appetite. He opened the refrigerator and got out a drink. He sat down at the kitchen table and looked at all the magnets that were stuck to the door. Trisha always liked to buy a magnet from wherever they had gone. Through the years the refrigerator became the pallet for the painting of their worldly travels. As he sat there drinking his mind started to calm and he started to relax. He got up and started over to the living room. He grabbed the remote and turned on the TV. As he sat on the couch he looked at the entertainment system and all the pictures that were there. Like a time machine the pictures were all placed in a line of years. Dawn when she was a baby, Dawn when she was 5, Dawn when she was 9. Vacation pictures hung from the wall along with a large family portrait.

Dr. Sinclair finally reached the point every parent does when they realize that time is moving at an alarming rate. That it seems that another year passes with every blink and that his little girl wasn't a little girl and sooner or later she would spread her wings and fly. He had tried to keep her enclosed and safe as much as he could. He tried to project her by acting hard and stern, especially when it came to her dating boys. He made sure that any boy that came to the door knew who he was and that he had a gun and wasn't afraid to use it. Sure he would never do something like that but he wanted to put the fear of God into any guy that looked Dawn's way.

He stood up and took the picture of Dawn when she was 9 off the entertainment system and held it in his hand. He was beside himself and fell into his own little world. Daydreaming so deep that he never heard the door open and Dawn and Trisha walked in. Trisha could see that he was in an emotional state of mind and motioned to Dawn to head upstairs. Just as his memories started to trigger a tear he realized that they were home.

"Honey, you ok?"

"Yes." He slightly growled.

He very rarely showed that side of himself to his family and he wasn't about to start tonight. It wasn't that he wanted to appear mean; he just didn't want to appear weak. If he could only realize that it was his emotions that his family needed to see.

"What are you doing?"

"Just looking at Dawn when she was younger."

"Seems like yesterday, doesn't it?"

"Trisha, I realize that I have been preoccupied lately. I just want you to know that things will get better once I finish this book. I am almost done. Please hold on for a little more. I am sorry for being here but not being here. If you know what I mean."

Trisha was caught off guard by his statement and for a second or two stood in complete shock. She wondered if he was feeling OK, or what had happened for him to talk like this. This was so unlike him. Usually he acted like a rock. This was sometimes a good thing. He was always the strong one that she could lean on, even though he was often times absent for emotional support.

"Honey are you OK?"

"Yes, I am fine, I just took some time to take an inventory of my life and I realize that life has been passing me by. Especially Dawn's life I don't want to look back and see that I made a name for myself and lost my family."

"Don't worry Darling, we're still here, but I am glad that you have come back to planet earth. I was worried there for a while that you weren't coming back, that you had bigger and better things to do than be married to me."

As she was speaking he walked over to the stereo and put in a cd.

As he walked over to her and took her hand in his the song, "I'll be seeing you", started. He pulled her close and started to dance with her in the living room. Being overwhelmed with emotions her eyes started to well up with tears. It had been a long time since he had done anything like this before.

Through all of this Dawn was creeping down the stairs like a little kid trying to get a glimpse of Santa Clause on Christmas Eve. She thought she would see them in another fight on sitting on opposite sides of the couch but when she saw them dancing she almost screamed. At first she almost ran to the living room to get in between both of them like she was eight, but before she did, she realized that this was their moment and that they needed the time together. Just when she thought her covert operation was a success both parents in unison told her, "Go to bed".

She went up to her room listening to the music with each step. The night was like Christmas to her. It had been so long since it seemed like the two of them were happily married and now it seemed for the moment they were on the road to recovery.

    Dawn got ready for bed and lay down. Her mind was at ease and she was relaxed. For the first time in weeks she gently slipped off to sleep

Chapter 2

The day started like any other that summer, hot, hot like an oven, especially in the house. It had been the third day of the heat wave and the heat was starting to affect everyone.

Dawn woke up slow and grumpy as usual with the summer heat. With it being so hot in the house it didn't seem like she actually got to sleep until 2:00 a.m. and now it was so hot she couldn't sleep much longer than 8:00 am. She got up out of bed and headed to the bathroom. As she passed the kitchen her parents were sitting there eating breakfast.

"Morning Sunshine." her father remarked playfully.

"Don't remind me."

She scuffled off to the bathroom and soon would reappear.

"Mom, can't we turn on the air conditioning now? This heat is unbearable."

"Well, well who is going to pay for it you?"

"No, it's just so hot in here."

"I agree, Trisha, let's turn it on. I would rather pay a higher electric bill than die of heat stroke." Mr. Sinclair told his wife.

"Ok, I will admit, it is pretty hot in here."

Trisha went over to the thermostat and turned on the air conditioning. She hated to pay a higher electric bill and tried to keep it off as long as they could stand. The same went for the winter; she would try and keep from turning the heat on as long as she could. Everyone breathed a sigh of relief as they heard the air conditioner turn on and felt the blast of cool air.

"Well, don't just sit there; we need to shut the windows." Trisha exclaimed.

They all scurried around the house shutting the windows before any precious cool air could escape.

After the windows were all shut Dawn headed back to her bed room.

"What are you going to do now Dawn?" Her father asked.

"Nothing much."

"Look, you mother has to work today and I have to go to the college for a couple of hours. Why don't you come along with me and go swimming at the pool? After you mother is done we can go out to eat. Sound like a plan?"

Trisha and Dawn agreed and Dawn headed to her bedroom to change her clothes.

"I have to go Bill, love you see you tonight. I will text you where to meet, OK?"

"Love you too, that will be fine."

Trisha headed to the garage and into her car. Bill looked out the door and waved goodbye. He would always say a prayer to ensure her safety anytime she went anywhere. Though he tried not to show it and kept it to himself he was always afraid that she might be killed someday.

He went back to the table and started gathering up the things that he would need for the day. Once he got it all together he was ready to go. He might have been ready, but Dawn was another story.

"Dawn, are you ready to go?"

"Almost."

"What do you mean almost, you were almost ready 20 minutes ago? Come on and hurry up. Bring your bathing suit and a towel. What else do you need?"

Her father impatience when it came to getting ready always annoyed her. She always felt that he was clueless when it came to how long it takes a woman to get ready.

After a few more bangs on the door and a couple, "Let's go" Dawn was ready and heading for the garage.

"Where are you going?"

"I was going to the car; you said I was going over to the college with you to swim."

"Dawn, do you forget that we don't even live a mile away from the college? We are going to walk."

"But Dad, it's like 100 degrees out there."

"It's good exercise."

So they both left the house and after he locked the door they headed down the street to the college. About half way there her father was about done. He wished now that he would have driven the car. Then he realized that he was supposed to meet Trisha later for dinner.

"I hope she wants to go some place close or I'll have to walk home to get the car." He thought to himself.

Just about this time, Dawn had come to the same conclusion.

"Dad, aren't we going out with Mom for dinner later?"

"I know, I know, I should have driven the car. You never know she might want to go to The Saratoga."

"Hopefully for your sake, you look like you are about to pass out."

"Hey little lady, let's see how good you do when you are my age."

"I forgot, you're old"

"Watch it." He replied jokingly.

After what seemed to take forever they arrive at the college.

"Look Dawn, I have one lecture today and I have some paper work to do. Here is some money for lunch. Stay out of trouble and meet me back in my office around 3:00. Remember to make sure that all these college guys know how old you are and who you are. OK?"

"OK, Dad, don't worry. I wouldn't cause you any trouble. Everyone here knows who I am. Lighten up, I am 17, I know how to take care of myself."

"That reminds me, what swimsuit did you bring?"

"My two piece, why."

An icy chill went through his body.

"Nothing I just wish you would wear something else. This place is full of guys looking for girls."

"Don't worry Dad, no one is interested."

That last statement didn't ease his mind much. He knew that she was a pretty girl whether she knew it or not and sooner or later guys would be calling.

"I love you." He told her as he walked to his office and she walked to the recreation center.

It was part of the summer quarter at college and Dr. Sinclair only had one lecture a week. It was for the students that had to retake the class or for the ones that wanted to jump-start the next coming year. To his relief he entered the coolness of the Science building and headed to his office. The college was like a ghost town in the summer. There were very few students around and even less staff. This was the part of the year that he enjoyed the most. He could set his own pace and usually wasn't rushed trying to deal with a few hundred students at a time. The summer schedule was easy, one lecture a week for 9 weeks. As Dr. Sinclair entered his office he put his briefcase on his desk and looked to see if he had any mail waiting. Since everyone would try to get on his good side, he never had a want for someone volunteering to help him with picking up mail or doing any other menial tasks. He looked through the mail and saw nothing of importance but one letter. He read it and put it in his briefcase. He then sat there and took a look at the mountain of paper work that he had to do for the day. Dr. Sinclair hated paper work. If he could get one of his eager beaver students to do it for him he would. He looked at the pile again and then at the clock. It was time to start the lecture. He entered the lecture room five minutes early and most of the students had already arrived. Dr. Sinclair was more lenient in the summer than he was during the rest of the year. He figured why make the summer any more stressful than it had to be. He would have all year to squeeze the best out of his students. He would wait to the precise time that the lecture was supposed to start and then he would start whether the students were ready or not. Dr. Sinclair wasn't a stuff- shirt and was well liked by the students and the staff. He had a great sense of humor but knew when to be serious or not. He did give a little more work than most, and most of that would require a lot of research. He was a hands-on professor and had been around the world to research his field. His class, Myth and Legends of the world was a unique one. For the most part students either loved it or hated it. It wasn't the doctor's teaching style; it was more the material that they had to study.

"Welcome students to the summer quarter. I am Dr. Bill Sinclair and welcome to Myths and Legends and human history. The purpose of this class is to show that even though a legend may appear so fantastic that it couldn't be true, there usually is some sort of starting point based around fact that starts the whole thing going."

He started asking the students if anyone knew the difference between a myth and a legend. After a moment or two of blank stars and wrong answers he proceeded.

"A myth is a story that tries to explain a natural occurrence, like thunder and lightning. Thor for instance is the Norse god of thunder and associated with storms. As technology increased myths became outrageous fairy tales.

A legend on the other hand is a story based on truth, at least the foundation of the story is. The story itself has been embellished throughout the telling. The Centaur legend for example, a creature half man and half horse, we would say this is ridiculous, but there is a possible start of the legend. When a culture that knew nothing of horses or men riding on them met with a horse riding culture, people started to talk about strange creatures, half man and half horse. And so the story gets repeated over and over and through the years these creatures become terrible and violent creatures that should be feared. Even in America, certain men like Daniel Boone and Jim Bowie became so well known for their exploits in the American wilderness that they became living legends.

Legends have also been introduced into society as morality tales. Like the couple making out in the car only to hear that the killer with the hook hand is on the loose. The girl get's scared and the couple leaves in a hurry. When they arrive at her house they find that there is a hook connected to the door handle of the car, scary maybe but true, unlikely. So in this class we will investigate known legends and myths and try to find the foundation or starting point to some of them, any questions?"

A young man raised his hand and Dr. Sinclair called on him.

"What about vampires, are they myth or legend?"

"That is a good question. Considering that the vampire has been a feared creature as far back as the early Persian Empire. But since there has never been any physical proof of an actual vampire, I would consider them more myth than anything. To date that has only ever been one official investigation of a vampire. Sure there have been many stories of vampires killing people but can they be proven, no. They fall under a category of fear and superstition. Like the old house on the corner that some old lady lives in, it's just an old house with a lady that doesn't come out much, but it doesn't take long for stories to surface about the house being haunted and that the old lady is a witch of some sort. You see it is far easier to accept the story as true rather than go up to the house and knock on the door and try to get to know the lady. Once someone proves the story to be untrue, the excitement is gone. We as humans tend to believe what we want to believe, even though that belief at times might be clearly ridiculous, especially when we don't understand what is truly happening. In fact, they would often reopen graves to make sure that the person was truly dead, only to find that blood or fluid was seeping from the mouth or that the body looked bloated or even made noise on occasion. We now know that this is the natural process of decomposition. Knowing this now, we can conclude that vampires are nothing more than a figment of our imagination or fear. Now thanks to authors and film makers the idea has become more real. I hope that answers your question."

"Yes, thank you."

"For your first assignment I want you all to find a legend or myth and research its beginnings and what the myth or legend was referring to and if there is a truth behind the story. We will meet back here in a week, happy hunting."

He dismissed the class and then went back to his office. He pulled the letter out of his briefcase and opened it up. It had a stamp from Slovenia on it. Being in the kind of research he often received letters from around the world with new legends and stories that people had come up with. To his dismay most were simple hoaxes or were written by some crack pot somewhere.

He started reading the letter. It seemed at first that is was just another nut from the other side of the world trying to get attention for something or other, but the more he read the more he was enticed. According to the letter someone had actual proof that vampires had existed and that they still did. Naturally he was skeptical, it was his job to be the skeptic, but this person had dates and addresses and even a dig site showing evidence of not just one vampire but a whole community of them. He tried to dismiss the letter at first but then he thought, "What would someone have to gain over this?"

He finished the letter and put in back in the briefcase and then set off to the President's office. He was intrigued and if he could sell the idea to him, a trip to Slovenia might be possible. He arrived and talked to him about all the procedures to be used and contacts to be made before any plans could be started.

Meanwhile Dawn had made it to the pool locker room and changed into her bathing suit and then went to the pool. The pool was large and very nice. It was just not a place to meet people, at least not Dawn. Dawn's father had made sure that every college age boy knew who Dawn was and who he was. This made meeting boys at the pool pretty hard. Sure she was a pretty girl, but most of the guys were too afraid to go over and talk to her. On occasion some guy that was new, or wasn't afraid would come and approach her. But it wouldn't take long for someone else to come along and whisper into their ears and then they would politely leave.

It often times made Dawn feel like she had a disease or something. At this point and time, she wasn't aware that her Dad had put a sign on her back saying keep away. Dawn's father wasn't trying to been mean; he just wanted to keep the college creeps away from his daughter.

After an hour or two swimming and hanging out at the pool by herself, she decided to change and wander around for awhile. Eventually she ended up at her father's office where she sat down and started browsing the internet on his computer. Dawn was surprised to find that her father was doing searches on vampires and Slovenia.

"Must be something for his new book" She thought to herself.

Dawn jumped as her father walked in.

"You're not looking at porn are you?"

"Dad, really, I don't do things like that!"

"I know, I was just kidding, the firewall of the college wouldn't let you even if you wanted to."

"I was looking at the research you were doing. What are all the searches on vampires and Slovenia?"

"Just some research maybe something to put in my next book."

Just as she thought, one thing Dawn's father was, he was predictable.

"Look at the time. We better see where your mother wants to eat. We might have to walk home, remember?"

"How could I forget?"

He texted Trisha and she told them to meet her at "The Saratoga".

"That's good, we can walk to there."

"Wonderful" Dawn interjected.

On the walk over to the restaurant Dawn and her father talked about their day.

"Pretty boring, I don't know what you have told everyone about me and now everyone at the college acts like I have a disease." She told him.

"All I said is that the guys better know that it's hands off."

"Dad, I'm not a little kid anymore."

"Yes I know that's exactly why I told them that. And dressed in your two piece bathing suit I am sure you could attract guys like bees to honey. Some day you will understand."

"Yeah right."

Her father kept a stern face but inside he had to laugh a little. He knew that Dawn needed a little freedom, but he also knew what college boys were like and he had no intention on one of them dating his daughter. At least that is what he would tell her. Deep in his heart he knew that some day she would meet someone and they would hit it off and the next thing is they get married and start their own life. It was just the way life worked he didn't have to enjoy the thought of his little girl leaving the nest though.

Though her father often times tried to hide his emotions he really was an emotional person. Just the thought of his little girl leaving the nest almost brought him to tears. He quickly tried to change the subject to something funny to get his mind off of things.

It was still hot when they started walking to the restaurant. By the time they arrived Bill was hot, sweaty and famished. Dawn seemed more bothered by the heat than hungry. Trisha had already arrived and had a table waiting. She rose to meet Bill and he gave her a kiss and said hello.

"What's the matter with you Dawn?" her mother asked.

"Nothing, just a long day doing nothing."

"Well tomorrow maybe you can clean out the refrigerator for me, or wash the clothes or clean the bathroom. Would that suit you better?"

At this point Dawn knew she had crossed the line and that she was stuck.

"I get it." She replied mournfully.

"Are you hungry?" Her mother asked.

"A little, hot more than anything. Being hot just takes away your appetite."

"And how was you day today Honey?" Bill interjected.

"Fine, though you wonder what goes through people's head sometimes."

"What do you mean?"

"Oh, some nimrod came in to the ER because he said that he was constipated. I was surprised that he didn't call 911 and ask for an ambulance. Other than that it was a slow day. No big deals just some small injuries and one case that a box of Fiber All would fix."

There was a slight pause and then they all started to laugh. By this time the waitress had come over and asked if they were ready to order. They all ordered and had a good dinner though Bill was preoccupied with something. They finished paid the bill and headed to the car.

"Where is your car Bill?" Trisha asked.

"I left it at home, we walked here."

"Are you going to walk home?"

"I wasn't planning on it do you want to kill me or something?"

"No, just get it."

They all got into Trisha's car and headed home. When they arrived the air conditioning was on and the house was cool. Dawn headed to the living room to watch some TV and her parents headed to her dad's office to talk about some things. They seemed happy when they walked into the office, but Dawn knew that very rarely was the case. She really hated the little meetings that they would have at times. Often she could hear them arguing. Her Dad would often lose his temper and start yelling after a while. She always was afraid that her parents marriage was about to fall apart and if it did, what would happen to her. This time was different though and they didn't seem to be arguing, they seem to be talking about something important.

"Trisha, I received this letter today. It is from someone in Slovenia saying that they have proof of vampires, proof that vampires are still in existence today. I talked to Oscar and he said that if I can verify the source and make some contacts that he will fund the research for me to go to Slovenia to check out the dig."

Trisha just looked at him with a shallow stare.

"Don't you see what this could do? If this turns out to be true, it would make me the most famous anthropologist in the world."

"Or the biggest crackpot the world has ever seen." She interjected before he had time to say anything else.

"Thanks a lot Trisha; you know I was looking for some more material for my second book. Why do you have to make fun of me?"

"I am not making fun of you, it's just the fact that people honestly think that vampires still exist or that they existed at all. It's just ludicrous to me."

"Real or not, it's my job to prove it right or wrong. You know that. I have been doing this for 20 years now."

"Are we going to be able to go with you this time?"

"It doesn't look like it. Slovenia is still considered an active war zone."

"Wonderful. You go on playing Indiana Jones and I have to sit here worried if you are ever coming home or not."

"You know I would take you both if I could. You act as if I like leaving you and Dawn."

"Well you just always seem to want to go on some dig or find some new evidence for this or that and you never seem to want to be home anymore. I just wish you would get as excited over us as much as you job. It really hurts my feelings. I feel like you love your job more than me and Dawn."

Bill really did love his family, he just seemed to lose his way at times. He would often times forget what was more important, his family or his job. Even though he could see that the stress of this news was weighing heavily on Trisha. He could see the tears welling up in her eyes. Before a tear had time to fall he took her in his arms and gave her a big bear hug.

"I'm sorry; I will make it up to you somehow. Plan a vacation, anywhere and we will go when I get back."

"Really?"

"Really, anywhere you want."

"Alaska? Hawaii?"

"Sure, anywhere, I love you. You and Dawn mean everything to me. Don't worry, I will be OK, it will be alright. I shouldn't be gone for more than 4 weeks."

"Four weeks, that's half the summer without you here." She said mournfully.

"It could be less."

"Or it could be more." She interrupted.

"What would you have me do?"

"Nothing, you figure it out. I am going to bed."

Through all of this Dawn could only here muffled sounds coming from the office. For once her father was staying calm and there was no yelling. She even thought that her dad might have learned how to control himself, but when her mother came out of the room teary eyed she knew something was wrong.

"I am going to bed, I love you Dawn. I have to work tomorrow, and don't forget to clean out the refrigerator tomorrow. OK?"

"OK, Good night, I love you too."

When her father left the room Dawn intercepted him in the hallway.

"What's going on, what is wrong with Mom?"

"It's OK, I will explain it later. She was just a little upset over my plans for the summer. It will all work out. Don't worry your pretty little head over it. OK?"

"OK, but I still want to know what is going on. You shouldn't make Mom cry like that!"

"Calm down Sunshine, I wasn't yelling at her, I might just be gone for a month, maybe a little longer, to do some research."

"I should have known."

At first it appeared to Bill that he might be suffering from déjà vu and would have to repeat the same conversation that he had with Trisha.

"This is between your mother and I, we will work it out. We plan on going on a real vacation when I come back. OK?"

"Where to?"

"Where ever you and Mom agree on. I am going to bed. I will see you in the morning. I love you have a good night's sleep."

"I love you too." Dawn told him.

With that he kissed her on her forehead and headed for the bedroom. Dawn went back to watching the TV. She lost interest in what she was watching. Now she had to think where she wanted to go for vacation. She turned of the TV and went to her room and turned on her computer. She started surfing the web for places that they might go. Telling her that it was up to her and Mom was like giving a kid the key to the candy store. For now she didn't know where he was headed and had no reason to worry about his return. For now all she had to do is find the best place in the world to go on vacation.

Before she knew it she had spent hours on the internet when she looked at the clock and it was after one o'clock.

"Oh, crud I better get to sleep, Mom will kill me if I sleep in tomorrow, with all that I have to do." She thought to herself.

She changed into her pajamas and got ready for bed. She got in the bed and tried to sleep, she was still exited over the thought of where to go. Eventually she nodded off and fell asleep.

Before she knew it, Dawn was awoken by the sound of her father banging on her door to get up. As usual she was like a turtle. Eventually she walked into the kitchen to see both parents there. She got up just in time to see her father off to work. She gave him a kiss and said goodbye. Bill then disappeared through the garage door and off to work he went.

"Well, little lady, according to you, you need a job to do today. I thought cleaning out the refrigerator would be fitting."

"Really?" Dawn said in horror.

"Yes, really. Take everything out, one shelf at a time and then wash the shelf and then put the stuff back in a timely matter. Can you do that?"

"I guess."

"This shouldn't take you that long, an hour or two. Do you understand?"

"Yes."

"Oh, one thing, I don't want to come home with a mess bigger than when I left. Clean one shelf at a time. Not all of them at once. OK."

"I got it."

"I have to get to work. Have a good day. I love you."

"I love you to. Have a good day."

With that her mother headed off to work, and left Dawn there by herself. Even though Dawn was 17 she still felt a little strange being by herself. Well, she still had the dog to keep her company. Dawn had already figured it would take her an hour to clean the refrigerator and her parents wouldn't be back for at least eight hours. She reached into the cabinet and got out a box of cereal. She was sure to test it first before she actually filled her bowl and put milk on it. She didn't want to repeat the fiasco of yesterday. She tasted a piece of cereal and it appeared fresh. She filled her bowl to over flowing and poured on the milk, in typical Dawn fashion she walked into the living room with her breakfast and turned on the TV and started to watch some game show.

"This is the life." She thought to herself.

She really didn't look forward to cleaning out the refrigerator, the last time she did, she almost threw up. You never knew what you would find in the back of the thing. Her father had a bad habit of putting leftovers in there and forgetting about them.

About an hour had past when the phone rang. She checked the caller ID, and as usual, it was her father.

"Hello Dad."

"Hello, are you all right?"

"Yes, everything is fine."

"Have you started cleaning the refrigerator yet?"

"Not really."

"So you haven't? Get to it. It better be done before I call at lunch time. There is no reason why it should take you longer than that. I love you. Talk to you later."

"Love you to, bye."

She hung up the phone and let out a disgusted sigh. She knew not to play games when her father talked to her that sternly.

"Well, I better get it done."

She rinsed her bowl and put in the dishwasher.

"Lord help me."

She started at the top shelf and started removing everything from it. After removing the first layer of juice bottles there seemed to be a hoard of jars that they all had forgotten about. Jars of old olives and pickles, half used ketchup and mustard all pushed back and forgotten about. She had removed all the items and started to sponge clean the shelf when the phone range. It startled her and she rose up quickly banging her head on the inside of the refrigerator.

"Ouch!"

She looked at the caller id and it was her mother this time.

"Hello, Mom."

"Just called to see how you were doing."

"I am all right; I just banged my head off the inside of the refrigerator."

"Should I call 911, are you going to live?" Her mother asked sarcastically.

"Yes, Mother, I will live."

Sometimes her mother sarcasm really got on her nerves.

"How is it coming, making any progress?"

"Yes, I am sponging the first shelf. What do you want me to do with the old stuff that I find? Some of this stuff is really disgusting."

"Throw it out, what do think you should do with it? Eat it."

"NOOOOOOOOOO"

"Don't get smart with me, just use your head. You do have a brain, use it. See you later, love you."

"Love you to, Bye."

Even though both parents kept a watchful eye on her and it drove her crazy it times, it also gave her a good feeling that they loved her and tried to protect her.

"I know I need some music." She thought to herself.

She went and turned the radio on the sound system and cranked up the sound. As the music started so did her motivation. She returned to her job and started sponging off the shelf. She got lost in the songs and the job didn't seem that bad, at least the first shelf. After the first shelf she put the articles back in and started on the second and third. Everything was going well until she reached the crispers. She opened the crisper only to find a bag of prepackaged salad that had been in there for ages. She reached in to grab it finding that some of the lettuce had already started to decompose and turn to liquid. Just the consistency of the package was enough to make her sick but as she picked it up the package opened and Dawn got a whiff of the contents.

"OH my Gosh!" she said partly gagging.

As she stood up her father happened to be standing behind her. She didn't hear him coming in because the music was so loud.

As she screamed and jumped the contents of the bag flew into the air and all over her.

"Daddy!"

"What? I just came back for lunch."

She would have said more, but she started to head for the bathroom as the smell of the rotting lettuce filled her nostrils.

"Dawn, are you ok?"

All he could hear at this point was Dawn gagging in the bathroom. He walked over to the door and began to knock.

"Are you OK?"

"Yes, as soon as I change my clothes. You scared me and I spilled some rotten lettuce on myself!"

By this time the whole kitchen was filled with the aroma of the bag.

"I see what you mean, we better open a window. I'll throw the bag in the garbage outside."

Bill lifted a window and then picked up the bag off the floor. He treated it like it was toxic waste and carefully carried it to the garbage can in the garage.

"Dawn, I'm no longer hungry, I am going back to work. Will you be ok?"

"Yes, I will be out in a minute. I am almost done. I will see you later."

After a minute or two he left to go back to the college and she went back to finish her job. Thus was Dawn's life. It seemed all the same, just a different day. So mundane nothing exciting ever happened in her world or so it seemed. She was like so many kids her age. Always looking for something more exciting out of life but stuck in the rut of just being in a so called normal life.

She finally finished the job only minutes before her mother returned from work. She hurried to make sure everything was finished and put back into its place before her mother entered the room. As she closed the refrigerator door she started to hear her mother banging on the garage door. Dawn walked over to the door like she had bricks tied to her feet. She finally arrived and opened it.

"Thanks, what took you so long?"

"I came as soon as I heard you knocking." Dawn replied.

"Well, just don't stand there. Help me unload the car."

"Yes mom!"

"And can you do it without the attitude."

"Yes."

With that Dawn started to help unload the groceries from her mother's car. Her mother was putting everything away as Dawn brought in the rest of the things.

"The refrigerator looks good." Her mother told her.

"Thanks, it was really sick in there, it smelled horrible." Dawn answered her.

"Well, it happens, welcome to adulthood. You have to keep things neat and clean or things like that will happen."

"I get it, I get it." Dawn said with a scowl.

After they put all of the groceries away her mother started to make dinner and Dawn went up to her room. Dawn was bored and could only hope that there was going to be more to do for the rest of the summer than clean out the refrigerator. She was hoping that she and her family were going to go somewhere.

After dinner Dawn headed to the living room before being interrupted by her mother.

"Dawn, aren't you forgetting something?"

"Like what?"

"Like cleaning up and loading the dishwasher." Her mother scolded her.

"Oh, how could I forget?"

"You better get used to it Dawn, dishes are a part of life."

"Well, when I have my own place, maybe I will eat off of paper plates all the time." She retorted back.

"I bet your husband would love that." Her mother answered.

Dawn wanted to respond but knew better. She realized that she better keep her mouth shut before it got her in trouble. She took the dishes from the table with the best attitude that she could come up with.

She loaded the dishwasher and shut the door and then headed into the living room. As she entered the living room she could see her father sitting there watching the evening news.

"Really?" She said coyly as she entered the room.

"Yes, really, maybe if you watched the news a little now and then you would learn something little miss." Her father said sternly.

"Ok."

"I'm going up to my room. Maybe there are some new videos on the internet." She told him as she headed to her room.

"What do you expect Bill, it's just her age." Her mother told him as she entered the room and saw the look of disgust on his face.

"If you say so, I just don't understand kids these days." He answered.

"I guess it's the same with every generation, Bill, don't worry, she will grow out of it. We all did." Mrs. Sinclair answered with a laugh.

So the night began to end with their daily family routine. Dawn was in her room and her parents were in the living room watching the TV. Such was the lives of the Sinclair family.

Chapter 3

"Dawn are you going to sleep all day or what?" her mother yelled outside her door.

"What?"

"Are you going to sleep all day or what?" she repeated.

"I'm getting up."

"OK, you already missed breakfast and if you sleep any more you are going to miss lunch."

"OK, OK, I'm getting up and getting ready. Are we going any where today?"

"I don't know why?"

"I wanted to know what to put on."

"Put something on that you can cut the grass in."

"Isn't Dad here?"

"He had to go over to the college for a little bit. He said he wouldn't be long."

"OK"

Dawn got ready and headed for the garage. She opened up the door and then got on the riding mower. She always wondered why her dad wouldn't break down and buy a new mower in stead of using this old dinosaur they had.

She turned the key and it started right up, as usual. She put it in gear and drove out of the garage. She started cutting the grass when suddenly she heard a quick, bang! And then the mower suddenly stopped mowing. Instead is started to make a whining sound and she started to smell rubber burning.

Just as she realized something bad had happened, she turned off the mower. She was just getting off of it when her father pulled into the drive.

She walked over to the car and met him when he got out of it.

"Dad, something happened to the mower, again."

"What did you do to it?"

"I didn't do anything to it. I was going around the yard and I heard a bang and it stopped mowing."

"What did you hit?"

"I didn't hit anything."

After the initial shock of thinking that Dawn had ruined the mower was over Dr. Sinclair realized what she was wearing.

"What are you trying to do Dawn, drive the boys crazy or something? Go change your clothes. You're not going to cut grass in that get up."

"Dad, no one is watching. No one even cares."

"Oh they care all right, they care a lot. No girl of mine is going to be the show of the day."

"Dad, I wear this out at the swimming pool."

"I know, but I don't like it, I don't like it a bit. You are not a kid any more, Dawn."

"Really Dad, you mean I'm not your little girl anymore?"

That last statement would always get to him. She knew that she had him wrapped around her finger.

With misty eyes he would reply, "You'll always be my little girl, now go change your clothes."

With that she would go upstairs and put on a T-shirt over her top. It was enough to appease him for the moment, but he still cringed in fear over the boys in the neighborhood. Today would be no different. The guys seemed be walking down the street or hanging out in view of the yard. Dawn went about her business oblivious to her spectators; she simply went back and forth cutting the grass listening to the music on her mp3 player.

"You go change your clothes and so will I." He told her.

With that he disappeared into the house and within 15 minutes came out with his work clothes on. Even though he was a Dr. of Anthropology and a college professor he still liked to do things around the house. He would often drive Mom crazy because it always took him twice as long as he estimated to get things done.

"Is that real time, or Dad time?" Mom would always say when he told her how long it would take to do something.

"Well let's see what you did to it this time."

"Dad, I didn't do anything to it. It's just a piece of junk. Why can't we get another one?"

As first he ignored her remark but after looking at the damage to the mower deck he was starting to think that her idea might be a good one.

"Well it looks like the main bearing on the mower deck is shot."

"What's that mean?"

"It means you won't be cutting any grass today with the riding mower."

Dawn hated to hear that because she knew what it meant. She would have to go back to the garage and get the push mower out. At least it was a self propelled mower and she really didn't have to push it. She sluggishly turned on the mower and got in her whining mode; even though she knew in the house you had to whine under your breath.

Even though Dawn was in the popular click of girls at school, she never considered herself good looking. She always considered herself plain Jane. She never did realize that many of the boys in school thought she was the hottest thing since sliced bread. To the guys that live close buy, watching Dawn cut the grass was a spectator sport. Usually they would walk up and down the sidewalk trying to get a glimpse of her on the garden tractor. They all really thought it was a treat to watch her push mow. Every now and then one of them would get up enough courage to enter the yard and start to talk to her. Dawn never seemed to put two and two together about why boys were so ever present when she cut the grass. Her father knew all to well and would make his presence known if he was there. He knew full well what was going on.

As she started to go around the yard her dad went into the house and came out a few minutes later. The expression on his face was that of a kid right before he would open his Christmas presents. He waved to her and told her that he would be back. She waited till he drove off before she turned off the mower and headed into the house.

"Mom, what's wrong with dad?"

"What do you mean?"

"He looked like he just won the lottery or something."

"Oh that. He just came in and told me the mower broke again. I just told him to go buy another one. So he's headed to the store now."

"Boys and their toys." Dawn said.

"You don't know the half of it."

As Dawn went to head upstairs she was interrupted by her mother.

"Aren't you forgetting something, Dawn?"

"What?"

"Aren't you forgetting to finish the grass?"

"I just figured that I could do it with the new one when he came back."

"I guess you figured wrong. First of all it will take your father three hours to make up his mind. Second, he will have to have it delivered. Third, he will have to read the owners manual before he let's anyone use it. Fourth, no one will use it until he uses it. You know you father, so get out there and finish the yard."

"All right." She said.

Dawn headed back outside for her torture for the day.

As Dawn went around the yard for another pass Brandon walked down the sidewalk and said, "Hi"

If it would have been anyone else she would have gone on like nothing had happened, but it was Brandon.

Usually Dawn had a very level head and really wasn't interested in dating anyone in high school. She had dreams and she didn't want anything or anyone to interfere with them. But Brandon was different, he was the captain of the football team, he was tall and handsome and very popular, maybe too popular for Dawn's taste. He had quite the reputation to loving them and leaving them. This didn't seem to bother Dawn either, when it came to Dawn she had her head so far in the clouds that her decision making was often off track.

"Hi" she replied.

"How are you doing?" he asked as he walked onto the lawn.

Dawn's heart started to race as she realized that he was heading closer to her. She turned off the mower in order to actually hear what he had to say.

"What's happening?" he asked.

"Not much, just trying to get the grass cut. My dad went to buy another riding mower. Our old one just blew up, for the last time."

"What are you doing later?"

"Later, when?"

"Later this evening around 6:00 p.m."

"I don't know, why?"

"I just wanted to know if you wanted to go out to the Tastee freeze for an ice cream or something."

Dawn tried to stay calm and collected. She didn't want to appear excited but calm and cool.

"Really!" she blurted out.

"Yes."

"Give me a minute to ask my mother. Don't go any where, I will be right back."

"Ok, I will stay right here."

Dawn went into the house, leaving Brandon standing there in the hot sun. The other guys that were watching the whole thing started to leave, knowing that their chance with Dawn was now over. Brandon had the reputation that a girl had never turned him down for a date.

After some negotiations with her mother Dawn returned from the house.

"That will be fine, as long as I am back by 10:30 p.m."

"Ok, I didn't think it would take 4 ½ hours to get an ice cream, but OK. It's a date."

Dawn's thoughts went right to the moon when he said, "It's a date."

"What?" she asked

"It's a date."

"Oh, yeh, it's a date."

He said his goodbyes and told her that he would be back at 6:00 to pick her up. As he left Dawn there by the mower Dawns brain went into overdrive. It was 3:30 and she had to finish the grass before she was aloud to leave. She started the mower and pushed the throttle as high as it would go. It no longer was self propelled, she was pushing it along. Before she knew it, it was 4:00, but she was done.

Dawn started to panic when she realized that she only had two hours before he would return.

"I have to get ready."

She put the mower away and ran into the house and up to her bedroom. Her mother was at the kitchen counter preparing dinner. She smiled slightly and laughed to herself. There was nothing like that first date.

She was just finishing getting ready when there was a knock at the door. Dawn tried to get there before her mother had a chance to answer it. To Dawn's terror her mother had already opened the door and invited Brandon in. Luckily though Dawn's dad hadn't made it home yet to start the cross examination. Though her dad had a more direct way of asking Dawn's suitors questions, her mother was more indirect. Her mother had a way of asking questions that seemed to be innocent but left no question unanswered. Dawn knew not to rush downstairs and enter the fray. It was her first date with Brandon and she didn't want to ruin her relationship with her parents over an ice cream cone. Dawn nervously waited on the stairs until she heard her mother tell her that Brandon was there. She knew full well that her mother knew that she was there, but she didn't want to expose their facade to Brandon.

Brandon took the interrogation like a real trooper and smiled through the whole thing. He himself was happy that Dr. Sinclair wasn't there to grill him over certain things. Dr. Sinclair had quite the reputation around town when it came to boys asking his daughter out.

"Nice to have met you Mrs. Sinclair."

"You too, Brandon, have a good time."

Brandon opened the door and let Dawn out. Brandon walked to his car and opened the passenger side door to let Dawn in. Dawn was taken back for a moment. This was the first time that she had seen Brandon's car. She actually expected something sportier, like a Firebird or something. She never expected him to be driving an old Ford Escort. She entered the door and he gently shut it and headed to the other side.

Dawn's sense of smell was assaulted when he shut the door. The car smelled like old socks and sweaty gym clothes combined with burnt oil.

"Sorry about the smell. I can't seem to get rid of it. I just got this car a week ago. My mother said that everyone's first car should be a pile of junk and that my first car would be no different. Just so you know the smell isn't from me or my lack of hygiene. I really don't know how to get rid of it. I've Fabreezed it twice a day for a week and it still stinks. Thank God it has been a warm summer, so I can drive with the windows open."

As he turned the key he attempted to start the engine. After cranking it over a couple of times there was a loud bang and a cloud of white smoke appeared behind them but the engine did start this time.

"That's good; I thought we might have to push it to start it." He tried to tell her confidently.

By this time Dawn didn't know what to think. In reality it was rather funny and she wanted to break out in laughter but didn't want to hurt his feelings.

Though Brandon tried to stay as cool as he could he was really nervous inside. His opportunity to impress Dawn just went out the window like the smoke billowing from the tail pipe. To Dawn the car seemed to be some sort of antique. It was even a standard shift, and that was something that was totally alien to her. Brandon put in the clutch and tried to reverse out of the driveway. As he let out the clutch the car lurched backward and stalled.

"Sorry about that, I haven't got the hang of this manual shift yet."

He then started the car and he backed it gently out of the driveway. By this time a group of neighbor guys had started to mill around at the spectacle of the coolest kid in Saratoga Springs failing at driving a car. They all could look, but no one dared to laugh, at least while Brandon was watching. They all knew how Brandon was and that he had quite the temper at times.

Finally Brandon took command of the little car that could and they started down the street to the Tastee Freeze followed by a trail of white smoke.

Dr. Sinclair pulled into the driveway as they pulled away. He parked the car in the garage and headed into the house. When he got into the house he noticed Mrs. Sinclair looking out the living room window at the car leaving.

"Who was that?"

He noticed that she was laughing as she turned around to answer him.

"That was Dawn and Brandon. He came over to take her out to Tastee Freeze."

"What, you let him take Dawn out? What is so funny?"

"Hold on there Le Commandant. They are just going out to get an ice cream and I gave him the once over. I am laughing because of the car he was driving. It reminded me of when you picked me up for our first date.

His initial shock of the whole situation was turned to laughter as pondered back to that first date.

"Don't you remember Bill?"

"How could I forget? I tried to impress you and then I ended up having to push the car to get it started. I am sure I looked like a winner at that moment."

"Yeah, you should have heard what my dad had to say about it later on."

"I bet I bet it made his whole day."

"Actually he said that he appreciated the fact that you worked so hard to take me out. He knew, though he wouldn't admit it, that you were a good guy."

"Well, enough about Dawn, what happened? Did you get your new toy?"

"I sure did and it comes on Monday."

"Well, Christmas came early this year."

"I have an idea. It's just us; let's go out, we haven't been out by ourselves for a while."

"Really?" She said in shock. "I have to get ready."

"You look fine, let's go."

Mrs. Sinclair's heart skipped a beat. It had been months since they had been on a date night. And this time he initiated it. She was filled with hope in that their last discussion might have made a difference.

Brandon and Dawn headed to the Tastee Freeze. Dawn was thankful that it was only a mile or two away. The cars heater seemed to be running and it was as hot as an oven inside even with the windows down.

"I'm sorry Dawn; I can't seem to turn the heater off."

"It's OK."

She sat there as still as she could, she was starting to get to hot and soon she would want to throw up. She started to think that her dream date was starting to turn into a nightmare. She did feel bad for Brandon though, he seemed to be trying so hard to impress her, and so far he had failed at that.

They arrived at the Tastee Freeze trailing smoke like a crop duster over a field and everyone there was alerted to them because of the deafening screech caused from his brakes when they pulled into the parking lot. The place was packed and they had to park down the street a ways from the take out window. Just as he went to get out of the car it started to rain.

"What more could go wrong with this date?" he thought to himself.

At this point Dawn started to roll up her window and tried to keep a straight face.

Seeing that she would have to stand in the rain he asked her what she wanted.

"Just a Coke float."

"Ok."

He closed the door and headed to the window. He stood in line in the cool mist as he waited his turn. Dawn rolled the window back down, even though the mist had turned into a shower, she just had to let some of the smell out. Brandon finally reached the window and ordered two Coke floats. He handed the girl the money and in a few minutes she handed him the floats just as he headed to the car the clouds released their rain in a torrent. Dawn tried as quickly as she could to roll up the window to keep from getting soaked. Brandon ran to the car in order to escape the deluge. Just as he reached the drivers side door, Dawn opened the door to help him since his hands were full. The door hit his hand and almost knocked one of the floats out of his hand. The ball of ice cream that was in the cup rolled out and onto the ground. He had no time to react as by this time he was already soaked and entered the car.

He sat down and closed the door and handed Dawn the other float. She looked at him and his soaked appearance and the disgusted look on his face. For a moment she didn't know what do to, until he broke out laughing. She no longer could hold back and started laughing along.

"I am sorry Dawn; I thought this date would go so much better. I was doing my best to impress you. I am sure that you are impressed now."

"It's okay. It has been a memorable date, to say the least."

It was the thing to break the ice between them as they sat in the car and drank their floats. Well Dawn drank her float and Brandon drank his Coke, seeing that his ice cream lay on the ground next to the car.

At one point the rain came down so heavy that they couldn't even see the front of the car. As they sat there and talked, Brandon noticed another fault in his chariot. A small drip started to form above the passenger side of the dashboard.

"My mom was right; this really is a piece of crap."

"It's fine; my dad says that everyone's first car should be a piece of crap. It makes you appreciate the next one you get." She told him.

"I don't know Dawn; your dad has quite the reputation around town. Most guys are afraid too ask you out. They're afraid that he might shoot them or something."

"It's not that bad Brandon; he would only shoot you if you tried something with me. That's all."

"That makes me feel better."

The rain started to taper off and Brandon took the empty cups out to the garbage. Brandon might have felt that this first date was a total disaster but Dawn was so high she thought that she could fly. He entered the car and tried to start it. He turned the key with a resounding click.

"Come on, what now?" Brandon said in disgust.

"What's wrong?" Dawn asked, even though she knew enough that the battery was dead.

"The battery is dead. I am going to have to call my mom."

"Don't worry Brandon, let me call my dad, we just live down the street. We could even walk there and I could get the car and give it a jump."

"Ok." He responded.

The night was warm and the sun was just starting to set. Dawn didn't care about the car; at this point it was just a way to spend more time with Brandon. It was like they fit together so well. He knew how to make her laugh and he seemed to be her dream come true. At this point anything bad that she had heard about Brandon was far gone; all she could see at this point was her Prince Charming, even if his horse had died along the way. She knew that soon they would both look back at this disaster and laugh. It would be a memory that they would both enjoy.

It was a night like this that made Saratoga Springs such a nice place to live. The streets were safe and crime was low. It was a small town on the out skirts of Albany that still had all the charms of old time America. As the two of them walked down the street Dawn's parents passed them on the road. After realizing that it was Dawn and Brandon, Mr. Sinclair stopped the car and rolled down the window.

"Didn't you have a car when you picked Dawn up son?" He asked.

"Yes sir, it wouldn't start. Dawn said that you might be able to give us a hand.

"Ok, get in and I will go home and get my tools."

Both Dawn and Brandon stood there in a trance not knowing what to do when Mr. Sinclair interjected.

"Well you guys are you going to get in or do you want to walk back to the house?"

They both hurried to the car and got in the back seat. Dawn went to sit close to Brandon but when she saw her father's raised eyebrows in the rear view mirror she slid farther away.

"I think the battery is dead dad." Dawn said sheepishly.

"Ok, that might help to know what the problem is."

"As they pulled into the driveway he hit the button to lift the garage door. He stopped the car and then got out and walked into the garage. Mrs. Sinclair had gotten out and was headed for the door.

"Thanks for the evening, Bill, I will see you later." She said as she gave him a playful wink.

Her little display made his heart skip a beat and he forgot what he went into the garage for.

"The tools." He said to himself as he regained his composure.

He grabbed his toolbox, put it in the trunk, and then got back into the car. He pulled the car out of the garage and then they headed to the Tastee Freeze.

When they arrive he parked facing Brandon's car so it would be easier to give him a jump.

"Open the hood will you son?"

"Dad, his name is Brandon, OK?" Dawn interjected.

"Ok."

Brandon lifted the hood and Dr. Sinclair looked into the engine compartment. He looked at the battery terminals.

"Filthy, just filthy, these terminals are so corroded, no wonder your battery went dead. Give me a minute. I think we will have you running in a minute."

By this time it seemed that they had become some sort of side show and people were coming around to see what was wrong. One by one, guys started coming over.

"What's up Brandon, the piece of crap won't run or what." John Hoover asked.

"Yeah, that's right; the piece of crap won't run. What's it to you?" Brandon responded angrily.

"Ah, Brandon, don't go postal, I just wanted to see if I could help." John responded.

"I don't know do you know anything about cars?"

"Not really."

"Then what good are you, get out of here."

Dawn just stood there listening and watching her father clean of the battery terminals. Once the crowd realized that Brandon was in no mood for being made fun of they went back to eating their ice cream.

"Don't fret it son, we all had a first car, and they usually are hunks of junk. My first car was a winner too."

Brandon was actually taken back by Dr. Sinclair's knowledge of cars and motors. He was trying to show Brandon different problems with the motor and what could be fixed easily and what could not.

"I'm kind of surprised at you Mr. Sinclair."

"Why's that?"

"I didn't expect"

Dr. Sinclair interrupted him mid sentence.

"You didn't expect a college professor to know his way around an engine. Correct?"

"Yeah."

"Son, my grandfather owned a garage back in North Carolina. He started modifying cars to run moonshine back in the 20's. My father was a mechanic on a race team and both of them taught me all they could. I think my father was disappointed when I chose to go to college instead of a career in NASCAR on a race team."

"Try to start it now son."

Brandon opened the door, sat down and turned the key. To his surprise the car actually started.

"Thanks, Mr. Sinclair."

"Don't mention it. You take care now son."

Brandon looked at Dawn and said goodbye and proceeded to drive home. As he left Dr. Sinclair could tell that Dawn was upset about something.

"What's wrong Sunshine?"

"Dad, his name is Brandon, not son. Why did you treat him that way?"

"Come on Dawn, I treated him OK, what did you expect me to do. I got his car running, didn't I?"

"Yes, but what if he never calls me again?"

"Well, then he wasn't worth your time or energy."

Dawn didn't even acknowledge his last statement she just got into the car. She knew he was right, but this was Brandon, the man of her dreams, what was she going to do if he never asked her out again?

As they pulled into the garage Mrs. Sinclair was waiting for them.

"Everything OK?" she asked.

"Yes, his battery terminals just needed cleaning, nothing big, just a standard first car."

Mrs. Sinclair smiled slightly and started to chuckle a little.

"What's that all about?" Dawn asked.

"Well Dawn, when your father came to pick me up for our first date, we had to push the car in order to start it. So don't fret it, it happens to most people and their first car. It's just a fact of life."

Dawn went up stairs to call Jessica. She finally got a date with Brandon and she was on cloud nine regardless of how bad it went. Dawn could hardly feel the ground as she rushed up to her room to call her best friend to tell her the news. Her mother just smiled and laughed to herself as she sat down next to Bill.

"Remember those days, Bill?"

"Yes, every time I look at you, you're still the only one that I see."

Trisha's eyes started to fill with tears before he was even finished with his sentence. She had almost given up all hope to think that she was still appealing to him. At times she thought that he was no longer interested in her at all. For now he had made her day, her month for that matter. At that moment she felt as high as Dawn did as they watched the TV together.

Chapter 4

After their first date the summer seemed to even go faster. Dawn's head was in the clouds as she was completely infatuated with Brandon. She could hardly believe at times that they were actually dating, it all seemed like a dream to her. With her focus now on her and Brandon, Dawn wasn't so worried about her parents or their relationship any more. She was sleeping better and her stomach wasn't giving her the problems it usually would. For the first time, Dawn was in love.

Mrs. Sinclair often worried about Dawn at this time. She knew how much Dawn was enamored with Brandon and was afraid that she might get her heart broke in the near future. She knew that this was all part of life and growing up, but she still wished she could shield her from it. Mrs. Sinclair knew that Dawn was on the sled ride of her life and going down the hill as fast as she could. She remembered the excitement of the first love and all the joy and anticipation that it included. She just didn't want her daughter to lose her innocence through it all.

She tried to reign in Dawn at times and tried to teach Dawn how to act around Brandon. She told her how to act when at a restaurant and ordering dinner.

"Make sure that you let him order first, and always get something less than he does. Always keep a close eye on where his eyes are at and don't let him sweet talk you into anything. Understand?"

Dawn usually would reply with an unenthusiastic response.

"Dawn I mean it. Guys at this age are only one step above an ape. Most of the time all they want is one thing. Do you know what I mean?"

"You mean all they want to do is play Canasta?" Dawn replied sarcastically.

"Dawn, stop being such a smart mouth, at this age, all they mostly want to do is get their hands on you and possibly something more."

"Is that what dad wanted when he met you?"

"Dawn!" She replied just as her dad entered the room.

"What's going on in here?" he asked.

"Oh, nothing dad, mom was just telling me that you wanted nothing more from her than sex."

"What?"

"Bill, that's not what I said. I said that she should be careful with Brandon. Guys his age often have ulterior motives."

Dr. Sinclair's blood started to boil at the thought of some high school punk trying to take advantage of his daughter.

"Did Brandon do something to you Dawn?" He asked like a detective at a murder investigation.

"NO!"

"Are you sure? I only have to shoot one of them and all the others will get the message. You make sure that he knows I am not playing games. Understood?"

"I understand dad. Don't worry; he has the fear of God in him and the fear of you. Ok?"

"Trisha, have you had the talk with Dawn?"

"Bill!"

"Dad!"

They both responded at the same time.

Knowing that he was out gunned he retreated back to his office to let Dawn and Trisha work it out.

"Dawn, you know you could tell me if Brandon tried to go too far, right?"

"Yeah, mom, I know."

She didn't like to lie to her mother but there was no way she would ever tell her mother if Brandon tried something. Dawn had to laugh inwardly though. Even though Brandon and she had been out a few times now, Brandon showed no signs of romance toward her. He never made a motion to even kiss her. She thought at one time that he was saying goodnight that he was actually going to try and shake her hand. So far he was nothing more than a complete gentleman. He never once showed a side of himself that she didn't like. Dawn couldn't understand how so many stories there were about Brandon and him being a ladies man. So far all he appeared to be was a nerdy jock. Dawn didn't care about that though. He was nice and caring and made her laugh. He seemed to understand her and would listen to her when she started to rant. To Dawn their relationship seemed more on a grade school level more than anything. Brandon seemed completely backward at times and totally uncomfortable around her. He hardly ever called her more than twice a week and they never went out other than on Friday nights, but for now she was fine with the whole setup.

She was sure that her father was only kidding about some things that he would say, but she wasn't taking any chances.

"Can we talk about something else? Brandon has been nothing but nice to me. I am not sure if he even likes me that much. He hardly calls me and we've only been out a few times."

"Don't try and rush things Dawn, you have plenty of times for guys. Just don't let this relationship get in the way of your dreams. OK?"

"I get it mom. I'm not stupid; I'm not going to do something that I regret later."

"Good. What does everyone want for dinner?"

"How about pizza?" Dawn asked.

"Pizza again, I am so tired of pizza, how about chicken sandwiches and French fries?"

"Ok."

Dawn started to head for the living room.

"Dawn?"

"Yeah?"

"Do you think you might ask if I needed any help?"

"Oh, do you need any help?" she asked reluctantly.

"Yes, you can set the table."

"OK."

Dawn set the table and within 20 minutes dinner was ready. Mrs. Sinclair really didn't like throwing a box dinner together like this but days that she worked it was the best she could do.

Mrs. Sinclair took dinner out of the oven and told Dawn to get her father and tell him that dinner was ready.

"Dad, dinner is ready!" Dawn yelled.

"I could have done that, go into his office and get him."

"OK"

Dawn went into her dad's office and told him that dinner was done. She had to tell him more than once, because he was so deep in thought he didn't even notice that she was in the room.

"Ok, thanks Dawn, I will be right there."

As Dr. Sinclair sat down he saw the chicken sandwiches and fries.

"You know Trisha; I think with you working it is about time that Dawn learned to cook."

"What?" Dawn interjected.

"I said it's time for your mother to teach you to cook. You mother is gone all day a couple of times a week. There is no reason why you couldn't cook on those days. It's a good skill to have as you get older. I'm kind of worried about you Dawn, that if there wasn't a pizza in the freezer or a box of macaroni and cheese in the cabinet that you might starve to death."

"Not as long as Marcelloni's still delivers." Her mother said laughing slightly.

"It's time for you to grow up a little. You are big enough to start to take care of things. Sooner or later you will have to do it any way, if you ever plan on moving out of the house." Her father told her.

Even though dinner was quick and from a box, they sat and enjoyed it like a family. They all sat together and talked and enjoyed each others company.

Chapter 5

After a few dates to the movies and out to eat Dawn didn't know anything more about Brandon then she did when he first asked her out. She knew where he lived with his mother and that was about it. He seemed very guarded about anything about himself. He always seemed preoccupied with something, like he was always looking over his shoulder. The one thing that she did learn is that he was very protective of his mother. She only saw him get angry once and it was where someone had made reference to his mother. She was afraid that he was going to beat the other kid up, but other than that he was usually very calm and controlled.

Mrs. Sinclair was also curious about this young man that had eyes for her daughter. It seemed that no one in the neighborhood could tell her much of anything other than that he was a good leader and captain of the football team and that he and his mother lived on the other side of town in a rickety old trailer.

Being the person that she was Mrs. Sinclair took it upon herself to get to know the family better. In her investigation she found out that Mrs. Phillips worked at a local restaurant and where she lived. Mrs. Sinclair made a pie and headed over there one day to say hello. Just like the other neighbors said, the trailer was old but well kept. She knocked on the door and Mrs. Phillips came to the door.

"May I help you?" She asked.

"Mrs. Phillips, My name is Trisha Sinclair, Dawn's mother, I just wanted to say hello and get to know you a little better."

"Come on in."

Mrs. Sinclair entered the small but quaint little trailer. It brought her back to the memories of her parent's trailer when she was younger. She tried to be inconspicuous when she looked around. She found a lot of pictures of Brandon and a few of him and her but none with a father figure present.

"I am sorry that the house is such a mess. I worked late last night."

"No worry. Mrs. Phillips, we have all been there."

"Call me Kate, please, so Dawn is you daughter? I have been hearing a lot about her lately. Brandon doesn't tell me much about the girls he is dating. I think he watches me more than I watch him. He is very protective of me."

Mrs. Sinclair didn't offer much for conversation. She allowed Mrs. Phillips to do most of the talking. She always thought that a person would tell you what you wanted to know if you just let them talk.

"I guess you came to check up on the boy that no one knows anything about." Mrs. Phillips said.

"Well I just wanted to get to know him and his family. I just wanted to make sure that his intentions were good. I have only met him a few times. He seems very nice and Dawn thinks he set the moon."

"It's been hard on him, the last couple of years. We were moving quite a bit for a while until we found Saratoga Springs. It seemed like a nice place, pretty low key." Mrs. Phillips said.

"I am sorry if I am being to forward, but I don't see a father in any of your pictures."

"No, he's the one reason that we live here."

Mrs. Sinclair could see her eyes filling with tears and one slowly dripping from her face.

"I'm sorry. I didn't mean to upset you. Maybe it's time for me to go."

"No, stay, it's been so long since someone has taken the time to get to know either of us. I mean it hasn't been easy making friends. We have been trying to stay low key where ever we are."

"Can I ask why?" Mrs. Sinclair asked quietly.

"Well, let me gain my composure." She replied as she wiped another tear from her face.

"My husband, Frank and I met in college, at first he was charming. He was studying to become a pharmacist and soon after he graduated we got married. Our marriage was good at first. He had got a good job at a local pharmacy and things were good. We bought a house and started to settle down. I had my own piece of heaven for a while."

"What happened?" Mrs. Sinclair interjected.

"Well, I guess you can say life happened. I got pregnant with Brandon. We were so excited, at least I was. Frank acted like he was, but I found out later that it was all an act. Once Brandon was born something in Frank broke. He no longer was the loving man that I knew and loved. He started drinking and his view of me had changed. I became more of his servant and live in maid than a wife and friend. "

"I'm sorry."

"Well you haven't heard the best of it yet. For whatever reason he never showed too much affection for Brandon and to this day I do not know why. He never liked to hold him and he never really acted very affectionate towards him. Brandon was about five years old when Frank hit me for the first time. I don't know why I didn't leave right then. I guess I was codependent at that time. I figured I had no other option and that he had never hit me before that and it might be an isolated incident. As Brandon got older Frank's anger got worse and worse. He often told him that I had cheated on him and that he wasn't his real father and that I was nothing more than a whore. He often called him worthless and swore at him. All this went on until Brandon turned 12. Brandon was coming home from school and opened the door to see his father beating me. He had knocked me down and was beating me in the face. I guess Brandon had enough and something in him snapped. He ran over and jumped on Frank's back and started to stab him with a kitchen knife. Frank was 75 pounds heavier and 6 inches taller so it didn't take long for him to throw Brandon off of him. But Brandon was like an animal at this time. I could see in his eyes that he was going to teach his father a lesson. I guess all those years of being abused by Frank and watching me getting abused had taken its toll."

She stopped for a moment to wipe more tears from her eyes.

"I'm sorry. It still gets to me."

"Kate, you don't have to go on. I never imagined. I am sorry. I just came over to get to know you better. I am sorry."

"I will be fine. You know you can only hold it in so long. It's been so long since I have talked about it."

She wiped another tear from her eye and started again.

"Frank had thrown Brandon against the wall and sort of dazed him. Frank was crazy with rage at this point."

"You've done it now kid. I am going to teach you a lesson you will never forget." Frank told Brandon.

"Brandon had a look of terror and rage in his eyes. His father grabbed him and threw him onto the living room floor. Even though it must of hurt pretty bad, Brandon got up almost immediately and ran at his father. He ran at him like a linebacker, head down and ready for impact. The impact threw Frank back up against the wall with a thud."

"I didn't know you had it in you, you little SOB!" Frank yelled at Brandon.

Brandon had enough and he was ready to die if he had to in order to end it.

"Frank forced his hands down on Brandon's back and knocked him back on the ground. He then gave him a good kick to the stomach. At this point I had recovered enough to grab the only thing I had handy. I grabbed my cast iron frying pan and I hit him square in the head with all that was in me. Brandon was able to get up at this point and grabbed the knife that had fallen on the floor. He jumped on his father and started to stab him. I was totally overcome in terror at this point. I wasn't sure what to do. I wanted Frank dead at this point, but I didn't want Brandon to kill him, so I pulled Brandon off his father and then the police arrived. A neighbor heard what was going on and called the police."

"Did he kill him?"

"No, he did manage to stab him 8 times and broke his cheekbone."

"When the police and ambulance arrived they started asking questions. To my surprise they not only took Frank to the hospital, they arrested Brandon."

"For what?" Mrs. Sinclair said in shock.

"They said that until they could investigate what happened he was going to be charged with assault with a deadly weapon. I tried to tell them that he was only trying to protect me from Frank. "

"So what happened?"

"Well they did arrest Frank in the hospital and took him to jail a week later and they locked up Brandon in juvenile hall. I tried to get him out of there and went to see him every day. The DA prosecuted Frank and he got seven years in prison, and the state made Brandon take anger management courses."

"So that's when you moved here?"

"Oh no, that's not the whole story. When I was on the witness stand I could see that Frank was burning with anger. That someday he would get me and Brandon back for what was going to happen to him. I can still remember his icy stare when they handcuffed him and led him out of the court room. I knew that when he got out we wouldn't be safe. That's when I took Brandon and we disappeared. "

"You've been on the run for over seven years now?"

"Yes, what a life for a young kid, I wish we could live a normal life, but as long as Frank is out there I know he will search until he finds us. When he finds us he's going to kill me and maybe Brandon. All I can do is try and beat him at his own game."

"Is Frank still in prison?"

"No, he got out about two years ago. I still keep up with what's going on. There is a restraining order out against him. But it's only good in South Carolina. I did divorce him while he was in prison, but that's just another reason for him to come and kill us."

"Mrs. Sinclair I hope you can understand now why there is so much mystery about us. I just want to live in the hope that we can be safe some day. It keeps me up at night. I know it bothers Brandon, like I said before, he watches me quite close."

"Don't worry Kate; your secret is safe with me. I understand. I would do the same thing. You have to protect your family. This is a small town. I am sure that he couldn't show up without being noticed."

"Probably not, but who is going to care about a poor waitress that lives on the bad side of town."

"I care, don't worry. Do you have a picture of Frank? We will keep an eye out for him."

Kate went to the back of the trailer and came out with an old picture of Frank.

"This is about ten years old, but I am sure you can find a new picture of him on the internet." She told Mrs. Sinclair.

"Thanks. I'll give you a call. We will have to get together again. I am sorry that it took this long to introduce myself."

"I understand."

Mrs. Sinclair said her goodbyes and headed for her car. She got in and started to drive home. The whole way there she thanked God for the family she had and that she didn't have to worry about some crazy man stalking her.

Chapter 6

Dawn had plenty of friends but there was the special friend that she liked to hang out with the most. Jessica was the girl that Dawn was most connected to. Jessica and her would often hang out at the mall or just hang out at home. Talk for hours on the phone or just watch movies on a Friday night.

They had known each other since the second grade and had been friends ever since. Each was the others confidant and held all the secrets of the other. They trusted each other without question and never had a reason not to.

They seemed to be a perfect match for each other. One was the catalyst for the other. Without the other they both were quiet and didn't interact much but together they were ready to take on the world.

All this started to change once they became of dating age. Not that they weren't the best of friends anymore, just that their relationship changed somewhat. The fact that Dawn was more popular than Jessica often made Jessica feel isolated and less than adequate at times. Dawn seemed to have it all and Jessica felt at times that she was just the tag a long. To Dawn, Jessica was never a tag along and she loved her like the sister that she never had. She never realized how Jessica felt and that she stood in her shadow, to Dawn, Jessica was her equal, she never felt at odds or in competition with her, Jessica on the other hand often felt like she had to try and outshine Dawn.

Dawn was the pretty girl and Jessica was the girl next door. Jessica tried as hard as she could to equate herself with Dawn but she never felt like she could be as pretty as her.

All of this might have been too much for Jessica to bear if not for the fact that Dawn was genuine all the way. She would never do anything that would hurt Jessica and always seemed to be her biggest fan. She was always there for her and would be the one rooting for her to succeed.

They both were the kind of friend that you could talk to, yell at or down right fight with but at the end of the day they were still friends. They saw each other for who they were, not perfect but flawed.

All of this was true until Jim. They both met Jim in the parking lot of the mall, after they went through the mall shopping and eyeing up the guys as they walked by. Guys often times get the bad wrap at checking out the girls but the girls were jut as guilty. They headed to the parking lot to leave.

"So what's up with you and Brandon?" Jessica asked Dawn.

"Nothing really, we've only been out a couple of times. He calls me every now and then, but other than that, there is nothing to report."

"Come on Dawn, there has to be something. Give me all the juicy details. Have you and him made out yet?"

"Jessica! No, like I said he hasn't even kissed me yet. I think maybe he is afraid of my father."

"Maybe, but it might be better for you this way."

"What do you mean?"

"I mean, I hear a lot of stories about Brandon, and most of them aren't very good. I hear that he likes to love em and leave em if you know what I mean."

"Yeah, I have heard the stories too. But at this point I don't know what to think. Maybe I don't interest him or maybe I'm not his type."

"Well one thing is sure." Dawn said.

"What's that?"

"I'm not going to be the kind of girl that sits by the phone waiting for him to call. I mean if he wants to date me it's in his court, not mine. I will leave it up to him to decide. I am not going to waste my time on anyone that isn't interested in me."

"You go girl. Be the one in control; don't let your emotions get you going."

As they got to the car Jessica noticed that the car had a flat tire.

"Dawn, you have a flat tire."

"No dah! What are we going to do now?"

"Can't you change it?" Jessica asked.

"Not really, I am not sure what to do; I never had to change a tire before. Let me call my dad."

Just as she pulled her cell phone out of her purse a young man approached them.

"Hello ladies, can I help you?" He asked.

"No I think I have it under control." Dawn replied.

"You're Dawn Sinclair, aren't you?" He asked.

"Yes, do I know you?"

"No, but I work for your father. I am his intern for the summer. I recognized you from his photo on his desk."

"Pardon me, I am Jim."

"Nice to meet you, Jim."

"Do you know how to change a tire?" Jessica interrupted.

"Yes, I do. Can you open the trunk?"

Dawn went over to the drives side of the car to open the trunk with Jessica walking close behind like her shadow. She hit the button and the trunk opened. Jim reached in and got the jack and the spare tire out and started to jack up the car.

"He's cute, don't you think? If Brandon isn't interested why don't you try for him?"

"We just met, and by the way, I don't know anything about him."

"You don't, but your dad does. Maybe he would meet your dad's expectations."

"Jessica, get real. First of all I don't think any guy could meet my dad's expectations. Second, he is in college. My dad would have a fit, if a college guy asked me out."

Jim proceeded to change the tire and listen to the girls at the same time. He had to smile just a bit when he heard what they were saying, he knew far too well about Dawn and her father.

"I've got an idea Jessica."

"What's that?"

"Maybe you should ask him out on a date?"

"What?"

"Well, you seem to like him, and your dad would probably say yes. Why don't you see if he'd go out with you?"

"Are you nuts or something Dawn? Why would any college guy go out with me? I am not you."

"What do you mean by that?"

"I don't have your looks and I don't have your brains. Why would he be interested in going out with me?"

"Come on Jessica, you look just fine, you're pretty and you have brains. I didn't say to marry the guy. I said to ask him out and see what he says."

"You girls better get back while I jack up the car. I don't want anything to happen."

Neither girl could stop from noticing his chiseled physic and his handsome features.

"Stop staring Jessica."

"You too, Dawn."

Jim's face started to redden when he realized that he was on display.

"You're embarrassing him Jessica."

"Well, you are just as guilty as I am, Dawn."

Jim proceeded to take off the flat tire and started mounting the spare. After realizing that they had embarrassed their new friend both girls stepped back and remained silent for a minute or two. After the brief silence they started to talk about going back to school and other unrelated things. Jim put on the lug nuts and slightly tightened them and lowered the jack. Jessica couldn't stop from staring as his muscles as he torqued the lug nuts when the car was on the ground.

"All done, let me put this flat in your trunk. This is just a donut, so you will have to get the tire repaired soon. Ok?"

"Ok, thanks, what do I owe you?" Dawn asked.

"What's the world coming to, if a man can't help a woman in distress?"

"Nice to have met you, Jim." Jessica said.

"I never did get you name." Jim replied.

"It's Jessica."

"Nice to meet you Jessica, do you think maybe you and me could go out sometime?"

"Really?" Jessica replied in surprise.

"Sure, I'll call you; maybe we could go to dinner and movie sometime."

"Ok, sure."

"See you later Jim." Dawn said as they got into the car and started to pull out of the parking space.

They just started to drive off when Jessica let out a blood curdling scream. Dawn slammed on the brakes and the car came to a screeching halt.

"What's wrong?" Dawn asked nervously.

"My number, I forgot to give him my number."

Jim came running up to the car, seeing that Dawn had stopped so suddenly.

"Is everything OK?" Jim asked trying to catch his breath.

"We're fine, Jessica, just forgot to give you her phone number."

Jessica hurriedly wrote down her number on a piece of note paper and handed it to Jim through Dawn's window.

"Thanks." Jim said.

"Call me."

They all said their goodbyes and the girls headed out of the parking lot, this time without incident.

"Well I am sure that he won't call me now after all of that."

"What do you mean?"

"I mean, he probably thinks I am some sort of bozo after all of that."

"Don't worry Jessica. Like my mother tells me. What is meant to be will happen no matter how bad it might seem."

"You know Dawn, you mother is pretty cool sometimes."

"Jessica, are you crazy, she drives me crazy most of the time. I think your mother is cooler than my mother."

"I guess that's the way it will always be. It's just a matter of perspective."

"I guess so.", Dawn replied as they laughed at what just happened. "What do you want to do now?" Dawn asked.

"I don't know, what is there to do in this rinky dink town. Is there anything at the movies?"

She was right. Saratoga Springs wasn't known for much other than having two colleges in town. Other than that there never was much going on. The only good thing was that they were only twenty odd miles to Albany and there was always something going on there.

"We could take a ride to Albany." Jessica suggested.

"I can't tonight. I told my mother that I would be back before 10:00 p.m. Do you want to come over and spend the night? We could watch scary movies all night long." Dawn answered back.

"I can't do that, my mother gets all bent out of shape when I don't ask her first. I guess it's time to go home and watch reruns of Let's Make a Deal on the Game Show Network."

"Really? Anything is better than that. I am sure that we can figure out something."

"I guess, I will just go home and wait for Jim to call me. I'll just get a half gallon of ice cream and wait patiently."

"OK, I get the hint. I will drop you off at you house." Dawn replied.

"What are you going to do?" Jessica asked.

"Probably go home and watch reruns of Let's Make a Deal." Dawn answered.

It didn't take long to get to Jessica's house and Dawn dropped her off. She then headed to her house. Dawn had just entered the house and sat her purse down when her father walked in.

"What's up Sunshine?" Dad asked.

"Nothing much, how about with you?" Dawn responded.

"I met someone that works for you today."

"Who?"

"Your intern Jim."

"You did, did you? Where did you meet him?"

"I had a flat at the mall and he fixed it for me. Oh by the way he told me to either get the tire fixed or get a new tire because I am riding on a donut."

"That was nice of him. He's a pretty good kid so far."

"He seemed to be. He even asked Jessica for her phone number."

"He did, did he?"

"Don't worry Dad, he didn't ask for mine. Apparently you've scared him away too."

"Some day Dawn you will look back and thank me for keeping all of the creepy crawlies away. Don't worry when the right one comes along, you will know it, your mother will know it and I will surely know it."

"Okay dad." She said sarcastically.

"What's for dinner Dawn?"

"I don't know I just got here."

"Well I guess we will have to make something." He told her.

Dawn was filled with fear at the thought that her father was actually going to try and cook dinner. Only on a rare occasion did he ever make anything good. Usually his food was a complete failure, unfit for human consumption. There had been times that the dog wouldn't even eat some of his concoctions. She always had to laugh that a man with a PHD couldn't make a simple box of macaroni and cheese.

"Well, let's see what we can make." He said confidently.

"Dad?"

"Yes."

"I don't want you take this the wrong way. But I am afraid of the food you make when you try to cook. It's usually really bad."

Her dad stopped and looked at her. She thought at first that she had hurt his feelings and then he burst into laughter.

"I guess I don't have a good track record when it comes to cooking." He told her.

"Who could forget your black spaghetti sauce or your pork croquets? I know you try, but I would leave the cooking to mom."

Just about this time Trisha entered the room carrying a bag full of Chinese takeout.

"Mom, you saved the day, dad was about to try and cook something." Dawn let out with childish glee.

"I hope you had the phone ready to call the fire department. Can you help me with these?"

"I'm sorry sure."

"Funny." Dr. Sinclair answered sarcastically.

"Bill, everyone has a knack for something. Cooking isn't yours. But there is good news. The Army called and said that they were going to try and use some of your recipes as bio weapons."

"I get it, I get it. I stink at cooking. What did you get anyway?" He said.

"Did you get any rat on a stick?" He asked.

"Bill, you know I hate when you call it that. It's chicken Teriyaki." Trisha responded.

"I know it just doesn't seem like its chicken. It looks more like pork. I think something has been lost in translation. I really think its city chicken." He replied.

"Maybe, but it's hard for me to eat when you call it a rat."

"I'm sorry; from now on I could call it cat on a stick, or maybe squirrel or chipmunk."

"Bill just stop it I am hungry and I want to eat."

"Dawn, get out some plates and see what you father wants to drink. Please poor me an iced tea."

"Sure to wash down that rat on a stick." Dawn replied.

Rather than yelling at Dawn her anger was directed to Bill.

"Bill, see what you started. Now I am telling you both, I have had enough of your foolishness and I just want to sit down and eat. Ok? Enough is enough."

Dawn knew when her mother had enough and she wasn't about to push her buttons, there was no reason to ruin a perfectly good evening, and this one was going better than most. Dawn got the paper plates and poured the drinks and they all sat at the table and divided the Chinese food. It had been the first time in a while that they all had sat down for dinner at the same time. They spent the evening eating and talking. For once it seemed that the family was on the road to renewal. That her father actually was making good on his promise to be home more often. After dinner they all cleaned up their messes and went to the living room to watch one of their favorite movies together. As simple as it seemed Mrs. Sinclair was on cloud nine. She was afraid for a while that the family was just going to slowly drift apart, but for that moment she had hope. Hope that Bill would realize what he had to lose. They all sat on the couch and watch the movie and they all laughed and had a good time. They were a family again. After the movie was over Dawn went upstairs to get ready for bed and left her parents alone. This was always the time that Dawn did her best to eaves drop on them without them knowing. Usually it was to no avail. Both her parents seemed to be clairvoyant and always could tell that she was trying to listen. Even so their quiet time together was always a barometer to Dawn on how the family was doing. No matter how hard her parents tried, the noise of their squabbles always filtered upstairs and into her room. This night was different, the sounds were soft and there seemed to be no angry words being said. It just seemed like they were enjoying themselves.

There on the couch their love seemed to have been rekindled for the time being. Neither of them was caught in the day's chaos or worried about anything. Both were just enjoying the others company. It had been to long, way to long, since they both had an evening like this one. With their feeling for each other being renewed they decided to go to bed.

Dawn could here them giggling to each other like they were in high school as they walked past her door.

"Good night Dawn. We love you." They both said in unison and giggling afterward.

"Good night Love Birds, I love you too."

They looked at each like they had just met and felt the old spark that brought them together in the first place and then giggled some more.

"Really guys get a room." Dawn yelled from her bed.

"We already have one." Her mother replied.

Dawn just rolled over and went to sleep. On one hand she was glad that her parents seemed to be falling in love with each other again, on the other hand when she thought of her parents and their love life she wanted to be sick.

Chapter 7

The fair came once a year and everyone went. It was the last blow out that Saratoga Springs had before school started again. It was a time to hang out and see friends that you hadn't seen in a while. Dawn was planning on going with Jessica but Jessica told her that Jim was going. Dawn didn't want to seem like a third wheel so she told her that she might see her there. The fact that Brandon hadn't called to ask her to go to the fair troubled her. Sometimes the lapses in his calls often got on her nerves.

She would often get mad, thinking, "What does he think I do all day? Sit around and wait for him to call?"

Just as she started to go on a rant inside her bedroom by herself the phone rang.

"I am not going to get it. If it's him he can call back." She thought to herself.

After the third ring, her mother picked up the phone.

"Dawn. It's Brandon."

"Ok, Mom I got it."

She walked down the steps as fast as she could and still appear as not to be anticipating his call. She calmly took the phone from her mother and told her thanks.

Her mother smiled and went back to doing whatever she was doing before.

"Sound good, let me ask my mother" Her mother heard Dawn say.

"Mom, can I go to the fair with Brandon tonight?"

"Sure, just be back by 11:00 p.m."

"She said yes. Ok, I will be ready. See you then."

Her anger was gone, replaced by the joy that a date would give. All she could think of now was what to wear and the fact she had no time to get ready. She started into her frantic chaos mode as she ran up stairs.

It was two hours later about 6:00 p.m. when Brandon showed up. Mrs. Sinclair let him in and asked him to sit down. She yelled upstairs to Dawn telling her that he was there.

"Ok, I'm almost done." She yelled back.

"She should be ready in a minute or two." She told him unconvincingly

After a few minutes went by Mrs. Sinclair couldn't even figure out what was keeping her. She excused herself and headed up to Dawn's room.

"Dawn, what are you doing in there?" She asked as quietly as she could.

"Nothing Mom, I'm almost done."

With that last statement the door opened and Dawn appeared. She ran down the steps and into the living room.

"I'm sorry, let's go."

Brandon got up and headed to the door. He opened it for her and they headed to his car. Brandon's car hadn't changed. It was still the hunk of junk that he had before. This time though he seemed more confident that it would actually start after he put Dawn in the passenger seat.

Dawn noticed that he went into a quick trance of sorts as he turned the key. The car belched some white smoke but started right up. The motor started to rumble and he started to back out of her drive.

When Dawn could see that he was more relaxed she wanted to ask him what was going on before.

"Brandon, what was that thing you were doing, right before you tried to start the car?" she asked.

"I was making a quick prayer that it would start this time. You never really know about this thing. It seems every time I drive it somewhere something new is wrong with it or something has fallen off of it." He replied.

"OK then." She said.

After a short drive they arrived at the fair grounds. They had to follow the instructions of the parking attendants on where to park. You had to be careful at times because if it started raining the front field used as a parking lot often turned into a quagmire filled with immovable cars.

He parked the car and they headed to the entrance. He paid for their tickets and they headed in. After milling around for a minute or two they were met by Jessica and Jim. They all decided to get some fair food and headed over to the food court. Rather than a food court it was more like a street filled with food trailers all offering an array of different fair delights. There were candied apples, cotton candy, sausage sandwiches and even deep fried pickles for the brave at heart. Since the fair was only once a year most people who came usually overindulged at the food stands. But what was the fair for, if not to eat and drink and have fun with your friends. After each of them had their fill of sandwiches and cotton candy the girls decided to head for the rides. It was a decision that they all would soon regret.

Like an evil entity that lured her in with a promise of fun she headed right for the round-about. Even though this ride was legendary at making people sick, she just had to ride it.

"How about the round-about?" She asked excitedly.

"Sure" They all replied in unison.

They gave the operator their tickets and found a capsule to sit in. Dawn and the others were filled with excitement. All the others except Brandon, he was trying to keep his concern over the ride to himself.

"I can do this, I can do this." He mumbled to himself.

"Are you praying again, Brandon?" Dawn asked jokingly.

"Maybe a little."

Without being able to say anything more the ride started on its violent journey around and around.

Round and round they went. With every revolution the food in Brandon's stomach seemed to get an inch closer to his mouth. He tried to remain calm and cool and act like he had it all under control but he didn't. He was only moments away from releasing everything that was in his stomach. He was holding on to the safety bar harder and harder until his knuckles started to turn white. As his knuckles changed color so did his face. He was turning into a nice shade of green when Dawn looked over at him.

"Are you OK?" she yelled. It was hard to hear over all the screaming that was going on.

"Yeah why?" He answered nonchalantly.

"You just look like you are going to be sick."

"No I 'm fine. This is fun."

Dawn tried not to look at his contorted face and worry that he was about to get sick but she almost had to laugh at him trying to stay so cool and collected.

After what seemed to be another 10 minutes the ride was starting to slow down.

"I made it; I did it without throwing up." Brandon thought to himself.

He started to feel a little better until the ride came to a screeching halt and left his stomach a few feet behind. Without warning his stomach released its contents as he turned his head to reach over the side of the capsule they were in. The noise of the ride was overshadowed by the sound of Brandon throwing up. Some of the onlookers started to laugh while others felt sick themselves. The ride's operator realized that he had a potential puke fest on his hands and did his best to get the passengers off the ride. Dawn felt bad for him but had to get out of there and get out quick. If the smell of this ghastly horror reached her nostrils it would be over for her too. The man took out the key and opened the safety bar. Dawn jumped out of the capsule and headed for the exit. Brandon was left by himself for the operator to help out. He took a couple of steps and then threw up again. As people watched Brandon with sadistic enjoyment others decided that the ride was not for them and started towards another. What had been a 10 minute wait to ride the round-about had turned into a no wait line. The round-about had taken another victim and this time it was Brandon. The ride was inherently evil and put another notch on its belt for all of the people that is had made ill. After that year, it was a ride that other dared others to ride, knowing that at least one of them would lose their lunch after riding. As he reached the exit Dawn was there, still trying to care but keeping a slight distance between them.

"I'm sorry Brandon, but if I smell puke, I'm going to puke. Are you OK?"

"Yes. I think it's all done."

As soon as that sentence left his mouth and he took another step his body went into another convulsion and he threw up into the nearby trashcan. People started staring at him and treating him like he had a disease. As he started to walk towards the sea of people, it opened up and split in order for them to keep their distance from him. After another attack he finally reached a bench where he could sit down. Dawn came over to him with a cold coke.

"Sip on this, it will help."

"Thanks. I'm sorry. I didn't want to make a scene, so much for another good date. I am trying to wonder if dating is the right thing between you and me." He told her trying to keep from breathing in her direction.

"Don't worry. Some day we will sit back and laugh. It's not that bad. You're not the first person to get sick on that ride."

"I guess I should have told you that rides that go around and around have always made me sick. It was so bad when I was a kid I was banned from riding the paratroopers ride."

"Why didn't you tell me that when I suggested that we ride it?" Dawn said with concern.

"I don't know I didn't want you to think that I was a wimp or something. I'm not afraid to ride them, I just can't"

"Brandon, would you stop trying to impress me and be yourself. It would have been a lot better for you and that Carney over there if you would have just told me."

"I know. Just being a guy I guess." He said with a moan.

Dawn had to hold back the laughter and the puke in her own throat as she watched the poor ride operator hose off the capsule that they were in. She looked around and saw that Brandon wasn't the only victim of the ride and that there were at least three others affected by it. She wasn't sure if it was the ride by itself or Brandon's actions that cause them to get sick. Jim and Jessica decided to part ways with them at that point, hoping that their evening wouldn't be ruined any farther.

After about twenty minutes had passed, she asked. "What do you want to do now? Do you want to stay here or go home?"

"We can stay. I think I will be OK now."

"Do you want to ride some more rides?" She asked.

He smiled and started to laugh. "No I think I will pass on that one."

The rest of the evening went without incident and both of them had a good time. Around ten o'clock they headed to the car. Brandon opened the car door for Dawn and she got in. He went around and then got in the car and said his prayer as he tried to start the car. At first the car made a loud grinding noise as he turned the key. But after trying it again the engine started.

"That was close." Brandon said. "I wasn't sure that it was going to start."

"I was praying that time myself." Dawn said with a smile.

"Apparently it helped." He told her with a smile.

He drove out of the parking lot and headed for Dawn's house. After they arrived he walked her to the door.

"I hope you had a nice night. I am sorry about getting sick." He told her sincerely.

"It's fine, like I said we will all laugh about it one day."

After a brief moment of awkward silence he reached out and gave her a hug.

"Good night." He said as he headed back to his car and drove home.

"Good night." She replied as she headed into the house.

As she entered the house she saw her mother watching the TV.

"Is dad still at work?" She said with a scowl.

"No, he's upstairs finishing packing for tomorrow." Her mother replied.

"Did you guys have a nice night?"

"Yeah, it was fun. Brandon got sick on the round-about and threw up." She replied.

"Really?" Her mother replied rather amused.

"Yes, it was awful, I almost threw up myself. It's rather funny to think about now, even though Brandon was pretty embarrassed."

"I bet, did he throw up on you?" Her mother asked.

"No, Thank God for that."

"You better get ready for bed."

"But, Mom it's just 10:30." She retorted.

"Yes, I know but we all have to get up at 5:00 tomorrow to take your father to the airport, or did you forget?" Her mother responded.

"Yes I did. Good night, I love you." Dawn replied.

"I love you too."

She walked up the stairs and to her room. She knew she should go into her parent's bedroom and tell her father goodnight, but she just didn't feel like it. She got ready for bed and headed to her room and got into the bed. Just as she turned off the light there was a knock at the door.

"Dawn?" Her father called out.

"Yes?"

"Good night, I love you." He said as he opened the door.

"I love you too, Daddy." She replied.

He then walked over to her bed and kissed her on the forehead.

"Goodnight Sunshine." He said as only a father can say to his little girl.

"Goodnight." She responded as she reached out and hugged him like she was 4 years old again.

After their hug he stood up and headed out of the room and shut the door. His behavior took Dawn by surprise as she realized that he had the beginning of tears in his eyes. She rested her head on her pillow and relished in the thought of her father's love and fell asleep.

Chapter 8

The tire blew with a resounding thud as it suddenly went flat. Brandon's car started to slide across the highway as he tried to maintain control of it. He was able to keep control and safely make it to the shoulder of the road.
He got out of the car and cursed under his breath when he saw that the tire was completely ruined.

"Just add it to another thing wrong with this car." He muttered angrily.

He went to the trunk and got out the jack, tire iron and the spare.

He was so angry that he started to mumble swear words under his breath as he jacked up the car. Brandon really wasn't the one to swear but this car had pushed him to his breaking point. He often thought that he would have better luck and more money if he just started taking the bus.

He had the car up in the air and was removing the lug nuts when a man in a pickup truck stopped. The man parked the truck in front of Brandon's car and then proceeded to get out.

"Having some trouble there son?" The stranger asked.

Brandon turned his attention from the tire to the man standing to his side. A chill ran down his spine when he looked at him and realized who it was. He had seen that face a thousand times before and it was one that he would never forget.

"Son, did you hear me, are you having some trouble?"

It appeared to Brandon that the man didn't know who he was and Brandon was going to try and keep it that way. He turned his head to keep the man from getting a closer look at him. He hadn't seen his father in 7 years and had grown about 5 inches and put on another 45 pounds, he changed his hair color at his mother's request, and now it seems like his simple disguise worked for the time being.

"Nothing more than a flat tire, I'm almost done." He answered trying to shield his face from full view.

"Are you sure? "

"Yeah, thanks a lot though for the offer."

"Ok". The stranger replied and headed back to his truck. Brandon tracked him out of the corners of his eyes. He tried to make it seem like he wasn't watching him. All he had to do is lower the car and tighten the bolts and he would be done and gone.

After the man went in his truck he grabbed something and then headed back to Brandon. By this time Brandon was just finishing up tightening the bolts and getting ready to move on.

"I am new in town and I am looking for my son. I haven't seen him in a while. Do you happen to know him?"

The man showed Brandon an older picture of himself when he was younger. Brandon tried to keep his composure to ensure that he could maintain the ruse that he started.

"No, I don't know him. Are you sure he lives around here?" As he put the blown tire and jack back in the trunk. He shut the trunk and then headed for the drivers seat.

"I'm sorry mister that I can't help you, but I have some place I have to be."

"Ok, thanks for your help." The stranger replied.

Brandon started his car, put it in drive and looked to see if anyone was coming. Chills went down his spine as he pulled out onto the road not knowing if the man recognized him. Brandon knew that he had to call his mother, but he wasn't going to lead his crazy father to where she was. He pulled out his cell phone as he sped away from him. He dialed his mother's number. The phone started to ring and ring until he got the familiar, "The person you are trying to call is unavailable, please leave a message at the tone." He hung up and tried to call again, and again.

"Come on Mom, pick up." He thought to himself. For all he knew his father could have already found her and killed her by now. He knew that he had one place to be and that was in town at the diner. He drove far enough to make sure that his father couldn't see him anymore and he turned off onto a side street. He knew the layout of town like the back of his hand; it was something that his mother made him learn, just to make sure he always had a way of escaping danger. After what seemed like an eternity he arrived at the diner. He knew if his mother was inside she would be ok. His car screeched to a halt as he pulled into the parking space. He then opened the car door and ran to the diner entrance. His mother was waiting on a table when she saw him come through the door. She could tell by the look in his eye that something was wrong. She finished taking the people's order and then excused herself.

"He's here, Mom, he's here." He said to her so fast that she couldn't understand what he was saying.

"Calm down Brandon, who's here?" She asked.

"Dad, he's here, he just tried to help me fix the flat on my car. I came here as soon as I could. I was afraid that he might have gotten to you first."

"I'm fine, Brandon, how do you know it was him?"

"Mom, I could never forget his face."

His mother was filled with all sorts of emotions, fear, anger, disgust, to name a few.

"What right does he have to show up now?" She thought to herself.

"What are we going to do Mom?"

"Well, I will tell you the one thing we are not going to do?"

"What's that?"

"We are not going to run and I refuse to be afraid. If he wants me come and get me. This time though I will be ready. Do you understand?"

"I understand." Brandon replied.

Brandon knew that you could only push his mother so far and this was as far as she was going to go. She had grown stronger through the years and she wasn't about to let a crazy ex-husband ruin her life.

"Did he see where we lived?" She asked.

"No, I met him on the other side of town."

"Good, if he shows up, I'll be ready for him this time. I will be ok, Brandon, don't worry. I'm ok; go back to doing whatever you were doing."

Brandon left reluctantly and sat out in his car for a while before leaving. His mother was the one constant in his life and he wasn't about to let his crazy father take that away from him. If he had to this time he would finish the job that he started the last time that he attacked her.

"Come on crazy old man. This time it's just me and you." Brandon thought to himself.

Brandon waited a little longer until he could see his mother signaling him that she was OK and to go home.

Katherine tried to give Brandon the most normal life that she could. That's why after two years she stopped running and prepared herself for the reality that her husband would someday come after her. This time though she was ready. She wasn't the codependent frail woman that he had married. The life they had together and the life she lived after his incarceration made her strong. Strong and ready to fight and do whatever it took to keep Brandon safe. And so their bond became even stronger, he was young man driven to rise above his past and she was a mother working to see that he would.

Brandon didn't go home that night and spent the evening driving around town. He went up and down the streets looking for his father's car to no avail. He circled around the diner more than once to make sure that he wasn't there and that his mother was safe.

At 10:00 p.m. his mother called Brandon to make sure that he was home safe. She worked the late shift tonight and he would have to go to sleep before she got home. Brandon answered the phone and told her that he was fine and that he was going to bed and not to worry. She hung up the phone and went back to work. She tried to keep her concern from Brandon but it still worried her that Bill was out there lurking in the darkness somewhere.

After Brandon got off the phone he got in his car and headed back to town. He didn't want his mother to worry but he was going to make sure that she was going to be OK. He headed back to the diner making sure that he kept away from the parking lot so that his mother could not see him. He knew that she would be angry if she knew that he was still up and downtown watching over her like her guardian angel.

At about 12:00 the diner was about to close for the evening. Brandon had parked across the street behind a bush. From his vantage point he could still see the parking lot but hoped that she couldn't see him. He had grown tired and was nodding off to sleep when she came out of the door and said goodnight to one of the cooks. She got in her car and headed back home. By this time Brandon had fallen off to sleep and by the time he woke up she was gone.

"She's going to kill me." He thought.

"I have to get home before she does. But how can I do that."

Rather than driving like an idiot to beat his mother home, because he didn't know when she left, he decided to go home at a safe speed. He was about 3 miles from home when his cell phone started to ring. He knew it was his mother by the ringtone.

He picked it up and answered.

"Where in the world are you? Why aren't you here in bed?"

"I was parked watching to make sure that you were OK."

"I'm fine; get your butt back here now!"

"I am on my way. I'm sorry."

She hung up the phone. She thought maybe she was a little too hard on him, but she didn't want to have to worry about him any more than she had to.

"Mom" He said as he entered the trailer.

"Just go to bed. It's late and you won't want to get up in the morning. No more secret missions, alright?" She interrupted before he could say anything else.

"Yes Mom. Good night. I love you."

"I love you too, now go to bed."

She got herself a cup of tea and turned on the TV. She always liked to relax a little and watch the current events of the day before she went to bed. Though she wanted Brandon to think that she had it all together she really didn't. With every sound and howl of the wind she would be startled. No matter how much she wanted to think she wasn't going to let the thought of Frank ruin her evening, it did. At about 2:00 a.m. she went to her bedroom and got ready for bed. After brushing her teeth she went around the doors once again making sure that they were all locked and that she couldn't see anyone outside.

"God help us." She prayed as she tried to sleep.

She never was a very religious person but she often called on God when times got tough. She knew that she should be more committed to her faith or not at all but this was one of those times that she needed some extra peace. As she laid her head on the pillow the wind seemed to howl more than usual and every sound outside seemed to be magnified.

"I need you now Lord. Help me and my boy." She prayed again. It had been a hard day and she was one inch from being overwhelmed with all that had transpired. She closed her eyes and tried to sleep. A strange feeling of peace came over her and she didn't feel so overwhelmed.

"Thank you." She said as she was finally able to sleep.

Brandon on the other hand had a terrible nights sleep. He often got up in the night and wandered in the dark trailer making sure that no one was creeping around outside. He would then go back to bed and try to fall back to sleep. Usually he was awakened by another nightmare or noise from outside. He finally woke up to the sound of his alarm going off. He found it difficult to get up, considering that he was running on very little sleep. He dragged himself out of his bed and headed for the shower. After standing in the stream of the hot water he started to perk up. He got out of the shower put on his clothes and went to the kitchen to get some breakfast. To his surprise her mother was sitting there at the table.

"Good morning 007, how did you sleep?" She asked him.

"Horribly, I hardly slept at all, how about you?"

"I know what you mean. But don't worry Brandon, this will all work out"

"I know, but I don't want to take any chances. Last night I downloaded this app to your phone."

"You did what?" She said with a shocked tone in her voice.

"Look Mom, now I can see where you are at any given time. If you press 111 it will send a text to me that you are in trouble. OK?" He asked

"OK, son, but I think that it will all work out. I don't think your father will be around. Why would he risk going back to jail?" She said.

"Because he's nuts, that's why and he said that he was going to get you in the end and I believe him full well. Don't take this lightly Mom. He is crazy and I don't think prison has changed him for the better." He explained.

"I work tonight, remember?" She asked.

"Ok, I will make note of that." He responded.

Looking at the clock he finished eating grabbed his books, gave her a kiss and headed toward the door.

"Thanks for breakfast. I love you." He told her as he walked out the door.

"Don't worry Brandon, I will be fine." She responded.

"I know." He replied as he got in his car.

As he got in the car and shut the door he said his ritual prayer as he attempted to start the car. He turned the key and after a few cranks it started up with its normal billow of white smoke. She waved goodbye as he headed out of the driveway and headed to school with a cloud of smoke not far behind. Brandon's mom had to laugh a little at the sight and remembered better days when she was young and driving her father's "Blue Bomber". She closed and locked the door and started her morning routine. She took a cup of coffee and turned on the morning news. The day was like every other and there was no suspicion that it would be any different. Same stuff, just a different day. After the coffee she read a few chapters of the latest book she was reading and then headed off to take a shower and get ready for work.

Brandon made it to football camp without incident and without anything actually falling off of his car. At times the car seemed to be put together with Play-Doh and he never knew what might fall off of it and was a source of ridicule for Brandon. Even though he was the captain of the football time and the coolest kid in the school, the car null and voided some of his social status. Usually there was a laugh or two as he pulled into the parking lot. The kids knew though not to laugh too much or to make sure that Brandon didn't see you laughing. Brandon wasn't a push over and often times liked to throw his weight around. He had no problem being intimidating to kids, especially those in lower grades. Brandon tried to curtail this domineering aspect of his personality while Dawn was around. He tried to be more reserved and gentleman like around her. But there was always a situation or two that would cause his inner man to be made evident.

Brandon had an explosive temper and was often down in the principle's office to try and explain his actions or a fight that he might have been involved in. It wasn't that he liked to fight, just always having to look over his shoulder made him jumpy and on edge.

Chapter 9

After hitting the snooze button another time Dawn finally awoke as her mother pounded on her door.

"Dawn, you have to get up now. Your father is almost ready to leave."

Dawn would normally disregard the first warning and lay in bed until her mother would open the door but today was different. Today her father was leaving for a trip to Slovenia. Once she became fully conscience she wiped the sleep form her eyes and put on her robe as soon as she could. She put on her slippers and headed for the bathroom. Dawn had a way to do things and nothing; even the end of the world was going to change that.

She soon came down to the kitchen where her mother and father were talking.

"Good morning Sunshine", her father said jokingly.

"Good morning", she replied half asleep.

Her father was going over everything with her mother as they prepared to leave for the airport.

"Blah, blah, blah, blah, blah." is all that Dawn could here right now. She opened the cabinet and got out a box of cereal. She poured it and added the milk. This was the time that Dawn tried to wind up in the morning.

As her parents babbled on Dawn thought about the next few weeks and how it was going to be. Sure, her father leaving for a few weeks was nothing new, but she never did like to see him leave.

"Hurry up Dawn, we got to go!" her mother said.

"OK, I'm hurrying." Dawn replied with an attitude.

She finished her breakfast and ran up to her bedroom to get ready to leave. She didn't want to miss taking him to the airport. She loved her father even though at times he seemed to be light years away. She tried to stay focused as she got ready. She knew that this day was coming. He had given them the news a month ago. At first Dawn was excited; she thought that they were going to get to travel again.

"Not this time Princess. I am heading to Slovenia, it's still considered a war zone." she remembered him telling her when she asked if they were going with them.

"I promise when I get back we will go somewhere, alright?"

"OK", she said.

She often wondered sometimes how much her dad loved her and her mother. At times he seemed like there was nothing more important to him than his job. He was often times caught up in some research or preparing lesson plans, leaving Mrs. Sinclair and Dawn alone a lot of times.

"We are leaving in 15 minutes, with or without you Dawn!.", her mother shouted from downstairs.

Her mother yelling brought her back from her daydream and she proceeded to get ready. Though she tried as hard as she could at times, she never seemed to be on time for anything. It wasn't that she wanted to be late; she could never seem to manage her time correctly. Today was different though; she looked out the window and saw her father loading the trunk with his luggage.

"I better hurry, or they are going to leave me here."

She tried to enter high speed mode, but usually all that meant is that she would forget something and have to do it again. She worked frantically to get finished as she saw the minutes count down to their departure.

"We're leaving, now! Dawn!" her mother yelled.

With that Dawn came running down the stairs and headed for the door.

"Wait just a minute, young lady." Her mother interrupted.

"Let me take a look at you."

"Dawn, did you even look in the mirror this morning?"

"Yes, why, what is wrong?"

"Nothing that won't wait until we get back home, I wish you would try and slow your mind down and think about what you are doing."

"Yes, Mom, I will try harder, I'm sorry."

"Did you brush your teeth?"

"No", she said reluctantly.

"Well get in there and brush them. What do you think you are doing? I have raised you better than that. Now get up there."

Dawn ran up the stairs to brush her teeth as her father started honking the horn. Dad had been patience up to this point, but he had a plane to catch and he couldn't wait very much longer.

Dawn acted like she was connected to a lightning rod. She got out the toothpaste and squeezed some on her toothbrush, swished the brush around her mouth and then rinsed her mouth. She was done in less than a minute.

Dawn ran back downstairs to find the house empty. At first she was full of fear thinking that they had left her behind but then she heard the car horn again.

She ran out of the house locking the door behind her and opened the back door of the car.

"Dawn, get in, I can't miss this plane." her father said angrily.

She shut the door and they were off and by this point it seemed that everyone in the car was in a bad mood.

"Why must you be late for everything? Can't you hurry at all?" he said.

"I tried, I'm sorry."

"I have to be at the airport by 7:00. I can't miss this flight. You have to get it through that pretty little head of yours that the world doesn't revolve around you. Got it?"

"Yes sir".

Dawn's mother didn't seem to say much. She was angry, Dawn could see that, but Dawn's lateness was just some more added stress. She sat there not saying much of anything for a while. Dawn guessed she wanted to cool off a little before she said anything.

After seeing that her parents were not going to yell at her any longer Dawn put her head phones on and turned on her mp3. Going to the airport was never a happy thing, unless of course they were all going somewhere. Dawn drifted off into a daydream. She was thinking about the last time that they all went somewhere. Last year about this time they were headed to France. Her father was doing some research there so they all got to go. It was very exciting at first, but when it became apparent that he wouldn't be there for much of their site seeing the luster kind of wore off. Though it wasn't all bad, she and her mother went to the Eiffel tower and the Arc de Triomph and her dad was there for most dinners.

This obsession that Dawn's father had with his work and research was a sore spot to the family. It always seemed to take precedent over anything else that was happening. Though to him he thought that he was just trying to be the best he could be.

"Someone bought the Jones's place" Dawn's mother said.

"I never thought that place was going to sell. I bet you they got a good deal on it. I heard that Jack was ready to unload it. I heard he said that he couldn't afford to keep two mortgages for very much longer."

As they passed a new girl was standing in the driveway. She gave them a quick glance and Dawn gave her a quick wave.

"She looks around your age." Dawn's father interjected.

"Maybe." Dawn responded.

"Well you should find out here soon enough school's going to be starting pretty soon."

"Don't remind me."

They finally arrived at the airport parking lot. They parked and he got out his luggage. They entered the airport and they made their way to the security checkpoint.

"Well, this is as far as you guys go. I love you, I will miss you. I'll call when I get there."

"He'll miss us, I bet", Dawn thought.

He gave her mother a hug and a kiss and then gave her a hug.

"I love you Sunshine, be good for your mother, and don't drive her crazy. Please."

"I love you too Daddy, I will try."

They both watch sadly as he walked through security and headed to his plane. If it would have been five years earlier they both would have eyes filled with tears, this time though, they were use to the long absences and grew accustom to it.

Dawn was more hurt this time than sad. It always seemed to her that he didn't really care about what was going on at home. He always had some place to be or something else to do. It always seemed that home was the last thing that he had on his mind. This trip especially. Usually he seemed sad to go, but this time he appeared actually happy to leave.

They both silently headed back to the car and they got in.

"Don't resent him Dawn."

"What?"

"Don't resent your father. He loves us, this book of his is just very important to him. He'll be back in a few weeks. I am sure that he misses us more than we miss him."

"I bet."

"I know that he seems preoccupied lately, but he'll come back to us. Don't worry."

"Who's worried? He isn't here half the time when he is home anyway."

"I know I am sorry. Sometimes you get lost when you are a parent. You'll understand some day."

"I just hate the way he acts sometimes. It just seems that his job is so important and we are an afterthought."

"I know how you feel. But we just have to hang in there. Let's go get something to eat."

Even though she tried to keep a positive outlook, Dawn's mother often thought the same thing. She often wondered if the job was worth it, or if he actually did love her at times. He just often times seemed so distant. She knew that he was a good provider and they wanted for nothing, nothing but his presence. She just hoped that something would open his eyes to see what he had at home. She realized that he had already missed so much, Dawn was growing up so quickly and it was like every time she blinked she got taller and a little older.

Dawn tried to act as if she didn't care about her father leaving. But it was hard not to show that she did. This time seemed to be different. She often was worried that she might never see him again, she was mad at him, but she didn't hate him, she just felt left out sometimes.

By this time the morning had turned to early afternoon and they were both hungry.

"Well while your father has to eat airline food let's go somewhere nice."
"Like where?"
"What are you in the mood for?"
"I want a buffet."
"You and those buffets, you better watch what you are eating, sooner or later it is going to catch up with you."

Even though Dawn's mother wasn't a great fan of buffets it was hard for her to tell her no sometimes.

In a little while they arrived at the buffet. Eating late and the stress of her father leaving left Dawn famished. All she wanted to do now was eat.

Dawn's mother on the other hand was the opposite. She didn't want to eat anything. She was filled with worry. Something inside her told her that this trip was going to be different. She just didn't have a good feeling about it. She tried to talk him out of going this time, but he wouldn't have it. He told her that if this new information was true it would be the discovery of the century and that it would put him on a national book circuit for sure. By this time in their marriage Trisha didn't really care, all she wanted was her husband back again. It seemed like she had lost him to this new book and she wasn't sure that her marriage was going to survive. She had been a good wife all these years and put up with his traveling and neglect but it was all taking a toll.

"It will all change when he's done with this book." She would often reassure herself.

Still she had to be prepared if it didn't. She wasn't sure if she could hang on for another few years if it didn't get better. She also worried what an impact it all had on Dawn. She always had to weigh the damage that was being done, against the damage a divorce would do. She just wanted to go and cry on someone's shoulder at times or just stand there and scream at him and tell him to get a grip.

"God, I need your help, my marriage needs you help, my daughter needs your help. My life seems to be going down the tubes. Give me strength." She thought to herself as she sat at the table picking at her food.

"Don't worry Mom, he'll be OK."

"I know I just have a lot on my mind."

Dawn's mother wanted to tell Dawn what she was thinking, but she knew that this was not Dawn's cross to bear. Dawn tended to be a worry wart and she didn't want to add to her load of worry. She did need a friend though. At this point of her life, she seemed to be alone. Her best friend Shelly moved when her husband got a better job and they had only lived in this subdivision for 6 months. It was quite a change from their former neighborhood and left quite a gap in her social circle. Before Dawn's father got the new position at the college as the head of the Archeology department things were different. He was home more often and they lived in a more modest home. He was there for her and she had a few girlfriends. But since the change he seemed to have rocketed off to limbo and left her in the dust, she needed some support now more than ever.

"Mom, you better eat something or you're going to get sick."

"I don't know Dawn, eating this stuff just might make me sick."

"Come on, it's not that bad, who's complaining about food now?"

Dawn's mother smiled as she thought of all the times she had to tell Dawn to stop complaining and just eat it.

"All right, but I don't have to enjoy it."

There was a brief pause as both of them thought about their conversation and then they both burst into laughter.

All of these highs and lows in one day were almost two much for her to bear and she quieted herself and a tear formed in her eye.

"Mom, it will be fine, it will all work out."

"I'm sorry, just got a little overwhelmed there for a bit. Let's finish up and go home."

Dawn finished her food and then they headed for the car.

"I ate too much." Dawn said.

"No doubt"

"I think I'm going to take a nap when we get home."

"Sounds like a good idea." Dawn's mother replied.

As she walked through the door a strange feeling of loneliness came over Trisha, even though he'd only been gone a few hours he seemed to have been gone forever.

"I'm going to bed and take a nap."

"Go right ahead. I will call you when dinner is ready."

"Don't even mention food right now; I think I might throw up if I even think about it right now."

Her mother was beside herself and didn't know what do to. She went to the living room and turned on the TV. She surfed through the channels and stopped at one here and there.

"Women who used to be men who want to be men again." The TV announcer introduced his next set of guests.

"Really, where do they get these people?" She thought.

After clicking through countless game shows and talk shows she finally decided that she needed to laugh at something. She opened up the entertainment center and got out one of her favorite comedies. She put the DVD in the machine and sat down to watch.

No matter how many times she had seen this movie, it still would make her laugh. As she watched, her exhaustion slowly overtook her as she fell asleep on the couch.

Chapter 10

The next morning Mrs. Sinclair wasn't going to let her loneliness get the best of her. She remembered that yesterday she saw that a new family was moving in to the Jones's place. She decided that she would make a pie and Dawn and her would go over and welcome them to the neighborhood.

She yelled for Dawn to get up like she did most mornings. She often wondered how Dawn was going to make it in the real world once she had a job to go to. She could only pray that Dawn would make the right decisions for her life and that she would live up to her potential. After waiting another 5 minutes she yelled up to Dawn again.

"I'm getting up." Dawn growled from inside her room.

"Get up Dawn; we are going over to the old Jones's place to welcome the new family to the neighborhood."

"Do I have to? Come on Mom, who does that any more? We aren't living in the 50's anymore." Dawn complained.

"Well, maybe that's what's wrong with people nowadays. Nobody knows anybody else and they don't want too. Maybe if we all got to know each other things would be better."

"I will be down in a minute." Even though she knew it would be more like a half an hour.

Mrs. Sinclair went back to her preparation. She had all the ingredients and started putting them all together. Before long she had the oven preheated and was putting a delicious apple pie in the oven. By this time Dawn had shifted into gear and headed downstairs to eat her breakfast. Her hair looked as if she was sticking her finger in the light socket.

"Did you even comb your hair?" Mrs. Sinclair asked trying to hold back the laughter.

"No, but I will after I eat my breakfast." Dawn said trying to reassure her mother that she really knew what she was doing.

"Yeah, right." Her mother responded. "I bet you would have left the house looking like you got you head caught in a weed wacker."

"No I wouldn't, I'll comb it, I'll comb it." Dawn repeated as she poured herself a bowl of cereal.

"Did Dad call?" Dawn asked.

"No not yet. He wasn't supposed to get there till after 5:00 p.m. and then he had a 5 hour drive to the dig site. He said that there was a small hotel there and cell phone service was sketchy at best."

"I just wondered. I am going to go comb my hair now." Dawn said sarcastically.

"Good and don't forget to brush you teeth either." Her mother answered back.

"I won't." Dawn answered as she headed back to her room.

Even though neither of them wanted to show it, both were nervous about Mr. Sinclair. He had never ventured into a hostile war zone before. They both were praying that he would be alright and that he would return safe and sound in a few weeks.

After another hour, Mrs. Sinclair was ready to pull the pie out of the oven.

"Dawn as soon as this pie is cool we are going over to the Jones's house." She yelled up to Dawn.

"I'm almost ready."

Sometimes Dawn was like a snail getting ready. Mrs. Sinclair often times would get frustrated at her snail pace when it came to getting ready, but then she had to remember that she wasn't the fastest either. She pulled the pie out of the oven and set it on the counter and headed upstairs to see what Dawn was really doing.

As she opened the door she could see Dawn sitting at her desk with her ear buds in listening to music. She seemed ready to go but why she was still up in her room was a mystery to her mother.

"What are you doing?" Mrs. Sinclair asked as Dawn nearly jumped out of her seat.

"What?" Dawn answered as if she was in her own little world.

"Take out your ear phones and get down stairs, it's time to go." Mrs. Sinclair said angrily.

"Alright, already, I'm ready." Dawn retorted.

Dawn got up and headed down to the garage. Her mother headed to the kitchen and grabbed the pie. Dawn walked into the garage and closed the door behind her.

"Would you like to open the door, Dawn, my hands are full." Her mother yelled through the door.

"Sorry Mom." Dawn replied as she opened the door. "Do you need help?"

"Yes, take this pie and don't drop it." Mrs. Sinclair said.

Dawn slowly headed to the car making sure that she was being as careful as she could be not to drop the pie. She placed the pie on the roof and opened the car door. She then grabbed the pie and slid into the seat and shut the door. Her mother was in the car by this time and opened the garage door. Within minutes of leaving their garage they had arrived. The Jones's house was about a mile away so they could have even walked seeing that it was such a nice day.

The Jones's house as they knew it hadn't been lived in for a few years and was showing some wear and tear. The owner had moved and tried to sell it for almost two years before taking a loss on it. He was just happy to get rid of it after paying for an empty house for so long. The house was built in the 50's and was a simple two story cape cod, just like the many others that were in the neighborhood.

As they pulled up it looked as if no one was home. There was no car in the driveway and the curtains were all pulled. Mrs. Sinclair got out and took the pie from Dawn, and then the two headed for the front door. Mrs. Sinclair stepped up to the door and rang the door bell. After a minute had passed she pressed it again.

"Don't." Mrs. Sinclair scolded Dawn as she went to press the door bell again.

"I guess they aren't home." Dawn said with a sigh of relief.

The door finally opened right before they started to leave.

"Hello, may I help you?" The woman at the door asked.

"Hello, I am Trisha Sinclair and this is my daughter Dawn. We just wanted to welcome you to the neighborhood." Mrs. Sinclair said.

"Come in, come in." The woman said as she opened the door and invited them in.

As they entered the house their eyes had to adjust to the dimmed lights. The curtains were all pulled and there was very little light in the house.

"Let me turn a light on in here." The woman said as she could see the two were having trouble seeing in the dim light.

As the room got brighter Mrs. Sinclair handed the woman the pie.

"I hope you like apple." Mrs. Sinclair said.

As the light increased they could see that the woman was dressed like she was going out somewhere special. She had her hair all done up and she was dressed for a night on the town.

"Of course, it's my favorite." The woman paused for a moment. "Where are my manners? My name is, Destiny Smith. Sit down please."

"I hope we weren't interrupting you. You look like you were headed somewhere."

"No not at all, my daughter and I." She stopped in mid sentence.

"I don't know where my mind is today. Let me get my daughter Grace, she is up in her room. We just got done putting everything where it needed to be."

She left the room and headed somewhere in search of her daughter.

She seemed to hesitate a little when she revealed her last name. It was kind of strange but was soon forgotten as they sat in the living room. The room was filled with dated furniture and was in perfect condition. Nothing was out of place and the room looked spotless. Mrs. Sinclair was surprised to see that the room was in such a condition seeing that it had been empty so long.

In a few moments she had returned with her daughter next to her.

"Let me introduce my daughter, Grace." She told them energetically.

"Hello." Grace said in a slight mumble as she raised her head just enough to look at her guests.

"She's a little shy around strangers." Her mother said.

Destiny headed to the kitchen to cut up the pie to serve.

"What would you all like to drink with your pie?" She asked. "I have ice tea, water and milk. I am sorry; we haven't had a chance to get to the grocery store yet. We just moved in yesterday."

Dawn and Mrs. Sinclair gave their drink request to Destiny and Grace brought in the drinks as Destiny brought each person a piece of the pie.

"I love what you have done with the place." Mrs. Sinclair said.

"I take it that you've been in here before." Destiny answered.

"Yes, we go to church with the man who owned it. He had it on the market for sometime."

Destiny seemed preoccupied with everything and couldn't seem to sit still. She was constantly looking around the room and repositioning anything that was out of place, but she recoiled a bit when Mrs. Sinclair mentioned church.

Grace didn't say much and usually had to be prodded by her mother in order to speak or converse.

"What grade are you in Grace?" Mrs. Sinclair asked.

"I am a senior." Grace replied.

"Wow, that's exciting. Dawn is a senior too but you don't look old enough to be a senior." Mrs. Sinclair said politely

"Well, she isn't but she got to jump a few grades. She's a smart cookie, she is." Her mother responded proudly.

In all of this Grace seemed to be like a turtle trying it's best to withdraw from the whole conversation. She didn't say much and seemed to be embarrassed by her mother's accolades for her. She just sat in the corner and said very little. She never spoke unless she was spoken to.

After a while Mrs. Sinclair and Mrs. Smith talked like old friends. Mrs. Sinclair was telling her all about Saratoga Springs. Where to go to eat and what to do on the weekends and how nice a town it was. Mrs. Smith didn't indulge in much information about herself or where Grace and she were from or much about their family. She let Mrs. Sinclair do most of the talking. They were on their third glass of sweet tea when Mrs. Sinclair decided that it was time to leave. She didn't want to overwhelm them for the first day that they were there and didn't want to wear out their welcome.

They all said their goodbyes and Grace mumbled hers as she rose to escort them out of the house.

"It was a pleasure to meet you Grace." Mrs. Sinclair said.

"Maybe we can get together or go to the mall one of these days." Dawn said to Grace.

"That sounds nice." Grace responded in a whispered hush.

"Thanks for coming over. It was nice to visit with you." Mrs. Smith said energetically.

"No problem. We will be seeing you again. I am sure." Mrs. Sinclair replied as she headed out the door.

She and Dawn got into the car, shut the doors and buckled their seatbelts as they started for home. Neither of them said anything until they were well out of view of the Smith's house.

"That was different." Dawn said.

"What do you mean, they seemed nice." Mrs. Sinclair answered.

"Yes, they were nice, but Graces' mother was a little over the top. Don't you think? How she fussed with everything and couldn't sit still. And I have met some shy people in my life but Grace is the shyest one yet." She said.

"Well, you shouldn't judge people that you just met, Dawn. Maybe Mrs. Smith has OCD or something like that, and just because Grace is shy doesn't mean she isn't a nice girl."

"I never said that she wasn't a nice girl. She seemed very nice, when she spoke. But she just sat there staring at us like she was off in her own little world or something. She just didn't seem to want to be there, is all that I am saying. And what about that room, it looked like they were from another time or something didn't it?"

"I have to agree with you on that. That couch looked like my mothers, especially with the plastic cover on it."

Dawn was about to add another observation but her mother interrupted her.

"That's enough talk about the neighbors. I am sure that they might be thinking the same thing about us right now, let's get to know them. I am sure that they might have a lot to offer. Grace and you might just hit it off and become good friends." Mrs. Sinclair said.

"Ok, enough said." Dawn agreed as their arrived home.

As they got out of the car and entered the house Mrs. Sinclair noticed that the phone was flashing saying that she had a voice mail. She threw her purse into the couch as she rushed to pick it up and hear the message. While they were out Mr. Sinclair had called. She pushed the button and listened to the message like a school girl reading a note from her boyfriend.

"Hello, is anyone there? Hello, Trisha, are you there? I guess not. I am here in Slovenia. What a trip, first the flight and then this bus ride. I didn't have cell service when I got off the plane that's why I didn't call. I'm at the hotel now. Tomorrow we are supposed to head over to the dig. I love you and I miss you Trisha, I wish that I could reach through the phone and hold you. Tell Dawn that I miss my little girl. I will ca." Then the message ended.

A tear had rolled off of Mrs. Sinclair's nose as Dawn and her listened. Dawn could see that her mother was shaken by his call.

"Don't worry mom, he'll be fine." Dawn told her mother.

"I know, I just miss him and I'm sad that I wasn't here to talk to him."

"Maybe he will call back later. It sounded like he said he was going to call again when the machine cut him off." Dawn reassured her mother.

"Hopefully." She said trying to hold back the tears.

As Dawn headed to her room Mrs. Sinclair yelled up to her what she wanted for dinner.

"Whatever." Dawn yelled back.

Even though she was trying to hold it together and keep her thoughts on what she was doing, Mrs. Sinclair wasn't focused on making dinner. She had decided to make chili and went on compiling the ingredients and went to work. She mixed all the ingredients and put it in a pot and let it slow cook for an hour. After the timer went off she yelled for Dawn to come down for dinner. Dawn arrived quickly and set the table for two. She poured her mother a glass of water and she poured herself some grapefruit juice. Her mother placed a piece of cornbread in each bowl and scooped out a serving of chili and laid it on top of it, she added some cheese and some sour cream and they both sat down to eat.

"Dawn!" Her mother scolded as she went to take a bite of chili.

"I'm sorry, I forgot." She replied.

"That means that you can pray for dinner and pray for you father."

"Thank you for this food and keep Dad safe." She said in a quick prayer.

"Short and quick." Her mother said sarcastically.

Dawn was smiling in anticipation of the chili, but her smile quickly turned to a frown.

"Yuck!" She said in a knee jerk fashion.

"Dawn, what is the matter with you. You always liked my chili. Why would you do that?" She said with a hurt inflection in her voice.

"I am sorry mom, but this isn't right, just taste it."

"OK." She replied as she ate a spoonful of chili.

The smile was erased from her face as quickly as it was from Dawn's.

"You're right, yuk." She said.

"Mom, what did you do to the chili? It doesn't taste like chili it tastes like cinnamon."

"I'm not sure. I thought I did everything the way I usually do. Let me take a look."

She got up from the table and opened the pantry to see what ingredients that she had used. Sure enough there was a bottle of cinnamon out in front. "

"Well it looks like I used cinnamon instead of chili powder. I guess I wasn't concentrating on what I was doing."

"You don't expect me to eat this slop do you?" Dawn asked in disgust.

"Dawn, don't call it slop. You could live off it if you had to, it just doesn't taste good, but you don't have to eat it."

"Do you want to order pizza?" Dawn asked.

"Not really, but at this hour of the evening it seems like the best choice."

Dawn picked up the phone and made the order. The man told them that it would be about twenty minutes for them to pick it up. They both sat on the couch and turned on the TV. At first Dawn was afraid to really react to the dinner debacle and sat in silence next to her mother until she looked at her and their eyes met and they broke out in laughter.

"Dawn, when you tell this story to your friends, be kind." Her mother laughed.

As their laughter subsided Dawn got ready to go to the pizza shop to pick up the pizza. Mrs. Sinclair was staying behind this time; she didn't want to take any chance of missing another phone call form Mr. Sinclair.

"I'm home!" Dawn shouted as she entered the house.

"Ok!" Her mother yelled back from her room.

She looked at the phone and saw that she was talking on it. Apparently her father called back. Dawn wanted to talk to her dad but was willing to let her mother have a turn. She got out two paper plates and put some pizza on each and then sat on the couch and turned on the TV.

"Dawn!" Her mother yelled to her from the bedroom.

"Yeah?" She called back.

"Pick up the phone if you want to talk to you father."

"OK." She gladly responded

"Hi, Daddy, how are you?" She asked. When it came to her father, she always acted like a little kid. She was Daddy's little girl and would always be.

"Good, Sunshine, how are you doing? Your mother tells me that you guys had some good chili tonight."

"Really, it was just awful; she used cinnamon instead of chili powder. We ended up getting pizza. It was funny though. Are you OK? Are you safe?" Dawn said is a hurried sentence.

"I am alright, everything is fine. It just took forever to get here. I just want to get done and get home. I miss you, I love you. Be good for your mother and try not to drive her crazy. OK?" He asked sincerely.

They couldn't see him, but tears were running down his face and his voice was shaking. He missed them far more than either of them would ever know.

"I love you Sunshine. Put your mother on the phone." He said.

"I love you too Daddy, I miss you." She said as she hung up the phone.

In a short time afterward her mother came down the stairs wiping tears from her eyes.

"Let's eat." She said as she tried to compose herself.

It was always hard for Dawn to see her parents in this state so she said nothing and the two of them had a quiet dinner together. After dinner Dawn went to her room and got ready for bed and her mother sat on the couch and watched some TV. Mrs. Sinclair might have been sitting in front of the TV but she wasn't watching it, she was too busy worrying about her husband and praying to God that he would bring him back home again safe.

Chapter 11

Dawn's mother went to work in the morning so Dawn had the day to herself. Dawn knew the rules not to leave town and that she should be home before ten. Dawn was usually good at following the rules even though there had been many times that she had been late with her curfew. The funny thing was that Brandon had never once kept her out past her curfew and that he was always on time. He always said to Dawn that he never wanted to do anything to ruin her parents trust in him. Sometimes Brandon's willingness to be a straight arrow with most things was kind of boring for Dawn. There was so many times that she just wanted to do something wild and free but the Brandon would always restrain her and tell her to calm down. Brandon was good for Dawn for the time being. The only problem with Brandon was that he didn't seem very interested in Dawn and that after going out doing the summer he still didn't call her much. At times she wondered if he really wanted to date her after all. He still was guarded and wasn't very affectionate. He always treated her nice but he only hugged her on occasions and hadn't even kissed her yet.

The summer was flying by faster than Dawn could think of. Dawn called Jessica to see what she was doing and to see if she wanted to go to the mall. Jessica said sure and Dawn asked her if she cared if the new girl, Grace tagged along, Jessica said she didn't care and that she would wait for her to pick her up. Dawn called Grace and asked her if she wanted to go to the mall. At first Grace seemed apprehensive but Dawn could hear her mother in the background telling her to go have some fun before school started. Grace then told Dawn that she would love to go and hang out for a while. Dawn told her that she would pick her up in about 20 minutes and that Jessica would be coming. Grace told her that would be fine and that she would be ready. After about 30 minutes Dawn showed up at Grace's house. At this point Grace didn't realize that Dawn was almost late for everything. Dawn pulled up the driveway and Grace told her mother goodbye and she walked to the car. She opened the door and got in.

"Hello Grace." Dawn said happily.

"Hi Dawn. How are you?" Grace replied.

"I'm just peachy. We have to go pick up Jessica and then we can go to the mall."

"Sounds good."

"What's that on the radio?" Grace asked.

"You never heard this song." Dawn replied.

"No, I am not into the new stuff, I like the oldies."

"You mean like Elvis and the Beatles." Dawn asked.

"No, the big bands and stuff like that."

"Grace, what in the world is a big band?" Dawn asked.

"It was just the style of music in the forties. I like it. My mother likes it. It's just something that we listen to together."

"Grace, you really have to get into the present times. No girl our age is going to listen to music that our parents like. It's just not normal." Dawn went on.

"Have you ever heard any big band music?" Grace asked.

"Yeah, maybe I guess when I go over to my grandmothers and we watch Lawrence Welk reruns." She said.

"Do you have an mp3? " Dawn asked.

"Yes, why?." Grace responded.

"Well I know one thing that we have to do today."

"What's that?" Grace asked inquisitively.

"I'm going to download some new music into it; I won't let a friend of mine be tortured by her parent's old fogy music."

"Dawn, it really isn't that bad. It's one thing that my mother and I relate to. You know, sometimes we don't see eye to eye."

"Tell me about it. I don't thing I see eye to eye with my mother at all. I love her; really I do with all my heart. I just can't understand the way she thinks at times." Dawn said.

"I know, I guess it's just the way it has always been and it will always be." Grace responded.

By this time they arrived at Jessica's house and she got into the car. Jessica could tell that they had been talking and wanted to get in on the conversations.

"What's going on?" Jessica asked.

"Jessica, this is Grace. Grace this is Jessica." Dawn introduced them.

"Nice to meet you Jessica." Grace said nicely.

"Same to you." Jessica replied.

"So what were you guys talking about?"

"Oh, I was just telling Grace that she can't go another day listening to big band music and that I was going to load her MP3 with some good music."

"Big band music, what's that?" Jessica asked.

"I said the same thing Jessica. It's just the music that our grandparents listen to." Dawn said.

Though Dawn and Jessica meant well, Grace felt bad that she didn't fit in and that she seemed to be the odd man out. Grace knew that big band music had gone out a long time ago but she still liked the sound that they had and she loved the time period.

They all talked and laughed as they headed to the mall. For once in a long time Grace seemed to have found a friend or two. Real friends, friends that didn't care that she wore outdated clothes or listened to outdated music. Just friends she could hang out with and have a good time.

They arrived at the mall and went around shopping here and there. Grace again seemed out of place. She seemed to have very little to no fashion sense and seemed frozen in the forties when it came to fashion. She watched and listened as Jessica and Dawn went on and on about the newest pare of jeans or the new shirts that were coming out.

After a while Dawn realized that this was all a little much for Grace. The one thing that Dawn didn't want to do was to single out Grace any more that she already was, she also realized that Grace was constantly scanning the people around them. She seemed like a scared mouse trying to keep away from a cat.

After a long day of shopping and eating dinner at the food court the three of them headed to the care and back home. Neither Dawn nor Jessica had bought anything for themselves but they did get Grace a new pair of jeans. Even though

Grace had protested and said that she had never even owned a pair and that she didn't even wear pants that often.

They headed to Jessica's first and dropped her off. She said goodbye and headed inside her house as they headed to Grace's. As they got to Grace's house Grace went to get out of the car and then reached out and gave Dawn a hug.

"Thanks." Grace said with misty eyes.

"For what?" Dawn replied.

"For being a friend and treating me to a great day."

"No problem. I am sure there will be more like it. Just you wait and see." Dawn reassured Grace.

Grace said goodbye and Dawn headed home.

"Hi Mom." Dawn said as she saw her mother sitting on the couch as she entered the house.

"It would have been nice if you could have told me where you were." Her mother said.

"I'm sorry that I didn't text you that I was going to the mall with Grace and Jessica."

"And how did it go?" Her mother asked.

"Fine, just Grace is a little backward to say the least."

"What do you mean?" Her mother replied.

"Well for one thing. She likes to listen to big band music. I didn't even know what that was, so I downloaded some good music onto her MP3"

"Good music you say, some might question your choice in music."

"I know mom, but I don't think that I could ever like your music. It's just too old."

"Dawn!" Her mother interjected.

"Well, I am sorry. I just can't get into your generation music."

"And I can't see what you see in yours." Her mother replied.

With the last statement a smile formed on Dawn's face.

"What's so funny little miss?" Her mother asked.

"Oh, it was just what Grace and I were talking about before. That she couldn't see eye to eye with her mother either and that it was just the way it would always be."

Her mother was almost agitated by the discussion when she looked back at her and her mother arguments of music and the fashions of the day.

"I guess you're right on that one, Sunshine." She said. "I guess you right."

"How was your day, Grace?" Her mother asked lovely.

"Mom, I saw Alberto at the mall." Grace replied in a panic.

"What?"

"Mom, listen to me. I saw Alberto at the mall." She replied annoyed that her mother seemed to be oblivious to what she had just said.

"Are you sure it was him?"

"Yes, it was him." She said with a tremor in her voice.

"Did he see you?"

"I'm not sure."

"Why would he be here?" Her mother asked inquisitively.

"Apparently Leopold didn't like the outcome of the situation." Grace replied.

"If he thinks he can intimidate us that easily he has another thing coming." Her mother replied angrily.

"I told him I have everything I need to expose him and I would if he didn't let us out."

"Grace, why? You just signed your own death warrant." Her mother said with tears in her eyes.

"It doesn't matter anymore mom, I am tired. I am tired of this life."

"Don't worry Grace, it will all work out, I promise." Her mother told her as she gave her a hug

Chapter 12

The day that everyone under the age of 19 head dreaded had come to pass. It was the first day of school. Moans and groans from every house that had school children were in full swing. The Sinclair home was no exception, and Dawn was one of the biggest whiners on the block when it came to the first day of school. Even though she had the alarm set she had hit the snooze button four times and had fallen back asleep. She was asleep at least until her mother barged into her room and commanded her to wakeup.

"Dawn, get your butt out of that bed and get ready for school. You can't be late for the first day of school and I have to get to work. It's time that you start acting like a mature young adult. Now get up!" Her mother demanded.

"OK, OK, I'm up. I'm up." She said as she pulled herself out of the bed and into an upright position.

She attempted to wake up as she started to her motor running and get ready for the first day of torture for the rest of the year.

"Dawn you have ten minutes to get your rear out here or you're not going to eat breakfast." Her mother warned.

"OK Mom, I'll be out in a minute."

Dawn did her best to shift into high gear and get things done. One thing she didn't want to miss breakfast. With only a minute to spare Dawn arrived in the kitchen and started to get her breakfast ready.

"I work tonight so you will have to make your own dinner tonight? Is that OK." Mrs. Sinclair asked Dawn.

"Yeah, I am sure that I can make a box of macaroni and cheese. When will you be home?"

"Around nine o'clock. So do your homework and your chores and the rest of the time is yours, so don't waste it. OK?" Mrs. Sinclair said.

"I won't, don't worry." Dawn replied.

She would have said more but then she looked at the clock and saw that the bus would soon be there. She finished her breakfast and gathered her things as she ran to the door.

"I love you, have a good day." Her mother told her as she headed out the door.

"I love you too, see you later." Dawn replied as she shut the door.

Dawn walked out the door as her mother watched her from the window in the door. Dawn hated that her mother still treated her like she was five and this was her first day of school, but it also made Dawn feel good that her mother still cared.

The bus came around the same time it came last year and as Dawn got on she found her seat next to Rebecca like she did so many times before. It wasn't that they had assigned seats it was just the way it was.

"Hi, Dawn, did you have a nice summer, how are things with you?" Rebecca said as she started her morning rant.

"Fine, how was yours?" Dawn replied, knowing full well what she would start asking Rebecca a question.

"Oh, it was fine, there were the highs and lows, and I did get to go here and there and blah, blah, blah, blah." Was all that Dawn could hear after a while.

Rebecca was a nice girl, but apparently no one at home ever listened to her much. The whole school was Rebecca's tabloid and she knew almost everything about everybody there. If something happened Rebecca knew about it, though most of the times she didn't have the whole story but one that had been passed down from student to student and by the time Rebecca got her information the story had already been embellished quite a bit. Dawn didn't mind much, Rebecca kept her in touch with what was going on at school, but she always had to remember never to forget the source of her information.

As the bus stopped, the weary prisoners got up from their seats to enter another year of their prison sentence. One by one they left the bus and headed for the door. Each seemed to have a ball and chain attached to his ankle as they all hobbled to their lockers and then their home rooms. The first day of school was always a drag, it was the last day of the summer and the first day of boredom, or so Dawn thought. She really didn't hate school, it was a place to meet with friends and socialize, and except for the homework part she'd probably love the place. But there was something about that last subject that the teachers were unwilling to give up. She got to her locker and then to her home room. It was the same old thing that she had been through all the years before, meet the teacher, get your books, learn a little and get some homework.

Dawn and all the others that had been there more than a year looked on in amusement as they watched the seventh graders wander around aimlessly. It didn't take long for Dawn to remember the time she was one of those lost souls trying to find her way in the new school.

As Dawn headed to her locker she saw a seventh grader do the unthinkable. A poor seventh grader actually was so lost that he asked a senior for directions. Everyone knew that you never ask another student for directions especially an older one.

As Dawn started to walk toward him she could just hear the end of the conversation.

"Yeah, your home room is just down that hallway. When you pass the swimming pool it will be on your left." The senior said trying to hold back his laughter.

By the time Dawn reach the seniors the poor kid had started his journey into the unknown.

"Brandon, how could you?" Dawn scolded him playfully. "That wasn't very nice of you."

"Maybe not, but it was funny. Come on, don't you remember being a seventh grader?" Brandon responded with a laugh.

"Yes, I do, and it wasn't nice then and it isn't nice now." She said with a slight inflection in her voice.

"Come on Dawn, some teacher will see him wandering the halls and tell him where to go. And think about it, in a few years he will be the one sending the new kids on some wild goose chase."

"Probably so, but I can't see the poor kid wander around like that. I have to show him where to go."

"Always the saint." He told her playfully. "Don't be mad, are we still on for Friday after the game."

"Yeah, I guess so, unless I find you giving out more bad directions." She told him with a smile.

With that she gave him a wink and then headed for the poor lost sheep heading down the hallway almost the sea of students. She tried to walk as fast as she could without running, she didn't want to get into trouble or knock someone down. After a slight jaunt she caught up with him.

She almost broke into laughter as she saw the poor look on his face.

"What's your name?" She asked him.

"Joshua, what's yours." He answered.

"It's Dawn. Well Joshua I heard what those senior boys told you and they didn't give you good directions."

"I figured that. I didn't know who to ask. I figured that they weren't telling me the truth, but what am I supposed to do." He answered.

"Where do you want to go?"

"My schedule said, Mrs. Crenshaw in room 212." He said disgusted.

"That's upstairs. Go up those stairs and go to the right, she will be right there." Dawn told him like a duck leading a duckling.

"Thanks Dawn." Joshua said in relief as he headed for the stairs.

Dawn smiled and headed to her home room. To Dawn she did nothing, to Joshua she just made his day. Not only did she tell him where to go but Joshua told all of his friends for the rest of the day that a hot senior girl actually talked to him in the morning. That day Joshua always smiled as he saw Dawn in the morning. He figured that the odds were against him and her actually dating some day but it was a good fantasy for the time being.

Dawn arrived at Mr. Gunter's room as she found a seat. After the 8:00 a.m. bell sounded and Mr. Gunter started the class. He told everyone that where they found to sit would be their seat for the rest of the year. He handed out every students schedule for the next 6 weeks and handed them their books. This would be repeated as each class began for the rest of the day. It was all paper work and formalities. When Dawn reached her third period class she met Grace ready to go in. Brandon was also there and ready to enter. Dawn quickly met them and introduced them.

"Hello Brandon", Dawn said.

"This is Grace."

"Grace this is Brandon"

"Hello, Grace said sheepishly."

"This is Grace's first day. She's just moved here."

"Nice to meet you", Brandon responded.

Grace extended her hand and Brandon gave her a friendly shake.

Brandon flinched like he was in pain for a split second. He let go of Graces hand immediately. He looked at Grace with a disdainful look.

"I got to go." He said as he headed to class.

"That was weird". Dawn said.

"That guy is no good for you Dawn. All he wants from you is sex."

"That's kind of forward don't you think. You just met the guy."

"Don't worry; I have a knack about people. I am very good at looking into their intentions and his intentions aren't good."

"Grace, I have been dating Brandon for three months now and he hasn't done anything in the way of pressuring me for sex. Really, you shouldn't go and say things about people that you don't even know. That's the way rumors get started."

Dawn's grandmother always told her that nothing good ever came out of a rumor, that they were nothing more than the Devil's own tongue.

"Just wait, Dawn, it might not be today, maybe not tomorrow, but sooner or later he will try to put his moves on you. Trust me."

With that the four minute warning signal was sounding and they both knew that they better get to their home room and quickly.

Sometimes she really questions some of the things that she had to learn anyhow. What was chemistry really going to teach me in the real world? As Dawn pondered all of these things in her head the teacher introduced Grace and told her to sit next to Dawn. Even though she was a pretty girl she looked peculiar dressed in old style clothes, the kind that they wore back in the fifties or something. As she sat down you could the whispers around the room of how she looked.

Dawn just couldn't seem to concentrate that day. It just seemed like everything was more interesting then whatever she was supposed to be learning, for whatever reason her mind kept on wandering. Maybe it was just the weather or the first week of school blahs.

"Dawn", the teacher said.

"Dawn? Who was Nathan Hale?"

With that Dawn snapped out of her trance and tried to answer the question like she actually was listening. Even to the surprise of the teacher, who definitely could see that she was preoccupied, she got the answer correct.

"Very good"

"Really, why couldn't they wait a week to give us something to do?" She thought to herself.

The teacher started on to the next topic and Dawn tried with all her might to stay focused. This really wasn't like Dawn; usually she was always on time, very organized and sharp as tack. Today though was different. All she could think about was what Grace had said about Brandon. It really started to bother her that Grace would be so quick to judge someone without even getting to know them. Or maybe Grace did have a knack about reading people.

After another totally uninteresting class the lunch signal rang. Dawn got her books and started to the cafeteria. By the time that she got there she could see that the cultural lines had been drawn and the groups were set for the rest of the year. It kind of made her remember the previous years that she sat with the popular girls at lunch.

Dawn watched as Grace sat down at the lunch room. Dawn knew that being the new kid was hard and it wasn't that long ago that she was the one sitting there all alone.

Grace was a little different to say the least. She seemed to be in her own little world, at least when it came to fashion. She was dressed like she was going to a retro sock hop or something. Most kids didn't even think that dresses like the one she had on still existed. She watched as kids went by and made their jabs and insults at Grace, but she seemed to handle it well.

Dawn watched and watched all the time knowing what the right thing to do was. She should just get up and befriend her, sit down and get to know her. But what would everyone else think. Dawn was no longer the one that had to sit alone; she was one of the girls that others tried to sit with, that all seemed like a life time ago that she was the new awkward one.

After watching and pondering a while Dawn knew that she could not sit there any longer, she would have to do the right thing.

"What is Dawn going to do?" One of the girls said as Dawn headed to Grace's table.

"I don't know that new kid is really out there."

Dawn left it all behind her as she reached Grace.

"Hi Grace, can I sit here?"

"Sure."

As she sat down she could feel that every eye from the popular table was now on her. She realized that her social standing could be destroyed by this.

"What does it matter? She needs someone just like I did." She thought to herself

"Rough being the new kid, I know... This school can be tough, but it's OK after you get to know some of the kids." She told Grace.

"Thanks, it seems like I don't fit in here to well. Not much of a fashionista, if you know what I mean. I just like the old style of clothes, old movies, and stuff like that." Grace replied.

With that the bell rang and lunch was over. As she got up and started towards her next class some of her friends started to ask what she was doing.

"Why would you even give a girl like that the time of day, Dawn?"

"Yeah, what were you thinking, are you trying to ruin your social status or something."

"That girl seems to have zero fashion sense; did you get a look at what she was wearing?

For the most part none of them had much of anything to say nice about Grace. How could they be so mean, how could anyone judge someone so easily just by what they were wearing? The biggest question that Dawn was asking was, am I one of those kids? Have I become one of those shallow kids that never get to know someone, just judge them on appearance? She started to her class, but was very uneasy about the whole affair. She knew in her heart that she had to make the right decision, whatever the consequence.

School seemed to drag on all day. 45 minutes and another class, another syllabus to look over, register their books, find new seats, all the fun that one person could handle. Soon enough it was time for the afternoon announcements and then off to the bus, the first day was over.

The whole time on the bus, Dawn was bombarded by Rebecca with questions and thoughts about the first day. Dawn had already had enough stimuli for the day; she really didn't need all of this chatter. The bus seemed louder than ever and it just seemed that all she could think about was Dawn. There was just something about her that she couldn't get out of her head.

As she got off the bus and headed for the door Dawn was just glad to be home. She unlocked the door and went in and sat her book bag on her chair in the kitchen she remembered that her mother was working and that she would have to make her own dinner. She opened the cupboards and looked for anything that was fast and easy. Like usual she found the one thing that she could make and that she liked to eat, macaroni and cheese. She got out a pot and some water and turned on the stove and set the timer then turned on the TV. All she wanted to do is sit and relax for a minute. She was busy watching some talk show when the timer went off. She got up drained the macaroni and put the ingredients in the pot and started mixing it together when the phone rang.

She read the caller id and saw this it was her mother.

"Hi, mom." She said as she picked up the phone.

"Just wanted to see if you got home safe." Her mother asked caringly.

"Yeah, I'm good, just making some Mac and cheese."

"I should have known anything happen today?"

"No not really just getting our books and learning our schedule. Junk like that." Dawn told her.

"OK, I will be home later. Have a good night. I love you."

"I love you too." Dawn said as she hung up the phone.

After eating her dinner and watching some more TV she decided to get on her homework. She opened her history and started her assignment. Dawn like most kids her age hated homework. She tried to hold off doing it for as long as possible but she knew that her mother would be mad if she hadn't done it by the time she got home. In fact the night would turn into another mundane school night that Dawn was so used to. She would do her homework and then take a shower and then get ready for bed. If she had enough time she would browse the internet, call Jessica or watch some more TV. After what seemed to be an eternity for Dawn she finished her homework and thought about what she could do next. She figured that she should get her shower out of the way and then do something else, proving to her mother that she was able to take care of herself without her parents prodding.

She went back downstairs and turned on the TV and waited for her mother to return. After a half hour her mother entered the living room through the garage door.

"Hello Sunshine." She said cheerfully.

"Hi, Mom, did you have a good day?" Dawn asked.

"Pretty good, how about you?" Her mother replied.

"OK, even though I sat at the nerd table."

"What?" Her mother responded with shock.

"The Nerds, it's the lunch table that all of the computer nerds and the AV kids sit at."

"Why did you do that?"

"Well, I was sitting with the girls I usually sit with when we all saw Grace looking for a seat."

"Then what happened?"

"Well, they started laughing at her and making jokes about how she looked. I didn't like it so I went and sat with the rest of the nerds where she found a seat."

"That's nice Dawn, I am glad to know that you did the right thing." Her mother congratulated her.

"Maybe, I am not sure right now. It seems that my social status has sunk to a new low." Dawn said in disgust.

"Don't worry Dawn. It will all work out. You did the right thing. That's all that matters. In a year you will be in college and who's going to care where you sat at the lunch table. The point is you did the right thing." Her mother said trying to convince her that it wouldn't matter in the greater scope of things.

"I guess. I am going to go to bed. Love you." She told her mother as she headed to her room.

"Love you too. Good night." Her mother replied.

The rest of the week was about as mundane as the first day, going to class, trying to listen, getting homework. The only thing different was lunch. Dawn still had some second thoughts on her decision to quit the "Stuck ups" and move to the loser table. She didn't want to be a stuck up, but she didn't want to be a nerd either. She wanted to be accepted where ever she sat. Her head was filled with conflicting ideas as she headed for the cafeteria.

She went through the lunch line and picked what she was going to eat and headed to Grace's table.

By this time of the week things had normalized and everything was pretty calm. Apparently the girls that she thought were her friends found someone else to occupy her space and fill the void. They didn't want to unsettle the course of the universe or something. Grace had managed to find some other nice kids that chose to sit with them.

"Dawn, are you OK", Brandon said as she sat down.

"Sure, why?"

"You bought a tuna fish sandwich."

"Yeah, so what?" she replied.

"You don't like tuna fish; you said that it makes you sick."

"I must be loosing my mind or something. I wasn't paying attention at all. I had no idea what I bought. Good thing you said something. I might have puked if I actually would have tasted that."

"Earth to Dawn", Brandon said playfully.

"Yeah, I know, I just can't get into today. It just seems like I can't concentrate on anything today. Everything is so boring today. I need to wake up or something."

After that she asked Brandon and Grace if they wanted it and then the other people at the table.

"Sure", Biff said, "Nothing wrong with that"

Biff wasn't his real name that was Bill. When he was in 5th grade someone said that he reminded them of Biff from the Hardy Boys mystery stories, and the nickname stuck. From then on, no one called him Bill, it was Biff. He really didn't care much about it. His mother always told him that they give nicknames to people that they like, so he accepted the fact the he was, Biff. He also was the kind of kid that would eat practically anything. In fact Dawn never saw him turn down any food that was offered to him. The worst thing about him was that no matter what he ate, and he was always eating, he remained thin. It was enough for Dawn to hate him.

"Anybody else have anything that they don't want?" Biff asked the other outcasts at the table.

At that point Dawn realized that she was sitting in the company of the "Untouchables". Kids from the AV club, the computer nerds, kids that didn't fit into the main stream group.

"Man, did I take a step down, I mean, I took a leap off a cliff." She thought to herself.

It wasn't that she didn't like these kids or that there was something wrong with them, it was just that a week ago she was on the head of the social ladder and now she was on the lowest rung. The more she thought about it though the more she began to feel good about herself. She was glad that she broke away from the group of "Stuck Ups".

"Who cares what people think", Dawn said out loud.

Everyone at the table looked at her as she realized that what she thought, she had just said out loud.

"Don't mind me; I am just out in left field today."

Dawn noticed that even in the company of outcasts and so called losers, Grace still didn't seem to fit in. She always seemed to be the one thing that didn't fit. No matter where she was, she always seemed to be the odd man out. It was something that Dawn couldn't put her finger on. Grace was smart; in fact she knew history like a computer. She could recite the "Gettysburg Address" by memory and knew all kinds of dates and facts. Maybe the "cool" girls resented her for this. Even though she kept to herself there was no competing with her on an intellectual level. She was also a pretty though her clothes were definitely out of date, but she always dressed nice and was clean. She never had any sort of odor about her. Maybe it was her dark eyes. They were the darkest eyes that she had ever seen, black as night and they didn't seem to give off a reflection.

"I will see you later Dawn, I have to go to the library." Grace said.

"I'll call you later."

"OK Dawn, see you around."

Brandon watched and waited until she was out of hearing range.

"She's a weird one; I will say that about her."

"Brandon, be nice, we can't all be as popular as you."

"S-o-r-r-y, Miss Dawn. I didn't mean to hurt your feelings."

"Just give her a chance. It's her first week in a new school. That's a lot to get use to. We all have a first day"

"Well, well, haven't we gotten all mushy on us."

The rest of the group just kept on doing what they were doing. They had heard all of this before. Being told that they were weird or strange was nothing new to them.

"You know Brandon, sometimes you can be a real jerk."

"I'm sorry, I shouldn't have said that."

"By the way, are we still on for the football game tomorrow night?" Brandon asked.

"Yeah, I will disregard the fact that you are jerk this time. "

With that the signal for lunch to end sounded and the chaos of the herd would start. 150 kids would get up and try to exit the cafeteria while 150 other kids would try and enter it. Like two freight trains heading straight towards each other. For the most part exiting kids would bear to the left and entering ones would be on the right. Every now and then for whatever reason someone would try and go against the current. Today it was Bills turn to be the lone salmon heading upstream. He was in a hurry when he attempted to rush into the swelling crowd. He hugged the wall to keep from getting pushed into the churning sea of people. As he got around the corner and into the main hallway the groups started to thin, unhindered by this he started to run down the hall, loaded with a number of books and he wasn't paying attention to where he was going. He was hugging the wall when Grace opened the door of the library not knowing that a speeding freight train was headed her way. The door opened out and Bill hit the door at full speed, the only thing keeping him from breaking his breastbone was the mass of books that he held in front of him. Everyone could see the pain that the collision caused by the look on his face but rather than facing the jeers of all the onlookers he kept on running like nothing ever happened.

"Did you see that? Dawn asked Brandon.

"Yeah, wasn't it hilarious?"

"Yes it was, but I wonder if he is OK."

"Even if he isn't he would never admit that he wasn't." Brandon replied.

"What do you mean?"

"I mean he's a guy, and to be a manly man, you have to mean to do whatever you do."

After Brandon's explanation Dawn had a hard time keeping her composure. She didn't really want to laugh at Bill, but it was funny.

In all of this chaos, Grace simply stood there and waited for Bill to pass and then shut the door. Dawn saw a slight smile appear; it seemed that everyone that witnessed the affair except Bill was laughing, just another reason for people to laugh at the poor guy. But like most things at school, they soon would be forgotten for some other person's fool hardy actions.

Soon the school day would end and Dawn headed for the bus. She entered and sat next to Rebecca and as usual Rebecca had to fill Dawn in on all the days' events at school.

"Did you hear?"

"Hear what?" Dawn responded.

"Hear about Bill Wagner. I guess he was running down the hall and that weird girl Grace tripped him."

"What are you talking about? I was there. Grace didn't trip him. Bill was running down the hall and Grace opened the door and Bill ran right into it. Rebecca I don't know where you get your information from but it never seems to be completely right."

"I was close" she answered back.

Dawn saw at that point the problems with rumors and what effect only telling one part of the story might have.

Rebecca started on another story of the day as Dawn saw Grace walking down the street. Just like in school she walked alone while the others walked in groups.

"That's sad" she said.

"What's sad?" Rebecca asked.

"Grace, she's walking home all alone, like she doesn't have a friend in the world."

"Well, maybe if she wasn't so weird, maybe she would have a friend to walk with."

"Well, Rebecca, if people would try and get to know her, maybe they would find out that she's a nice girl. She's just shy." Dawn answered back

"You know Dawn, why don't you join Greenpeace or something. You seem to always want to save the world or something."

Dawn was taken back by that comment. Before this she didn't think that Rebecca even knew what Greenpeace was.

"I just don't like to see anyone be alone."

"You have changed, I mean changed a lot since last year. I mean, last year you wouldn't have cared at all about the new weird girl. You would have been the one making fun of her, you and all of your cheerleader buddies."

"I am ashamed to say that you are probably right. But look anyone can change. We don't have to stay the same. I didn't like the person that I had become; I finally saw that my actions affected other people. I felt really bad about the people that I hurt, so I am trying to change."

"Whatever you say Dawn, I will believe it when I see it", Rebecca muttered to herself.

The whole conversation put Dawn on edge. Maybe she couldn't undo the damage that she caused, but she didn't want to cause any more. She truly did want to change. She didn't want to be popular at the cost of someone else.

"Are you going to get off the bus, Dawn?" Rebecca asked.

"What?"

"Are you going to get off the bus? Earth to Dawn, are you there?"

Dawn was unaware that the bus had arrived at her stop. She said goodbye to Rebecca and walked off the bus.

Chapter 13

Dawn knocked on the door like she always did and Grace's mother met her at the door.

"Come on in, how are you?" She asked.

"Good Mrs. Smith, how are you?" She replied.

"Fine, fine, Grace is up in her room. "

"Thanks"

As Dawn left she couldn't help but notice Mrs. Smith was in front of the mirror with the hair brush in her hand mumbling about something. She often felt sad for the woman; it seemed as though she was in her own world and had this fixation about her looks.

She headed to Grace's room down the hall. Even though she had been there a dozen times before she was still surprised how the house looked like inside. It was always well kept but looked like a house from the "Andy Griffin Show." All of the furniture looked old, like it belonged in a museum or something.

Grace was waiting for Dawn and she had the door open. Dawn was again shocked. Grace actually had on some make up and she appeared to be painting her nails.

"How do you like it?" Grace asked Dawn.

Dawn had to think for a second. She really didn't know what to say, Grace never wore makeup or painted her nails and this was certainly a change for her.

"It looks great. What's up with all of this?" Dawn asked.

"What do you mean?"

"Well, yesterday you were still wearing poodle skirts and no makeup, why such an abrupt change all of a sudden?"

"I don't know. I was tired of living in the past. I guess I wanted to start to be like everyone else. I wanted to try and fit in."

For the first time since they met, Dawn actually got to see Grace for how beautiful she really was. She went from the girl next door to Hollywood in a few hours.

"Well, I do see one problem with all of this Grace."

"What's that?"

"I am not sure that the loser table will let you sit there any more, we may need a bigger table because I am sure that the guys who never noticed you before are going to notice you now." She said.

"Come on Dawn, what boy is going to be interested in me? I hear what people say about me. It wasn't that I wanted to be weird, I just like that time period. It was simple, not as fast paced. "

"I know kids are mean. They are the real losers though."

"Well, which color do you think, black or red, or maybe a hot pink."

"I think you need red. We don't want to send the world into a total tailspin."

"You're funny Dawn. Thanks."

"For what?"

"For being my friend."

"No problem, thanks for being mine."

They spent the rest of the time they had painting nails, putting on makeup and talking about guys. For the first time since they met Grace had finally seemed to come out of her shell. She finally emerged from the 1950's and entered a brave new world.

The next day at school there was quite the buzz around the school. Everyone was talking about the new girl that showed up for school. Little did most of them know that the new girl was just the plain old Grace wrapped up like a Christmas present. Her new appearance looked good and she was quite the show stopper. She was turning heads of every guy down the hall and she filled the hearts of the girls with indignation.

"Who does she think she is?" She heard one of the girls say.

"Yesterday she was a reject from a rerun and now she thinks she's Marilyn Monroe." She heard one of the cheerleaders say.

Grace was very uncomfortable through all of this. She never realized that by changing her clothes, letting her hair down and putting on some make up would create such a stir. She was wishing now that she would have left her old clothes on and forgot the idea of a new me. She entered home room amongst the stares and whispers. She knew that her face must be red and not because of the blush that she was wearing.

"Wow!" Biff said as she sat in her seat next to him.

"Are still going to eat with us at the lunch table, Grace?" Jeff King asked.

"Of course, why wouldn't I?" She replied.

"Have you taken a look in the mirror lately? I didn't expect someone looking like you to sit here any more. You've changed quite a bit in a day."

She was just about to respond to him when Mr. Gunter walked into the room. A hush came over the room immediately. Mr. Gunter liked order and a quiet classroom. The rumor was that his face was made of hardened clay and it would crack if he ever smiled. He was a tough teacher but fair and he actually liked to try and teach. He just had his own way of doing things. He was stiff and rigid and liked doing things "old school". He didn't have much time for fashion and hated the way teens were influenced by culture. Even he was shocked by Grace's transformation, but didn't say anything.

"There goes another teen influence by peer pressure." He thought.

It wasn't that Grace was pressured into changing, she had just come to the conclusion that she could live in the 1950's or move on to bigger and better things. She didn't want to turn into her mother who seemed lost in her own private world.

Once the class had started it still was evident that only Grace's outward appearance had changed. She still was the soft spoken brainiac that they all knew and some loathed at times.

Soon it was lunch and everything was getting back to normal. Like usual there was a large mob of kids leaving the lunch room as a new mob of kids tried to enter it.

Grace got through the lunch line and got her lunch and went to the loser table and sat down like she always did. Biff was there along with Jim who was engaged in a conversation about the newest Sci-Fi movie that was coming out.

Raymond was there along with Bob talking about the latest technology. To them nothing had changed much. She was still Grace to them and still belonged to their club. They welcomed her just like they always did and treated her in their geek fashion. Even though they didn't show it on the outside most of them had to take a second look at the new girl sitting at their table. Brandon came over and sat down along with Dawn.

"Looking pretty good there, Grace." Brandon said.

"Brandon!" Dawn said as she playfully hit him.

"You look very nice today Grace, by all the things I hear, you have made quite the impression." Dawn told her.

"Yeah, I bet I can beat her at chess now that she is the new socialite of the school." Biff taunted her.

"You wish, Biff, I still could beat you with my eyes closed." She retorted back.

"Oooooooooooooooooo!" The other nerds said in unison.

"That's sounds like a challenge" Bob replied.

"You name the place and the time and I will be there. Just make sure you bring enough tissues to wipe the tears away when I beat you." She said back.

"Oooooooooooooooooo!" The nerds said again.

"You're on, Grace, prepare to be defeated." Biff said confidently.

This banter between them might have lasted all lunch long but was interrupted when Sam Green came over to the table.

"Hello Grace, you look nice today." He said to her.

Like a group of fathers watching over their daughter when a date comes to the house, the nerds all gave him a look of death.

"How dare he try to invade the lair of the geeks?" They all thought to themselves.

Grace might be the new pretty girl but she was still one of their own, they weren't going to let Mr. Studly into their group so easily. Grace could feel their disdain for him and told them to calm down.

"Don't worry; I'm still in the club, guys."

He sat down next to Grace and started to talk. Grace seemed preoccupied and wasn't really listening to him. She had more important things to do at the moment. Grace's outside might have changed but she was still Grace on the inside. As Sam talked on and on she slowly inched her hand next to his. She softly laid it upon his. Sam's eyes lit up like he had just been electrocuted. Like a surge of energy was flowing through his body he stood up without warning, causing a slight stir at the table.

"I'll see you around Grace." He said to her as he walked away from the table.

"I'll see you later." She replied nicely.

"What was that all about?" Dawn asked.

"Nothing, I guess he had to go somewhere." Grace replied.

The nerds went back to their lunches and conversations but Dawn pondered what had just happened. It brought her back to the time that she introduced Brandon to Grace and that she went to shake his hand and he responded the same way. She tried to get Brandon to tell her why he acted the way he did but all he would say is that she was weird.

The day went on as usual, slowly, minute by minute, hour by hour the occupants waited and waited for their relief to come. The split second the bell sounded the students headed to the buses like a herd of stampeding buffalo.

Brandon told Dawn that he had to stay over for football so he couldn't take her home today.

"Oh well, that just means that I don't have to walk home today." She thought to herself. Though she would never tell Brandon it, she often times was embarrassed to be in his car. The old jalopy smelled terribly and if you didn't smell it coming you could hear it. It always sounded like it had 5000 marbles rolling around the engine. And if that didn't get you the trail of white smoke that it left would. There were also the multiple layers of paint that it had, she wasn't sure if it was a yellow car or a gray car. Brandon always told her that he would like to get it painted once he saved some money. She always wished that it would roll over a hill and be lost to time.

She got on the bus and sat down next to Rebecca.

"Hi Dawn, how are you today?" She asked.

"Fine Rebecca, what do you have to tell me today?" Dawn replied.

"Nothing much, nothing more than Grace changing her whole look. But you already knew that right?"

"Yes, I did, Rebecca."

As they headed down the street she saw the kids walking home from school. It was a little different today. Usually Grace walked by herself with some other kids in front and sometimes making fun of her. This time though Grace was walking with Biff. Apparently Grace's physical change had affected Biff's outlook on her. Sure Biff was the Chess Captain of the school and he was quite the nerd, but he was a nice guy. They both seemed content as they walked down the sidewalk. Dawn was quite moved by the scene. For once she didn't feel sorrow for Grace.

"There she is now, walking with Biff the Stiff." Rebecca said laughingly.

"Rebecca, can't you say anything nice about anybody?" Dawn said scolding her.

"It's true, he's about as dry as toast if you ask me."

"I didn't ask you Rebecca. You came up with that one on your own." Dawn replied.

"You know Dawn I don't think that you like to hear me talk at times." Rebecca said with a slight hint of hurt in her voice.

"I just wish you would say nice things about people and not always be such a bummer." Dawn told her.

The conversation struck a nerve with Rebecca and she didn't talk for the rest of the ride to Dawn's house.

Dawn didn't want to hurt Rebecca's feelings, but Rebecca was like a walking talking version of the Nation Enquirer with legs. If there was any news to report or any rumors on campus, she would surely know, even though her sources of information were only about ½ right ½ the time.

As the Bus came close to Dawn's house she noticed a strange car in the driveway. A man, who appeared to be Dr. Monroe from the college, was leaving the house.

"That's weird, what would he be doing at the house."

At first Dawn was tempted to think that her mother and the Dr. might be having an affair, but then her common sense took over and she dismissed the notion.

The bus arrived at her house and she got off and headed to the door.

As she entered the house her mother met her. Dawn could tell that she had been crying and that something was terribly wrong.

"What's wrong and why was Dr. Monroe here?"

"It's your father."

"What about him?"

"Dawn, I don't know how to say this, so I am just going to tell you. You father was killed in Slovenia."

Emotions swelled within her like a lightning strike.

"That can't be, we just talked to him last night. What happened?"

Dawn's mother tried to stay strong for Dawn, she knew that night was coming and she could fall apart then.

"It seems that their group was attacked by rebels. Everyone was killed but one intern."

"This can't be happening. I hate him, I hate him. Why did he even have to go there in the first place?"

Dawn was starting to lose control when her mother reached out and hugged her.

"I know Baby, I know."

The hug calmed her down a bit and kept her from becoming hysterical and after five minutes or so she began to regain her composure.

"What do we do now?"

"We grieve, we heal and we go on living."

"That's king of cold Mom, you act like it doesn't matter to you at all."

"Of course it matters. I just lost the love of my life and I will never be the same. My life will always be empty because of this. But my life is not going to end because of it. Look Dawn, this is just the beginning. I have to hold it together. Do you know how much work has to be done?"

"No."

"I have a funeral to plan; I have to get everything in order. I have bills that will need paying. Your Dad did all that. Now I have to do it all. I just had my heart ripped out of my chest but I have to keep it together for now. There will be plenty of time for me to sit in the dark and cry and wonder what I am going to do and how I am going to do it. And for now I need you to go to your room and let it all out. Soon this place will be filled with good intentioned friends and loved ones. Soon we will have to stand in a receiving line and greet people and soon we will have to bury your father."

Dawn headed to her room still numb at what had just happened. It still didn't seem real to her. She just talked to him last night. At least she got to say she loved him one last time. Like a wave her emotions started to swell up within her and she started to cry again. After a few minutes she started to calm down. She went to her desk and got out her photo album. As she started to look at the photos another wave came in and so did the tears. Her tears would be interrupted by the phone. Just as her mother said, it was Aunt Kathy giving her condolences and told her it might take her a day or two before she could be there. Her mother picked up the downstairs phone and she went back to her crying.

It seemed as soon as her mother got off the phone with one person another person called.

"This is crazy." She thought to herself.

"Mom, was right, this is a whirlwind."

It might have been a whirlwind, but it kept her mother busy and if she was busy she didn't have time to lose control. Dawn's mother knew that she seemed to come off a little cold but for now it was the only way she could keep it together. She felt like someone had reached into her chest and pulled out her heart, but for the sake of Dawn, she would have to keep it together.

Soon after the phone calls started, so did the visitors. There were the neighbors coming over to say they were sorry and then church people.

Dawn's mother kept it together like the strong woman she was. Dawn on the other hand wished that they all would just go home.

"Why can't they just leave us alone for now? Don't they know how hard this is?"

"Don't worry Dawn, this will all be over in a few days and then we will be on our own."

Her mother's last statement hit home and Dawn realized for once what her mother was trying to say. Like it or not, she would have to deal with the pain of what all this meant. Her dad wasn't coming home and it was just her mother and her from now on.

"I'm going for a walk, I need to think."

"Ok, tell Grace I said hello."

It always surprised Dawn how much her mother knew about her. It was almost like she could read her mind at times.

"I will."

She gave her a hug and then she started down the street. It seemed like the whole neighborhood was watching her walk along as she headed for Grace's house. It seemed to take eternity for her to get there but she finally made it. She held her emotions in the whole walk there. There was no way that she was going to let any of her neighbors see her lose it.

She rang the doorbell and Grace answered it.

"Come in"

"What's wrong Dawn?"

"My Father has been killed in Slovenia", she tried to tell Grace what had happened between bouts of tears. Grace reached out and held her. This was strange to Dawn, because Grace very rarely ever touched her, or anyone else for that matter. In a matter of seconds during the embrace Grace's eyes filled with tears as she joined Dawn. This was also peculiar, considering that she never saw Grace show much emotion before either.

"I'm sorry."

Both of them cried for a while until Grace's eyes met Dawn's and she had a feeling of calm.

"Just hang in there. Things will be OK, you will never be the same, but you have to be strong for your mother. She's going to have enough to deal with in the next couple of months and she's going to need your support. Be there for her, she's going to need your love and support. OK?"

Dawn was taken back by Grace's comment. She expected her to be clueless to the situation. But she always seemed to be wiser than her years. She then remembered that Grace had lost her father years ago, and that it seemed to throw her mother into her own little world.

"I will try. This is just so unfair. There was so much that I needed to tell him. There was so much that we hadn't done together. I was kind of mean to him when he left. I was so mad. I couldn't understand why he had to leave; now he is gone for good."

"Let it all out, cry and scream, let it all go and then you will go on. You can't let his death end your life too."

As they talked together it seemed like Grace had read her mind, or had over heard the conversation that she just had with her mother. It just seemed like her mother was feeding Grace with the words to say through an ear piece or something.

Grace had a way about her, something that seemed to calm Dawn. Just a look into her eyes and a peace would come over her. It was very strange to Dawn at times. It seemed like she had an aura of peace around her. Dawn would spend the rest of the day with Grace but never put to mind the pain that her mother was feeling and if she needed Dawn to be there. At this point though there was a storm of emotions going on inside her. She couldn't worry about her mother or anyone else at that moment.

Chapter 14

The day came and everything was set, the doors opened to the funeral home and people started to stroll in, one after another came to pay their respects. Dr. Sinclair was well known and well liked and Dawn's mother was very active in the community. It was a great show of support from all of those that loved Dawn's father. This though really didn't matter much to Dawn. All she wanted was for it to be over. With every new person and introduction from her mother Dawn just wanted to scream and burst into tears.

At one point as Dawn's eyes started to fill with tears her mother handed her a tissue.

"You're allowed to cry, just hang on; it will all be over in a little while."

"Thanks Mom."

The crowd slowed a bit to allow Dawn to wipe her tears and to give her some space.

Over and over she would shake hands with many people that she never met and probably would never meet again. Though this time didn't mean much to her, it meant everything for her mother. It seemed that her mother found great comfort and joy in the fact that so many came out to see her father for the last time. Though Dawn could not see past her mother's smile, a piece of her mother would slowly die with each passing person. It was one of Dawn's greatest flaws, she rarely saw past the outward appearance of a person and tried to see the inner most being of a person.

It would be through this catastrophe that Dawn would finally realize the error of her ways and see how shallow she had been. That she herself was a victim of her own devices. That her so called friends didn't even show up to pay their respects. No, it was the strange girl from down the street that came to say she was sorry.

"I am sorry for your loss." Grace told Dawn.

"I am sorry." She said as she gave Mrs. Smith a hug.

"Thank you Grace, I needed that." She said.

Dawn noticed that her mother's demeanor changed at that point and the calming spirit that Grace had seemed to come over her mother.

Grace exited the line and then sat down in the back by herself as usual. After Grace arrived, so did the other nerds from school.

Dawn started to look inward to herself and realized that she was just like the other kids at school. She was part of the clicks that made fun of the kids that seemed to care about the other kids. She was part of the shallow girls that didn't look past what a person wore and never got to know what was behind the face and get to know the true character of a person. She was full of shame at this point, ashamed at herself for all the times that she had made fun of them and acted like they weren't as good as her. Unable to handle the new influx of emotions, she started to break down and cry.

"Excuse me Mom; I have to get some air."

"Go ahead, I understand."

She walked out of the room and tried to find a place of solitude in the midst of the crowd. The only place she could find was in the woman's bathroom. She made sure that she was all alone before she broke down. She entered the empty stall and sat on the toilet. Tears came like a river as she sat there by herself. They weren't tears of grief for her father but tears of anguish over her own failures. She wondered how she had turned out this way. In fact she knew that her parents would be so disappointed if they had any idea that she had acted like this.

"Dawn, are you OK?" she heard Grace ask.

She was taken off guard, considering that she didn't hear anyone come in.

"I feel terrible, Grace"

"That's understandable."

"No, I feel terrible for who I am, and what I have done. I've acted terribly to some of those kids and they are the ones that came to see me, while my so called friends didn't even show up. How is it that you have been my friend through all of this? A year ago I would have been making fun of you too."

"But you didn't Dawn, it's never too late to change, remember. You taught me that. We can all be better people, none of us are perfect."

Dawn was going to say something but was interrupted when someone else came into the bathroom. She wiped her tears and left with Grace. When she arrived back at the receiving line it seemed to be bigger than ever.

"Where have all these people come from. I think that everyone in town came tonight." She whispered to her mother.

"You father did make an impression on people."

Dawn looked out onto the group but couldn't find Grace. It looked like she had left. It wasn't like her to leave without saying goodbye. But Dawn was sure that she had her reasons. She looked at the clock and sighed when she saw that there was still another half an hour of this torture to endure. Just as is seemed that the crowd started to thin more people started to filter in. Her so called friends from school finally arrived; even some of the football team came. This caught Dawn off guard, just when she had lost hope in her friends they all of a sudden showed up. Even though each of them was nice and seemed sincere a rift had been created between Dawn and them. She realized at that point that she had to change; she had to look into the heart of a person, not just at their appearance, that outcasts and misfits had things to offer too, but for now she had to remain focused on trying to be strong and shake each hand and give an occasional hug.

Finally the time had come and the last person went through the line. The last relative said goodbye. They had endured the torture of the moment and now were alone again. Mrs. Sinclair was overcome with grief as she looked over at her husband and the thought that tomorrow would be the last time she would ever see him again. As tears started to flow down her mother's face Dawn realized that she was quite absent for her mother in the past couple of days. That she was more engrossed with her own grief and pain than to worry about how her mother had felt. Her tears started to flow once more as she reached out to her mother and gave her a hug.

"I'm sorry Mom"

"For what?"

"For leaving you alone for the past couple of days, I never thought about your pain."

"It's OK, it's easy to do, it's just hard to see your father there and realize that he isn't coming home. We better get home; we have another big day tomorrow."

Mrs. Sinclair gained control of herself and wiped the tears from her eyes and blew her nose.

"Let's go home."

They both entered the car and headed home. Another day over and one more to go, then it would be apparent to both of them that it was just them against the world.

The morning would come way too soon and they both would be up and getting ready for the funeral. There was nothing either one of them could say so they got ready in relative silence. Neither of them really felt like eating anything and they just kept to themselves until it was time to leave. For once Dawn was ready and her mother didn't even have to call her. She went to the car without a sound and her mother followed her. The day was looking like it was going to be nice, the sun was shining and the clouds were moving past with the breeze.

"How could such a day be so beautiful? It should be filled with black clouds and rain." Dawn thought to herself.

Though both Dawn and her mother were filled with raw emotions neither would say a word. That was until some idiot driver cut them off and they almost had an accident. Mrs. Sinclair laid on the horn and blasted the idiot in front of her. She gave him a look that could have killed him. At that instance she was so filled with emotions that she almost hit the gas instead of the break.

"Mom!" Dawn yelled.

Dawn's voice broke the silence and brought both of them out of their trance.

"What are you doing?" Dawn asked.

"Nothing, I just got caught up in the moment. I better get my head out of the clouds and watch what I am doing."

Mrs. Sinclair reached over and turned on the radio. She had left his cd of classical music in the stereo and it started playing.

"Yuck, this is music to die to." Dawn interjected without thinking.

Once the words left her mouth Dawn knew that she had misspoke. It was just something that she always said to her father every time he turned it on.

"I'm sorry Mom, I didn't think, I "

"I know." Her mother interrupted.

"It's going to be OK."

They arrived at the funeral home and the director politely met them at the door.

"Good morning ladies."

"Good morning." They both replied in unison.

The funeral was to start at 11:00 but they were there at 10:00. Mrs. Sinclair didn't want to worry about anyone being there so they could make their last goodbye together and alone. At this point Dawn wasn't really sure what to do. She looked at the casket and still had a hard time wrapping her thoughts around the whole ordeal. It just didn't seem real yet, she thought that he would enter the door and tell them that there was a big mistake and that he really wasn't dead.

But reality finally took over; with each glance into the cold casket she realized the finality of it all.

"Mom, there is still one thing that bothers me in all of this."

"What's that?"

"Who would have done this? What gain would anyone have to kill him? He was on a research trip. It just seems too pointless."

"I can't answer that question Sweetheart. God only knows the answer to that one."

With that response anger filled Dawn's thoughts.

"Why did she even mention God right now?" She thought to herself.

"Where was God when they were attacking him? How can this be fair? Her father wouldn't have hurt anyone. Where was God now?"

A thousand questions bombarded her mind as she stood there in the silence. As she pondered her thoughts a song came over the sound system that she recognized. It reminded her that life was temporary and that any moment her life could be extinguished too. She had to remember that her father's body was dead but that his soul lived on; it was the foundation to all that she believed in. She was suddenly filled with peace and a feeling of comfort came over her. This was the first time that death had visited her but surely would not be the last.

Soon, just like the night before people started arriving. Not as many as the night before but Dawn was still surprised by the shear number of visitors. Again people came to show their respects to a man that had made an impact on their lives.

"What did Dad do to have such an impact on so many people?" Dawn thought to herself.

The time finally came and the pastor arrived. It was time to start the funeral. Dawn and her mother sat down and the pastor began the eulogy.

To Dawn's surprise the pastor didn't speak much about Dad and his accomplishments but about his faith and what it meant to him. The pastor was directing his sermon more about eternity than the death of her father. He offered words of hope for those who had died and that all those in attendance could have that hope too. Dawn felt it was more like a revival meeting than that of a funeral. The mood went from that of a sorrowful goodbye to a joyous thought of the reunion that they would someday have. It was such a moving sermon that it brought many there to tears.

Still it was hard for Dawn to focus at times. She still was filled with conflicting emotions that were warring deep inside her. She still was angry and hurt, that her father would leave them alone and that God would take him away from them. She just felt like standing up and screaming, "This is so unfair!" but she stood fast and kept it all inside.

They both went to bed that night, wondering about life and what would happen next, two broken hearted souls clinging to the hope they would one day see their loved one again. That didn't ease the loneliness at times, or fill the gap created by his absence, it was way too large for anyone person to fill, and no person could ever take his place; he was loved and would never be forgotten. He was gone, but he left a legacy branded into the hearts of the ones that loved him. One had lost a husband, friend and lover, the other a dad and father, both had lost the man that held their hearts. This would either pull them together or drive them apart. They could either share their grief and loneliness and help each other through it or keep it inside and push the other away. It was a choice that both of them had to make, a choice that neither had wanted but had been thrust into by such a tragedy. Either way, it was just the two of them now. They could either let the sorrow crush them or step up and deal with the pain and loss and go on with life.

Chapter 15

As the days wore on, their lives readjusted and they went back to their old schedules. Mrs. Sinclair went back to work and Dawn went back to school. Grace was even a bigger help now, more than ever. Grace seemed to read Dawn's mind. She could just tell what Dawn needed and when she needed propped up. She was still the same old shy Grace but something about her had changed. She no longer seemed so self absorbed, but now she seemed to be reaching out to help someone else. Dawn's loss seemed to bring Grace out of her own little world and pushed her into Dawn's. She started to interact more with the kids at the table. She seemed brighter and more cheerful. She smiled more. Even though she was still on the weird side, she was slowly stepping up to a less weird state more towards normal. Everyone seemed to take notice of her change, though the other kids still made fun of her and called her names, the other geeks and nerds took notice and she actually started to fit in with them. Granted this wasn't much higher on the social scale as she was before, she at least now was part of a group of friends that she seemed to relate to. She was like the caterpillar finally turned into the butterfly.

Dawn and Grace became even closer during all of this. Instead of quietly sitting in the shadows watching the world go by Grace was actually interjecting and being part of the conversation. This was a side of Grace that Dawn had never seen. Sure, Grace was always polite and never said anything bad about anything or anyone, but she never seemed to be there mentally. Physically she was, but her mind always seemed to be light years away.

The two actually went to the mall to shop on more than one occasion and Grace was actually trying on clothes that were in style. Dawn couldn't help but to think that all Grace needed was a friend, someone that didn't care what clothes she wore or how odd she might have acted, but a friend none the less. Dawn at this point realized that she might have lost the shallow wannabes that she hung out with, but she gained the one thing that she wanted so desperately. Not just a friend, but a soul sister, someone that knew her inside and out, someone that she could share her inmost feelings with, without the fear that she would ever tell. The kind of friend that would walk through fire for you, that was what Grace had turned into.

In all of the chaos of her father's death Dawn's relationship with Grace had blossomed into more than a friendship and more of a sister to sister relationship. Without realizing it, Dawn's relationship with Jessica had suffered considerably in all of the emotion turmoil of what had happened. Jessica started to feel like the one being left out and started to resent Grace at the thought that she had stolen her best friend. To Jessica it seemed that Dawn was no longer interested in her and that Grace was her new best friend. Jessica tried to remain civil to Grace but at times the tension between the three was very evident. Dawn always tried to tell Jessica that nothing between them had changed and that she still was her best friend, but that their little group had added a new member. Even so Jessica started to distance herself from Dawn, even though Dawn's heart would break at the thought of loosing Jessica as a friend, Jessica was sure that Grace had taken her long held position. Dawn tried her best to include both of them in all that she did. She always made sure she invited both of them to go to the mall or out to eat, but it seemed that a riff had been created that neither of them could fix. Dawn was held in an emotional quandary, she wasn't sure what to do, she wanted to be friends with Jessica but she also wanted to be friends with Grace. She didn't want to have to choose between the two.

Chapter 16

With the arrival of Brandon's father, Brandon's emotions started to run wild. He was caught in a whirlwind of anger, fear and hatred all swirling around in his mind at one time. Not only were his emotions running wild, so were his hormones.

Dawn on the other hand was still in her realm of darkness since her father had died. She still was grieving and at times couldn't see the light at the end of the tunnel. To her life seemed to be slowly drifting into oblivion. She no longer had the hopes and dreams she once held and her ambition had all but left her. She was slowly being strangled by the weight of her loss and she was slipping into a deep depression.

Brandon was on the height of his emotions while Dawn was on the depth of hers. Both of their emotions were high, just at opposite ends of the spectrum.

As they pulled into the park and Brandon turned off the car, they both sat there in the silence for a while. The night was warm and the sky was clear and Brandon opened up the sun roof so they could see the stars. They sat there for a while looking at the night sky. Dawn wasn't even in the car, in her mind she was somewhere else thinking about her life and how things had turned out. Brandon wasn't sure what to do and sat there in the silence staring up at the night sky.

"Do you think people in heaven can see us down here?" She asked breaking the silence.

"I don't know, I never thought about it much." Brandon replied.

"I just wonder if they can see what's happening. I just wonder what my dad is doing right now. I really miss him." She said as she started to cry.

"Dawn, I am sure that he is up in heaven smiling. He knows that you and your mother are going to make it. He knows that he taught you the right way to live and that some day you will be up there too." Brandon said with caring and compassion as he reached out to hold her.

As they hugged the storm raging in both of them came together and a fire started in each of them. Brandon's fire was fueled by raw emotion and hormones while Dawn's was fueled by hurt and depression. As they held each other and began to kiss their passion ignited. This was the first time that their passions were released as their kissing began to become heavy.

Brandon was driven by his desire for Dawn and Dawn was driven by her need to be loved and embraced by a man. Brandon was a perfect surrogate for the moment and she began to get lost in her emotional hurricane as Brandon was lost in his. As these two super storms collided destruction was sure to follow.

Both were lost in the moment as Brandon's hands started to wander around different areas of Dawn's body, whether he consciously started to feel the off limits zone or unintentionally moved in that direction was known only to God and him. Dawn might have been an emotional wreck but she hadn't lost her common sense. Within seconds of the violation she snapped out of her dream world and back to reality.

"What do you think you're doing?" She snapped at Brandon.

"What?" Brandon replied not knowing what to say.

"Don't act innocent with me Brandon; what do you think you're doing?" She asked him again.

"You think that just because I'm sad and depressed that you could get alone with me and put your moves on me?" She scolded him.

"I." He was going to say something when she interrupted him.

"You know Brandon, I thought that you were different, but you are the same as any other guy. I think my father was right. You're one step higher than an ape."

"I didn't mean anything Baby. I just got a little carried away. I'm sorry." Brandon tried to apologize.

"You know that's right. It's the first and last time it will ever happen because you and I are through." She yelled at him as she opened the car door.

"Where are you going?" He demanded.

"I'm going home." She responded.

"What are you going to do walk home, from here?" He asked caringly.

"Maybe, maybe I will just call my mother and explain to here what you were trying to do."

"Look Dawn, I'm sorry. You can break up with me, but let me drive you home. It's dark and I wouldn't want anything to happen to you here." He told her sincerely.

"I don't want you to drive me home; I am never getting in a car with you again. You are nothing more than a creep!" She shouted as she started to walk away from the car.

That last comment struck a nerve with Brandon, he was sorry that he went too far but calling him a creep wasn't helping his ego.

"Have it your way, you stuck up little princess!" He shouted as he drove down the road.

As she watched his tail lights head down the road Dawn started to think that she might have over reacted and that she shouldn't have called him a creep. She also became aware that she was in the middle of the park at night and was about three miles from home. At first she thought to call her mother, but then decided that she didn't want to have to explain why she was in the woods this late at night and why Brandon dropped her off, so she called the person that would understand, Grace.

She frantically tried to find her cell phone in her purse in the dark. She looked around to make sure that no one was around. She dialed Grace's number and stood there hoping that she was home.

"Pick up Grace." She said as she became more and more frightened from her surroundings. The phone rang and rang and rang with no answer, so she had no choice but to call Jessica. Jessica was still a friend but the two of them hadn't spent any real time with each other in a while, so Dawn wasn't sure what Jessica would say.

After ringing about five times Jessica picked up the phone.

"Hi Dawn." She said as she picked up the phone.

"Jessica, I need your help. Can you pick me up? I am in the park and I need a ride home." She said frantically.

"What are you doing in the park at night?" Jessica asked in disbelief.

"It's a long story. Brandon and I had a fight and I got out of the car and he left." She said.

"Can you pick me up; I really don't want to have to tell my mother?"

"No problem. Give me about 10 minutes to get there." She said trying to reassure her.

Those ten minutes felt like 3 hours before Jessica arrived. Dawn definitely could fill the chill in the air and she was starting to feel cold, adding to the fact that she was sure that there was some goon lurking in the woods ready to attack her. With every crunch or rattle in the woods her fear level increased. She started to pace around, thinking that a moving target would be harder to catch and it help to keep her warm.

"Where are you Jessie?" She muttered to herself as she waited in the darkness.

Even though Dawn had bruised his ego, Brandon still cared for Dawn. He didn't drive far when he realized that he just left her in the middle of the park at night. He turned the car around and started back to her. He could see her standing on the side of the road as he returned. She was trying to keep herself warm with the light jacket she had on.

Dawn was happy at first because she thought that Jessica had finally arrived but then she realized by the noise and the smoke that Brandon was coming back.

He rolled the window down as he pulled up along side her.

"Baby, get in the car. I promise I will not do anything I will just take you home." He said.

"I won't get in that car. I told you to leave me alone." She snapped back at him.

"Come on Dawn, it's cold and you're out here in the dark. It may not be safe."

"Like you really care, all you wanted from me is something I am not going to give you."

"I told you that I was sorry. I wasn't thinking. Just let me take you home." He told her as he tried to remain calm.

"You were thinking alright, you were thinking how far I can get with Dawn!" She scolded him.

The more he tried to reason with her to at least get in the car and wait for Jessica the angrier she got.

"Have it your way then." He said one last time as he started to pull away.

She watched as he drove down the street and turned around and drove back to her and pulled off the road.

"What are you doing now?" She asked him.

"You don't have to get in the car but I am not going to let you stand out here in the dark, is that OK, Princess?" He told her.

"Whatever." She responded coyly.

Jessica finally arrived and Dawn opened the door.

"Thanks a lot!" She said to him as she got into Jessica's car.

As they set off to Dawn's house Brandon put his car in drive and headed for home too. Things definitely didn't go as planned for him and he wasn't sure what was going to happen next. He thought that there might be hope for Dawn and him when she calmed down a little, but he still had to prepare for the thought that it was over between them.

Both Dawn and Jessica remained silent for the ride to Dawn's house. She knew that Dawn didn't want to talk and that she would tell her what happened when she was ready. Before long they arrived at Dawn's house and she thanked her for the help and then watched her drive off before she entered the house. Her mother was sitting there in the semi darkness watching the TV waiting for Dawn to return like she always did.

"Did Brandon get another car?" Her mother asked

"What?"

"Did Brandon get another car; I couldn't hear it this time when he dropped you off." She asked again.

"No, that was Jessica. Brandon had some car trouble so I called her to take me home." Dawn replied, trying to keep the real reason why Jessica brought her home. She really didn't want to lie to her mother but she didn't want to explain the evening to her either. There would be a time for that, maybe when she was around 40 years old, but not tonight.

"Did she take Brandon home too?" Her mother asked trying to get to the bottom of the mystery.

"I don't know, I wasn't waiting around to see." She retorted back at her with a slight attitude.

"Dawn, what happened?" Her mother asked.

"If you must know, Brandon and I broke up and then I called Grace to come and pick me up, but she didn't answer so I had to call Jessica, OK, that's what happened. Can I go to bed now; I really don't feel like talking about it right now. Is that OK?" Dawn replied with a definite attitude this time.

"I'm sorry, Dawn. I know how much you liked him. Good night, I love you." She said as she rose up and gave her a hug.

It took everything within Dawn to keep from loosing it and start crying, but she kept it in this long and she wasn't about to break down in front of her mother now.

"I love you too. I will see you in the morning." Dawn said.

Dawn was quietly shocked at her mother's response. Maybe it was because Dad wasn't there to give her questions on what happened or maybe that her mother knew the pain of a breakup and realized that she needed some space.

Mrs. Sinclair tried to keep a cool look about her, but inside she wanted to know what had happened. They appeared to be a happy couple and Brandon appeared to be a nice guy, so the question that remained is why they broke up. Dawn left her mother to ponder the newest mystery of the family as she got ready for bed. Later as she headed to her bedroom she could hear Dawn quietly crying in her room. It broke her heart to know that Dawn had suffered another heart break so close to her father's death, but this time she knew that Dawn was going to have to deal with this one herself. She got ready for bed, said some extra prayers for Dawn and fell asleep.

Chapter 17

Mrs. Sinclair let Dawn sleep in that Saturday, they had nothing planned and she figured Dawn didn't get to bed until late. Eventually Dawn woke up and headed downstairs.

"Good morning Sunshine." Mrs. Sinclair said.

"Good morning." Dawn grumbled back.

"You alright?" Mrs. Sinclair asked with care.

"Yes, I will be. Right now I just want something to eat." Dawn responded in a sleepy haze.

It was about 10 o'clock and the phone began to ring. Mrs. Sinclair was about to pick it up as Dawn shouted. "Don't who is it?"

"It says Brandon's Mother's number."

"Let it ring, I don't want to talk to him right now." Dawn told her mother.

"Ok."

Dawn went back to the process of getting her breakfast ready. Dawn in the morning wasn't usually focused on anything. Usually it took her awhile to wake up so she was often in a fog of sorts. Today was no different as she started to pour cereal into a bowl. She had about twice the amount of cereal in the bowl mounded like a pyramid when she asked. "Dawn, what are you doing?"

"I'm getting some cereal. Why?"

"Will you pay attention? There is no way you are going to eat that much cereal. Put some of that back." Mrs. Sinclair scolded her.

Dawn reluctantly scooped up the excess cereal and put it back in the box.

"Is that better?" She asked with a glare in her eyes.

"Yes. Don't do that again, watch what you are doing." Mrs. Sinclair said as she headed for the living room to let Dawn eat in peace.

Dawn was about half way through her bowl of cereal when the phone rang again and it was Brandon again. She told her mother that it was Brandon and let it ring and she did. Every time Brandon just hung up and didn't leave a message. Apparently he knew that someone else might get the message and wanted to leave the reasons for their breakup between them.

After about the ninth call Mrs. Sinclair said, "Dawn, you can't hide from him forever you are going to have to talk to him sooner or later."

"I'll talk to him all right, but not today, the ape." Dawn answered back as she finished her cereal and put her bowl in the sink.

"What did you call him?" Mrs. Sinclair asked inquisitively.

"An ape, it was just a slip of the tongue. I am going to get ready, do you mind if I go out with Grace to the mall or something?" She asked politely.

"No, go ahead, why don't you call and we all can get something to eat for dinner. Sound like a plan?" Mrs. Sinclair replied.

"Sure, sounds good." Dawn said as she headed to her room.

Call it mother's intuition or esp. but it only took a few seconds for Mrs. Sinclair to solve the mystery of their breakup after Dawn called Brandon an ape. Mr. Sinclair often went on tirades about guys with Dawn and called them apes when it came to their hormones or what every guy their age wanted. She had a slight shudder of fear run through her when she thought what might have happened the night before. Dawn headed to the bathroom to get ready for the day and Mrs. Sinclair headed to her bedroom for some quiet time. This was the time that every parent of a daughter dreaded, getting the news that some guy had tried to take advantage of them or worse that their little girl had gone too far willingly. She knew that she could confront Dawn about what happened or let Dawn handle the situation herself. But when she realized that Dawn appeared to handle herself the right way and took care of the situation, she decided that Dawn was using her common sense and wouldn't press her on what happened that night, but she was going to keep a watchful eye on Brandon from now on if he ever came around again.

After Mrs. Sinclair sat and meditated for a while on what to do next Dawn knocked on the door. "I called Grace but she didn't answer so Jessica and I are going over to the mall for a while, OK? I'll call you later about dinner. Love you."

Dawn's mother opened the door before she was finished speaking.

"Alright, I love you, drive safe." Her mother said as she gave her hug.

They both walked down the stairs and they headed for the garage. Dawn thought that her mother was acting strange because she rarely followed her into the garage.

She got into the car and hit the garage door opener button and the door started to open.

Her mother stood by the door as she started the car. As Dawn put the car in reverse and started to pull out her mother waved and said. "Dawn."

Dawn immediately put on the brake and rolled down the window.

"Did you need something?" She asked

"No, but just remember that I know how to use a gun, just like your father." She replied as she gave her Dawn a playful wink.

As she pressed on the gas she didn't know what to think, until she made it to the end of the driveway. She gave her mother a last smile and wave and headed to Jessica's house. Shock flowed through her like she had put her finger in the light socket. She realized that somehow her mother knew what had happened between her and Brandon.

After Dawn left Mrs. Sinclair headed to Mr. Sinclair's office. The college had sent over his belongings and now it was her sad job of going through them. She had put the boxes in his office on the floor. She picked one up and put it on the desk. It was full of notes and handwritten pages for his next book. She felt like taking a match to all of them at that minute.

"Cursed book, if it wasn't for it, he will still be alive." She thought to herself.

She tried to keep calm as she pulled the papers out of the box and tried to keep them in some order. It seemed that most of the book was already typed and there were only a few chapters left that were still handwritten. She separated the typed from the handwritten and then pulled out some more papers from the box. In one of the piles of paper was a yellow sheet that didn't match the other papers in the pile. She was intrigued at what the paper said.

"I spent my life chasing rainbows while the flowers of my garden went unkempt.

I saw the beauty in the sunset yet missed the beauty of the flowers that I had planted.

With all that I am ready to fade from view

All that I did was meaningless because my flowers grew and bloomed;

Yet I never took the time to be captivated by their beauty or held in awe by their scent.

I was a fool not to see the beauty I held in the garden I planted."

Tears filled her eyes as she realized that it was the last thing that he had written before he left. It was the final eulogy of his life and how he felt about Dawn and her, overcome with feelings she slouched into the chair and held her head in her hands and began to cry.

Some hours later as Dawn returned from her day with Jessica. Her mother met her at the door. Dawn was kind of worried that her mother was going to ask her what happened between her and Brandon the night before but she didn't. She saw that her mother was holding a yellow sheet of paper.

"Dawn, I know that you thought you father didn't care. But I found something in his papers. It was the last thing he wrote before he left for Slovenia." Her mother told her in a shaky voice.

Dawn took the paper from her mother and started to read the lines of the poem. Her eyes filled with tears just like her mother's before and her mother reached out to console her.

"It's OK Dawn, its OK." Her mother told her.

"No it isn't, it can never be OK." Dawn answered back.

"What do you mean, Dawn?"

"I was so mad when he left. I acted like I hated him. I acted like he didn't care and now I can't tell him I love him." She said in between tears.

"I know, it's just how life is some time. We all have done things that we cannot change. He knew you didn't mean it. I just wanted you to see that he did care and he was concerned that he wasn't as close to you as he should have been." Her mother said.

"Can I have this?" Dawn asked.

"Sure." Her mother responded.

Dawn headed upstairs and lay on her bed and cried, the pain she felt was knowing there was no way to tell him that she loved him.

She sat up and looked around her room and saw a picture of her family. She took it off the wall and took the back of it off. She slid the picture out and put the paper in front of it and then put the frame back together and put it back on the wall. His last words would be her guide with dealing with the ones that she loved. When she started to take for granted the loved ones that she had around her, all she had to do was read that poem. From this day on she would treat each day like it was her last, and live every day to its fullest. She was no longer going to walk in grief but she was going to bask in the sunlight of each day, happy to be alive and surrounded by people who loved her.

Chapter 18

Dawn was often alone at nights since her father had died. Her mother tried to get the hospital to change her hours, but for now both of them had to live with it. So rather than sit there watching TV or surfing the internet, Dawn would go over to Grace's house or vice versa. Grace seemed to be a walking talking computer at times and she seemed to have all the answers when it came to homework. She was very philosophical and had many intellectual thoughts of classic books that they had to read. She often times though showed signs of disdain and boredom when it came to certain subjects. Many of the books she could recite by memory, and even though Grace very rarely ever spoke Spanish Dawn was sure that she was fluent. This was always the puzzle to Dawn, when it came to Grace. She often thought that Grace belonged in college, not high school and that she was a step above anyone that she knew when it came to intelligence.

So there they would be, Dawn and Grace doing homework, Dawn would be trying to keep up with Grace who seemed to be like a run away freight train.

This day was no different as the two had finished their homework and were sitting in the living room watching an old movie when Dawn noticed that a car pulled into the driveway. She looked out the window to see who it was.

The car was an older model but was still in good condition. It was something that Dawn wasn't used to, since she had been going out with Brandon.

She couldn't help but wonder who was going to get out of it. As she looked and pondered a slender well dressed man got out of the car.

"Grace, do you know this guy? He's a real hunk." Dawn said with excitement.

"Yeah, he's my brother." Grace replied laughingly.

"Oh." Dawn replied as the smile left her face.

"It's OK, he is good looking." Grace told her as she began to snicker as she went to open the door.

Just as there was a knock at the door Grace opened it to let her brother in.

"Hello sis." The man said as he picked up Grace and gave her a hug.

"Hi, Max." Grace replied in a gleeful tone.

After swinging her around a little he let her down.

"Oh, I am sorry. Where are my manners? Dawn this is my brother Max, Max this is my best friend Dawn."

Dawn rose from the couch to greet him and he reach out his hand to shake hers.

"Very nice to meet you." Dawn said.

"Likewise, any friend of my sisters is a friend of mine." He responded.

Just then Mrs. Smith entered the room.

"Who was at the door?" She asked not seeing Max at first.

"Max!" She screamed as she rushed over to give him a hug.

"How have you been?" She asked excitedly.

"Fine, Mom, just fine. And how are you?"

"I am good, everything is good. Sit down. Are you thirsty, do you want something to eat?"

"No Ma, I am fine." He said respectfully.

At this point Dawn seemed out of place and a little uncomfortable seeing that they were having a family reunion of sorts.

"Grace, I will see you tomorrow, I can see you and your brother have a lot of catching up to do." Dawn said.

"That's OK Dawn, you don't have to go. You're just like family. Stay, you can get to know Max." Grace replied.

"Are you sure?"

"Yes, I am sure. Come and get to know the rest of the family."

With that they all went into the kitchen and sat at the table and talked. This was the first time that Max had been with the family in two years, so they were all excited to see him. They sat there and asked what he had been doing and they told him what new things were going on.

At one point Dawn was overwhelmed with the memory of her family talks around the table and realized how much she missed her father and almost started to cry.

"Are you OK?" Max asked Dawn as their eyes met.

For the first time Dawn got to look into those dark eyes. Eyes so dark they were like looking into a well and not being able to see the bottom. He had eyes just like his mother and sister. With that look calm over her that she couldn't explain. It was like a blanket of peace had come over her and she began to calm down.

"Yeah, I'm fine." Thanks for asking.

"I better get home. It's getting late." Dawn said as she looked at the clock.

"Are you sure, you just got here?" Mrs. Smith said.

"Yeah, I better go, thanks for the evening and nice to meet you Max."

"Likewise, the pleasure was all mine." Max replied as he stood up to walk her to the door.

It kind of took Dawn by surprise. Max seemed to be an extra ordinary gentleman. Grace got up and told her goodbye as Dawn walked to the car and drove home.

For the next four hours the three of them sat around the table drinking iced tea and talking. Max was back and it was a joyous time and they all were happy to see each other.

Seeing Grace and her family so happy, set Dawn into a tailspin of emotions. The fact that she would never see her father again hit her like a freight train. She started to feel the weight of loss on her shoulders and the never ending feeling of guilt she had. She now regretted all the times that she took her father for granted and the times that she often fought with him. As she started to get close to her house she pulled herself together so her mother wouldn't see that she had been crying. She pulled the car into the garage, shut the door and after wiping the tears away from her eyes and trying to fix her makeup she headed for the door. As she opened the door she saw her mother sitting there on the couch watching the TV waiting for her to come home.

"Hi Mom."

"Hello Sunshine, did you have fun?"

With that statement the tears started to flow from Dawn's eyes once more.

"What's the matter Honey?" Her mother asked as she got up from the couch.

"Nothing much just that, Grace's brother came over and they were all happy and talking to him so I left to let them catch up on old times and when I came in here you called me Sunshine. You never call me Sunshine, only Dad did." She said trying to hold herself together.

"I'm sorry Dawn, I didn't mean anything." She told her as she gave her a hug.

"I'm sorry, just seeing them so happy threw me for a loop."

"It's OK, it's OK." Her mother softly whispered over and over.

The two stood there for several minutes as her mother tried to calm her down. She knew that Dawn would make it, but that she was still in a volatile emotional state.

"Thanks Mom, I am going to bed." Dawn told her mother as she headed upstairs.

"Goodnight, I love you." Her mother replied.

"I love you too."

Dawn regained her composure and got ready for bed and fell asleep, little did she realize that her mother cried herself to sleep.

The next morning Dawn realized that she had a decision to make about where her life was heading. She could let the loss of her father end her life or use it as another stepping stone and go on. She was often filled with guilt or remorse that she was forgetting her father but she knew that grief would be a large weight around her neck.

She decided that today would be the last time that she would allow her emotions to run wild and that she would remember her father and not be grieved by him. She had taken a great loss but so had so many others in the world and who was she to think that she was any different than any others that had suffered such a tragedy. She allowed herself one more 'good cry' before she started the day and decided that this experience would just be another thread in the tapestry of her life, today she became an adult.

Chapter 19

At school Dawn made sure that she avoided any contact with Brandon at any cost. She didn't want to talk to him; she didn't even want to see him. As she walked down the hall she saw Grace standing next to her locker.

"How late did you stay up last night?" Dawn asked.

"Till around 2:00 a.m. , though my mother went to bed around 12:00."

"I take it you guys had a good time?"

"The best, I haven't seen Max in two years. He has always been a good brother to me. We always get along and he knows how to cheer my mother and me up. It was really nice."

"I am glad. He seemed like a great guy." Dawn replied.

"He is, you should get to know him better. I know you want to."

"Grace!" Dawn said with a smile.

"It's OK, Dawn; you're not the first girl to be attracted to my brother."

"Just give some time Grace before you have me marrying him, OK?"

"OK." Grace replied with a snicker as they headed off to class.

The day seemed to drag on and on, as Dawn tried her best to keep her distance from Brandon, finally the lunch bell sounded and Dawn headed for the cafeteria, she went through the lunch line and bought her lunch and headed to the loser table. Since Dawn had broken social protocol the table had started to grow in numbers. The table now included other social outcasts other than just the geeks.

As she sat down everyone at the table hushed their talking and primarily kept to themselves. The group had become aware of her emotions and didn't want to set her off.

"I'm fine guys, let's get back to normal." She told them.

They all looked at her in disbelief and went back to their quieted lunch time.

"I mean it guys, I 'm fine. I just want to get back to normal. OK." She said trying to reassure them that talking was OK.

With her last statement someone at the table took the liberty to start normal conversations again and within minutes the whole table was busy talking among themselves about the events of the day.

To Dawn's surprise Brandon came over and sat down like nothing had happened.

"Hey losers." He said as he sat down next to Dawn.

"You have some nerve, sitting here, don't you think?" She responded.

"This is the misfits table isn't it? And right now I'm just another misfit."

At this point everyone at the table was glaring at Brandon. Dawn hadn't told anyone what had happened but Grace but everyone there knew that something had happened between them.

"I have nothing to say to you Brandon, I told you before, it's over."

Brandon went to reach over and touch Dawn but was intercepted by Grace's hand. As Grace's hand touched Brandon's a surge of energy flowed through him like a lightning bolt making him jump to his feet.

"You're one crazy witch!" He shouted at Grace.

"Have it your way Princess." He scolded Dawn as he walked to another area of the lunch room.

"Grace, what did you do to him?" Dawn asked.

"All I did was touch his hand, I didn't do anything to him." She replied.

Everyone at the table noticed what happened when Grace touched Brandon but no one said a word.

As Brandon walked away Dawn realized that her relationship was over and another wave of emotion was about to come over her. This time though she was in control and not her emotions. She decided at that point that happiness was a choice and she was going to choose to be happy. With this new feeling of joy that had replaced the crushing feeling of loss, she went from the deepest of deeps to the highest of highs. Again her emotions had gotten the best of her and without thinking she was ready to do something on an impulse.

Without thinking twice Dawn filled a teaspoon full of corn from her plate and launched it over at Bill sitting at the far side of the table. Without warning Bill was hit with a flying barrage of corn.

Bill lunged back quickly after being hit with the flying vegetables.

"Who did that?" He asked with confusion in his voice.

Dawn had done her best to keep anyone from seeing what she did, but seeing that she was the only one there with corn on her plate left no room for question. It only took Bill a matter of seconds to come to the conclusion that Dawn had opened fire on him and he in turn threw his dinner roll at her. She saw what he had planned and had time enough to duck from the flying piece of bread, instead of hitting her it landed in Jim's soup.

"What's going on here?" Jim retorted as he looked over at Bill.

Bill looked innocently at Jim as he replied, "You got nothing on me."

At this point Jim hadn't seen the corn hit Bill and was more interested in the book he was reading than flying vegetables.

What happened next went down as a school legend. No one really knew who started the next barrage of flying food, even though Jim appeared to be the guilty culprit. Before anyone said another word, a heap of mash potatoes flew across the length of the table and hit Christopher and then pandemonium broke out. Everyone at the table seemed to have lost their sense of where they were and started to throw parts of their lunch at the other people at the table.

Just as Miguel was ready to throw his dinner roll Mrs. Sims bellowed out, "What in the world is going on here? Stop this. Stop this right now!"

Whatever was going through Miguel's mind at this point was only known between him and God; after Mrs. Sims ordered the food fight to stop, he threw the dinner roll which bounced off of Grace's head.

"That's it mister, you just got yourself a one way ticket to the principle's office. In fact all of you here at this table did." She bellowed once again as she ordered all at the table to head to the office.

All at once they stood and headed to the office, still covered with potatoes and corn and anything else used in the battle. Each one held a stoic face as they headed to their impending doom. As they walked past the others in the room, the other students were mystified of what had just happened.

After a moment or two someone in the crowd yelled. "Way to go!"

The rest of the crowd started to clap and yell as the condemned members of the loser table headed to certain detention.

As they headed away from the lunch room they all started to smile as they could hear Mrs. Sims yelling at the remaining students.

"This type of behavior will not be tolerated; quiet down or you will be heading to the office next."

Everyone quieted down, they all knew that at this point, Mrs. Sims meant business and she wasn't in a mood to be messed with.

As the group of delinquents headed around the corner and no longer could be seen by those in the cafeteria they all took the time to look at each other.

Bill had potatoes in his hair. Jim had corn down the front of his shirt. Dawn had butter stuck to her shoulder and Miguel had some spaghetti on his belly. Grace didn't go unscathed as she tried to fix her prim and proper state of dress.

After each one had the few seconds to see each other and to think over what had happened they all broke out in laughter in unison. The laughter was short lived though, as they entered the door to the main office. Each of them knew that they were going to get it, because food fights vary rarely ever happened at school. All of them became silent as they entered the office to the surprise of the secretary sitting there.

"May I help you?" She said in shock as she saw the food hanging on each of them.

Dawn, feeling that she was the one responsible for the fight spoke up.

"Mrs. Sims sent us down here, I started a food fight."

"What?" The secretary asked in disbelief.

"Mrs. Sims sent us down here because I started a food fight." Dawn repeated.

The secretary picked up the phone and called the principle.

"I've got about six students here, something about a food fight." They overheard her say.

Each was sitting in their own little world of terror as the thought of having to explain their behavior to their parents or the amount of detention that they were sure to receive, or maybe even a suspension.

By this time the lunch bell had rung and Mrs. Sims entered the office to make sure that group had arrived like they were told.

"Can you believe this?" Mrs. Sims asked the secretary.

"Who would have ever thought that the members of the chess club and science fair would have started something like this?" She rambled on.

"Do you want me to tell Mr. Stevens that you are here?" The secretary asked.

"Yes, I want to make sure that he knows what happened here."

The secretary picked up the phone and called Mr. Stevens and informed him that Mrs. Sims was there also.

At this point Mr. Stevens was disgusted. Now he not only had to find out something about a food fight but now Mrs. Sims was involved. To him Mrs. Sims was the cranky old teacher that forgot why she went into teaching and should have retired years ago.

After a few minutes more of waiting the phone rang and the secretary told them all that the principle was ready to see them. Usually in a matter such as this Mr. Stevens would talk to each student individually to make an unbiased decision on what had happened but seeing that Mrs. Sims was going to sit in on the proceeding he wanted to buffer himself along with the students from her wrath.

Mr. Stevens was noticeably shocked as each member of the loser table entered the room. He found it hard to believe that some of his best students were standing in front of him covered with pieces of someone's lunch.

"What do we have here?" Mr. Stevens said as his office filled up with students.

"Well, I will tell you, Mr. Stevens." Mrs. Sims broke in.

"As I saw it, Dawn here threw corn at Bill and then Bill threw a roll and then someone threw mashed potatoes and before my very eyes the whole table was throwing food. This is just disgraceful. Just totally disgraceful that such a good group of students would stoop so low."

"Thank you Mrs. Sims, for your eyewitness testimony. That is all I need from you. You can go back to class now." Mr. Stevens said.

"Yes sir." Mrs. Sims replied as she left the room in an angry huff.

They all could hear her ranting and raving as she left the main office as she headed back to her class.

"Well, is this true, Dawn, did you instigate a food fight?" He asked.

"Yes, I did." Dawn answered rather sheepishly.

The others of the group were taken back at the fact that Dawn admitted to the crime.

"No, she didn't, I did." Bill interjected. "I started the fight."

"No, I did." Christopher added.

"No I did." Miguel said.

Even Grace stepped up and said that she herself started the fight.

"Now let me get this straight, each of you is telling me that you started this fight?"

"Yes". They all said in unison.

"You all realize that the person that started the fight is the one that is most responsible and is going to get the larger punishment?" He asked them solemnly.

"Yes." They responded again in unison.

"How am I going to explain to anyone that some of the best students in the school had a food fight during lunch? This hasn't happened since I was in school." He said as a slight grin appeared on his face.

As each of the members of the team saw his face they realized that it might not be as bad as it was first thought to be. They later found out, by Bill's research into the archives of the school newspaper that the principle himself was involved in a rather large full lunch room food fight on his last day of school.

"Nevertheless, someone has to pay for such behavior, but after hearing the evidence set before me and that Dawn's tripping and falling into Bill caused the incident, I will show some sort of leniency. The only thing that I require is that none of you discuss the punishment with anyone outside of this room. Is that understood?" He ordered like a sergeant in front of a platoon.

"Yes sir." They responded.

"First of all this will be written down as an accident where Dawn's tray fell on Bill and Bill's tray fell on Bill and so on and so forth. Understand?"

"Yes sir."

"Second, each of you will be remanded to the lunch room each day for a week where you will empty the trash and clean the tables. Is that understood?"

"Yes sir."

"If I hear anyone talking about this in the halls or out in the street, I will give each of you a year's detention. Is that understood?" He said sternly.

"Yes sir."

"Get out of here, all of you, and get cleaned up."

"Yes sir, and thank you sir." They all said in unison.

As they started to leave the office the principle asked Dawn to stay. Each thought that she still might get something more, because they all knew that Mr. Stevens knew the truth.

"Sit down Dawn." He told her as everyone else left the room.

"What's going on Dawn?"

"What do you mean?" She replied.

"Come on Dawn, you have a 4.0 grade average. You are part of the National Honor Society. What is going on?"

"I just got caught up in the moment sir. This was the first day that I have been happy since my father died."

Mr. Stevens knew the answer before he asked the question but he just wanted Dawn to say what she was feeling.

"I understand. Just don't let something like this happen again. OK?" He asked in a caring voice.

"I won't and I am sorry, thank you for not suspending any of us. I really did start the whole thing. It just got wild and out of hand before I knew what had happened." She said with tears in her eyes.

"It will be OK and so will you. You better get cleaned up and back to class." He told her like a father to a child.

At that moment Dawn got to see the principle for something more than a principle. She always had this idea of Mr. Stevens as a tyrant of sorts loving to punish guilty students. This time she saw a man that cared about the students that were under his leadership and hadn't forgotten what being a kid was.

"Oh, Dawn, I have a reputation to keep up, so keep this to yourself, won't you?" He asked.

"Yes sir and thanks again." She told him as she left the room and headed for the gym.

The rest of the day went without event as the last bell of the day sounded and the stampeding mob headed for the buses.

As usual Rebecca started her daily rant as Dawn sat down beside her.

"To bad about you and Brandon." She said to Dawn.

"What?" Dawn replied.

"To bad that you and Brandon broke up." She answered.

"Who told you that?" Dawn asked inquisitively.

"Everyone knows Dawn, there are no secrets at Saratoga High for long. The rumor is that you weren't his type of girl and he had to let you off easy. Didn't want to get to serious. He didn't want to see you get your heart broke later on." Rebecca said like a news anchor giving the daily news report.

"Are you kidding me? He didn't break up with me, I broke up with him!" She said angrily.

"Hold on there Dawn, I am just the messenger here. All I do is relay the information, I don't create it." Rebecca responded.

"Well, Rebecca I wish you would consider the source of your information sometimes before you start spreading it around the school."

"You know Dawn; I don't know why I sit with you sometimes, all you ever seem to do is yell at me." Rebecca responded.

"Maybe I wouldn't yell at you if you could stop spreading rumors." Dawn answered angrily.

"Whatever." Rebecca said with a sigh.

"Yeah, whatever" Dawn added as they sat in the silence for the rest of the ride home.

. It seems that Brandon had embellished his account of the relationship and had left out some key pieces of information.

Chapter 20

After the incident at the lunch table Brandon used his influence to start a smear campaign against Grace. He did all that he could to have people bully her or make fun of her in some way or another. People started messing with Grace's locker, writing, Witch, on it more than once and even cracking eggs in it. It had seemed that Brandon was able to turn the senior class against her over night.

This was nothing new to Grace. She had heard it all before. If it wasn't about the clothes she wore it was about the way she looked. She wasn't going to waste her time on even being bothered by it.

Dawn on the other hand was infuriated by it all. There was no reason for the rest of the senior class to be involved in Brandon and her break up. Grace had nothing to do with it, and how dare he try to ruin her reputation over this. All it did for Dawn was show that Brandon could act like a real child at times.

The geeks were angry too, Grace was one of theirs and no one was going to hurt one of their own. What the geeks lacked in brawn, they made up in brains, sure, none of them would be very good in a fight, but they could fight in other ways. They tolerated most of the behavior until someone messed with Grace's locker. They all had enough at that point and decided to take action. Christopher and Miguel were both chemistry majors and they came up with a plan for retaliating. Between the two of them they mixed up some sort of potion that would create a foul odor that filled up Brandon's locker. In fact it was so foul that once he opened it, all of his books and his coat became impregnated with the terrible stench. The janitor had to be called to wash the inside of the locker to try and get rid of the smell.

This just made Brandon more angry than usual. He knew that the nerds had something to do with it, but he couldn't prove it. He also knew that all he had to do is beat up one of them and the others would cower in fear, or so he thought.

Brandon's plan was simple, just get one of the nerds alone and put the fear of God into him. He made sure that he wasn't alone and that he had plenty of help to carry out his plan. The plan was really simple, get Bill alone after gym class. They cornered him while he was getting changed and dragged him to the showers. One of Brandon's goons held him while Brandon did a good job at punching him in the stomach. Brandon didn't want to hit him in the face. If there were no physical marks on Bill, it was just his word against Brandon and his goon.

While Bill was getting beaten up, Christopher and Miguel started to wonder where he was as they waited outside by the gym. After a while they decided to see what was taking him so long. They were shocked to find that the locker room was empty but the showers were running. They went over to find that Bill was lying on the shower floor. They turned off the showers and ran in to help him.

"Bill, who did this?" Christopher asked him.

"Brandon Phillips." He said with a moan.

"Let's get him up. We can take him to the principal's office." Miguel said in haste.

"No." Bill responded.

"Why, Bill, I am tired of Brandon thinking he can do whatever he wants. He acts like he runs the school." Miguel said.

"Yeah me too." Christopher added.

"Don't worry guys. Brandon is going to pay. But we are going to do this my way." Bill said in-between breaths.

"Help me get to class." Bill asked the two.

"I will be fine, but Brandon is going to regret this. I promise you that." Bill said.

They both helped him to his feet and escorted him out of the locker room. Bill tried his best to hide the pain and act like nothing had happened. He wanted to make sure that Brandon would think that he was too afraid to say anything about the attack.

Bill had enough and was going to make Brandon pay the price. He spent the rest of the day trying to get the geeks to meet in the library after school, every member but Dawn. He was afraid that she was a little too close to Brandon to be involved.

Bill sent a message to another member and they sent the message to another till everyone had been notified. At the end of the day they all were assembled in the library, everyone except Grace. Bill thought at first that Grace had bailed on them and wasn't really one of them, but just has he was thinking the worst of Grace she walked into the room.

"Grace, we have to know, are you with us?" Bill asked in a hush.

"I'm here, aren't I?" She responded.

"Here is the plan." Bill said, to the group like they were generals planning for an attack.

Bill had it all planned out and everyone at the meeting had their own notebook to take notes. Each had an individual task according to their special talents. Then Bill explained that he himself couldn't be part of any of the retaliation. Brandon was sure to know that he was involved but there could be no association with Bill for the plan to work. After about a half an hour Bill asked the group if they understood what they were to do and they all responded with a nod. They all knew that Brandon drove to school everyday and decided that they would have to do it while school was in session. It was a risky endeavor but at this point they were all tired of Brandon and his band of football goons.

The next couple of days Bill played the cowering victim when it came to Brandon, if Brandon looked at him wrong Bill played like he was scared and walked the other way. Brandon's own ego wouldn't let him see that he was being played by a wimpy nerd.

The day finally came that they were ready to bring their plan to fruition. They had decided that they couldn't pull of the stunt during lunch because someone was bound to realize that one of them was not in lunch. Since Christopher and Miguel shared a study hall it was decided that they would get a pass to the library then they would head to Brandon's car, do the deed and then proceed to the library. So being the sly agents that they were they showed the teacher their passes for the library and acted as if they were headed there. They both knew that they only had about 10 minutes to spare before someone would realize that they weren't where they were supposed to be, so they had to be quick. Brandon always tried to park in the same place so they knew where his car should be, so they both tried to be as inconspicuous as they could be. To keep people from seeing them leave the school together they decided to split up, one would take the exit near the band room and the other would take the exit near the vocational shop. Miguel arrived a little before Christopher and like a well oiled machine they went to work. The school had very little problems in the parking lot and had no cameras poised on them so they felt pretty confident that they could pull off their crime without any witnesses. Since Brandon's car was an older model, Christopher was able to open the hood without having to be in the driver's seat. As he lifted the hood Miguel loosened the wing nut to the air cleaner and removed the cover. He then poured a generous amount of liquid pig manure around the ring of the container and put the lid back on and tightened up the nut again. He then took the rest of the liquid and poured it onto the manifold of the car. Christopher then lowered the hood like nothing had ever happened. After they were finished they both separated and then headed the way they came to get to the library before someone noticed that they were gone. Miguel made it to the library first handed the librarian his pass and then signed in. Christopher then arrived about a minute later and did the same. They found a table and opened their books and just gave each other a friendly smile. They both felt confident that they had gotten away with the crime of the century; now all they had to do was wait.

    Bill could hardly contain his excitement when he saw Christopher and Miguel at the end of school. He knew that he had to keep it together and didn't want to ruin their plan and expose what they had done. Every time they saw each other in the hall they simply smiled at each other and said "oink". No one seemed to hear what they said or didn't care as each of them headed to their bus. Dawn noticed the slight eye contact and heard their code word but wasn't sure at the time what to think. Bill had planned to stay after to make sure that there were witnesses to where he was after their little stink bomb went off. Since he drove to school Brandon was never in a hurry to get to a bus and took his time leaving the school so after the main herd had emptied into their cattle cars he headed to his car. He got in and started the car and as usual it coughed and bellowed out a cloud of white smoke. He let the car run for a minute and then put it in drive and headed to the pizza shop where the rest of the football team was. It was a cold afternoon so Brandon had set the heater on high as he headed down the street. As the car's motor heated up the smell of cooked manure started to fill the car, at first it was just a slight fragrance filling the air but once the manifold became hot the car was filled with an unbearable stench. Brandon rolled the window down to escape the smell but doing so only let more smell in as the smoke from the liquid started to pour out from under the hood.

    "What is going on?" He said as he started to gag.

    Brandon had decided that he could make it to the pizza shop before he would stop to figure out where the smell was coming from. As he entered the parking lot some of the football team was outside hanging out waiting for him to arrive. As he got closer to them they could smell the horrid stench coming from his car. He stopped the car and opened the door with a gag.

"Man Brandon, why does your car smell like that?" Keith asked.

"I don't know?" He responded in between gags.

The rest of the team started to move away and headed for the restaurant as they all got a whiff of the odor.

As Brandon opened the hood to see what was causing the odor George came over to see what the problem was.

"Smells like someone put pig poop on your manifold Brandon." He said jokingly.

"No da, Bubba, how long did you have to think before you came to that conclusion?" He replied back.

"Whatever you jerk." He responded as he walked away from the car.

Phase one of the nerds retaliation was complete but the war was far from over.

"That stinking nerd, I'll get him for this, if it is the last thing that I do." He said out loud.

He got back into the car and headed to the do-it-yourself car wash. He opened the hood and put his money in the machine and started to spray the engine off. Little did he realize that soaking down the engine didn't do the car any good. After he sprayed off the manifold he put the wand back, shut the hood and got back in the car and attempted to start it. Then he tried to start it again, and again. He had almost ran the battery down to nothing when he decided that the car wasn't going to start and to call his mother.

After telling his mother what had happened she arranged for a tow truck to take the car to the local garage. She showed up around the same time as the tow truck did. As the man attached the car he reassured them both that once the engine had time to dry out it would start right up. The man lifted the car and drove off to the garage and Brandon and his mother headed for home.

"Tell me again why you were spraying off your car's engine?" She asked.

"I was trying to get the crap off the manifold." He told her.

"What?"

"Someone put crap on my manifold and the whole car started to smell like a pig pen so I drove it to the car wash and tried to wash the motor."

"Who would do something like that?"

"I am not sure, but I have my suspicions." Brandon replied while mumbling to himself about Bill.

"What's going on Brandon? Did you do something to someone?"

"No mom, I have it under control."

"It's just since you broke up with Dawn, you haven't been acting the same."

"Don't mention that slut's name." He told her angrily.

Without a mention Mrs. Phillips reached over and slapped Brandon's mouth.

"Don't you ever call a girl that!" She responded.

Brandon was caught off guard and started to raise his hand to hit his mother.

"Just try it and you'll be out on the street." She said sternly.

"I'm sorry mom. I wasn't thinking."

"You can say that again. I don't know what is going on, but you better get your act together!"

"I will." He replied

Nothing more was said as they arrived home and they got out and walked into their trailer. All Brandon did do is reach out and give his mother a hug.

"Sorry mom." He said with a shaking voice.

"It's OK; just don't let it happen again." She said in a stern but loving tone.

"Did you get anything to eat?" She asked him as they pulled into their parking space.

"No, I was too busy trying to get that smell out of my car."

"Are you hungry?"

"Yes, hungry and mad." He grumbled back.

"Calm down angry man and get ready for dinner." She told him trying to keep a straight face.

For the rest of the weekend Brandon was stewing over who had sabotaged his car. On Saturday afternoon the garage called and said that the car had dried out and that they could pick it up. Mrs. Phillips had to work that afternoon so she took Brandon down to the garage to get the car. He could see the car in the parking lot as they arrived and they both got out after she parked the car. The garage owner came out to greet them.

"All it needed was to dry out, but it might take a few days to get the smell out of the car. I would suggest riding with the windows open for a while." He told them both.

"But he could freeze to death." Mrs. Phillips responded.

"Well freezing might be a better way to go rather than smelling that." He said trying to hold back the laughter.

"Mom, it's not that bad." Brandon told her as he walked over to the car and opened the door.

Mrs. Phillip paid the man and told him thanks as she said goodbye to Brandon. She almost started to laugh uncontrollably as she saw Brandon's face as he got in the car. She held it together though as she got in her car and drove off to work. The car would start but the smell was still as strong as the night before. Brandon did what the mechanic had suggested and road with the windows down. The cold was more bearable than the stench for the time being. He went back to the trailer and looked for some air freshener and started to spray the inside of the car. Over and over he washed the inside of the car until the smell was somewhat tolerable. During the whole procedure he went over and over in his mind how he was going to get Bill for this. After cleaning the inside of the car for the tenth time he decided that it would have to do and headed inside where he did nothing but watch TV for the rest of the day. He was too embarrassed to do anything with anyone and he wasn't about to have anyone ride in his car at this point.

The next morning Brandon slept in like he did most Sunday's. When he finally got up he went out to the living room to see his mother watching some TV evangelist.

"Mom, what are you doing?" He asked.

"What? I'm just watching a church service. What's wrong with that?" She replied.

"Nothing, I just never thought of you as someone who ever went to church or even believed in that stuff."

"Well maybe we should go to church; it wouldn't hurt anything or anybody. Maybe it would be good to find some other nice people."

"Really mom, religion makes me sick sometimes. Religious people are nothing but a bunch of hypocrites that sit around and tell you what you can and cannot do, just a bunch of hogwash if you ask me." He told her bluntly.

"Brandon; not all church people are hypocrites. Dawn's family is religious and they seemed genuine. You can't form you opinion about a group of people based on a few bad ones in the group."

"Maybe, but I don't trust them. Not one of them. All they want is your money." He shot back.

Brandon never thought much about God and sometimes he wondered where God was in the first place. He wasn't about to get tied in to some fairytale hocus pocus. Mrs. Phillips on the other hand wanted more out of life. She was starting to think that maybe there was a better way to live and that going to church may help her in her private life, and maybe help her socially. Being a single mother she didn't have much time for a social life, but church might bring her together with some other nice women at least. Brandon just shook his head as he headed for the door.

"Where are you going?" His mother asked.

"Just outside, I wanted to see if the car still smelled like a pig took a dump in it." He said in mopey voice.

"OK." She responded with a chuckle.

"Some day you will look back on this and laugh." She reassured him.

"Maybe, but it just makes me mad, right now." He answered as he left the trailer.

She laughed out loud as she looked through the window to see Brandon's face in disgust as he opened the door and sat down in the driver's seat.

"I guess it still smells." She said to herself.

The next day as Brandon headed for school the car actually started to smell a lot less. He had left the windows open all night and prayed that it wouldn't rain. In the morning the smell had dissipated quite a lot but there was still an essence that kept him driving in the cold with the windows open. He rolled into the school parking lot like usual and parked. Everyone was staring at him as he got out of the car; apparently the "pig poop" incident had got around the school.

"What are you all looking at?" He said angrily.

Since their breakup Brandon had become quite angry with the world. Everyone went back to what they were doing as Brandon headed into the school. Little did Brandon realize that the smell in the car had impregnated his clothes with a faint smell. He knew something was wrong as people started to whisper as he passed them. He couldn't tell what was wrong until he arrived at his locker and some of his buddies were waiting for him.

"Man, do you stink!" George said as he laughed out loud.

"He's right. You smell like you were sleeping with a pig or something." Another one of his cohorts said.

"The rest just moved a step back from Brandon and laughed under their breath.

"Laugh all you want you bunch of Bozos, but I am going to make Bill pay for this."

"How do you know he did it? I saw him in the band room, he couldn't have done it."

"I realize that genius. He might not have done it himself but one of his friends did."

"Oh." George replied.

Brandon had to understand that George might be a good football player but he wasn't the sharpest tool in the shed.

Brandon thought Bill was nothing more than a wimpy nerd but one thing he didn't realize was how well connected Bill and his band of geeks were in the school. Bill had connections through the library, shop and even the kitchen staff. He often worked on peoples computers at school and only asked for favors now and then. He might be a nerd but he was well liked nerd. Making Bill pay was going to be harder than Brandon thought. Every thing he did resulted in the nerds retaliating.

Bill on the other hand was well thought out, being a chess master; he was always two steps in front of a situation. Just when you thought you had him cornered, he had won the game. The war between Brandon and him was nothing different, Brandon might have won round one, but the war was just beginning. Bill could see the whole picture and not just some petty instances between them. He was going to give Brandon an attitude adjustment nerd style.

"Nice cologne Brandon." Bill said as he walked past.

"What did you say, Nerd boy?" Brandon growled back.

"Nothing, nothing at all." Bill said in a coy fashion.

"I'll tell you this Nerd boy, don't you ever touch my car again or you're a dead man."

"I don't know what you're talking about Brandon. I didn't touch your car."

"Maybe not, but one of your nerd buddies did. That I'm sure."

"You have nothing on me or anyone else Brandon, so stop making accusations and take a bath, because you stink."

With that last statement Brandon grabbed Bill and was going to knock his books out of his hand when a teaching walked by.

"Is there a problem Mr. Phillips?" Mr. Halet asked.

"No sir, no problem, is there Bill?"

"No, nothing at all Mr. Halet." Bill answered.

With that Mr. Halet shook his head and headed to his home room class.

"You're lucky he happened to walk by you little wimp. I'm going to squash you like a bug some day." He threatened Bill.

"Ok, Brandon." Bill answered.

"Just one thing you need to know."

"Yeah, what's that?"

"If you grab a tiger by the tail you better watch out for its mouth." Bill answered as he proceeded to his home room.

"What did he mean by that?" George asked.

"Don't worry about it. We better get to class." Brandon said as they headed for home room.

Chapter 21

Going to home room was hard, not just for Brandon but also for Dawn. They sat next to each other and at this point neither of them wanted to be anywhere near the other. Dawn usually kept to herself and so did Brandon. He knew that he wasn't one of Dawn's favorite people right now.

So they both made the best of things and tried to keep out of each others way. Eventually they might learn to tolerate each other but for now they would keep their distance. So far, home room was just another 15 minutes of torture for both of them. Today was a little different though, as Brandon walked into the room he could hear the room busing about his car and how he smelt like pig poop.

"I hope your happy Princess." He said to Dawn.

"What are you talking about?"

"Don't act so innocent. I know it was one of your loser friends that sabotaged my car."

"Look Brandon, I don't know anything about it. All I know is what Rebecca told me on the bus."

"Well, who did she say did it?"

"She said that she didn't know. Just that someone put pig poop on your car"

"Well, I am sure that Bill had something to do with because of what I." Brandon stopped short of saying that he beat Bill up.

"Did what? What were you going to say?"

"Nothing, just tell Bill and your other losers that I'll get even, don't you worry."

"Brandon, calm down it could have been anyone. Bill isn't the only one that you've bullied here at school. I suggest that you better watch your self."

"Funny; Princess."

"Stop calling me that you jerk."

"Why don't you try and make me, Princess."

The whole interaction might have gone into a more heated mode but the teacher walked in and started to take roll. Both of them sat there in a huff for the rest of home room.

After the bell sounded everyone headed to their next class, lucky for both of them that was the only class that they shared.

The rest of the morning was just as boring as most and then came lunch. Dawn headed to lunch like the rest of the herd. She went through the line and got her usual chicken salad. Most of the geeks were already seated and smiling from ear to ear when Dawn sat down.

"What did you guys do?" Dawn asked in a shock.

"We did nothing." Bill interjected.

"I know you didn't do anything Bill you were in the band with me. But I am asking Chris and Ken what they did?" She demanded.

"Like Bill said, they have nothing on us. Let's just keep that way alright, Dawn?" Ken replied.

"You guys, you better watch yourselves." Dawn replied.

With that everyone finished eating and nothing more was said. At this point they all knew that the less anyone knew the better. As Dawn scanned the group she could tell that none of them could really keep a secret that well. Just by reading their faces she could tell who had something to do with it.

Through the next couple of weeks there was trouble brewing. It was a war between the football thugs and the nerds. The thugs had the brawn but the nerds had the brains and it seemed that the brains were winning. The thugs under estimated the toughness of the nerds and thought all they would have to do is beat one of them up and the battle would be over, but the nerds wouldn't give up that easy. They might not have the power of the football players but being beat up and being made fun of was nothing new to any of them, they were use to it, to them it was just another day in the park. The football players on the other hand weren't always prepared for the nerd's retaliation. The other problem was that the football players could never blame anything directly to anyone of them. For the most part all of the battle between the groups was pretty harmless. There was the pig manure prank and then they toilet papered, Brandon's trailer, they replace the water in the team's water bottles with vinegar, nothing big, just things to make sure that Brandon knew that they were still in control.

All of this planning behind her back always made Dawn feel uncomfortable, but the nerds had decided to keep her out of it for plausible deniability. She knew that the loser table was behind all of the pranks against the football team but they wouldn't ever tell her anything, but the one thing she didn't know is Grace's involvement in most of them. Dawn would have been totally flabbergasted if she would have known that Grace was the mastermind behind some of the group's best pranks. Dawn hoped that as the days past so would the war between the groups and that everyone would learn to get along with each other. She was doing her best to get along with Brandon and forget the past and move on, but she wasn't so sure that the football team was going to forgive and forget.

Since their breakup Dawn was spending more time with Grace and at the Smith house. This always gave Dawn ample time for her to talk to Max when he was there. Dawn tried to stay calm and cool when he was there but she often would get the giggles when she tried to talk to him. She was always a little giddy when he was there. Even though Dawn thought she was hiding her attraction to Max she was only fooling herself. Dawn was beside herself with the thought of this tall handsome stranger being attracted to her. He seemed to be her ideal man and possessed all the qualities that she was looking for. He was kind and funny and she never once saw him lose his temper or even raise his voice. He cared for his family and waited on his mother and always treated Grace with love and respect. In fact the three of them seemed to have a stronger bond than most families. All three of them seemed to like each other and each others company, in fact when Dawn was there all they did is talk to each other or play board games. When Dawn observed them they all seemed to be part of an episode from some long lost black and white TV show.

The fact that the family as a whole seemed to be a little backward and possibly a little boring at times didn't change Dawn's outlook on the situation. She still liked hanging out at Grace's house when her mother was working.

Dawn was always a little worried about the situation though, she was afraid that her relationship with Grace might change if she and Max actually got together. She loved the thought that Max and her would actually go on a date, but not at the expense of her relationship with Grace. She liked Max, but she loved Grace, she loved her like the sister that she never had.

With every day that past Dawn's thoughts of Brandon would fade and her thoughts of Max increased, but she was more guarded this time considering what had happened between her and Brandon. She also wanted to make sure that no matter who she liked or was dating that it wouldn't interfere with her dreams.

Grace had changed also in this time and she often came over and stayed with Dawn on nights that her mother worked. Grace had certainly blossomed and Dawn seemed to be the catalyst that ignited the spark in Grace. Apart from each other both of them tended to be shy and sit in the shadows, but when you put them together they seemed to fuel the other's creativity. They seemed to be able to read each other's mind; at least Grace could, and finish each other's sentences.

In all of this time Dawn and Grace moved closer together while Dawn and Jessica moved slowly apart. Dawn never intended on their relationship to slowly fade but it just seemed since her father died and Jessica started dating that the two grew apart. Not that they weren't still friends, they just weren't the friends that they used to be. Jessica at times seemed uncomfortable around Grace and seemed to look at her in a strange way. That was the problem with Grace, you either loved her or she gave you the creeps for some reason. Dawn and Jessica still talked on the phone, but not as much and they still went out, but Jessica tried to distance herself from Grace without hurting Dawn's feelings. Jessica still thought of Dawn as her best friend, but there was just something about Grace that she didn't like, maybe it was her mannerisms, or the dark cold eyes or the way she seemed to know what a person was going to say or think. It all seemed just a little too weird for her. Jessica was still waiting for Jim to return from Slovenia when he recovered from his wounds. She hadn't seen him in months but they were able to keep in touch via email. Jim had mentioned that he might be returning to Louisiana to finish his schooling there and might not return to Saratoga Springs. This was something that Jessica hated to think about, she didn't know Jim very well but they did get to go out for a few months and she really liked him and he seemed to like her. So all she could do is send him emails and pray he would return to her.

Chapter 22

Another day had come and Dawn was running to catch the bus as usual. The bus was just about to leave as she bolted out the door and ran toward it. She got on and sat down next to Rebecca. Now Rebecca was a nice girl, but did she like to talk, and talk about almost anything. Dawn was not sure if she didn't have anyone to talk to at home or wasn't allowed to talk. But sometimes all she wanted to do is tell her to be quiet. Dawn of course would never do that and she politely shook her head and acted like she was interested in the latest babble that she had to report.

"News is that you and Grace's brother are an item." She told Dawn.

Dawn wasn't really listening by this point so Rebecca continued.

"Well, is it true?"

"What?" Dawn replied.

"You and what's his name, Max, isn't it? Are you going out? News is that you and he are a hot item."

"Where in the world did you hear that from?" Dawn retorted angrily.

"Whoa there Dawn, I didn't mean to upset you, but Brandon says that he saw you two making out behind the Tastee Freez the other night."

"Are you kidding me, that liar, I mean I haven't even been on a date with Max, he hasn't even ask me on a date. We are just friends, wait till I see Brandon!"

As the bus stopped at the school and Dawn got off, it seemed that all eyes were watching her. It seemed that Brandon had done his best to spread the rumors of her and Max throughout the school.

By this time Dawn's anger was apparent and everyone knew just to leave her alone. They all could see the fire in her eyes and where she was headed.

Like a cruise missile locked on to its target Dawn headed straight for Brandon's locker. He was surrounded by a group of boys when they saw her heading their way. They could feel the vibes coming off of her and decided to move out of the way.

"What in the world are you doing, telling lies about me?" She yelled at him.

"What do you mean?" He responded as if there was nothing wrong.

"You know exactly what I mean, telling everyone that I was making out with Max"

"That's his name, I couldn't remember. What's the big deal? Would you rather me tell everyone that you and I did it in the back of my car?"

Brandon's entourage gathered just in range to hear the exchange between them.

"That's another lie, you jerk, that's the whole reason that we broke up and you know it."

"Says you, the way I see it, you just go from one guy to the next. Some people would call you a slu"

Before he could get out the rest of the sentence, Dawn reared back and kneed Brandon before he could finish. He let out a groan and fell to the floor.

"You witch!" he mumbled as he convulsed in pain.

Brandon's set of goons seemed ready to retaliate when a teacher stepped in and asked what was going on.

Before either of them had time to explain he told them both to head to the principals office.

Two of Brandon's friends picked him up and helped him down the hall, while Dawn still in a heat of rage held her head high.

Kids looked and stared and whispered, but she walked on like she owned the school.

"No one is going to ruin my reputation like this." She thought.

As they got closer to the principal's office Dawn started to consider the repercussions of what she had just done. It started to hit her that she could get suspended for this. She started to worry what her mother was going to say. Her head started to slowly droop the closer she got.

"I guess I should have thought this through." She thought to herself.

They got to the office and told the secretary why they were there. She told them that it would be a minute and told them to sit down.

Sitting there she wondered if the principal was really busy or this was just a mind game that they played. Just to make you sit there and worry about what was going to happen. Still, having to sit next to Brandon was enough to make her blood boil. She couldn't even look at him in fear that she would attack him again.

The time had finally come and her fate was sealed as they were called into the office.

"So, what happened hear?" The principal asked.

"This witch here kneed me in the groin." Brandon growled.

"Is that true Dawn?"

"Yes, but only because he told everyone that I had sex with him in the back of his car and he was about to call me a slut. And given the chance I would do it again, he is nothing but a jerk and a liar!"

By this time Dawn's anger level had rebounded and she was noticeably upset.

"Is that true Brandon?"

"She is just a crazy woman, principal, I can't help it that she is having second thoughts about what happened between me and her. And another thing, I didn't call her a slut. Ask anyone of the guys that were there."

"I am sure I would get an unbiased account of what happen, right?"

"Of course, do I look like a liar to you?"

The principal knew that Brandon was lying, but at this point it was just a he said she said incident. The only thing he could do is suspend both of them for 3 days.

"There is no way I can come to a conclusion in this matter. I tend to lean to Dawn's side of the story Brandon, but to be fair I will suspend both of you for 3 days for fighting."

Dawn's heart sank inside her chest.

"Three days suspension, what is my mother going to say?" she thought to herself.

"You can both call your parents to come pick you up. I hope that this will be the last time that I ever have you in my office for something like this. Is that understood?"

"Yes sir", they both responded in unison.

So there they sat as they waited for their parents to arrive. Brandon seemed to be a pillar of stone, while Dawn had become fidgety. This was the first time that anything like this had happened to her. In fact before this she was an honor student. She had never been in any kind of trouble before.

Brandon on the other hand was known for trouble. It seemed to follow him around like a cloud, if there was a fight he never was to far away. This would be his second suspension this year.

Brandon's mother was the first to arrive. He simply drove up to the school and Brandon got up to leave.

"See you around, Slut" he whispered as he walked away.

Dawn at this point was too preoccupied to even think about what he said. All she could think about is what she was going to say to her mother.

It seemed like an eternity for her mother to arrive. Dawn saw her pull into the parking lot and then get out of her car.

"Here she comes" She thought to herself.

Dawn's mother wanted answers and she wasn't going to leave until she got some. She entered the reception area and asked to talk to the principal.

She was told to wait a moment and have a seat and the principal would see her in a minute. Without saying a word to Dawn she sat down next to her. Dawn could see the disappointment in her eyes and could feel the anger flowing out of her.

She was about to say, "I'm sorry" when her mother stopped her short and told her not to speak.

"Could this day get any worse?" she thought to herself.

"Welcome, Mrs. Sinclair, how are you today?"

"I've been better", she responded.

With that they disappeared behind a close door. Dawn could only imagine what they were saying. She hoped that this would all work out somehow.

Within a few minutes her mother reappeared and she told her to get her things and to head for the car. She still seemed angry but not as much.

As her mother got in the car Dawn was about to give her account of what had happened but her mother stopped her.

"Dawn, I was very disappointed and angry when I got that call this morning, but after talking to the principal I calmed down. I was able to negotiate that this would not be on your permanent record, even though you still will be suspended. Now you can tell me what happened."

"Well I got on the school bus this morning and Rebecca was asking me about Max and me. Things like: how long have we been dating and when did we decided to become a couple. I told her that we weren't a couple, but she told me that she heard from Brandon that he saw us making out behind the Tastee Freez the other night. I was so angry that I went to talk to Brandon; he told me that I would have to live with it and the fact that he told everyone that I had done it with him in his car a while back. He was about to call me a slut when I kneed him. I know I should have walked away but he made me so mad. I just did it without thinking. I'm sorry."

"Good for you, I would have done the same thing. It's a good thing that your dad isn't here I would hate to think what he would have done to him. I know you are going through a lot of emotions right now, but you have to learn to control your anger. OK?"

"I love you Mom", she said with tear filled eyes.

"It's going to be fine, I love you too. Let's go home"

The rest of the afternoon was filled with her talking on the phone trying to get her assignments for the next three days.

Chapter 23

After losing another battle to the nerds, Brandon decided to take matters into his own hands and go for the leader of the nerds, Grace. He was filled with rage at the thought of the nerds being able to make him look like a total fool at times. He knew that they had to have some sort of inside information, that none of them were that smart and that Grace knew far too much about him and his habits.

"I'll get that witch, if it's the last thing. I will make her pay." He told his football goons.

Brandon figured that he would be able to at least scare Grace into submission if he could get her alone for a minute or two, so he devised a plan to get her alone. After all of the planning was done he decided to take his top goon with him. They made a plan to get her alone and corner her in a corner hallway off of the shop wing of the school. They got one of their girl friends to send Grace a note, supposedly from Dawn to meet her there after school. Though Grace could have easily asked Dawn what she wanted she didn't mention it to her at all. In fact she made no mention of the meeting with anyone in the club. She simply headed to the shop wing after school like the note told her to.

As she walked down the hall it became apparent that she was the only one there and that she had been tricked. Just as she went to turn around and head home Brandon and his goon appeared from around the corner.

"Going somewhere?" Brandon asked her.

"Just going home." She responded.

"Not so fast Gracie, let's have a talk." Brandon told her as he started to walk closer to her.

"I told you Brandon, I am going home and I am going home now. Get out of my way before you and your goon get hurt." She told them forcefully.

"Yeah right, what are you going to do, pretty girl." George told Grace.

By this time Brandon and George had cornered Grace and blocked her way of escape.

"Tell your nerd friends that the war is over." He told her angrily.

"Who said it was over, we have yet to begin to fight." She answered him sarcastically.

"I don't want to have to hurt you, but I will."

"Give it you best shot, you blow hard!" She yelled at him.

With that George went to put his hand over Grace's mouth, but before he could reach around her, she grabbed his arm and whipped him into the wall where he landed with a thud.

"What the?" Brandon said in disbelief.

Brandon's reflexes switched on as he was going to show Grace who was boss. He was enraged and meant to do her some sort of harm as he reached to grab her. But just like she did to the goon, she was able to grab Brandon's arms first. This time though she didn't whip Brandon into the wall she just gripped his wrist with all her might. Brandon watched in terror as her face changed and her eyes glowed like fire. His body was hit with a bolt of energy that caused him to fall to his knees. He wanted to break free but he couldn't control his own body and was paralyzed by her grip.

George had gotten up and recovered from his whip into the wall and watched as Brandon's face became contorted and he started cry like a child.

By this time some other people at arrived and were watching the interaction between Brandon and Grace when George went over to Grace and was going to hit her. Grace released Brandon as he fell to the floor and caught George's fist with her own hand and force him to the floor crying in pain.

It was quite a show for the other kids that were staring in disbelief at what they had just witnessed. Grace had single handedly beaten up Brandon and the top football goon of the school.

"Like I said, we have yet to begin to fight." Grace told both of them.

"Let that be a lesson to leave the nerds alone. OK?"

"Yes." George replied.

"You'll pay; you'll pay for this you witch!" Brandon screamed back at her.

"How is that Brandon, I don't think you can handle a rematch." One of the onlookers said to him.

Grace brushed herself off and headed to the exit as the rest of the kids stood around making remarks and jeers towards Brandon. He at one time was the king of the school, but as of today, he was nothing more than a has-been.

"Get away from me, you bunch of creeps!" He shouted as he got and headed to the door.

"What are you going to do, Brandon? Grace really kicked your butt." Paul Simpson said.

"Well I will kick your butt if you don't shut up, how's that?"

"I'm so scarred." Paul replied.

With that Brandon reared back and knocked Paul right on the floor with a right punch just as the principle walked into the crowd.

"That's it, you just got your self another 3 day suspension Brandon. Get to the office now, you included George" He demanded.

"Are you OK?" The principle asked Paul.

"I think so."

"I don't want anyone else to go any where until I find out what is going on here. Do you all understand?" He said sternly.

After asking the crowd what happened he headed to the office to find Brandon and George waiting for him.

"Mrs. Todd, please call Mrs. Smith and tell her that I need to talk to her about Grace." The principle told the secretary.

"Yes sir." She replied.

"Brandon you can sit here until your mother arrives and as for you George you just earned yourself a three day suspension. I called your mother and she will be here soon, so sit there till she gets here, understood?" "

"Yes sir." George replied as he hung his head in shame.

Mrs. Phillips had arrived and she and Brandon headed to the principal's office. After about ten minutes the door opened the Brandon and his mother exited. His mother was noticeable upset as they headed for the door. Neither of them said anything as they headed for their cars.

The next three days the school was a bee's hive of rumors. Everyone was talking about how Grace had beaten up Brandon and George. Everyone knew that Brandon and George got suspended but Grace didn't show up for school for the next three days either. In fact Grace seemed to disappear. Dawn had called numerous times and even headed to Grace's house, but no one answered.

She was worried about Grace, all she knew about what had happened is what she heard, and most of that was from Rebecca. At this point she didn't know what to think, all she wanted to do is make sure that she was alright.

After three days Brandon and George showed up to school, the both seemed like beaten wolves that had been beat down from alpha males to omega ones. Brandon was told during his suspension that he was on the verge of loosing his scholarship if he didn't get his act together, so he knew that he had to change or find a new career path. He was going to do his best to leave the past behind and head for a new future. He didn't want to disappoint his mother any more than he already had. He had worked to hard to get the scholarship in the first place, he didn't want to sabotage it, and from now on he was going to be on the straight and narrow.

The story about the fight had three days of embellishments so by the time Grace showed back up to school everyone was looking at her in a weird way. She returned to school, without makeup and was wearing one of her old skirts. After all the strides that Grace had taken to fit in, this one incident sent her back to the beginning. Before she was just the shy new girl, but now she was the weird witch, the kids now treated Grace like she was some sort of witch that had super powers.

Dawn hadn't scene Grace since the fight and was excited to see her arrive at school.

"Grace, how are you?" She said vibrantly.

"I'm fine, I guess." She said shyly.

"I tried to call and I even stopped at your house but you didn't seem to be home."

"Yeah, I'm sorry about that, we went away for a few days." She whispered back to Dawn.

Dawn was going to ask her some more questions when it became evident that Grace didn't want to talk about the matter any more.

"I'll see you at lunch, OK?" Dawn asked

"I'll be there." Grace responded as she headed for class.

Dawn saw that Brandon and George were the only ones hanging out at his locker any more. It seemed that he also had fallen from his position and now was just another regular kid. Since the fight only George stood by him, while the rest of his football buddies left him alone. Even though she would have never told him so, Dawn felt like Brandon should be allowed back at the loser table, this time as a true member along with George. As the warning bell sounded she fell out of her trance and headed for her home room to sit next to Brandon. Before the fight there was always tension between them, now it seemed that each had come to except the other and let the past be the past.

Later as Dawn headed to the cafeteria and bought her lunch she headed to her seat. The table was pretty quiet; no one seemed to be saying much at all. As

Grace bought her lunch and headed to the table Dawn could see that all eyes were on her and that everyone was saying things to her as she walked by, Grace didn't say anything but stopped most of the comments when she stopped and stared at a few in the crowd. A quiet hush came over the room as she sat at her seat.

Everyone sat there in relative quiet not knowing what to say.

"Good to have you back." Bill said to Grace.

With that all of the other losers joined in to welcome her back. No matter what, she had earned their trust and friendship and she would always belong to their group. This meant everything to Grace; the losers were the first group that stuck with her when everyone else turned on her. Her face brighten and she smiled as she realized that she was in the presence of true friends and not a bunch of shallow fair weather ones. The table started back to its racket as everyone started to talk about their usual stuff, they left Grace alone, making sure not to mention what happened the week before. Like some many times before, time would erase the events of the year and things would eventually get back to normal.

After school Dawn called Grace but Grace told her she didn't feel like talking much and just wanted to chill out for the evening. Dawn understood and hung up the phone; she then prepared herself some macaroni and cheese and sat there wondering what to do for the rest of the night.

"I guess I could get my homework done." She thought to herself.

She put her dirty dishes in the dishwasher and headed upstairs to do her homework.

"I lead such an exciting life." She said to herself in disgust.

She spent the rest of the evening doing her homework and getting ready for bed. After her mother came home she talked to her for a while and went to bed.

"Same stuff different day" She said as she got under the covers and turned out the light.

Chapter 24

The days went by and it was apparent that Brandon had changed and it was for the better. The thought of loosing his free ride to college hit a nerve with him and he was making sure that he didn't mess it up. He was doing his best to be more polite and had left the war with the nerds behind him. He had more important matters at hand, his mother and college. He was also starting to relax when it came to his father. He hadn't seen or heard from him again since the incident on the side of the road and was hoping that he did the right thing and left town, even though he knew in his heart of heart's that wasn't true. He realized that Frank was like a crouching lion in the grass, patiently waiting for the time to pounce. He knew that Frank was waiting for the right time to act, so Brandon wanted to be ready for just that moment. He had installed a GPS tracker on his mother's phone along with speed dial to his cell phone so she could call him with one touch of a button. He still was on the lookout for Frank and still held stakeouts at the diner when his mother worked late. His mother had made it apparent that she wasn't going to move this time and she was tired of running, so Brandon was making sure that he was able to watch over her.

So the day started like any other, he got up took and shower, ate his breakfast, his mother worked the night before so he didn't wake her up and headed for school. He got into his car and turned the key.

"Come on Puff." He said as he attempted to start the car.

After a belch and a slight bang the car started with its usual puff of smoke and the rumble of the engine. Off he went with a trail of smoke behind him as he headed for school. As he parked the car he headed to his locker and headed straight to class, he no longer stood around his locker in the morning, since no one hung out with him any more. He headed to class and found his seat and sat quietly beside himself reading his history homework. Soon enough class was about to start when Brandon felt his cell phone vibrate he immediately pulled it out of his pocket trying to keep it hidden from the teacher. He didn't want to get detention over a simple text. It was from his mother so he made sure that he took a look at it.

"hel m"

At first he thought that she must have hit button by accident and sent him a bogus text. But once he had a minute to analyze it he realized what it meant.

"Help me!"

He got up from his desk and ran out of the door to everyone's amazement.

"Who just left?" Mrs. Jackson asked.

"Brandon, he left in a real hurry." One of the girls in the first row said.

She headed to the door to see where he was headed only to see him running for the door.

"Brandon, slow down!" She yelled down the hallway.

Brandon hit the doors hard and out he went. He didn't hear her or pay any attention to anyone. He was in a desperate situation and he was going to make sure that his mother was safe. He ran to the parking lot and got in his car. He turned the key and to his amazement it actually started. In his haste he jammed the gear shift into reverse and squealed his tires as he pulled out of the parking space. He slammed on the brakes missing a parked car by only inches. He jammed the gear shift into drive and pushed the gas clear to the floor. He peeled out of the parking lot in a cloud of smoke and screeching tires.

He sped down the street as fast as his hunk of junk would take him. He didn't have far to go and he knew the streets well. He was in a dangerous state of mind seeing that he wasn't watching how fast he was going just watching where he was going. He had gone through his third red light when he gained the attention of a police officer. The officer pulled out of traffic and hit his lights and headed after Brandon. Brandon was too engulfed in his own fear to even realize that he was being chased by the police.

"Just another mile and I will be there." He thought to himself.

Before long there several other police cars in hot pursuit. Brandon was only focused on getting to the park and getting to his mother. He was like a panicked husband whose wife had gone into labor.

He slid into the entrance of the park and started down the Avenue of the Pines. If he had brought her into the park he would be along this road. He slammed on his breaks as he noticed the car that Frank was driving the day before. He opened the car door and headed towards the car. The trunk was open but there was no sign of Frank or his mother. He ran into the woods where it seemed that a path was made.

"Hold on Mom, I'm coming." He thought to himself.

Chapter 25

The air was crisp that morning and the signs of winter were everywhere. The days were becoming shorter and the nights were colder. Most of the birds had left and the trees were bare. It was days like this that the park was often deserted, it was nothing like the summer days when people would be walking through it in masses and having a good time enjoying their time outside. On days like this only the diehard runners and creepers were in the park. He sat there alone in the eerie silence hearing nothing but the wind rustling through the trees. He liked to sit and listen, it was something that never got old to him. The air was still and cold as he sat there besides himself pondering what he was going to do next. Fate seemed to have brought him there and like a leaf tossed in the wind he probably wouldn't stay long. He tried to lose himself in the golden silence of the deserted park pondering his plans and the meaning of life amongst the stillness of the day when his thoughts were interrupted with the sound of screeching tires and a car door slamming.

"That's odd." He thought to himself as he stood up.

Though he was on a nature trail he wasn't far from the parking area and hearing screeching tires wasn't normal since the speed limit in the park was only ten miles an hour.

"I told you I would make you pay." He heard a man say as he started walking toward the commotion.

As Brandon arrived on the seen he could see his father's car parked next to the woods. He hit the brakes hard and his car screeched to a stop. He jumped out of the car as fast as he could. As he got closer he saw a path that led into the woods. He ran down the path as fast as he could. The sound of sirens and police cars started to fill the air as the police converged on the area. His mind was racing and he was breathing hard as he entered the clearing. He could see his mother lying close to a hole in the ground and his father being held up by his head by a wild looking man with eyes that were blazing like fire, the same way Grace's did the other day.

In the confusion of the moment Brandon wasn't sure what was going on.

"What are you doing?" He yelled at the man.

Brandon's scream was enough to break the man's concentration as he looked Brandon in the face. This time Brandon got a good look at the man as the man dropped Brandon's father in disgust. Brandon's father hit the ground with a thud as the man ran into the woods. Brandon tried to remain calm as he ran over to his mother lying on the ground. He saw the hole and the shovel and it became apparent that his father was going to murder his mother and bury her there in the woods. He kneeled over his mother and checked to see if she was still alive. Just as he was checking to see if she had a pulse, he was interrupted.

"Don't move boy; get on the ground with your hands behind your head." The policeman yelled.

"But my mo" He was interrupted as the policeman pushed him to the ground and grabbed his hands.

"But my mother, my mother." Brandon started to yell as the policeman started to put the hand cuffs on him.

At this time, another officer emerged and radioed in that he needed an ambulance at the park. He then headed to Brandon's mother and tried to assess her condition. Brandon was trying his best not to resist at this point, all he wanted was to make sure that his mother was still alive and that she was OK.

"She has a pulse and she's still breathing, but she's not awake." The office exclaimed.

"What about that old man over there?" The arresting officer asked.

As the other officer headed to Brandon's father, four more officers appeared out of the woods.

"Is this the suspect?" The newly arrived officer asked the arresting officer.

"This is the speeder, who those people are and what is going on, I have no idea" The officer answered

"He's alive, and awake. He keeps mumbling some sort of gibberish over and over." The assessing office told the rest of the police standing there.

The arresting officer put Brandon in the back of the police care as the other officers watched his mother's condition while they all waited for the ambulance.

"What's your name son?"

"Brandon, Brandon Phillips. Is my mom going to be alright?"

"I think so son. What in the world is going on here and why were you running from us?"

Brandon's mind was racing and he was trying to tell his story the best he could but it was hard for him to think straight under the conditions.

"I wasn't running from you, I was just trying to get to the park to help my mother."

"How did you know she was here and why did you think she was in trouble?"

"I worry about my mother a lot and I installed this locator on her cell phone. I got this strange text from her and saw that she was at the park when she should have been at work."

"Was that strange or something, maybe she needed a day off."

"My mother would have never gone to the park without telling me or skipped work without calling off first."

Even though he was listening to the officer he couldn't help but look out of the car and watch his mother on the ground.

"Is my mother going to be alright?" He asked again.

"She's still breathing and she has a pulse. The ambulance should be here any moment."

"I left school got in my car and drove here as fast as I could. I'm sorry I wasn't thinking. I didn't even realize that you were behind me."

"Then what?" The office asked.

"When I got to the park I saw the car parked there so I parked and I got out of my car and headed down the path. I found my mother there and a man holding the old man by the head, I screamed and the man ran away, and then you guys showed up. That's what happened."

"Did you get a good look of the man holding the old man by the neck?" The office asked intuitively.

"Know I didn't. He apparently saw me and ran into the woods." Brandon replied.

The officer grabbed his radio and called for dispatch saying that there was a possible suspect roaming through the park. The radio became alive with chatter as the police dispatch tried to coordinate a search for the perpetrator.

As the officer completed the interrogation he opened up the car door and let Brandon out. He took of the handcuffs and told Brandon to call 911 the next time and that they would handle the situation.

"I've waive any citations this time for your reckless driving. You'll mighty lucky boy that you didn't kill anyone out there today. But under the circumstance I probably would have done the same thing." He told him compassionately.

The ambulance arrived just as Brandon was headed to his mother. Just like before he was told to get out of the way while the EMT's tried to asses his mother's condition. After doing the once over they made sure that she was still alive they put on a neck brace and put her on a back board.

"Is she going to be OK, is she going to be OK?" He kept on rambling with the EMT's.

"She seems to be fine; she might just have been knocked out. We have to get her to the hospital. I am not sure what might be wrong." The EMT told him.

While the one EMT worked on his mother, the other EMT worked on his father. His father was awake but didn't seem coherent. He was sitting up and pale as a ghost but kept on rambling on about some man. Brandon hadn't taken the time until now to even look at his father. As he stopped and stared he was shocked at what he saw. The man he knew as his father was around fifty years old; this man was clearly in his seventies.

"How does he look?" The one EMT asked the other.

"He seems fine physically, but he appears to be in some sort of shock. He keeps repeating, "make it stop, make it stop". He replied.

They were putting Brandon's mother into the ambulance when the second one arrived.

"What we got?" The EMT asked the others.

"An old man who seems to be in shock." He replied

With that they loaded him on a gurney and set him to the hospital. As they loaded Brandon's mother on the ambulance and it started out of the parking lot Brandon went to get into his car.

Since Brandon knew that his mother should be ok he had time to relax. He took a moment to look around him to see all the commotion going on. There were police cars all over and he could see at least two K-9 units. As Brandon left and the ambulance pulled away the officer shook his head in disbelief. He was an 18 year veteran of the police force but this was one of the most bizarre cases he had been involved in yet.

The officer stayed at the scene trying to figure out what had happened. He ran license plates on Frank's truck and did a search for Frank from his driver's license. Frank's criminal record came up with the details of just being released from prison for attempted murder of his wife. The officer's mind started to go over things. Brandon's mother had a different name than Frank's wife, but it made sense that it might be his ex-wife. But if it was, why didn't Brandon tell him that he knew the man as his Father.

"This is getting weirder by the minute." He thought to himself.

Saratoga Springs had its share of crime but nothing like this. After about an hour he finished his investigation and called a tow truck and headed over to Brandon's trailer. As he arrived he saw that the trailer door was wide open and blowing in the wind. He got out of the car and pulled his gun. He slowly entered the house and asked if anyone was there. As he entered he could see the evidence of a struggle and that Brandon's mother was definitely taken by force. He checked all the rooms of the house to make sure that there were no other victims or perpetrators in the home and then called the crime lab to have them process the trailer for evidence; he then headed to the hospital.

"Hi, mom." Max said as he entered the house

"Hello, Max." she said with a tremor of fear in her voice.

"You scared me; I didn't hear you come in. Did you have a nice day?"

"Yes, nothing knew, same stuff different day."

For once, his mother put down her brush and stepped away from the mirror.

"You know Max, I haven't seen you in two years. What have you been doing all that time? I know you and Grace did Skip on the computer or something but you rarely ever asked to talk to me. Why?" She asked as though her feelings were hurt.

"Its Skype mom, not skip." He replied.

"Skype, skip, whatever, you know what I mean. Now answer the question. Why were you so distant?"

"I don't know that last time I saw you, you were ranting and raving about my father and all that he did. I just thought it was best to give you some room. I didn't want to aggravate your condition."

"My condition, my condition." She replied angrily as her disposition changed.

"My mind might be twisted with this obsessive compulsions but I still am all together her and don't you forget it. I am no more senile than you are. I know what I am and what you are. I just find it hard to think that your father would think that he was giving us some sort of gift. He cursed us with this existence and I have a hard time forgiving him." She told him sternly.

"I'm sorry. I just thought."

"You just thought that I was some old woman that had lost her mind. I know. But I have all my faculties and I know what is going on here. I was just hoping that Grace and I could start another life here." She interrupted.

"I'm sorry." He said sincerely.

He spent the rest of the evening conversing with his mother. It was nice, even though at times she would scold him for this or that. He thought that he had lost her to dementia years ago, but she seemed to have returned, at least for the time being.

Chapter 26

After being questioned by the police Brandon was still in shock at what happened. He was glad that his mother was still alive but he couldn't stop thinking about Max and what he did to Frank. He tried to drive as safe as he could even though he was speeding quite a bit to get to the hospital. By the time he arrived they had given his mother a set of x-rays and were going to give her a cat scan to make sure that she didn't have a brain injury.

After hastily entering the emergency room he was escorted to the family waiting room where he waited impatiently. He wasn't one to pray, he never even considered that there was a God before this. But this was a different circumstance.

"Lord, if you are there, help my mother. She's all I have." He prayed quietly.

As he raised his head he realized that he wasn't alone and there were about a half dozen people in the room, all waiting, all praying, all hoping that their loved one would be OK. Brandon usually didn't have time to think about what other people were feeling. Not that he was selfish; he just wanted to keep his mother safe. For once he could see that he wasn't alone; there were plenty of people in his same situation. The room was filled with despair and hopelessness. Just by looking at some of the people he could see that all hope was lost and all they were waiting for was the doctor.

As the door opened they all were gripped with the anticipation that it would be their doctor coming to tell them that everything was going to work out. All their hearts waned in disappointment when it wasn't a doctor at all. A finely dress man opened the door and scanned the room. On seeing the man he was looking for he went over to him like an arrow shot from a bow. The man sitting by himself in the corner got up to meet him.

"Hello pastor, thanks for coming." He said sadly.

"How is she?" The man asked caringly.

"I do not know they are trying to get her to respond. They think that it was a stroke. They aren't sure if she'll make it or not." He replied as tears filled his eyes.

The gentleman was deeply moved and took him by the hands and started to pray with him.

Not coming from a religious family, Brandon was enticed by the meeting. He was intrigued that someone would do something like that for someone else. Or to think that God would hear their prayers, or that He even cared. It wasn't that Brandon didn't believe in God, he was never taught about Him. He watched the man after praying with the first man went to the next group and talked to them and then asked if he could pray with them too. To Brandon's surprise no one of them said no. They all accepted the prayers willingly and respectfully and said thank you when he was finished. By this time Brandon wasn't sure what to make of all this and was a little frightened by it all.

"Hello son. How are you?" The man asked.

"I'm OK."

"I'm Reverend Johnston. Who are you waiting for?"

"Hello, I am Brandon and I'm waiting for my mother, she was beaten up pretty badly." Brandon replied with a shaking voice.

"What's your mother's name?"

"Katherine."

"Well Brandon, do you mind if I pray for you?" He asked gently.

"No, I guess not." Brandon replied sheepishly.

Brandon winced slightly as the Reverend put his hands on his shoulders and started to pray.

"Lord, we know that you have a purpose and a plan for all of us. We pray that you would touch Katherine right now and heal her by your power and love. Show both Brandon and Katherine love and grace that they might know you and not just know of you." He prayed.

He finished the prayer with amen while Brandon stood there not realizing that the prayer was ended. The door opened and everyone's attentions were focused on the door again. The doctor looked in the room and his eyes met the man in the corner. Even a blind man could see the despair that was in the doctor's eyes and the man broke into tears.

"I'm sorry Mr. Brown; there was nothing we could do. I am sorry for your loss." The doctor said matter of fact.

"Can I see her?"

"Yes, you may, come with me."

"Thank you pastor, she's dancing with Jesus now." He said with a strange expression on his face.

Brandon was lost in the man at this point. His expression changed. He went from hopelessness and despair, to sadness and hope. It was the strangest think he ever saw. Brandon was so caught up in the moment that he actually asked the reverend a question.

"Reverend?" He asked.

"Yes, son."

"What was that all about, that man just lost his wife, but he seemed relieved or something. It was kind of strange."

"Well Brandon, Mrs. Brown was a Christian, and when a Christian dies they go to heaven. Mr. Brown knows this and he knows that some day he will see her again in heaven."

"Really? I'm sorry sir. My family has never been very religious. We only go to church on Christmas and Easter, if that. I know about Jesus, but that's about it. I'm not sure that I really believe that God is up there. You know what I mean?" He said ashamedly.

Just as the pastor was going to give Brandon his selling point on belief and faith the door opened again. Everyone looked, hoping that it would be their turn. The doctor opened the door called "Brandon Phillips".

"That's me."

"You're mother is going to be fine. She not awake yet. She has a broken leg and a broken wrist and some bad bruises but no brain damage. She will recover."

"Can I see her?"

"Yes, come with me."

He almost left without acknowledging the pastor there.

"Thanks pastor. Thanks for everything."

"Sure thing Brandon, look me up. I'm at First Christian Church."

"OK, maybe you'll see me there on Sunday."

The reverend knew in his heart that he probably wouldn't see him again; Brandon was like most people after the trauma they would probably forget their need for God.

He was shocked as he entered the ICU. Her leg was in a cast along with her hand and a tube in her nose and an IV connected to her arm.

"She's still sedated and she isn't conscience yet, but she should come out of it in an hour or two. Don't worry, she'll be alright."

"Thanks" He said as he went to his mother's bedside.

"Hi, Mom." He said as she lay there motionless.

"The doctor said that you will be OK. You have a broken leg and wrist, but other than that, nothing permanent. They got him, Mom, they got him. Someone got there before I did and took care of him. He's in the hospital too."

As the night wore on and the doctor assured Brandon that his mother would be fine, so Brandon took some time to relax. He sat next to his mother's bed just thinking of the days events

"Where am I?" She asked quietly as she slowly awoke.

"You're in the hospital. You are going to be alright." Brandon replied.

"What happened?" She asked

Brandon was about to answer when a policeman entered the room.

"Mrs. Phillips; I am glad to see you're awake, I am detective Jones may I ask you some questions? The doctor said it's OK, as long as you are up to it."

"Sure." She said in a whisper as she pressed the control to allow her to sit up.

"Do you remember what happened today? Do you know who attacked you?" The officer asked.

"I remember getting ready for work and opening the door of the trailer when someone grabbed me and put something over my face. I remember getting sleepy. "

"Is that all you remember?"

"I started to wake up when he opened the trunk. I acted like I was asleep. I was hoping to get enough strength to get up and run, but I still felt disorientated. He took me out of the trunk and then threw me on the ground. I tried to keep quiet, but it hurt a lot. I was lying there trying to get it together when I heard Frank yelling."

"What was he yelling?"

"No! Make it stop, make it stop. That's the last thing I remember. I can't remember anything else until now?" She replied.

"You called him Frank; did you know your attacker?" The officer asked.

"Yes, it was my ex-husband. I hadn't seen him in years, but he always said that he would find me some day and kill me."

"One more question, Mrs. Phillips. Did you see anyone else there in the park with you and your ex-husband?"

"No, but I could tell someone else was there, but I couldn't roll over to see who it was." She replied.

"Thank you for your help, Mrs. Phillips, get some rest and get better. You have a good son over there. If it wasn't for him, your ex-husband might have gotten away with killing you. I'll give you a call in a day or two Brandon; I just have to get your statement to finish the investigation."

"OK" Brandon responded.

Even though he tried to remain cool, the officer could tell that he was trying to hide something. Brandon watched as the officer had left and he told his mother to get some sleep and that he would be back in the morning. As kissed her on the cheek and left her get some sleep. The officer met him outside the door and asked him to follow him into the family waiting room for intensive care.

"Brandon, I am trying to understand what is going on here. Your mother knew that Frank was her ex husband and your father, but you told me you didn't know who he was, is that right?" He asked inquisitively.

"Yes, that is right. I hadn't seen my father since he went to jail. That was seven years ago. The man I saw at the park looked old. My father is only around 50 years old and the last time that I saw him he didn't have white hair." Brandon responded with slight tone of disdain in his voice.

"I looked up your father's criminal record and it said that he served time for attempted murder. But that anything about you has been sealed because you are a minor. Would you like to tell me anything about him or about the day he tried to kill your mother?"

"Not really, but I will." Brandon answered.

"It was like this. For years my mother and I took abuse from my drunken worthless father. He used to call her all kinds of names and hit her. I was just a kid and didn't know what to do. I just knew that she deserved better and that some day I was going to get her out of there. She just seemed to take it all and try to hide me from the abuse, but he liked to hit me too at times."

"OK, what happened that day?" The officer asked.

"I came in one day from school to hear a scuffle in the kitchen. When I walked in, my mother was on her back on the floor and my father was trying to strangle her."

"So, what did you do?"

"You know, I didn't think to long about it. I just knew he was going to kill her if I didn't try and stop him. So I grabbed a kitchen knife, jumped on his back and stabbed him."

"Did that stop him, did he go down?"

"No, he was in a drunken rage; I am not sure how deep I actually stabbed him. He threw me off his back and I dropped the knife. He picked me up and threw me into the living room. He was really drunk and disoriented and couldn't stand up or walk very well so it took him a while to reach me. I was scared. I was trying my best to get away from him. He did reach me and picked me up again and threw me into the doorway of the kitchen."

"What happened next?" The officer asked like someone being read a murder mystery.

"Like I said before, he was so mad and nothing seemed to faze him. He pinned me to the floor and started punching me in the face.

"You are a worthless piece of crap! Just like your mother, I'm going to kill both of you!" He yelled at me as he started to choke me.

"How did you get away?"

"I wouldn't have, but by this time my mother was conscience and she had grabbed a frying pan and hit him square in the head with it. One thing you didn't do is threaten to kill her baby."

"Did that do the trick, did it knock him out?"

"Yes it did. Then I went and got the knife again and started to stab him over and over and over until my mother pulled me off of him and the police arrived. Apparently the neighbors heard what was going on and called the cops."

"So that's when he went to jail?"

"Yeah, both of us."

"What?"

"Yeah, the police charged him at first with aggravated assault and charged me with attempted murder."

"You've got to be kidding me?"

"No I'm not, what justice." Brandon said sarcastically.

"So what happened to him and how did you and your mother end up here?"

"The charges against him were changed to attempted murder and mine were dropped but I had to take anger management classes, after I spent a month in juvenile hall. He was found guilty and sentenced to seven years, my mother have been on the run ever since. "

"You've been on the run all this time?" The office asked with shock in his voice.

"Yes, but it seemed like we finally found a safe haven here. My mother actually felt safe and so did I, until now."

"Alright, you filled in all the gaps. Just tell me about this person you saw in the park."

"I didn't get a good look at him. All I saw was him holding Frank by the head. When I arrived he dropped him and ran into the woods. That's all I can say." Brandon answered with a slight tremor in his voice.

"That will do son, I got all I need. Go take care of your mother. She needs you." The officer told him as he slapped him on the back.

"You're a good kid, Brandon. Don't worry; Frank is going away for a long time this time."

"Thanks." Brandon answered sincerely.

Brandon headed back to his mother's room as the officer completed his paperwork. Brandon still felt a little jittery with everything that had happened and he hoped that the officer would believe his story, but he would worry about that later. Now he had to worry about his mother.

Things still didn't completely add up to the officer. His gut told him that Brandon wasn't telling him the whole story. "Maybe he was afraid he was going back to juvi." The officer thought to himself.

"What a night, maybe the old man can tell me about the man in the park. What difference does it make any how? Frank deserves anything he gets at this point." The officer mumbled to himself.

He was about to call it quits for the day but the police officer inside him wouldn't let him. He knew that he had to finish the investigation regardless of what he felt and headed to Frank's room.

As Brandon entered his mother's room a doctor was looking over her condition.

"Is she going to be all right?" He asked nervously.

"Yes, Brandon, she is going to be fine. I gave her a pain killer and a sedative. She should be able to leave in a day or two. Go home; you've had a busy day. She will be fine."

Brandon walked over to her side and kissed his mother's head.

"I love you mom, I will be back in the morning." He told her.

As Brandon headed home officer Jones talked to the doctor about Frank's condition.

"There is nothing physically wrong with him that I can find. He has had some sort of physiological shock. He isn't able to say much more than, "No, and make it stop!" at this point." The doctor told him.

"Do you think that he will recover and how old is he?"

"He may recover, the mind is a strange thing, but you never know. I would put his age around seventy," The doctor answered.

The detective told him thanks and headed to his car. The more he investigated this case the more convoluted it became.

As Brandon came home, he pulled into the parking space. There was a police officer still there.

"We're just about finished here. We are still taking evidence so you can't go in yet." The policeman told him.

He waited impatiently for another 10 minutes as they finished their jobs and left his trailer. As he walked in he saw that the kitchen was a complete mess. It seemed that his father dragged his mother in there before he put her in the car. He rearranged everything and threw out some broken dishes and then went to his room. He had no desire to take a shower, he was completely drained of energy by the amount of stress that he had been through and all he wanted to do is go to sleep. He couldn't help be relieved just for the fact that his mother would be alright and that his father was in custody. But as he lay there on the bed, even though his body was exhausted, his mind was racing. He couldn't help but think of what he saw at the park.

"But what about those eyes and the look on his face?" He asked himself staring at the ceiling trying to sleep.

"His eyes were just like Grace's."

.As the minutes turned to hours and he lay there looking at the numbers on the clock he decided to get up.

"If you can't sleep you might as well waste time playing video games." He thought to himself.

After an hour or two he fell asleep on the couch due to exhaustion.

Later that evening when everything went quiet at the hospital the nurses had just finished their rounds as they shut out the lights to the patients could get some rest. The hospital floor became quiet other than for the nurses talking at their station. Frank was sleeping peacefully after they gave him a sedative to calm him down. Nothing was out of the ordinary and it was everything as usual.

A tall nurse walked down the hall and into Frank's room. The room was dark so the nurse turned on the over the bed lighting so he could see what he was doing. He took a once over at Frank and saw that he was resting peacefully and that his vital signs were good and normal.

He took a look at the door and started to retrieve his stethoscope from his pocket and put it around his neck. He then bent over Frank and took a good look at his face. He stood there bent for a moment and then slightly slapped Frank in the face. Initially Frank didn't wake up so he slapped him a little harder. Slowly Frank woke up from his chemically induced sleep to find his attacker staring him in the eyes. As Frank realized that someone was determined to do him harm he went to push the call button on the bed but his attacker grabbed his arm and put his hand on his mouth so he couldn't scream.

"Don't worry, this won't hurt a bit." The attacker whispered with a slight sneer.

Just like at the park, the attacker pulled Frank up to him by cupping his head in his hands like a ball. He then stared into Franks eyes. Frank immediately started to tremble and shake. Frank wanted to scream but couldn't he was frozen in fear, hypnotized by the attackers gaze.

"Just go to sleep, just go to sleep." The attacker whispered.

By this time Frank's strength was drained and he couldn't even resist him even if he wanted to. His attacker kept his hands firm on Frank's head as his life was slowly drained from him, with a final gasp Frank died as he watched the heart monitor flat line. When alarm sounded he laid Frank's head back in the bed, with the care of handling a new born baby. He knew that he only had moments before the room would be filled with an express team that would try and revive him.

He simply entered the bathroom and closed the door behind him. Within a minute the charge nurse had rushed into the room to see what had happened and saw that Frank was in cardiac arrest. She grabbed the phone and dialed the number to summon the express team to the room. As the express team ran to the room to try and save Frank's life his attacker simply waited for everyone's attention to be drawn to saving his life and he walked out of the room. Dressed like a nurse and playing the part well, no one ever questioned his being there as he simply walked to the stairs and headed out of the hospital.

After working on Frank for about 12 minutes the decision was made to call the time of death and except the reality that Frank had left the world never to return. The physician in charge called the time and called for the morgue to come and pick up the body. Since he was a suspect in a kidnapping, detective Jones was called and informed that he had died.

The detective had just laid his head on his pillow when the phone range. He wanted to let it ring and get some sleep but the detective in him wouldn't let him do that. He picked up the phone and got the news about Frank and told the hospital that he would be there shortly.

"So much for a good nights sleep." He said out loud as he hung up the phone.

After a short drive he arrived as the hospital and asked the physician what happened.

"He simply died. There's nothing else I can say. There was no physical trauma to his body. He simply stopped living." The doctor told them.

"Isn't that a little strange doctor? That an old man comes in here suffering some form of shock and within a few hours is dead. And you have no other reason other than natural causes?" The detective asked.

"That's it detective. He was an older gentleman. I cannot explain his trauma; I can only tell you that he had no physical trauma to his body. Apparently the shock to his brain was far more severe than we suspected." The doctor answered.

"If you say so doctor, but this case gets stranger by the hour. It just doesn't seem right. Are you sure that no one came in here?" He asked.

"I am sure, the charge nurse had just finished her rounds when the alarm sounded that his heart had stopped. Simple as that, I know that this sounds cold, but he just died, most likely of old age. The medical examiner will do an autopsy on him tomorrow. Now if that is all, I need to get back to work." The doctor told him.

"I think that will do it, Thanks." The detective responded as he left for the attendants to take care of Frank's lifeless body.

The detective filled in the rest of his notes as he headed to the stairs to his car outside. He would call the next day for the results from the medical examiners autopsy. He got into his car and started back home, hoping that he could get a few hours of sleep.

Chapter 27

Dawn woke up and got ready for school. She was running late so she had to hurry. She wanted to blame the inventor of "snooze button" for her being late.

"If it wasn't for that little button to push, she might have gotten up on time." She thought to herself.

She tried to get ready before her mother got up, to ensure that there would be no drama in the morning. She got dress and put her makeup on and got her stuff as she headed for the bus stop. She could here the alarm going off in her mother's bed room so she knew she better be heading out the door. She left the house locking the door behind her just as she saw the school bus heading her way.

"That was close." She thought to herself as she breathed a sigh of relief.

She walked to the middle and sat next to Rebecca as she always did. As usually Rebecca started on her daily rant about this or that Dawn knew just to sit there politely and act like she was really listening.

"Did you hear the news Dawn?"

"What news?"

"You can't tell me you didn't hear about Brandon and the psycho that's on the loose, can you?" Rebecca said in disbelief.

"Really I didn't I didn't watch any TV last night and I went to bed early. What happened?"

"Well, the way I hear it, some psycho attacked Brandon's mother, took her to the park to kill her but Brandon found them before he had a chance to kill her. When Brandon got there he caught the killer trying to kill some old guy and his mother." Rebecca said excitedly.

"Did they catch the guy?"

"No, that's the crazy thing. Brandon said the guy ran into the woods, so there is some psycho still on the loose. You better lock you windows and doors at night Dawn."

Realizing that Rebecca wasn't always the best when it came to telling accurate stories she pulled out her cell phone. She quickly dialed her home phone. The phone rang twice and her mother picked it up.

"Hello, what's wrong Dawn?"

"Mom, turn on the TV, Brandon's mother was attacked last night and the guy who did it is still on the loose, I just wanted to warn you, I have to go."

She hung up before her mother had a chance to say anything.

"What?" Her mother said as she hung up the phone in shock.

She went over and turned on the TV to find out that there was much to do about nothing on that early in the morning. She turned it back off and turned on the computer. Most of the time local news was better found on the internet than the Albany TV stations. After a few minutes of searching she found a small article explaining what had happened at the park and that the suspect was still on the loose. The thought of some psycho hiding in the shadows gave her a chill as she went through the house making sure that all the doors and windows were locked.

Later that morning the coroner was about to do Frank's autopsy. He had called the detective Jones to report his findings.

"So what do you have doc?" The detective asked.

"This one is a strange one Brian."

"What do you mean?"

"I mean the chart says that he was 50 years old, but after my examination I would suggest that he was more about 80 years old. His internal organs show definite age and decay. His liver was showing sign of cirrhosis and it looks like he had the beginnings of renal failure."

"Could it be that he just lived a hard life? He did spend the last 7 years in prison."

"That could account for it, but I would say that his body was in a state of accelerated aging."

"Well, what did he die of?"

"It looked like he died of natural causes."

"But did he? You seem a little hesitant there?"

"Well, it had elevated levels of adrenalin in his blood stream."

"How elevated and what does that mean?"

"I mean really elevated. Like off the charts elevated, like enough to kill him out right."

"How does that happen?"

"Well the chart says that they injected him with epinephrine in order to jump start his heart."

"OK, does that account for the elevated levels?"

"Maybe, but I don't think this much.

"So what do you think happened?"

"It is possible in the rush and confusion of the evening that they gave him too much and just didn't chart it down. I doubt that it would have helped any how the way his internal organs were damaged."

"What if they didn't give him too much?"

"Look Brian, on the record, this man died of natural causes due to advanced aging of his internal organs due to drug and alcohol abuse."

"What about off the record?"

"Off the record I would say that this man could have been driven into cardiac arrest by fear."

"Are you telling me that he was scared to death?"

"That's what it looks like, but this would make me look like a complete crack pot if I wrote that down in official cause of death."

"I understand."

"This is the other thing that I found." He said as he held Frank's lifeless head in his hands.

"I found a set of finger impressions around his neck, like someone was holding him up with his head,"

"That matches the witness' story, that he saw someone holding him by the head." The officer responded.

"I also found another set of impressions around his face.

"Are they the same person?"

149

"I couldn't get any finger prints from the body so I can't say for sure.

"You said that they are on his face?" The officer asked perplexed.

"It looks like someone had their hands pressed around his face, like they were looking into his face when he was lying on the ground or in the bed. It could have been a nurse or a doctor trying to get him to respond when they entered the room."

"But you couldn't get any finger prints?"

"No, but if they had gloves on like they should, then I couldn't get them anyway."

"Thanks Doc. I guess this investigation is over." The officer said as he left the room and headed back to the station to do his paperwork.

Chapter 28

Mrs. Sinclair milled around the emergency room, it was a slow night and she was bored. She was looking over charts and seeing if anything needed to be done, but tonight she was all caught up. Working at the hospital was routine, there was an occasional trauma, but for the most part it was just some non-life-threatening event that needed attention. Just as she sat down at the nurse's station the phone began to ring. The charge nurse picked it up and started to talk to the person on the line. She wasn't on it long when she hung it up and looked at Mrs. Sinclair.

"Trisha that was the ambulance, they are bringing in a teenager that seems to have been hit by a car. She has no vital signs so far."

The ER doctor and team of nurses awaited the ambulance as it pulled up to the emergency room.

"We have a teenage girl, no id; she seems to have been hit with a car. She has no vital signs. We have been doing CPR since we picked her up on the scene."

"The EMT told the doctor as they wheeled the patient into a room.

Mrs. Sinclair was in the room awaiting the patient and the doctor's assessment of the situation. She was shocked when she saw the condition that the girl was in. Her face was severely injured and she seemed to have no signs of life. As she took another look at her and the clothes she was wearing she realized who the patient was.

"That's Grace Smith?"

"You know who this girl is?" The doctor asked as he was rushing around trying to find a pulse or some sign of life.

"Yes, she is my daughter's best friend."

She knew that she had to remain professional but she couldn't help but become noticeable emotional.

"Come on Grace." She whispered as she reached out and held her hand.

The charge nurse could tell that Mrs. Sinclair's hands were shaking and she appeared to be whispering as she stood close to Grace.

"I am going to call the time of death." The doctor said rather abruptly.

"No!" Mrs. Sinclair interrupted.

"I'm sorry Trisha; she was dead before they even brought her in here."

"Excuse me." She replied as she walked out of the room.

It was not like her to leave her responsibilities but this was something that she never expected. She never thought she would see someone so young and who she knew die in front of her.

"Trisha?" The charge nurse asked her.

"Yes."

"Would you want to call the next of kin, or should I?"

"I will." She said with a slight tremor in her voice.

"Are you sure, I can do it."

"No, I will be fine." She replied as she picked up the phone.

The charge nurse left her alone as she made the call to Grace's mother. After making the call she gently hung up the phone.

"Her mother will be here in about 5 minutes. I told her that Grace was in an accident, but didn't tell her that she was dead."

"OK, I will inform the doctor that she will be here soon and he can break the news to her himself."

"OK, I need to use the restroom." She told the charge nurse matter of fact.

"OK."

Mrs. Sinclair headed to the restroom, numb from head to foot. She wanted to cry but she knew that she couldn't. Grace's mother would be there soon and would need a shoulder to cry on. She had to hold it together for a while, at least until she told Dawn.

"Jesus, how am I going to tell Dawn?" She thought out load.

As Mrs. Smith entered the emergency room they all knew who she was by the look on her face. The registrar at the window simply opened the emergency doors and directed her to the room where Grace was.

"I am Mrs. Smith, Grace's mother, is she OK? Is she OK?" She said franticly.

"Mrs. Smith, I am sorry for your loss, but Grace seems to have been struck with a car and was severely injured. There was nothing we could do."

"What do you mean, where is she, I need to see her, I need to see her."

"She's in here, but please brace yourself for what you are going to see." The doctor told her as he opened the door.

"No!" She screamed as she entered the room.

Mrs. Smith was babbling on and on and was almost at the point of hysteria as Mrs. Sinclair entered the room. Mrs. Sinclair didn't say anything she just reach out and gave her a hug as Mrs. Smith sobbed onto Mrs. Sinclair shoulder. The doctor gave Mrs. Sinclair a look and he walked out the door and closed it behind him.

"What am I going to do, she was my life, she was all I lived for. What kind of person would hit someone and drive off?" She said

"Where was she?"

"At the park, walking. That is all that we know at this point. The police are still at the scene trying to figure out what happened."

Just then Mrs. Sinclair's pastor entered the room.

"Mrs. Smith this is my pastor, reverend Fitzgerald." Trisha told Mrs. Smith.

"I haven't had a need for your religion yet, and I don't think I need it now. Thank you for coming, but no thank you."

Both Trisha and the reverend were taken back a little by her demeanor and with that the reverend excused himself and left.

As Mrs. Smith sat in the family room crying, the investigating detective quietly walked in.

"I am sorry for the intrusion, Mrs. Smith, and I an am sorry for your loss but I need to ask you a few questions."

"About what?" She answered with a slight agitation in her voice.

"I just need to know if there was anyone that might have wanted to hurt Grace."

"What, why would anyone want to hurt her? She was a nice girl. I don't know anyone that would want to hurt her. Why?"

"It's just routine there were no witnesses to the crime, I just want to cover all the bases."

"There was nothing routine about what happened to my daughter!" She replied.

"I am sorry; I didn't mean it that way. I just want to find the person who did this and make him pay." He reassured her apologetically.

"I'm sorry for yelling at you, I know that you are only trying to do your job. Please find out who did this." She told him with tears in her eyes.

"I will do everything in my power to find out." He replied as he walked out and left her in the room alone.

Hit and runs were rare in Saratoga Springs. It was a small town and it didn't take long for a secret to get out. He put out an APB out for any vehicles that had some resent front end damage to them. He also called on the local repair shops to make a report if anyone brought a car in with front end damage.

That night Grace's demise along with the facts of the hit and run were released to the news in hopes that anyone that saw anything or had any information would come forward.

After about 15 minutes they came to take Grace to the morgue and get her ready to be shipped to the funeral home. They took Mrs. Smith to the office to fill out the needed paper work to release her body.

Mrs. Sinclair knew that by law she couldn't tell anyone what had happened until the police made the case public, but she didn't want Dawn to find out by way of the news. She excused herself again and went out to her car to use her cell phone.

She dialed her home number and waited for Dawn to answer the phone.

"Hello." Dawn answered.

"Dawn are you alright?" Mrs. Sinclair asked.

"Yeah, why?" Dawn replied.

"I just wanted to make sure that you were OK."

"I'm fine, what's wrong, you seem upset."

"Dawn, I didn't want you to see this on the evening news who hear about it on the bus tomorrow."

"What?" Dawn interrupted.

"Are you sitting down?"

"Yes, what has happened?" She said slightly agitated.

"Dawn, Grace was hit by a car this evening and was killed."

Her mother heard a slight bang as the phone fell out of Dawn's hand and hit the floor. She then heard Dawn starting to scream. She stayed on the phone listening and waiting for Dawn to pick it back up. After a while she started to call Dawn's name.

"Dawn, Dawn. Are you there?"

"Yes, I'm here. But I don't understand, I just got done talking to her a few hours ago."

"I know it's hard to believe but it's true. I was here at the hospital when they brought her in."

"Can I see her?"

"No, her body is being shipped over to the funeral home now."

"How did this happen, where was she?"

"I guess she was talking a walk in the park, apparently it was a hit and run."

"Mom, I have to go, this is too much for me to process right now. I will see you when you get home." She told her mother between tears.

"I love you Dawn."

"I love you too. " She told her mother as she hung up the phone.

Mrs. Sinclair tried to compose herself and then headed back to the emergency room.

"Trisha, I want you to get your stuff and go home. It's been a rough night, and we will be OK for the rest of the evening without you." The charge nurse told her.

"Thank you." She said politely as she got her purse and headed back to her car.

She was used to seeing people die in the ER but this was far to close to home not to affect her. All she wanted to do now is head home and comfort Dawn for a while.

At the park the police were trying to put together what had happened. There was very little information, just a 911 call made by the person that found her in the ditch.

"I was just walking through the park and I saw this girl laying face down in the ditch. I tried to see if she was still alive as I called 911." The witness told the police.

"Did you see how she ended up in the ditch?" The officer asked him.

"No, I just was walking here and happened to see her there if I would have gone another way, who knows when someone would have found her."

"After you called, what did you do?"

"I rolled her over and saw if I could give her CPR. I couldn't get a pulse and her face was pretty battered. I was over whelmed by the sight of her face. I couldn't give her mouth to mouth. I just couldn't. I almost threw up just kneeling there waiting for the ambulance."

"OK, I understand. Thanks for your help; you are free to go now."

"Were they able to revive her at the hospital?" He asked caringly.

"No, she was pronounced dead on arrival."

The stranger lowered his head and slowly walked away, visibly shaken by the thought that the girl that he tried to help had died.

"Sometimes I hate this job." The officer whispered to himself as he watched the stranger walk away.

After he made sure that any loose ends and any evidence was taken into account he headed to the hospital. He was torn as he drove to the hospital, he had seen all types of car accidents before but this one struck him right in the heart. He could only imagine loosing his own child in such a heinous way. He was determined to find out who did this to this poor little girl.

He entered the hospital to find that the atmosphere was thick and filled with emotion. He tried not to bring attention to himself as he approached the front desk. He asked for the head physician and the nurse sent him back to the emergency department. He introduced himself to the doctor and told him why he was there.

"Doctor, I just need to finish my investigation on the girl that was brought in here earlier, from apparent hit and run."

"Yes, officer, what do you need to know?"

"Was it a car that caused her facial trauma, or was it something else?"

"I would say at this moment that her injury seemed to be caused buy a fast moving vehicle of some sort. She had massive facial trauma. Basically her whole face was fractured along with her skull. It seemed that she died instantly. Were there any witnesses that saw what happened?"

"No, just the person that called 911. He said that he found her in the ditch in this condition."

"What a shame. Who would hit someone with a car and then drive off like nothing happened?"

"Doesn't make sense, does it Doctor?"

"Know, you just wonder about people sometimes. I don't know how you police officers do it."

"Do what?"

"Deal with people at their very worst."

"Sometimes its hard Doctor, sometimes it's very hard."

The officer thanked the doctor for the information and finished filled out his paperwork. Over the course of his career he had to investigate homicides, rapes and all sorts of cruelty but this was different, this was personal to him and he vowed to find the person responsible. His sleepy little town had just become marred by the loss of this little girl by the hand of some irresponsible coward and he was going to make them pay.

As Mrs. Sinclair entered the house she found Dawn sitting in the living room with the lights off staring into space.

"Dawn! Are you alright?" She asked her trying to break her out of her trance.

"Dawn!" She said again, but this time a little louder.

"Yes." Dawn finally responded.

"Are you OK?"

"Not really, I was just sitting here thinking. I don't know what to do."

Mrs. Sinclair could see that she had been crying and that she seemed to be in a state of shock.

"I don't know what to do either." Her mother told her.

"What?"

"I mean, I don't know what to say. I don't know what to do, but to say I am sorry."

"I just can't believe that she's gone. She stopped over here before she headed to the park. She asked me if I wanted to take a walk and I told her no. That was the last time that I saw her." Dawn said in a quivering voice.

"I am going to bed." She told her mother matter of fact.

"All right, try to get some rest." Her mother replied lovingly.

Dawn was so upset that she didn't brush her teeth or even get into her pajamas; she just pulled the covers of the bed back and slid in with her street clothes on. She really couldn't sleep but she just wanted to be alone for now. First her father and now her best friend, she could only imagine what could happen next. She would lay there for a few more hours staring at the ceiling thinking about Grace and all the memories that she had with her, she then slowly faded off to a horrible nights sleep.

The next morning Mrs. Sinclair let Dawn sleep in; she didn't get her up to go to school

"There's plenty of time for school, she just needs a little time." She thought to herself.

Dawn woke up a few hours later to find the house empty. Her mother went to work. She did leave her a note to take it easy today and that she loves her. Even though her emotions were not as frayed as the day before, she still had a hard time keeping from crying. She went to the cupboard and got out the cereal and then got out the milk. She poured the milk and then slowly ate her breakfast. The breakfast was like the rest of the day. It was slow and long as she sat there most of the day looking at the TV but not paying any attention to what was on. It was around 2 o'clock that the phone rang and she picked it up. It was Max and he was calling to give Dawn all the information about the viewing at the funeral home.

"We are trying to keep this a small viewing to keep the stress low on my mother. We are not putting the details in the newspaper to keep the amount of visitors to a minimum. I hope you and your mother will be there."

"Yes, I will be there. Tell your mother that I am sorry about her loss."

"I will. Try and have a good day. Bye."

At that point Dawn felt like the whole world was closing in. It was happening so suddenly. Tomorrow would be the last time she would get to say goodbye. It was so sudden. She went back up to her room and cried some more.

"Dawn, I'm home." Her mother yelled as she entered from the garage.

Dawn came down the steps to welcome her mother home.

"I bought some chocolate ice cream. I thought a little comfort food would help."

"OK, I didn't really feel like eating much."

"I know, but a little ice cream will help calm your emotions."

Mrs. Sinclair went to the kitchen and got out two bowls and put a few scoops of ice cream in each.

"Here you go."

They both started to eat it in silence when Mrs. Sinclair started to chuckle.

"What's so funny?"

"I was just thinking about your father. He was never happy with a scoop or two. He always wanted"

"A glutton man portion." Dawn interrupted.

The statement broke the tension of the room and lightened up the mood.

"How about the time he tried to make honey baked ham. Remember, the dog wouldn't even eat that stuff." Dawn said

"How could I forget, we had company over and everyone is thinking that they are going to have a great dinner. What a let down. We ended up having to go out that night."

"He tried, but he was a terrible cook." Dawn said.

"That he was. I often was filled with fear, when he told me he had mad a special dinner for me. I know he tried, but I never saw him create too much of anything good."

"How about his fire chicken?" Dawn interjected.

"Yeah, that was another one of his failed concoctions. Made from the flames of Hell itself I think. Even he had to admit that it was too hot to eat."

With each passing memory their mood lightened a bit, both were still sad but it was far better to remember the good things rather than to be filled with the grief of the day. They sat there swapping stories like girl scouts around the camp fire and eating the ice cream. Before long both had eaten a half gallon and the time had flown away. For once in the past months, time had gotten away from both of them. They had forgotten their grief for a moment and remembered their happier times.

It was a strange thing to get used to referring to her father in the past tense. She often still felt like he was going to come through the door one night.

For Mrs. Sinclair the nights were the hardest of them all. Sleeping in a bed that she shared with him for so many years and now the bed seemed so much bigger and so much colder. The place where she felt safe and warm in his embrace was now a place of loneliness and cold. She now would often wake up thinking that he would be there but she would soon realize that it was only a dream, that her nightmare was still a reality and that she would have to go on without him. So much of her life was wrapped around him. He was the strong arm when she needed him; he was the one thing that she could always trust in. Sure he had his faults and no one knew them better than her., but now she came to realize that there would never be another like him and that her soul mate was gone and she would die of a broken heart someday. Mrs. Sinclair was a strong woman though and was not about to let her husbands death be the end of hers. She would go on, not the same person, changed, tainted by grief, but she would survive. She realized that she still had something more important in the world than herself and that was Dawn. If for no other reason she had to go on and show Dawn that life was always worth living no matter what the circumstances it might bring. She was going to roll up her sleeves and do whatever it took to make it. She would show the world, that she might be down, but she wasn't out. This latest event might have knocked her down a notch or two but she would rise back to the occasion. But for now she just wanted to cry. And she did, she cried a lot, but with every day, it seemed that she shed one less tear and that the burden was slowly being lightened.

Chapter 29

Brandon got up in a rush as he saw that he slept in and that he had missed the bus and would have to drive to school. He got dressed, opened the refrigerator door and chugged some milk from the container. He put the lid back on and put the miniscule amount left back in the refrigerator. He then ran out the door and into the car. He hastily made his prayer and attempted to start it. To his surprise it actually started on the first attempt and away he went. He slammed the car into reverse as his tires squealed as he left the small driveway, slamming it into drive he hit the gas pedal as his tires left a skid mark as he headed for school.

He arrived in the school parking with only a few minutes to spare, he would have to hurry if didn't want to be late. He noticed that some of the kids gave him a strange look as he got out of the car and headed for the door. He was just about to walk into the school when he noticed that there was a small crowd around his car and some of the kids were taking pictures of it with their phones. He immediately turned around and headed back to see what all the fuss was about.

"What's going on? Why are you guys taking pictures of my car?" He asked.

He was shocked when one of them pointed to the bumper of the car. It appeared to be dented quite a bit and the fender had a slight crease to it.

"It looks like you hit something, Brandon." One of the kids said to him.

With that statement a chill went through the crowd as they all started to head for the door.

"What's going on?" He asked the kid.

"Didn't you hear? Last night someone ran over Grace Smith in the park and killed her. The police were asking for information about any cars that had front end damage."

"Well it wasn't me, if that's what you are implying." He said angrily.

"I didn't say that it was, you just asked what was going on and I told you. I have to get to class." He said as he headed for the door.

Brandon spent the next couple of minutes looking at his car and the damage. He had no idea what had happened or how it got there. After looking another time he headed for the door. By the time he got to the door the principle was there waiting for him.

"Good morning Brandon, could you come with me." He told him.

"Sure, what is this all about? I'm not late or anything?"

"No, I just need to talk to you for a minute."

The two walked to the principles office and the principle asked Brandon to have a seat.

"How is you mother doing?" The principle asked.

"Just fine, she is doing well, it could have been much worse, much worse."

"How are you doing?"

"I am fine, why?"

"I just wanted to know how you were doing."

After taking another couple of minutes talking between them Brandon became annoyed.

"Mr. Burnell, I don't know what is going on here, but why am I here. What have I done? I just want to go to class, is that OK?" He said as he stood up and turned to leave the room.

The office had a window that faced the parking lot. Brandon was filled with horror to see that someone was attempting to tow his car.

"What in the world?" He said as he headed for the door.

"Sit down Brandon."

"What?" He asked as he took anther step to the door.

"Sit down!" The principle said again, but this time with authority.

"Mr. Burnell that is my car that someone is towing away, all I want to do is find out why."

At that moment the phone rang and the principle picked it up.

"Let them in." Brandon heard him say.

As the door opened up two police officers emerged and stood next to the door.

"Brandon Phillips?" the one officer asked.

"Yes."

"Where were you last night around 8 o'clock?"

"I was at the hospital tending to my mother." Brandon replied with annoyance.

"Brandon, how did you car get the damage to its front end?"

"I do not know, I got up this morning and I was late and didn't notice it until I got to school this morning."

"Brandon, how old are you?"

"18, why?"

"Because, Brandon I am placing you under arrest for the hit and run of Grace Smith."

"What, are you kidding me? This is ridiculous. Why in the world would I hit someone with my car?"

"Please place you hands behind you back." The office told him sternly as the other officer read him his Miranda rights.

Brandon submitted without incident and put his hands behind his back as the officer put the handcuffs on him and lead him out of the office.

It was very shocking to everyone in the office area to see Brandon being escorted out of the school in handcuffs. Within seconds of the incident texts were being made all over the school about the incident. Even though cell phone use during school hours was prohibited phones were going off all over campus. The incident had become such a distraction in most of the classes that some of the teachers left the classes to go to the office to find out what really happened.

The principle seeing that things were getting out of control quickly got on the PA system

"This is principle Burnell, and I would like to address the incident that happened this morning with a student and that student has been taken out of school by the police. Please remember that cell phones are prohibited during school hours and that he would give out any other information as it became available."

By this time everyone had enough time to come up with their own theory of what happened. In the fray of people taking sides whether on not that they thought Brandon had killed Grace, Bill surprising was his biggest advocate.

"I don't believe it. I know we had our differences but I can't believe that he would have done something like that." Bill said matter of fact.

"I don't know Bill, you should have been here the day that Grace beat him up, he was pretty mad. In fact he almost broke my jaw that day." Paul told him.

"Come on Paul, do you think he would actually kill a person just because he lost a fight?"

"Not just a fight, a fight with a little girl, and she kicked his butt, she humiliated him."

"Maybe so, but I still don't think he was capable of all of that."

"I don't know Bill, what I hear, is that he came here after he was in juvi for trying to kill his father or something."

"There you go again, Paul, just another rumor, who knows what's true or not."

"If you say so Bill, I just thought that you would be ready to crucify him after all that he did to you lately."

"It just doesn't add up, it just doesn't make sense. That is all that I am saying."

After their discussion the teacher took control of the class and asked everyone to be quiet. As she started teaching the shock of what had happened finally hit Bill like a freight train, he fell into a trance completely consumed by the events of the day. Finding out that the first girl that took notice of him was killed the night before and that the person that seems to have done it was Brandon was too much for him to take. He got up slowly and walked to the teacher's desk.

"I need to go to the nurse's office if that would be alright?" He asked respectively.

The teacher could see by the look on his face that something was definitely wrong with Bill. He was pale and it looked like he was about to throw up.

"Sure, I hope you're feeling better."

Bill left the room without saying a word and headed to the nurse's office. Every step was agony for him. He was filled with disbelief and anguish. Finally his stomach had all it was going to take, and as he walked past a garbage can he started to throw up in it. Kids walking down the hall tried to keep their distance from the kid loosing his lunch in the garbage can. After emptying his stomach of all its contents he then finished his walk to the nurse's office white as ghost. After telling the nurse his story she called his mother to have him picked him up and take him home.

As Brandon was escorted into the police station he was finger printed and photographed and then put at a desk in order to make his one phone call. Since the incident with his father, his mother and he always had a lawyer. His mother always wanted to know her rights and where she stood within the law when it came to Frank. Brandon knew the phone number by heart and made the call. After talking to the receptionist he tried to explain the situation and the lawyer said that he was on his way and would be there in about an hour.

"That was my lawyer and told me not to say anything until he arrives." Brandon told the detective.

"Brandon, we haven't even charged you with anything. What makes you think that you need a lawyer? Did you do something?" The detective prodded him.

"I know my rights, I have the right to a lawyer and I am using my right to a lawyer" He replied with irritation.

"All I was saying is most innocent people don't need a lawyer."

"I thought that we are all innocent until proven guilty or did I miss something there?" Brandon retorted back.

At that point the officer realized that Brandon was an intelligent person and knew how to handle himself and that this case was neither cut nor dry. The officer took off his handcuffs and led Brandon into an interview room. For someone that was under suspicion of killing someone with their car, Brandon was quite calm and cool. The detective had interviewed countless suspects before but known seem to be this calm before. He thought that maybe Brandon didn't have anything to do with it.

"Would you like a drink?" The detective asked.

"No, thank you." Brandon answered.

The detective placed a tape recorder on the desk and then started the interview.

"What is your name?" He asked Brandon.

"I am not going to answer any questions until my lawyer arrives." Brandon angrily answered back.

"All I did was asked your name." the detective answered. "What do you have to hide?"

Brandon said nothing but stared right into the detective's eyes.

It seemed to take forever for his lawyer to arrive. After introducing himself and taking a minute to confer with Brandon the lawyer allowed the interview to start.

"Can I begin?" The detective asked the lawyer with disdain.

"Go ahead."

"Brandon Phillips."

"Brandon, where were you last night around 8 p.m.?" The detective asked him.

"I was at the hospital with my mother."

"Can anyone verify this?"

"My mother."

"Was you mother in the same room with you last night?"

"Yes, she was resting."

"So, if you were to leave the hospital, she probably would not have seen you?"

"I guess not."

"So I am going to ask you again. Where were you last night around 8 p.m.?"

"I was at the hospital with my mother."

"Isn't it true that you had a fight with Grace Smith on Friday and that you told her that you were going to make you pay?"

"I didn't kill Grace Smith!'

"I suggest that you charge my client or we are going to leave." Brandon's lawyer told the detective.

"We will hold you until tomorrow to see what the District Attorney wants to charge you with.

"You mean I have to stay in jail for the next day? Can they do that?" Brandon asked his lawyer in a panic.

"Yes, but don't worry, it will only be for a day. I will make sure that they have a writ of habeas corpus by the morning."

The detective led Brandon out into the hall and handed him over to another officer to take him to a holding cell. He then picked up the phone and called the crime lab to see if they had finished processing the car. The crime lab told him that they were still working on it but so far they could find no physical evidence linking the car with Grace's hit and run.

"Don't worry Brandon, this will all work out. I will be back tomorrow." The lawyer said as he left.

They took him to the processing officer who took an inventory or Brandon's belongings and then gave him an orange jumpsuit to put on. After he put it on he gave his clothes to the officer and he added them to Brandon's inventory and after Brandon signed the receipt they lead him to the holding cell. To Brandon's relief there were no other people in any of the cells, for the time being he was the only one there. The jailer opened the door and Brandon walked in and sat on the nearest cot. Since he had nothing else to do he laid there and stared at the ceiling and waited for the next day to come.

For most of the day Dawn stayed up in her room and laid there staring at the ceiling. She couldn't believe that Grace was gone and that someone could be that heartless to run her over with a car and not even stop to see if they could help. She was filled with sorrow and anger. She was sad that Grace was gone and angry at the person responsible. She also felt so guilty that she didn't walk with her that night. The silence was broken with the phone ringing. She figured that her mother would get it and if she didn't they would call back so she went back to her trance staring at the ceiling.

"Dawn, Pick up the phone, it's Jessica." Her mother shouted up the stairs.

Dawn was actually excited to hear that Jessica had called. They had grown apart since her dad was killed and Jim was injured.

"Hi Dawn, how are you. I thought I should call and see how you were doing. I haven't talked to you in so long."

"Hi, Jessica, I'm fine, it's good to hear from you, I was hoping we could get together again, like old times."

"I would like that." Jessica replied.

"Dawn did you hear the latest news?"

"No, I have been here all day, I haven't had anything on, all I've done most of the day is staring at the ceiling."

"Are you ready for this?"

"Yes."

"This morning the police came and arrested Brandon and towed his car away. They think that he was the one that killed Grace."

"You have to be kidding me. Where did you hear that from, Rebecca?"

"No, I saw it myself. Everyone at school was talking about it."

"I can't believe it; he would have never done something that terrible. He's not like that."

"Believe it or not, they did arrest him and tow his car.

"You know Jessica this is all getting to weird for me. I don't know what is going on. Why in the world would he kill Grace?"

"I guess he was still pretty angry about what Grace did to him last week."

"Come on, they had a fight, you don't go and kill someone over a stupid little fight."

"I guess, we should get together when every thing calms down. I miss hanging out with you."

"Me too, thanks for calling." Dawn said as she hung up the phone.

"Mom!" Dawn screamed at the top of her lungs.

Not knowing what was going on her mother came running up the stares as if Dawn was an infant and had fallen out of the crib.

"What's wrong?" Her mother shouted as she opened the door.

"Mom, you are never going to believe this. They arrested Brandon for killing Grace."

"What?" Her mother stared at her bewildered.

"Mom, are you there? That was Jessica and she said that they arrested Brandon this morning for killing Grace."

"That doesn't sound right. I would never think that Brandon could ever do something like that."

"That's what I told Jessica, but she said that they towed his car because it had some kind of damage."

"Mom, this town has gotten complete weird lately. Who would have ever thought anything could have happened like this here."

"You have that right."

The phone call from Jessica seemed to release the flood waters of information. Before long the phone was ringing off the hook with people calling and asking Dawn if they had heard about Brandon. Each one had their own opinion about it and each of them needed to share it with Dawn. For the most part, Brandon was loosing in the court of public opinion. Even though he was yet to be formally charged with anything and there was no evidence to link him to the crime, the kids at school were turning against him.

While Dawn's phone rang continuously for hours, Brandon sat alone in his jail cell with nothing more to do then to lay there and think. He was beginning to think that he was going to die from boredom but then they let another person into the jail cell. Brandon didn't get up he simply followed the person with his eyes as they let him in and then they locked the door.

"Hey, what's up." The man said with a gruff voice.

"Nothing, just sitting here. What about with you?"

"They got me for assault and battery. I guess my old lady called the cops on me. I can't wait till I get out of here after I post bail."

"Ok." Brandon responded.

Brandon was on his guard not to say much at all. He knew that the police often times used people to testify against people later.

"What are you in here for?" The man asked.

"I don't know, they haven't charged me. They are making me wait till tomorrow."

"Well, what did they arrest you for?" The man replied with agitation.

"Murder, or better a hit and run."

"You mean you're the one that hit the girl in the park?"

"No I am not the one that hit the girl in the park. I am the one that they think hit the girl in the park."

"Do you have a lawyer yet?"

"Yes."

"That was quick. I guess you want to cover your rear, don't you?"

"You know mister, what business is this to you. I don't know you from Adam. As far as I know you are an under cover cop just trying to get me to incriminate myself. So why don't you just go over to the other corner and leave me alone." Brandon said angrily.

"Have it your way kid. But you have to be one heartless human being to do something like that."

"Yeah, about as heartless as someone who beats up a woman, right?" Brandon retorted.

With that last statement the man's face turned red with anger.

"Listen here kid, you know nothing about it. She was asking for it, she drove me to it, so there. At least I didn't run her over with my car and leave her in a ditch to die." The man answered back.

Rather than continue the banter between them Brandon just left it go and lay back on his cot. The man laid back on his, even though he was visible still upset he decided to leave Brandon alone for the time being. After that Brandon's time of solitude was over. In a few minutes they brought in another honorable citizen. He entered the cell and looked around and saw Brandon laying there and then he saw the first man sitting on the cot in the other corner. He could tell that Brandon was in no mood to talk so he went over to the first man and started to talk to him. Brandon tried not to move but look at them both out of the corner of his eye. At this point he was concerned that the two might try and attack him. As the new guy sat next to the first man they started to whisper amongst themselves. After a quick conversation the new guy stood up and started to walk over to Brandon's cot.

"So you're the guy that killed the little girl in the park?" He said with disgust.

Brandon laid there and acted like he didn't hear the man.

"Hey kid, I said, you're the one that killed the girl in the park." The man said again slightly raising his voice.

Again Brandon just laid there like a stone, acting as if the man didn't even exist. The man had walked closer to Brandon by this time.

"Hey kid, I am talking to you. You think you're tough or something?"

The man had arrived at Brandon's cot and was standing over him staring down at Brandon with an angry scowl.

"I heard you mister. Just leave me alone. I don't want to talk to you or anyone else. I am just waiting for my bail to be set."

"OK, punk." The man answered and went and sat down next to the wife beater.

Brandon started to worry to himself that if these two guys thought he was guilty, who else on the outside, thought he was guilty.

Later on a drunk driver was brought in but he did little, other than lay on a cot and sleep off his drunkenness. For the most part for the rest of the evening Brandon sat there keeping to himself and saying as least as possible.

That night Brandon laid there pondering the day and what was going to happen tomorrow all the while trying to keep a good watch on the other guys in the room.

That night the detective in charge of the investigation kept on hounding the CSI lab on whether the car had been processed or not. Every time they told him that they were working on it and they would get back with him. Eventually a CSI technician delivered the report to the detective. It was one sheet of paper.

"Here is your report detective." The technician told him.

"This is it?"

"Yes it is."

"What no, trace of hair, blood or fabric?"

"Nothing, the car is clean. There are no fibers, hairs, blood. Nothing, all I can tell you for sure is that he hit something with the car. But as it stands now, it doesn't appear that this car was used in the hit and run."

"Thank you." The detective told the tech as he walked away.

"What is going on here?" He thought to himself. "This makes no sense at all. If he hit her, there should be some evidence left behind. No one could clean the car that good."

The news intrigued the detective enough that he started from scratch and took a look at the investigation from the beginning. He started to go through the only witness' statement and the medical examiner's report.

"All he said is that he found her in the ditch and he saw a car going by that matched Brandon's." He thought to himself as he read the report again.

"Cause of death: Severe trauma to the face and head." The report read.

Something wasn't right. Everything pointed to Brandon but none of the pieces to the puzzle fit.

As he read the reports over and over there was something about the witness that stuck out to him, but he couldn't figure out what.

After he had looked through the files another dozen times he decided that he had enough and would get ready to go home. He cleaned up his desk and went to put on his jacket when he looked at the witness' name; John Villisca.

Even before he had finished typing the auto fill had filled in the name for him.

"I knew it; I knew that I had head of that name before." The detective thought to himself.

"Villisca axe murders." The search engine provided.

The detective went to tell his partner what he had found when he looked up and realized that everyone had left for the day and he was the only detective there at the time. He decided that it all could wait till the morning and headed home. Even though he had left the station the questions about the case and the new found information about the witness wouldn't allow him to sleep. It was all he could think of. He kept on trying to tie up all of the loose ends but things still didn't make any sense.

Chapter 30

Brandon got up from his bunk and started to walk around. He was tired, very tired. He barely slept at all the night before. He still didn't trust the other guys in the cell with him and was always looking over his shoulder.

An officer came around with some "breakfast", if that's what you want to call it, but Brandon was hungry and ate it, regardless of how awful it was. He was counting the seconds till his lawyer return and he would see what was going on.

For the detective on the case his morning was filled with calls to the D.A. on what they were going to do with Brandon. The D.A. didn't want to, but without any physical evidence linking the crime to Brandon they would have to let him go.

At 9:00 the officer came to the cell and called for Brandon and he opened the door and let him out. Brandon's lawyer was there and they proceeded to get his stuff from the processing office. As they walked the lawyer proceeded to tell Brandon that there was quite the media circus waiting for him as he would leave the police station and to let him do the talking. After signing his release and getting his wallet and car keys back they headed for the door, Brandon two steps behind the lawyer.

As they exited the building there seemed to be a hundred people around the exit. Reporters were there pushing their microphones into the lawyers face.

"What do you have to say about your client's release?" The one report asked.

"My client is innocent and the evidence proves this." The lawyer responded

"Why did they arrest your client then in the first place? Every thing points to him as the main suspect?" Another reporter asked.

"May I remind all those listening, that in this country a person is innocent until proven guilty. There was nothing to implicate my client and so they had to let him go."

"What about the death threats that your client has been receiving? Are you concerned that people may take the law into their own hands?"

"Let it be known that my client had nothing to do with the death of Grace Smith and that there in nothing that ties him to this tragedy and all of this coverage simply takes away from the fact that an innocent girl was killed and the person who did it is still out there." The lawyer answered as he quickly put Brandon into the car.

"Are you alright?" The lawyer asked Brandon.

"Yeah." He answered though he was a little shell shocked.

The lawyer talked about what was going to happen next and as long as he had nothing to do with Grace's death he had nothing to worry about. He told him that they could find no physical evidence linking his car was the one that hit Grace.

It wouldn't take long for them to arrive at Brandon's trailer. To both of their demise, there were people there waiting for them. This time along with some news reporters there were kids form school and neighbors as well.

"I gave our statement at the police station. My client has nothing to say." The lawyer said before the new reporters could even ask Brandon anything.

"Killer!" Someone yelled as the two entered the trailer.

It caused Brandon to twitch like he had been hit with a live wire. He was definitely shaken when he walked into the living room and saw his mother standing there. She had tears running down her face and he could see that the telephone was off the hook. She reached out and took her son and gave him the strongest hug of his life.

"I knew you couldn't do something like this. I just knew it." She told him as a set of new tears started to flow down her cheeks.

"Its OK mom, I'm fine, this will all blow over soon enough. I tried to tell them all that it wasn't me."

"Is there anything that I can do to help before I leave?" The lawyer asked.

"No, thank you, thank you for getting my boy back." Mrs. Phillips said.

"I will be in touch. Try to stay low for awhile. It seems that some people have already convicted you. Just wait it out. They will find the person that did this soon enough." He said assuredly as he left.

The crowd started up again as he shut the door and headed to his car. Brandon and his mother could see that they might have some tough times on the way.

"Why is the phone off the hook?" Brandon asked his mother.

"I just got tired of it ringing continuously. People would call and ask questions or call and threaten us."

"What?"

"Some idiots were calling threatening to do what the justice system couldn't."

"Mom, maybe we should get out of here for a while, it might not be safe." Brandon told her.

"Look son, I am tire of running. I told you before that no one not even your father was going to make me run this time and I am telling you now that I am going no where."

"OK." He said as he gave her another hug.

"I love you mom."

"I love you too."

"Are you hungry?" She asked.

"Yeah, the stuff they gave us for breakfast shouldn't have even been called food. I am not sure what it was."

"Well, what do you want?"

"Anything, it doesn't matter, just something to wash that taste out of my mouth."

She laughed a little as she headed for the kitchen to fix some breakfast. She was filled with joy and elation to know that even though the crowd might think he was guilty she knew that he wasn't and that he was home again.

Brandon turned on the TV. He was still in a state of shock of what had transpired in the last two days and still couldn't believe that it was happening. He was also concerned that the people of the town not only thought he was getting away with murder but that some of them might just take the law into their own hands. At least he felt safe in the house, and had made up his mind that he wasn't going to leave it unless there was a fire.

Later that day as the D.A. headed out of the courthouse he was approached by a reporter.

"Why did you choose not to charge Brandon Phillips for the death of Grace Smith?"

"I can not hold a person without cause or evidence. Yes Brandon Phillips was a suspect but after we reviewed all of the evidence there was none, absolutely no evidence to tie Brandon Phillips to this case. Now excuse me I have to be somewhere." The D.A. said as he got into his car.

The news crew was satisfied that they got their story and packed up all of their equipment and headed to Albany.

Detective Sayers was seated at his desk as his partner Detective Jones came in to the building and sat at his desk.

"Did you even go home last night, Brian? Have you been here all night? You look like crap?"

"I went home but thinking about this case kept me up all night. This is getting weirder by the moment." The detective told his partner.

"Why is that?" Detective Sayers replied.

"Well I Googled the witness' name last night and the Villisca axe murders."

"What?"

"Yeah, the witness' name is the same name as the town in Iowa where a family was murdered in 1912. I am starting to think that the Brandon kid had little or nothing to do with this and that the witness might be our new suspect."

The detective called the dispatch officer and asked to talk to the officer that took the witness statement the night that Grace was killed and asked if he could describe the witness. The officer gave his description to a sketch artist who tried his best to come up with a composite of the witness. They then gave the composite to all of the officers and told them to be on the lookout for the man and gave a copy to the local TV stations to see if they could get any information on his whereabouts. After they were done the two detectives headed back to the park to see if there was anything that might have been missed that night. After going to the park they headed downtown to see if anyone around had seen the witness.

To both of their surprise some people said that they had seen him around and he seemed new to town. Most people said that he seem to just show up and didn't think he was from Saratoga Springs.

For the next couple of days Mrs. Phillips had made arrangements with the principal that Brandon could get his assignments and work at home for the week to allow things to settle down before he went back to school. Two days after the police impounded his car Brandon received a phone call from the lawyer telling him that they had release his car from evidence and that he could go pick it up. That was wonderful news to Brandon but his mother had headed for work and he had no way to get there, so he started to make some phone calls to some of his friends in order to pick up his car from the police impound yard. One after the other made some sort of excuse why they couldn't drive him down there and then quickly got off the phone. It was like no one wanted to even be associated with him anymore. As a last resort he called, Bill.

Bill could hardly believe his ears when he picked up the phone and heard Brandon's voice on the other line.

"Bill, this is Brandon. I know things have been rough between us lately but I need some help." Bill heard Brandon say on the other line.

At first Bill was just ready to give him a piece of his mind and hang up the phone, but something inside wouldn't let him do it so he let Brandon talk.

"I can't find anyone to help me and I need to go down to the police impound yard to pick up my car. Could you give me a ride? Please." Brandon asked.

There was a brief period of silence to where Brandon was certain that Bill was just trying to come up with an excuse to say no. But to Brandon's amazement he said yes.

"Alright, I will be there in a minute or two." Bill told him.

"Thanks, thank you very much." Brandon said, like a kid at Christmas.

Chapter 31

The day started with clouds and a cold mist. Dawn could feel the cold in her bones as they arrived at the funeral home. As her mother parked the two popped their umbrellas and headed for the door. She still found it hard to believe that she was actually there, that Grace was really gone. It was just the other day that they were together watching movies and eating popcorn.

The family had decided to only have one day for a receiving line and then a small private ceremony at the end. Dawn knew that she had to go now if she ever wanted to say goodbye to here friend.

She tried to keep the tears from welling up in her eyes as she tried to stay strong as she entered the receiving line. There weren't that many people there so it didn't take her that long to meet up with Mrs. Smith standing there along with Max.

Dawn was surprised, for the first time, Mrs. Smith didn't seem self absorbed. She was well a dressed, but didn't seem to be worried about her appearance like so many times before. It seemed to Dawn that she would spend hours in front of a mirror making sure that every hair was in place and that every thing looked just right.

As her turn arrived she hugged her and Mrs. Smith reached out and hugged Dawn giving her a hug that seemed to transfer all of the feeling that Destiny felt into Dawn. It was almost overwhelming as Dawn tried to remain under control. Dawn knew that if she shed one tear she wouldn't be able to stop. No, this was a time to be strong. She would cry in the car on the way home or in her room.

Max could see what was going on and took a step over to his mother and released Dawn from her grip. Just as the hug from Mrs. Smith filled her with raw emotion a hug from Max calmed her down immediately. One look into those dark eyes of his and all fear and grief went away. As Dawn thought about it, everyone in the family had the same eyes, dark and hollow, like looking into a well and not being able to see the bottom.

"I am sorry for your loss; I loved her like a sister. I will miss her." She told Max as he released her from his embrace.

"It's OK we all loved her and she will be missed." Max said.

"Max this is my mother, Trisha." Dawn said as she introduced the two.

"Dawn, I want you to come over and help me with Graces' things." Mrs. Smith said mournfully.

"Alright, I'll be over as soon as I can?"

"That will be fine", Mrs. Smith answered.

With that the two found a seat in the back of the room. The room was filled with people but she didn't seem to know any of them. They all seemed to be looking at them, watching their every move. Dawn then realized that she seemed to be the only person from school that actually came to the funeral home.

Dawn realized that Grace was a little backwards, maybe a little weird at times but that was no reason not to come and say they were sorry.

As she sat down she seemed to be overwhelmed again with emotion. It seemed like the whole room was an empty pit filled with people without hope. They all seemed to have the same hopeless look on their face. Hollow eyes filled with despair. She seemed very much out of place, like a candle in a darkened cathedral, the only light in the midst of a darkness that could almost be felt. It was all too much for her to fully process. First she had to say goodbye to her father and now to her best friend. But as good as friends as they were, Grace was always guarded. She always seemed to be hiding something. Always watching what she said when it came to certain subjects. She always seemed to have a dark side to her, an area that no one was able to penetrate, a side that seemed beyond repair. Though Dawn always tried to get her to open up, she wouldn't. After a while Dawn left it alone, Grace always seemed like a fragile flower and Dawn didn't want to hurt her.

Sitting in the back Dawn's mind wandered to all of the times that Grace and she were together. All the fun they had and all the good times that they had together. Dawn still couldn't understand what would cause someone to hit her and drive off. What kind of person would run over someone and not stop to see if the person was alright, and what if it was Brandon that intentionally killed her? No matter who did it she was filled with anger towards the person that had taken Grace and all the potential that she had. Now the world could never know the person that Grace would have been.

Soon it became apparent to Dawn that she had to leave the funeral home. There was a presence there that didn't seem normal. Sure it was sad, dismal place, but this seemed to be presence that was more than she could understand. She wanted to stay for the ceremony but the gloom and despair was becoming to strong for her to bear. She whispered to her mother that she needed to leave and her mother agreed.

As they got in the car and her mother started to drive she became overwhelmed with a wave of emotions. Being in the car she was able to release her feelings. She started to cry uncontrollably as the thought of never being able to see her again became evident.

"It's alright Baby, let it out." Her mother said compassionately.

"I'm sorry mom; I tried to keep it together." She said in-between tears

After seeming like a hour their finally arrived at home. Mrs. Sinclair parked the car and went into the house. Dawn laid her purse on the floor and headed over to the freezer. She got out a half gallon of ice cream and got a spoon and sat down on the couch. She opened the lid and started to eat the ice cream straight from the container. She was in a state of sensory overload as she continued to eat and stare at the wall.

"Dawn, get yourself a bowl." Her mother scolded her after she went to take another spoonful

Her mother's statement brought her out of her trance, the stress and emotions of the day had finally overwhelmed her stomach, without warning her stomach decided to set free its contents. Before even realizing what happened she threw up on the living room rug. She stood up in shock and dropped the container and the spoon on the floor as she ran to the bathroom. All the emotions that she had bottled up finally released as she spent the next few minutes throwing up.

Finally there was nothing left to release, physically or emotionally she stood up and wiped off her mouth with some water and rinsed her mouth with some mouth wash. She stood there staring into the mirror on the wall, looking at her own grim reflection brought her back to the present as she remembered the vomit and ice cream in the living room. She ran out to the living room to find her mother picking up the container of ice cream and the smell of vomit hit her nose.

"I'm sorry." She said out loud as she headed to the kitchen for a bucket and a sponge.

"It's alright." Her mother replied.

As she returned with the water and the sponge she turned on the radio and began cleaning the place up. With the music and the smell she was able to leave her misery behind and started to drift off to a happier place. All that evening Dawn went over thoughts and memories of Grace. All the things that they did together, all the places they went and all the secrets they shared. After a few hours of sitting there pondering, the time had come to go to sleep. She got ready for bed, changed into her pajamas, brushed her teeth, told her mother goodnight and that she loved her as she headed for bed. As she pulled back the covers and got in the bed she decided to make sure from this day on that she lived every day like it was her last. To remember that she was never promised tomorrow, she was never promised another heart beat and that life was precious, and how much she cherished her mother.

Chapter 32

Dawn was too angry to feel sad when she headed back to school. She felt like telling everyone at school what she thought of them and that they weren't worthy of Grace's friendship and they all were the biggest losers she ever met. It became apparent at lunch that some of the girls did seem sad about what happened did approach Dawn to apologize for their behavior. For most however Grace was just another weird person that they would never see again.

Mrs. Smith had made arrangements so that Dawn was allowed to clean out Grace's locker and bring her belongings home and turn in her books. Dawn decided that she would wait till school was over because she didn't want anyone gawking at her as she cleaned out the locker. The last bell rang for the school day to end and so the herd of kids headed to their buses and Dawn headed for Grace's locker. The school was almost completely deserted as she opened the locker. It was just as Grace had left it, neat and perfectly arranged; she took a deep breath and started to sort books from belongings. She put the books in a milk crate that the office had supplied and put the other stuff in Grace's own book bag. After she was finished she headed over to Grace's house to help Mrs. Smith clean up her room. It was something that she dreaded thinking about, let alone, doing, but she said she would and Dawn knew that Mrs. Smith needed some help.

As she walked up to house and knocked on the door, Dawn got lost in her thoughts, it was if Grace wasn't gone, when Mrs. Grace opened the door Dawn jumped. For a moment Dawn thought that Grace was going to open the door.

"I'm sorry I startled you. I know, it's hard to think that she's really gone."

"How are you doing Mrs. Smith?" Dawn asked as she gave her a hug.

Mrs. Smith didn't look the way she usually did. She always was dressed like she was going to meet the president or someone, even though she rarely left the house. Her hair was always done up and she was always dressed to kill. Not today though, she was still in a robe and for the first time that Grace had ever seen her, her hair wasn't done. She wasn't standing in front of a mirror making sure that everything was just so.

As they entered the house Dawn realized that for once, she didn't see a mirror in the house. That was one thing about the house that she realized was different.

Dawn's feet seemed to be made of lead as she started up the stairs with Mrs. Smith. It was the longest set of stairs that she ever had to climb. She felt like she was walking up a dark hill not knowing what was on the other side when she got to the top. As they reached the top of the stars Mrs. Smith began to cry so Dawn reached out and gave her a hug. This was not a time for words but just companionship.

"I'm sorry Dawn; I just can't go in there. It's like if I go in there I come to realize that she's not coming home. I just can't take all of this right now, take whatever you want, Dawn, I know that Grace would have wanted that. I am going to my room. I need to be alone right now."

And with that Mrs. Smith left Dawn in front of Grace's door as she headed to her bedroom, softly crying as she walked.

As Dawn entered the room she was shocked to see it in the condition that it was, it looked like a tornado had gone through the room. Everything was in disarray and there were piles of clothes all over the place. Dawn was completely taken back as she entered the room. Every other time that she had been in Grace's room it was immaculately clean and everything was in its place, but not now. Dawn looked at the desk and saw that pens were all scattered on the top, this was something that she never saw before. Grace always had the pens in her exact order. The bed spread and sheets were off the bed and the mattress wasn't sitting in the frame like it should be, it was also out of position from normal. Grace always made sure that her bed was always six inches from the wall, even if she had to measure it. All of the drawers in her desk were pulled out and their contents were in heaps on the floor. Every drawer to her dresser was open and clothes were hanging out of them. It looked like someone had gone through Grace's room looking for something or that Mrs. Smith went a little crazy when she found out that Grace was killed. Dawn didn't have time to really think about all of this, all she wanted to do is get the job done and get out of there. Dawn sat down on the bed and took a look around. A tear fell from her face as she thought that this would be the last time she would be in this room. The totality of what happened finally hit her as she realized that Grace wouldn't be coming home. She would have broken down and start crying but in the quiet of the moment she could here Mrs. Smith sobbing quietly. She regained control of herself, one thing that she didn't want to do was to upset Mrs. Smith any more than she already was. Dawn sat on the bed she and was flushed with memories, there were so many good ones made there, so many nights they talked together about school, boys and other things.

As Dawn looked down at the floor she saw a small snow globe laying there she picked it up and she started to look at it closely. It was an ordinary snow globe like any other. The only thing strange about it was the date on the bottom. It had a date of 1940 on it.

"Wow, it must have been Grace's mothers or something."

Dawn moved from the bed to the chair in front of the desk and started to go through the drawers of the desk. The drawers had papers and notebooks stuffed in them with no order. Dawn pulled a pile out of the drawer and set it on the top of the desk. Dawn started to sort the papers and the notebooks out. The papers seemed just to be old homework and had no significance. There was a notebook she found labeled with the month and year. She opened it to find out that it was a journal that Grace had kept. It was of the last few days that she had on earth. For the most part the entries were pretty mundane and Dawn really didn't like reading it, it made her feel like she was invading her privacy. But Dawn hoped that maybe the journal would shed some light on why she took her own life. Dawn skimmed through the pages which revealed very little about her last days, but she stopped when she read, "I saw Phillip today. I suppose that Leopold sent him here. I guess my time is up."

"That's weird." Dawn thought to herself.

She was intrigued and turned the page only to find that the rest of the pages of the journal had been torn out.

Dawn went through the rest of the desk trying to find the missing pages to no avail. She realized that the notebooks were all labeled with a month and a year. Dawn was surprise when she opened one of them and started reading it. Each page had a date and something written about the day. She was surprised to think that Grace kept a diary, but she also thought that it might have been good therapy for her condition. For the most part the entries were as normal as anyone's life might have been. Simple entries like; "Went to the mall, couldn't find anything that I liked." Dawn not wanting to pry to much into Grace's personal life put the notebook down and opened up another drawer. It was filled with more notebooks. They too were thrown into the drawer in no particular order. Dawn sorted through them to see if there were any newer ones. She finally found one that was dated around the time Mrs. Sinclair and Dawn went to meet the Smiths. Dawn was intrigued with the journal and decided that she had to know what Grace was feeling and if her journals keep shed any light on her mental status.

She started to read the first page with nothing more than an entry; "Just another day." As she flipped through the pages there were more and more simple entries of how bored she was with life and she didn't know how much longer she could go around again. As she turned the page she almost missed a small entry. But as she went to turn the page she stopped and read the entry again.

"I met a Dawn today, her mother and she came over to welcome us to the neighborhood. She even tried to get to know me, I couldn't believe it. If she only knew the truth, I don't thing that she would be so nice."

Dawn wasn't sure of what to think about the entry.

With an entry like that Dawn had to sift through the notebooks again and look for an older one. She remembered that Grace moved to Saratoga Springs about the same time Dawn's dad was preparing to go to Bosnia.

After a minute or two looking through the piles of notebooks she found the one that was listed a month earlier than the other. She opened it up in anticipation of finding out something about the girl she thought she knew but now seemed like a stranger.

"Just arrive today and moved into the house. What a mess and what a headache. I hope this is the last time that we move for awhile. I am tired of moving every 5 years. Maybe some day I can get back to Hawaii, I miss it there. "

Dawn felt like she was reading the latest mystery novel by this time. With every page it seemed that the girl she called a sister was more complex than she could have ever imagined.

Dawn felt bad for Grace after realizing what torment she was in and the need to have everything documented that she did in life. It seemed that Grace had to have everything just the way she wanted it and not being in total control of everything seemed to drive her a little crazy.

Some of the pages had doodles on them while other had very detailed drawings. Some though had dark images that were startling for Dawn to see. Some were images of death and Grace's idea of hell. She seemed to be as hopeless as the rest of the ones that were at the funeral home. It seemed that everyone tied to Grace had the same dark cloud of despair over their heads.

The next daily entry almost caused Dawn to drop the notebook in disbelief.

"Went to the college today to see where Mr. Sinclair worked. Too many people there couldn't get him alone. Maybe I can try again tomorrow or maybe in the parking lot, going to be hard to do. Very well known and liked. "

"What in the world did Grace want to do with my father?" Dawn though to herself.

After she read the pages she placed them in her purse and went on with the job at hand.

She put the papers in a box along with the notebook and after the desk was clean she opened the closet. This was the one thing that Dawn always found peculiar about Grace. She always dressed like she was in the 1940's or something. She never seemed to have any fashion sense at all. Grace always said that it was the time she wished she lived in and that she like the clothes. It was one of the major factors of her exclusions in school. No one ever wanted to see past the oddly dressed girl and look at the person behind the dress. They all seemed so shallow to never notice what she had to offer. Only the outside seemed to matter to them.

Dawn was shocked as she opened the door to see that there were clothes all over the floor and boxes all piled in a heap in the corner.

"What happened here?" She thought.

She started to pick up the dresses that were on the floor and laid them on the bed. She was surprised at the amount of clothes that Grace had, though some of them seemed pretty dated and home made.

She took each dress and laid it on the bed as if each was once owned by a queen. She went through every pocket and made sure there was nothing in them. Mrs. Smith had told Dawn to take what she wanted and she would give away the rest. Dawn really didn't want any of the clothes, she would feel weird wearing a dead person's clothes and she really didn't like Grace's sense of style, so she put them all in the boxes for the mission.

As she finished the dresses she went on to the heap of boxes that were left. She sighed as she started to open each one and find out was inside each of them. For the most part there was nothing outstanding in any of them. Most were filled with shoes or hats.

"She loved to wear those hats." Dawn said out loud.

She took the hats out and looked at them. Some were very ornate and pretty, but Dawn couldn't see herself wearing one.

"These are something that my grandmother would wear." She said.

She put the hat back and started on another box. After what seemed to be a hundredth box of shoes she came to the bottom of the pile and could finally see the floor. The last box seemed to be a larger hat box than the rest and when she picked it up it was rather heavy. She carried the box to the bed and slowly opened the lid.

"What's this?" She mumbled to herself.

On the top of the pile was a mirror that filled the box.

"Why would you put a mirror in a box?" Dawn asked herself.

"She pulled the mirror out of the box and revealed an old photo album. She pulled the album out of the box and sat on the bed, proceeding to look through it just to be nosey and started to look at the pictures. It was at this moment that Dawn realized that there were no pictures in the house, no family portraits, no school pictures, nothing.

As she opened the album it was filled with old family photos. Most were in black and white but some were in color, but they were all faded from age.

"Why would anyone take black and white pictures in this day and age?" She wondered.

For the first time Dawn could see a picture of Grace's family. Mrs. Smith was young and beautiful and Mr. Smith was ruggedly handsome. In many of the pictures Max was in them, though he didn't look any different than he did now, in fact, Grace looked the same too. As Dawn started to think about the pictures, she started to look for some landmark or time stamp in order to see when the photos were taken. As she looked through the pages she came to a picture that shocked her. It was Grace blowing out the candles on her 16 birthday. That just didn't make sense. She knew Grace for over 2 years; she was easily 17 or 18. Dawn stopped for a minute and then thought about the picture again. Dawn suddenly realized that she never did find out when Grace's birthday was. Grace never talked about it and she never had a birthday party. As she looked at each picture more diligently she realized that there was not a TV in the house, just and old box, she later realized to be an old radio. The more pictures she looked at the more confused she became. The cars in the photos were old, they were big and boxy, and nothing like the cars of today, and in one of the pictures Dawn could see an old theater with the marquee showing, "The Maltese Falcon".

"What movie is that", she thought.

"I have never heard of that one."

Dawn was surprised to see that Grace was happy once and seemed to have friends at one time, if only Dawn could figure out when that was.

She carefully tried to peel the tape off the corner of the photo in order to get it out of the album without tearing it. As she slowly removed it she looked on the back. It simply had a date stamp on it. Aug 1940.

"That doesn't make any sense." She said to herself as she pondered the age of the photos.

After a minute or two she stopped pondering and started looking again. There were photos of Hawaii and their house and Grace's father in uniform. When she had looked through about half of the album the photos stopped and new paper articles filled the rest.

The first set of articles were from Hawaii and mentioned a car accident where four people were killed and another had a front page story dated Aug 1940 saying, "Night of the Capua, Community Gripped in Fear." As she thumbed through the pages they all were the same about people dying or being murdered. The articles made Dawn cringe; it seemed that Grace had some fixation with death or murder. After looking at another page she put the album back in the box and decided to get back to work. She had finished the closet and now she was working on the chest of drawers. It was filled with sweaters and the like, just like the rest of Grace's clothes, nice but severely outdated. A few hours later, but it seemed like an eternity by Dawn, she had finished. She had neatly sorted all of Grace's clothes and her belongings and had them ready to go.

She was almost scared to death when she turned to leave and Max was standing in front of her.

"I'm sorry; I didn't mean to startle you." Max said after he saw her jump.

"It's OK; I didn't know that you were here. I thought that only your mother was in the house."

"I just got back from taking care of some things." He replied.

"I should have knocked."

"That's alright, I just got finished. Everything is packed up and ready to go." She said with a slight tremor in her voice.

"We're all going to miss her." He told her.

She proceeded to show Max the way she had the boxes laid out and how she sorted them. She picked up the box that said Mom on it and gave them Grace's mother.

"I found some things that I am sure that you would want. I showed Max how I sorted everything so I am done." She said caringly.

"Thanks, Dawn. Thanks from the bottom of my heart. You will never know how much she loved you and how much your friendship meant to her." She told Dawn as she reached out and gave her a hug.

"Keep in touch Dawn; you will always be part of the family. I love you." She told Dawn with a mother's affection.

"I will Mrs. Smith, and I love you too." Dawn replied.

"Where are your manners Max? Walk the young lady to her car." She scolded Max.

"Pardon me, Dawn. I am sorry. I guess I wasn't paying attention." He replied.

She waved to Mrs. Smith as Max opened the door and they both headed outside. Max opened the door and helped Dawn get into the car. As she sat down she opened the window to say goodbye.

"Can we get together? There are some things I need to know about Grace." She asked Max.

"Should I call you?" He replied.

"Sure, we can set a time and date." She answered.

"Alright, then we will call it a date." He said with a slight smirk on his face.

At that instant Dawn realized that she had just asked Max out on a date and not the other way around. Her face flushed with red as she realized her social gaffe.

"OK then." She replied trying to keep her composure.

"See you then." Max told her as she started the car and drove off.

"Smooth Dawn, really smooth, dad would kill you if he knew that you asked a guy out." She thought to herself.

"I'll keep this one to myself. There's no reason to throw gas on the fire." She said as she headed for home.

Max went back into the house.

"You alright Mom?" He asked.

"I'm ok. She's a nice girl." She replied holding the box Dawn gave her on her lap.

"Yes, she is. Do you want anything to eat?"

"No, I am alright; I'm not really hungry right now." She told him.

"Ok, I have to go out for a while. I will back in a little while." He told her as he headed back out.

"You stay safe, and keep away from Leopold." She told him with a slight tremor in her voice.

"I will Mom. Take it easy. I will be ok. Love you." He replied as he kissed her head lovingly and headed for the door.

"Max?" She said right before he opened the door to walk out.

"Yes Mom?"

"You know the truth, right?"

"Yes, Mom, I know the truth." He said with a grim look on his face as he left the house.

Dawn arrived home to find her mother sitting at the kitchen table. She seemed to be in deep thought as she read some paperwork or something. Dawn tried to walk to her room hoping to go unnoticed but her mother stopped her.

"How did it go?" She asked.

"OK, I guess. It was very sad. I now know how you felt when you had to do it for Dad. I'm sorry I left you to do it by yourself. I just couldn't."

"It's OK. Everybody deals with grief differently. Was her mother there?"

"Yes, but she didn't say much and I heard her crying somewhere in the house, it was really sad, Max, showed up when I got done."

"Max?" She asked inquisitively.

"Yeah, Max. What are you implying Mom?"

"Nothing." She remarked with a playful smirk.

"I'm going to my room for a while." She told her mother shaking her head.

"What do you want for dinner?"

"It doesn't matter. I'm really not that hungry right now, anything but another pizza." She interjected before disappearing into her room.

Mrs. Sinclair realized that they might have had one to many pizzas from the local pizza shop.

Dawn went into her room and shut the door. She sat on her bed and opened her purse and opened the notebook papers again.

The last entry of the notebook simply said; "I saw Phillip today. Apparently Leopold has given the order. I am so tired and I am ready."

"Who are these people, and why would they want to kill her." She thought to herself.

It seemed the more that she was able to delve into Grace's private life the weirder thing became. She had to stop for a minute to keep from getting sucked into Grace's paranoid delusion and start to focus on something else. She pulled her homework out of her book bag and stated to go over the stuff that needed to be done. After reading through her assignments she pulled out her flash drive to edit some pictures for the PowerPoint presentation she was working on. After dozing off for the sixth time she decided she had enough and got ready for bed.

She woke up with the alarm so she got ready and came down to eat breakfast.

"Did you sleep well?" her mother asked.

"Not at all, I kept having nightmares about Grace, and it felt like someone was in the room with me at times. It was really weird."

"Did any of them have anything to do with Max?"

"No, Mom." She replied with a slight annoyance,

"We're just friend's mom, right now he is just trying to keep his mother in check after Grace's death. She really is kind of strange at times. She used to be totally self absorbed, sitting in front of a mirror for hours worried about the way she looked. Lately though she has been sitting in a chair mumbling to herself."

"Dawn, it could be her way of just dealing with the loss of her daughter. Loosing a child is the worst pain that there is. It might be the only way that she can cope with the loss."

"I realize that, she actually seems a little more normal lately. She hasn't been as vain as usual. The other day she actually opened the curtains and let the sun in. Usually the house is as dark as a cave. "

"Well, we all grieve in our own way."

"I guess."

"The bus is here, you better get out there."

"See you later Mom, I love you."

"I love you too, have a good day."

Chapter 33

Max called just as he said he would and set up a date with Dawn. She was overjoyed but she tried to stay as calm and cool as she could. She didn't want him to think that she was too anxious. Later Max pulled up to the house and knocked on the door. Dawn's mother opened the door and asked him to come in. His politeness even caught Mrs. Sinclair off guard. He seemed to be the most courteous person that she ever met. It even made her feel a little uncomfortable around him. Dawn wasn't ready as usual so Max had to wait in the living room and spent the time talking to Mrs. Sinclair. Mrs. Sinclair put the time to good use and tried her best to give him the third degree, though she tried to be very diplomatic about it. Max just sat there and answered her questions without a problem and waited patiently until Dawn came down. After the third time of Mrs. Sinclair telling her to hurry so they wouldn't be late Dawn finally arrived at the living room.

She apologized for making him late and after kissing her mother on the cheek told her goodbye and headed for the door and off to Max's car. Mrs. Sinclair watched through the door window as he opened the car door for her and off they went.

After they left Mrs. Sinclair sat on the couch and tried to analyze the new man in Dawn's life. So far she had nothing but good things about him, but that didn't keep her motherly instincts from kicking in.

He was a complete gentleman with good looking features, even though she noticed that he had a large scar on the side of his face from near the back of his ear almost down to his neck and he had the darkest eyes she had ever seen, just like Mrs. Smith and Grace. She noticed that he had large hands with long thin fingers but that his skin tone was whiter than most people's. After a few more minutes of deep thought she felt that Dawn would be ok and turned on the TV and waited for them to return.

As they arrived at the theater Max parked the car and opened the door for Dawn. She was always taken back by how courteous he was, he always treated her like a special lady and was never harsh or demanding. As they headed to the entrance Dawn noticed that Brandon was walking past. He simply looked at the two of them with a coy look of dislike and then his appearance suddenly changed. Brandon went to turn around and say something to Dawn but his better judgment took over and let them walk away.

"Someone you know?" Max asked.

"Just my old boyfriend, that's all."

That was all that was said and Max didn't bring it up again. Max bought the tickets as they came to the box office and then entered the theater. He proceeded to get some popcorn and drinks. As Max waited Dawn told him that she had to use the restroom and would be back. At this point Max became aware of someone staring at them. As he tried to see who it was the person went on acting like they were doing something else. Max made it seem like he didn't get a good look, but he did.

Out of the corner of his eye he could see Brandon staring at him through the lobby window. Brandon was looking at Max like he had seen him somewhere before. Max turned slowly and looked right at Brandon. Brandon looked back and mouthed "It was you." And then he walked away.

Soon the popcorn was ready along with the drinks and Dawn had returned. They gave the matron the tickets and he ripped them in half and told them where to go. As they entered the theater and found their sits Grace took off her coat and went to put it on the seat next to her. Max's whole body quivered as he looked at her as he noticed that she was wearing the necklace that Grace had given her.

"What's the matter Max? Is there a spider on me or something?" She asked inquisitively.

"Where did you get that necklace?" He asked abruptly.

The question shocked Dawn considering that he was nothing less than a perfect gentleman any time before.

"You sister gave it to me? Why, what is the problem? What is wrong with you?" She answered him slightly annoyed.

He was just about to answer her when he took a good look around the theater and became aware of the other people in the room. As they were seated Max saw a man sitting in the back row that he recognized.

They were a little early and there wasn't many people in the theater yet and Max tried to talk in a whisper.

"Dawn, you have to give me the necklace."

"What?"

"You have to give me the necklace, now." He tried to keep his voice down.

"What's wrong with you? Ever since you saw me wearing this you've been acting weird. You act like it's the Hope diamond or something."

"Dawn, I told you I would explain this all some day. But you have to trust me."

"I still don't understand."

Max leaned over and talked softly into her ear.

"Do you see that woman down front, with the brown hair?"

"Yes." She whispered back.

"Her name is Marie and the man in the back row is names Alberto. They're here to get that necklace."

"I'm not going to give this necklace up to anyone. Grace gave it to me the day she was killed. It was the last time I saw her alive and I am not about to give it you some stranger."

"If you don't give me the necklace, Dawn, they will take it, even if it means killing you and me." Max retorted in the softest tone he could.

At this point Dawn was scared and confused and went back to a feeling that Max was a little to far out there for her taste. She then reached back and unclasped the necklace and placed it in his hands.

"Do not leave the theater, understand?" He told her as he headed for the exit.

"OK." She whispered back.

He pulled out his cell phone as he left the theater. He dialed Leopold's number.

"This is Leopold." The voice on the other end answered.

"This is Max; I have the heart, call off your dogs now."

"What are you talking about?"

"Marie and Alberto are here, call them off. I have the heart."

"I am so happy to hear that Max. But as for Marie and Alberto, I have no idea why they are there. I did not send them there."

"Maybe you didn't but I am sure that you told them who might have the heart, right?"

"Max, don't get so upset. You know I only do things in order to maintain and protect our way of life. Don't worry I will make sure that nothing happens to your little friend. Just remember Max, who you are and what you belong to. You wouldn't want her to get hurt."

"I understand"

"Alberto should be headed your way, give it to him."

"OK"

With that Alberto appeared and Max handed him the necklace.

"I knew you would do the right thing, Old Boy. You shouldn't play with fire Max; you might end up getting burnt."

"Just take your prize and get away from me you wolf."

"What a nice thing to say Max. Have a great day, you never know who you might meet around here, now do you." Alberto said as he gave a slight grin.

Alberto left the lobby and Max went back to Dawn he saw that Marie was gone also.

"Well?" Dawn asked.

"Well, I gave it to Alberto. Leopold told me that there will be no more trouble."

"Max I don't understand the mystery about the necklace. What is the big deal?"

"I'll explain it all after the movie."

"You tell me that someone is here willing to kill me over a piece of jewelry and you want to watch the movie?"

"Well, let's go then."

They headed out of the theater and down to the diner as they sat down and the waitress came over to take their order.

"I just want a coke, I don't feel very hungry." Dawn told her.

"I'll have the bacon cheeseburger, and will you make it rare, with a coke also."

The waitress took the order and then left them alone.

"How can you eat, after what has just happened?"

"I am sorry about that; I just haven't eaten all day. I could eat a horse at this point."

"OK, OK, tell me what is going on and don't hold back, I want to know it all."

"OK, here goes, just wait until I am done until you freak out, OK?"

"OK."

"My name is Maximillian Cmerci. I was born in Warsaw Poland in 1810.
"That would make you over? 180 years old."
"I told you, to wait until you start with the questions."
"I'm sorry, go on."

I grew up a normal kid. Chopin lived in my neighborhood; his sister taught me how to play the piano. In 1830 my brother was part of an uprising against the Russians. My father told me to go down and get him before someone was killed. By the time I got there the Russians already had begun shooting people. It was mass hysteria. I finally found my brother lying on the ground dying from a gunshot. I was about to pick him up when one of the Russian pigs nearly cut my ear off with his sword."

With that Max pulled back the hair around his ear to show a long scar of where he was cut.

As I grabbed my ear he shot me and I fell to the ground and blacked out. I woke up with my father over me telling me to get up and get home. He said that he would get my brother and to meet him back at the apartment and to hurry before the Russians returned. He picked up my brother and threw him over his shoulder and we raced home before the Russians returned."

"So what does that have to do with anything?"
"It has to do with what I am."
"Well what are you?"
"I layman's terms, I am a vampire."

A shock went through Dawn's body like she was just told that she had cancer. This new man that she was attracted to just told her that he was a vampire, he instincts told her that he was a psycho and run but one look into his eyes and she was back to calm.

"So you are telling me that you are undead, is that it?" She asked with skepticism.

"No I am not undead, I am just a much alive as you are. I simply have a blood disease that gives me some abilities and a curse"

"What kind of abilities, can you run like a cheetah, do you crave blood and do you sleep in a coffin?" She asked mockingly.

"No, those are just legends, though we are strong, and we need blood at least once a year or we will slowly grow weaker and die."

"What is the curse?"

"Think about it Dawn, I am trapped in a twenty year old body, I never show signs of age. I have to go through life doing things over and over again. Do you realize how many degrees I hold, how many colleges I have attended?" He asked her.

"How many?"

"Let's see, I went to Oxford, Yale, Harvard, Princeton, Harvard Law School, John Hopkins Medical School just to name a few, I have 12 doctorates and 20 bachelor's degrees. I have been around the world 14 times; I've climbed Mount Everest three times and can speak 8 different languages. I have to move every 7 to 10 years because people start to wonder why I haven't aged. I have been every where and I have done everything that one human can do. I can never gain prominence or fame. My life will be lost to the pages of history like I never existed. Does that help explain some things?" He asked Dawn.

"Are you kidding me, that doesn't explain anything, other than you may be a raving lunatic of some sort. How do you expect me to believe something like this? I would have believed you better if you would have told me that you had been abducted by aliens."

"Look Dawn, my kind have been massacred for eons. We are creatures of legends. Some say we are the Devils children. But we are not; we are living breathing human beings just like you."

She was about to respond when the waitress came over with their order and then left.

"Well, enough said, I am famished. Are you sure you don't want a bite of my burger?"

"No, I don't want to become a vampire" Dawn retorted jokingly.

"It doesn't work that way. I would have to pass my blood to you."

"By the way, Max, you don't have pointed teeth, where are your vampire fangs."

"We don't have fangs, that's Hollywood"

Dawn still wasn't convinced that what he was talking about was real. To her he seemed like he had gone mad.

"I think it's time to go home now." She told him.

He put his burger down, took a sip of his drink and asked for the check. He left his unfinished meal and a tip and paid the bill as they left the restaurant.

"Alright, I know this is a lot to handle at one time." He told her as they headed for the car.

Max opened the car door and Dawn sat down, he shut the door and headed for the driver's seat. He got in the car and went to turn it on.

"Is there anything else that I should know?"

"Yes, and it wont be easy to hear."

"By this time, you couldn't tell me anything more shocking that what you already have."

"Brace yourself."

"I'm ready."

"Dawn, Grace was one of us. In fact she was the "Heart of Darkness"."

"You expect me to believe that Grace was a vampire too." She said trying to keep as calm as she could.

"Yes, that's why she had the necklace, it's called the "Heart of Darkness", and it proved that she was Leopold's highest ranking officer, his right hand man."

"An officer for what?"

"For the Network."

"What is this network you keep mentioning?"

"The 'Network' is a large group of people like us"

"Vampires, you mean." Dawn interrupted sarcastically.

"Let me rephrase, The 'Network' is a group of vampires that most of us belong to, and our leader is Leopold Robespierre He was the stately looking gentleman at Grace's funeral. The network allows us to live and hide in plain site; it provides us with identities and passports along with funds if we need them."

"Well, tell me this Max, if she was an assassin, who was she here in this little town to assassinate?"

"I am not sure for certain. But I think your father."

"Why would anyone want to kill my father? You are starting to act like we are all part of some sort of international conspiracy now."

"Dawn, look, I am not sure what was going on, or why they killed Grace, but I know that your father was somehow connected with it all. He had something or knew something that they wanted."

"Well, Dad was killed in Slovenia, not here. So how do you explain that one?"

"Like I said, I do not know all of the particulars. Before I take you home, do you mind stopping at my mother's house first?"

Dawn shuttered a little. Now she was afraid, what did he have in mind? For all she knew he was some sort of delusional psycho killer.

"Sure, what do you need there?"

She tried to play it cool and act as if nothing was wrong as she made sure her cell phone was on. She made sure that 911 was entered into it so all she had to do is push the call button.

"I just want to show you something. It will make all of this seem a little more real."

They arrived at Mrs. Cmirci's and knocked on the door. All the time Dawn had her cell phone in hand. Mrs. Smith answered the door and was happy to see both of them.

"Hello Dawn, this is a pleasant surprise Dawn, it's so nice to see you again."

"Hello Mrs. Smith, how are you."

"Fine, fine, welcome, come on in."

After entering Mrs. Smith told them that she would leave them alone and that she was going to bed.

Dawn started to feel even more uncomfortable at the thought of her leaving them alone. Max took Dawn by the hand and told her to come with him. She went willingly but inside she was next to screaming.

"I need to show you this."

They entered a room with a large floor length mirror on the wall.

"I want to you look at me and then look at my reflection in the mirror, ok."

"Ok." She replied, thinking that this was getting weirder and weirder every moment.

She took a long gaze at him and his dark eyes. Even though inside she felt ready to scream in terror, one look in his eyes and she was calm. She then looked at the mirror. She immediately stepped back in shock. She looked again at his reflection and then back at him.

"Look, Max, I don't know what kind of magic trick this is, but it isn't funny any more."

"It's no magic trick, it is who I am. The mirror shows how old I am."

It was as if the mirror held his true reflection of what he really looked like. To look at Max looked like a vibrant twenty year old. But in the mirror, he looked like a sad old man with white hair and wrinkles drawn all over his face. It was all too much for Dawn to take in.

"I need to go home now!"

"Alright, I'm not going to hurt you."

He reached out to touch her, but she pulled away from him quickly.

"Don't touch me, don't look at me. There is something that you do, when you look at me, isn't there? Can you hypnotize me with your eyes or something?"

She headed for the door, with Max close beside.

"It's not what it seems; forget what you've seen in the movies, I'm not like that, Mom is not like that."

"You mean, you mother is one of you, too?"

"Yes, I can tell you the story about her and Grace if you would like."

"You know Max, I have had enough of your stories for one night. I am going to home and going to bed."

"Let me drive you."

"NO! I can walk it, it's not that far."

He opened the door and she started for home. He watched her as she walked down the sidewalk. She watched him to make sure that he wasn't following her. She was filled with anger and disbelief and he was filled with sorrow and pain.

It seemed to take forever to get home, the home time the wind seemed to calling her name and she constantly felt like someone was following her. She finally arrived to an empty house as she unlocked the door and went in. Her mother was working so she would have to spend the rest of the evening by herself. She was completely freaked out but what had just happened and was trying to process the evening's events. For the first time in a long time she was afraid to be in the house alone. With every creek of the house and every blow of the wind she thought someone might be outside or worse, inside the house with her.

Like a young kid afraid of the dark she started to turn on every light in the house and then sat in the living room curled up on the couch and turned the TV on. She wanted to call someone and tell them what happened but she was afraid that they would probably think that she was crazy or something.

As she sat there trying to concentrate on the movie on the TV the phone rang. She was glad to talk to someone so she didn't even look at the caller id.

"Dawn, don't hang up, you have to listen to me." The voice said on the other side.

"Is this Brandon?" She said in a flash.

"Yes, don't hang up on me; I have to talk to you for a minute."

"Why should I talk to you, you're nothing but a jerk." She responded as she went to hang up the phone.

"Just listen, it's about the guy you were with tonight."

That sparked her attention enough to listen to what he had to say.

"So what about him are your jealous or something?"

"Maybe a little but that's not why I called. That guy"

"His name is Max and he is Grace's brother." She interrupted.

"OK; you have to stop seeing Max, he's not human or normal, there's something wrong with him."

"Brandon, what are you talking about, why are you trying to cause trouble."

"I'm not, I am telling you there is something about the guy that I would be afraid of."

"Like what, get to the point, Brandon, I am almost finished listening to you."

"Dawn, look, I am sorry for what happened and I had nothing to do with Grace's death, you have to believe me. But Max is the one that attacked my father. I am sure of it. I never saw him before tonight so I didn't know who he was."

"What do you mean attacked your father?"

"When I got to the park there was Max holding my father in his hands with this wild look on his face and his eyes were as red as the sunset. I yelled at him and then he dropped my father and ran into the woods."

"Did you tell this to the police?"

"Yes, but I didn't know who he was and I was afraid they would think I was crazy if I told him that he had red eyes."

"I can understand that, but that doesn't prove that it was Max or that he's not human."

Even though she was talking to Brandon trying to disprove his theory of Max, Dawn was thinking to herself that the story that he told her tonight might be true."

"Look, Grace, hate me all you want but there was something different with Grace too. She had some sort of power and you know it. Every time she touched me it was like she was punching me in the gut. Explain to me how a girl weighing 100 pounds beats up me and George?"

"Thanks for your concern, but I will be fine." She paused. "I don't hate you Brandon, but I do hope you get your act together, goodnight." She said politely as she hung up the phone.

She was even more shell shocked now than when she first got home. Now it seemed that Max might be telling her the truth and that he and his family were monsters.

The whole ordeal unnerved her quite a bit and she would have gone to bed but the wind was howling and she was afraid for the time being. She turned off the TV and went upstairs to her room. She decided if she was going to be scared she might as well do her homework. She plugged her flash drive into the computer and started to go through the folders when she saw a new one that she hadn't created.

"What the?" She muttered to herself.

The folder was called Grace, so he double clicked on it and the folder opened to show its contents. It was full of pictures; in fact it had the same pictures that were in the photo album in Grace's room. It appeared that Grace had scanned the pictures and somehow put them on Dawn's flash drive.

"How in the world did these get on my flash drive?" She thought.
After all of the thumbnails there was a text file named: "Read Me".
She was shocked to find that the file was a letter addressed to Dawn.

Dear Dawn,
By the time you read this, I most likely will be dead. I am sorry for what I am about to tell you and I am sure you may find it hard to believe.

I belong to a network of people; that most people would call "Vampires". I happen to be the best assassin in the network has, but that all changed when I met you.

I was sent to Saratoga Springs in order to kill you father. He was very close to revealing the actual existence of us and Leopold wouldn't let that happen. When I arrived I tried to do my job, but I was never able to get him alone and then he left.

That's when I met you. You were different; you actually tried to be my friend. It seemed like forever since anyone tried to do that. You tried to get to know me and included me in your group at school. I love you for that; it made all the difference in the world. You offered me the one thing that I needed more than anything, hope.

I decided that I could no longer be a part of the Network; in fact I told Leopold that I had the evidence that would expose him and the network to the world.

This is why they killed me.

The photo album is upstairs in my closet at the bottom of my hat boxes with a mirror on top of it. I hope you found it before they did. If you did find it give it to my mother or Max. You can trust my mother but I don't think in her mental state that she will be able to help you. You can also trust Max; he wouldn't ever do anything to hurt you. Don't trust Leopold, he will kill you in a blink of an eye, or Phillip if he shows up.

I love you like a sister and I hope you realize that because of you I finally could let go of my past and all the anger that I held.

I am sorry for everything and all the trouble that I have caused you and your family.
Love,
Grace.

The letter sent a chill through Dawn. Either the whole Smith family was crazy or what Max told her might be true. It was all a little too much for Dawn to process so she got ready for bed. She usually waited up for her mother to get home from work but she didn't want to answer a lot of questions about their date so she went to bed. As she crawled into the bed she pulled the covers up over her head like a 3 year old afraid of the dark.

"This can't be real." She whispered to herself as she fell asleep.

In the morning her mother was at the kitchen table as she walked down the stairs. She started her usual routine and sat at the table after preparing her morning cereal.

"Well, tell me how it went?" Her mother asked inquisitively.

"It was alright."

"Well what did you do?"

"Well, we went to the movies but then I didn't feel well so he took me back home."

"How do you feel now, any better?"

"I suppose, I guess I was just a little too nervous and it got the best of me."

"Well, don't worry; I am sure he will ask you out again."

"Yeah, maybe." She replied unenthusiastically.

Her mother went to say something but could tell that Dawn wasn't in the mood to talk so she let it go. Dawn on the other hand didn't like to lie to her mother, and technically she hadn't lied, she just didn't fill in all the details. At this point Dawn wasn't sure what to make of the Smith family and didn't want to get her mother involved.

After breakfast the two of them got ready and headed for church. Dawn was physically present but her mind was somewhere else. There was so much she had to think about and so many questions that still needed to be answered. She still wondered how anything that Max had told her was true but after reading the letter from Grace she wasn't all that sure. So for the day she sang the hymns and acted like she was listening to the sermon, but in reality she was as far away as China in her mind.

"Are you alright?" Her mother asked as they left the church and got into the car.

"Yes, why?" Dawn answered.

"Well, because you seemed totally preoccupied. What are you thinking about now?"

"I don't know, do we have to talk about this now?" Dawn answered with annoyance.

"No, I guess, not. I just want to make sure that you're alright, that's all."

"I'm fine, I just have so much to deal with right now."

"I know." Her mother said as she kissed Dawn's head.

As they arrived home Dawn seemed to come out of her trance and join the real world. She let Max and Grace go for the time being and relished in the afternoon with her mother. She realized that time was moving so fast and that her life was changing so quickly and that she didn't want to push her mother away. As they both were about to get out of the car her mother decided that she didn't feel like cooking and that they were going out for lunch. Dawn was thrilled with the idea as they headed into town. After lunch they spent the rest of the day at the mall, not as mother and daughter, but as friends.

Chapter 34

As Monday came and went Dawn had to keep up with her hectic schedule. Her personal life might have been in a tailspin but that didn't keep her from her responsibilities. She still had to keep up with her band duties, take her SAT test and figure out what she wanted to do for a career The College had agreed to allow Dawn to go there free because of the circumstances of her father death, so her college was already chosen for her. So Dawn tasted what life was really about and the roller coaster ride that it sometimes was, though she felt like she was more on a tilt a whirl than a rollercoaster. She felt more like her head was spinning and she was going nowhere. She had become so involved in making sure that she was going to excel her last year of high school that she almost forgot about Max. Just as she was overwhelmed with another day of assignments and things that she had to do to graduate, Max called. He apparently wanted to allow her to come to grips with every thing that he had told her about Grace and his family. She picked up the phone and he asked her if they could get together again. She was excited and looked at her calendar and conferred with her mother and came up with a date and time. They made plans to meet on Saturday for dinner and maybe a nice stroll through the park. With the plans set her little rendezvous with Max put a spark back in Dawn. Her mother laughed to herself when she saw the smile on Dawn's face as she hung up the phone. Dawn tried to remain calm and cool as she headed to her room but the change in her demeanor was quite evident. Even though she was quite excited about her date with Max she still was quite apprehensive about it all. She still wasn't sure what to think about everything but she was willing to give Max the benefit of the doubt. So far the Smith's had been nothing but nice to her and she wasn't about to throw it all away over this.

The promise of a new date with Max put the spring back in Dawn's step and it was quite evident to everyone that the Dawn that they use to know was back. It was apparent to everyone but Dawn that she was beaming and she had the look on her face like she was twelve and had a secret to tell. Brandon was quite miffed about Dawn's attitude and thought for sure that her new love interest had something to do with it. He was sure that he was an alien or vampire or something and he was going to take matters into his own hands in order to protect Dawn from him. Dawn seemed unaware of Brandon's burning anger as she left the room for the next class.

Before she realized it the lunch bell sounded as she headed for the cafeteria. Her head was in the clouds as she sat in her usual seat. Everyone there sat there staring at her as she sat down.

"What's up with you?" Bill asked.

"What do you mean?"

"I mean, what's up with you? You seem to have you head in the clouds or something." He responded.

"Oh, it's nothing, just enjoying the day. That's all. What's up with you?" She asked with a giddy laugh.

"Nothing much, same stuff, different day." He said sarcastically.

"That's good." She responded like she wasn't paying attention to anything he said.

Everyone else sat at the table, bewildered at her behavior. Just when they thought they had Dawn all figured out she would surprise them again.

Like a kid anticipating Christmas, Dawn was giddy with joy the whole week. The days were flying by as she couldn't wait for her next meeting with Max. By this time she had informed the rest of the losers that she had a date with Max and that she couldn't wait. It was kind of odd to Bill and the other guys but since there were no other girls left at the table she had to tell someone.

With each passing day and each time Brandon saw Dawn with her new found happiness it would make him even angrier. He still had to deal with the daily whispers of half the school thinking he got away with murder but it was his fixation with Max that made him the angriest.

"How could she be attracted to such a guy?" He thought to himself.

Every day that he returned home from school and his mother wasn't home he would boot up his computer and do some more research on myths and legends. At this point he was sure that Max was some sort of vampire or other creature of the night but was afraid to really tell anyone what he thought. He was afraid that anyone that he did tell would think that he was some sort of idiot for even believing that there were such creatures. Even though his common sense would tell him to step away and turn around his obsession with Dawn's safety would override such a thought. His behavior even started to worry his mother at some point. It seemed that he was slipping back into his old routine and that his grades were suffering. He assured her that he was just dealing with a lot at the moment and and that he would get his grades back up. She tried her best to believe him, but she wasn't sure what was going on.

Friday came and with it another football game.

"Keep it together girl." Dawn thought to herself as she marched with the band onto the football field.

She didn't want to cause another snafu like the suicide line incident. After this performance there was only one last home game and that would be senior night. All she had to do is get through this halftime and then she was free for the weekend. The band's performance went without incident and Saratoga Springs won the game. She came home and went to bed anticipating the next day and her date with the man of her dreams.

Dawn bolted out of bed as she heard the alarm go off. She got her robe on and headed to the kitchen. She was surprised to see her mother up and sitting at the table.

"Morning, Dawn." Her mother said.

"Good morning." She responded in a giddy fashion.

"You're bright eyed and bushy tailed this morning."

"What?" She asked in confusion.

"You know, bright eyed and bushy tailed, like a high strung squirrel.

"Mom, you really need to update your repertoire when it comes to these old sayings of yours."

"OK, I will try and learn the hip new verbiage that all the cool people use."

"OK, Mom." Dawn replied as she rolled her eyes.

"Kind of excited aren't you?" Her mother asked inquisitively.

"No, I just want this date to go right this time. I don't want to ruin it like last time."

"Don't worry, just remember."

"I know mom, go with the flow."

They both had a laugh as Dawn got her bowl out of the cupboard.

"Remember Dawn, none of us are perfect, and we all blow it sometimes. I assure you the more you get to know Max the more imperfections you are going to find."

"I know, I know." Dawn responded with a mouth full of cereal.

"Just take it slow, will you. I don't want Max to be a rebound boyfriend."

"I will mom, and I assure you, that he isn't." She told her confidently.

Even though it was only 9:30 in the morning Dawn began to rush like Max was going to be there in twenty minutes. Her nervousness became so apparent that her mother had to stop her and tell her to stop and take a breath. She did and then went back to getting ready. Even though she had the whole day to get ready and drive her mother crazy in the process she still wasn't ready by the time Max knocked on the door. Mrs. Sinclair invited him in and he graciously accepted as she showed him to his seat.

Mrs. Sinclair didn't want to give him the third degree this time so she tried to keep the conversation light. They talked about his mother and how she was doing and how the weather was unseasonably warm. She still couldn't get past his pale skin and those dark eyes. He always looked at her and anyone else for that matter, straight in the eyes. But that was one thing that got to her. There was never a reflection in them; they were always dark and hollow. He seemed to bring a cold dark presence with him, just like the one at the funeral home. She thought at the time it was just the sense of loss, but it seemed he carried a sense of despair about him. She became concerned that his dark spirit may corrupt Dawn's jovial fun loving one.

Dawn came down after a minute or two and after telling her mother goodbye they were off. Just as usual he gave her the royal princess treatment and opened the car door for her and gently held her hand as she got in and out. He was so cordial at times that Dawn wondered if it all was just an act and was trying to gain her trust.

"Where are you taking me?" She said with a giddy smile.

"No place special, just wait and he see." He said with a gentle smile.

He wouldn't tell her where they were headed but she was about to scream when they arrived at the Lake Ridge Restaurant. It was one of Saratoga Springs finest and she had never been there. She had heard stories about it but up until now it was just a dream to go there.

"Really?" She asked sheepishly as he parked the car.

"Really." He replied as he got out and opened her door.

As they entered he gave the maître d' his name and they were seated Dawn was beside herself. She never expected to end up on her second date with Max here, especially how the first one ended. She was also nervous that she was going to act inappropriately not knowing what all the rules and proper etiquette were when eating in such an establishment.

The waiter came over and as she was instructed by her mother waited for Max to order and then she made sure her order was less than his. He seemed to be aware of the custom and made sure that he ordered something that was at the top of the list so Dawn wouldn't be nervous about what she ordered. As the two sat there waiting for dinner to come, Max opened up the lines of conversation.

"Dawn, I need to ask you some questions." He said seriously.

"Alright, what do you need to know?" She replied.

"Two weeks before I arrived here I got a letter from Grace. She said that she met a girl that changed her whole outlook on life and that for once she had hope. How did you offer Grace hope?" He asked.

"I don't know, the only thing I did was be her friend and I invited her to my youth group."

"You mean Grace went to church with you?" He asked as if he couldn't believe what Dawn was saying.

"Yes, she went to church with me. What's the big deal?"

"The big deal is that the "church" has been massacring us for centuries. We have been branded as the children of the devil or even as demons at times. It was the church that hunted us down and killed off many of us. That is the big deal. We have been taught to not only fear the church but stay away from it and its members. We have been indoctrinated year after year that there is no hope of salvation for us anyway so why would we go? We've been told that we are condemned to hell and that heaven is unreachable. This is why I find it hard to believe that Grace went to church with you." He said to keep his voice down.

"Max, I don't know who has filled your mind full of these things but we all have hope. There is no one that is to far gone, as long as you're alive there is time to change. How could your soul be bound for hell when you did nothing to become this thing that you are? You have been lied to; you have the same hope that I have. All you have to do is believe. Grace did not tell me how she felt about church, but she didn't tell me much of how she was feeling anyhow. She always kept to herself. Actually, I didn't think she actually like it. She very rarely ever participated in the service at all. "

"What about my mother, did she go?"

"No, your mother was another story. She seemed to hate the church. My mother asked her once and that was the end of that."

Their dinner finally arrived as they sat there enjoying each others company. They talked between mouthfuls of food and for the most part the conversation was light. They were about half way done with the meal when Dawn decided that she needed to ask him some more questions.

"Grace told me that she saw Phillip here and the Leopold must have given the order. What did she mean by that?" She asked intently as the smile vanished from Max's face.

"I'm sorry I didn't mean to ruin the mood." She told him politely.

"It's alright; I guess the truth has to come out sooner or later. Apparently Grace had chosen to expose the network and Leopold put the order out to kill her." He said in a somber tone.

"Then Grace wasn't killed in an accidental hit and run, it was intentional?" She said with shock in her voice.

"Yes"

"And you know who did it?"

"I am not sure, but I have an idea."

"Then why don't you go to the police?"

"And tell them what? That Grace was a vampire and another vampire killed her." He said sarcastically.

"How do you know that a vampire did it, she was run over by a car. My mother said her face was completely crushed."

"That's what someone wanted the police to think. The reason the killer crushed her head was to hide the fact that Grace was drained. That is what killed her, not the car."

"What do you mean drained?" She asked.

"We heal very quickly so it is very hard to kills us in a conventional way. So, one thing a vampire can do is literally drain the life out of another. The only thing is that the vampire they drain reverts to they actual age."

"Wouldn't someone at the hospital notice that?"

"Maybe, but because it was apparent that she was dead they assumed that the accident was the cause of death."

"Tell me this, who would have believed her if she exposed this network. This all seems like some sort of fairy tale if you ask me?" She said in disbelief.

"It would have unless she had some sort of proof. She kept a diary and a photo album. It was the photo album that they are after. Apparently she kept a record of all the murders that she and Leopold were involved in. It could very well destroy the Network and put us all in danger."

When Max mentioned the photo album she flinched a little, she told him later that it was just a chill. In fact she wasn't sure if she should tell anyone that she gave the album to his mother and that Grace made a digital copy of it.

As they continued eating their conversation slowed and it allowed both of them to finish. Max asked for the check and then they headed out to the car.

Indian summer had started so the air was warm and was a perfect evening for a walk in the park, or at least to sit on a park bench and talk. Dawn still had another thousand questions to ask, it seemed for everyone that Max answered there were two more that she needed to ask. They sat there together in silence for a minute or two, Max seemed to be in deep thought and Dawn was still trying to come to grips with everything that he had told her.

"Is there anything else that you would like to know?" He said breaking the silence between them.

"Grace said that Phillip was here. Why was that important?"

"We haven't seen Phillip in quite a while. He was probably here to kill her." He said rather emotionless.

"What? He would kill his own sister?" She said in shock.

"Grace was our stepsister. My father married Destiny after Destiny's husband was killed in a training accident in Hawaii."

"Are you sure that your father didn't have anything to do with it?"

"No, I am not. I am sure though, that my father loved her and Grace."

"How can you be so sure?"

"If he didn't love them then he would have let them die after they had an auto accident. He couldn't bear to live life without them so he changed them. Neither of them thought it was a gift though, both Mom and Grace viewed it as a curse, Grace was completely filled with rage and Mom went crazy."

"What did Grace do?"

"She went on a rampage one night. She caused a car accident where she killed all four people involved. She broke into a house and killed a family. The whole incident became know as "The night of the Kaupa and she became a legend".

That last statement made Dawn's head spin. She remembered reading the old news story about the incident.

"What do you mean legend?"

"There still remember her as the "Lady in White", look it up on the internet. I am telling you the truth." He said trying to convince her that he wasn't crazy and that this was all real.

"There was such fear in the community and so many people involved in the investigation that I am sure that they would have caught her sooner or later."

"Well, what happened?"

"The Japanese attacked Pearl Harbor. Within a month, my father and I were deployed and Mom and Grace were shipped back to the mainland with all the other non-essential personnel."

"So, should I be afraid of Phillip?" She asked.

"Yes, he is completely twisted. Apparently he has made some sort of deal with Leopold to join the "Network" again."

"Why wasn't he in the "Network"?"

"Leopold banished him after the Zodiac killings."

"What? You're telling me that your brother is one of the most notorious killers of the twentieth century?"

"Yes, that is what I am saying. He brought so much publicity to himself that Leopold expelled him from the "Network" and warned him that he would have him killed if he ever did something like that again."

"Alright, I will, but tell me this, are you some legendary killer from the past?" She said sarcastically.

He hesitated at first until she asked the question again.

"Yes, I was one of two people involved in the White Chapel murders in 1888." He said nervously.

"Is that supposed to mean something to me?" She asked defensively.

"I'm sorry I should have explained, history will remember me as "Jack the Ripper".

Just the thought that she was sitting to someone that could be so vile made her stand up.

"What are you saying? You're telling me that you are "Jack the Ripper"?"

She went to leave when her eyes met his and calm came over her and she sat down.

"That is what I am saying. But what the history books and movies don't tell you is that there was more than one of us. That's why they never caught us."

"Let me guess, Phillip and you?"

"Yes."

"You know Max, just when I think that this relationship of ours cannot get any weirder you go and tell me that you're some serial killer lost to history. Are you crazy or something? This is far too weird for me at times. How do you expect me to believe any of this anymore?"

Even though Dawn sat down she put a few inches between her and Max. He seemed to have some ability to control her with a glance and it made her feel uncomfortable. In fact the whole conversation made her feel like getting up and running for her life.

"Please, Dawn, I know the more I tell you the crazier I seem, but I am as sane as anyone. What can I do to prove to you that this is real?"

"Well, you said that Grace had a photo album, but you are telling me that you have lived two hundred years and there is no evidence that you actually exist?"

"Since we age so slowly, we have to change identities about every 10 years so we move around a lot, but there are a few pictures of me."

"How do you change an identity?"

"We take it from someone else."

"You mean you murder them, don't you?" She said in disgust.

"Yes, that is what I mean, though we call it, "trading lives" in the network."

"Why, so you don't feel like the murderers that you are?"

"Maybe so."

"The more I get to know you the more I realize that you people are without consciences, you don't seem to care about anything but yourselves. I thought I knew Grace, but it seems that the person I know was nothing more than an act. She was just a violent killer." She said as her anger built up inside her.

"That was true about Grace, until she met you. She said that you were the first person in a long time that actually got to know her and treated her like a friend. That is why all of this happened. She didn't want any part of the network anymore. She told me that you offered her hope and that she had no desire to live this way."

A tear rolled off of Dawn's cheek as she realized that a simple act of kindness made such a difference in Grace's life.

"Dawn, I came here because I wanted the hope, I wanted what she had. You didn't know her, like I knew her. She was full of anger and rage and didn't care how many lives she ruined, until she met you."

A chill came over her as she started to consider the world that she had inadvertently entered into. A world so bizarre no one in there right mind would even consider its existence, a world without morals or civilized rules, where murder was just a way of life, a world of shadowy creatures that only appeared as people but were more like blood thirsty animals.

She really didn't know how to feel at this moment. She was filled with fear, fearful at the fact that this man that she was attracted to at best was insane and at worst was a cold blooded killer.

As the night wore on the air became colder and the wind started to pick up. She sat there with her hands together on her lap as she started to shiver.

"I guess it's time to get going." Max said as he realized that she was cold.

As they stood up he reached out and held her hand for the first time. A soothing gentle spirit came over Dawn and then a feeling of happiness. It happened so quickly and the fact that she didn't seem to have control over it that she let go of his hand.

"What did you just do?" She asked apparently upset.

"I just held you hand. I am sorry if I upset you." He said shyly.

"You did more than hold my hand. You did something. You made me feel what you were feeling. Didn't you?" She asked like a prosecutor in court.

"If I did I'm sorry, I didn't intend to."

Dawn kept her composer but she was really frightened now. If Max could control how she felt just by holding her hand or calm her by a simple glance, what would keep him from attacking her?

"Max, I want the truth and I want it now! What did you just do and what can you do?" She's said almost screaming.

He glanced at her and their eyes met, her anger went away and she was calm in an instant. This time though her calm demeanor didn't last.

"See you did it again. I don't know how you did it but I think you can hypnotize me with your eyes, am I right?" She said in disgust.

"Yes I can. I can also read your thoughts or implant mine. I can transfer emotions from you to me or the other way around." He said calmly.

"Max you are starting to scare me. I would say you were crazy but I knew that Grace could do it; I saw her do it to Brandon."

"We all can do it. That's why you became so upset at the funeral home; my mother's emotions were being transferred to you. That's why I gave you a hug, it let me transfer mine to you."

"Max, can we go home now?" She asked totally overwhelmed again.

"Sure." He said as he led her to the car.

As they walked she tried to keep her distance from her and avoided looking into his eyes. She just wanted to get through this night and try and process even more bizarre information then from their last date. Max could tell that her demeanor had changed and made no attempt to touch her and kept his distance. He realized that it all was a hard pill to swallow and she would either come to grips and accept who he was or run from him and leave him in her dust. Both of them were so focused on each other, neither of them noticed Brandon's car parked close by.

They returned to Dawn's house without incident and without a wood spoken between them. He stopped the car and opened her door and proceeded to lead her to the door as they got closer, it appeared that the door had been forced open and someone had broken into the house.

"Mom!" Dawn yelled into the house.

There was no answer. Dawn wasn't sure if her mother had made it home from work yet or if she was still in the house.

"What should we do?" she asked Max.

"Let's call the police and wait in the car until they come."

"But my mother could be in there, what then?"

"So could the thief, they will be here very quickly."

They dialed 911 and though Dawn didn't want to wait she waited with Max in the car. It only took 10 or 15 minutes for the police to arrive. They entered the house and turned on the lights. They searched the house and reported that there was no one in the house and that it was safe to go in. By this time Dawn's mother had returned from work to find the police at her house and that her house had been ransacked by some thief.

On entering she found that the house looked like a tornado had gone through it. Drawers all through the house were opened, clothes thrown all over the floor. It seemed apparent that the thief or thieves were looking for something in particular. The police told them to make a list of things that were stolen and to turn a copy into them and one to their insurance company and then they left. Dawn headed upstairs to see if anything was missing while her mother stood in disbelief at the mess that someone created.

"Is there anything that I can do?" Max offered politely.

"Thanks, but I don't think so. I just find it hard to believe that someone would think that we have something worth stealing." She replied in disgust.

"Dawn, Max is going to leave, do you want to say goodbye." She yelled up to Dawn.

"I will be right down." Dawn answered.

Dawn came down shortly and walked Max to the door. She didn't want to make a scene with her mother there so they walked out the door and stood there on the landing. She still didn't get close enough to touch him and would look directly at him.

"Max, I like you and I loved Grace, but I have to process this some more. I will call you, is that OK? I just need some time." She said in slight whisper.

"I understand." He replied as he said goodbye and walked to his car.

She watched him get in and drive off before she headed back into the house. She was shocked to see her mother standing there waiting for her to come back in.

"Well, did he?" She asked

"Did he what?" Dawn replied slightly confused.

"Did he kiss you?" Her mother asked inquisitively.

"Mom! No." She exclaimed.

"What would give you that idea?" She asked.

"Well you went back outside; I just thought maybe he was going to make his move."

"No, he didn't kiss me, and right now I don't have any time to think about that. I just want to know why someone would try and rob us."

"I wonder about that myself." Her mother replied shaking her head.

"Well let's try and get this place cleaned up." She told Dawn as she headed for the broom closet.

Dawn focus changed from Max to her mother as the two started the job of getting the house back in order.

"Well, how did it go?" Her mother asked as she picked up a broken knick knack off the floor.

"It was alright." She replied.

"Just alright, tell me details, where did you go to eat?"

"The Lake Ridge." Dawn said without emotion.

"The Lake Ridge, pretty impressive, you father only took me there twice and that was for one of our anniversaries."

"It was very nice and the food was really good, but I felt a little out of place. I was afraid that I was going to do something wrong and make a fool out of myself."

"That's understandable." Her mother reassured her.

"Well, what did you do after that?" She asked Dawn intuitively.

"Nothing much, we went over to the park and talked."

"He didn't take you over there to make out did he?"

"No, of course not, he has always been a perfect gentleman. We just went there and talked. I probably asked him a million questions about Dawn. There was so much that I wanted to ask him, but it started to get cold so we came back home."

"OK then. It's late and you better get ready for bed."

Dawn agreed and headed upstairs and her mother followed a few moments later.

Driving home to his mother's house light went off in Max's brain. He still couldn't fill all the pieces together but he started to put it all together and it was all starting to make sense to him. He arrived home to find that his mother had gone to bed and that is where he was headed.

After a long night of tossing and turning Max woke up and headed downstairs. He passed his mother's room to hear her weeping again.

"Are you alright, Mom?"

"I will be I guess, do you want me to make you some breakfast?"

"Know, I don't have time I have a meeting to go to."

"Have a good day"

"I love you Mom"

"I love you too Maximillian."

He wanted to stay and talk but he knew that what he had to do was too important to postpone. He had to go into town and meet with Leopold. It would take him a few hours to get to the city so he had a lot of time to ponder on everything that had happened. He hadn't made an appointment and wasn't even sure that Leopold was there so he might be taking a long drive for nothing. He finally reached his destination and parked the car and then headed for the entrance of Leopold's office. As he entered the office he was greeted by the receptionist.

"May I help you?"

"I am here to see Leopold."

"May I ask who is calling?"

"Margaret, you know who I am, just tell him that I am here to talk to him." He replied angrily.

"I have Maximillian Cmerci here to see you sir." He heard her say.

"I am sorry but Leopold is not available right now, can you come back tomorrow?"

"No I cannot!" He replied as he headed for the door.

She got and tried to stop him as he opened the door to Leopold's office.

"I am sorry so, he just rushed in." She told Leopold.

"It's alright, Margret. Can you make sure that we won't be disturbed?"

"Yes, sir."

"Maximillian, how are you?"

"Don't be coy with me Leopold, now you won't see me?"

"I didn't say that Max old boy, I just said that I was busy and could you come back tomorrow. You must gain control of yourself. What is wrong?"

"You know exactly what is wrong; it just took me a while to figure this all out."

"Fill me in friend, what are you upset about?"

"Doctor Sinclair, why did you kill him? And why did you order Grace drained?

"Look Max, Doctor Sinclair was about to release a book confirming the existence of us."

"But who would have listened, they would have thought he was crazy." Max interjected.

"That's true, but he was an expert on myth and legends and people actually did listen to what he had to say. I felt that it would be better for us all, if he was out of the picture."

"I understand, but why Grace. She was your closest confidant, if you were willing to kill her, then which of us is safe?" Max asked.

"I had to, she had everything on us. She had photos; she had records of me, old records and records as old as the revolution. She was threatening to go public with her own story. I couldn't let that happen. She said that she was tired of living this lifestyle and that she was going to expose us all. I had to contain the situation.

"But why did you use Phillip to do it?"

"Well; Phillip contacted me and asked to come back to the fold about the same time that Grace decided to go rouge. So I figured what a better test of loyalty than to have him kill his own sister. I realize that she was you sister and I am sorry that I had to do it, but I have to look at the overall picture here."

"Why couldn't you have told me, I could have taken her to Azil, there would have been no one to listen to her then. She would have calmed down."

"Max, she knew the rules as well as you do. You know as well as I, she could never live with herself after Hawaii, I am surprised that she lived this long is this state. It is a sad fact that many of us are very fragile beings, I am sorry, but you will see that it had to be done in the end." He said like a father that had just paddled his son.

"Sometimes Leopold you are a heartless demon. I wonder if there is any compassion left in that dark soul of yours."

"Come now Max, I have spent years trying to preserve our way of life. You know that if it was up to the rest of the world, we all would be dead; they would hunt us down and kill us. Remember Max, we will defend what we have here."

"What is that supposed to mean?"

"You're relationship with Dawn might just prove to be more dangerous than you think."

"Now you are spying on me?"

"Not, spying Max, just making sure that you are staying committed to the cause."

"And what cause it that Leopold?" he responded angrily.

"Our survival."

"Max, you know that you can't stay there, neither can you mother. There are too many unanswered questions and too many loose ends, just be careful Max, this is a slippery slope that you are on."

"What would you have me do, this is the closest thing to home that Mom or me have had in a long time." Max responded in a huff.

"Max you must realize that the closer you get to this girl the more danger she is in." Leopold said in a menacing tone.

"I swear Leopold, you better leave her alone. You maybe able to control me, but you leave her alone." Max responded angrily.

"Calm down Max, make it easy on yourself. Let her go or make us one of us, either way you will have to choose, or I will have to choose for you." He said like the tyrant that he was.

"I understand and I swear my allegiance to you and the Network." He said sheepishly as he bowed and kissed Leopold's ring.

"I know you will do the right thing Max, you always have. Now if you will excuse me I have some work that needs done." Leopold said nonchalantly.

Max left the room like the servant that he was, like a wolf with his tail between his legs. The meeting left Max shaken, he was so angry he felt like blowing the lid off the Network himself, but he knew that he couldn't do that. He also realized that he was putting Dawn and her mother in danger and would have to make a decision. He constantly switched back and forth to what decision that he would make as he drove the long trip home. He was torn; Dawn was the first person in a long time that reminded him that he was still human and still had a choice about the life the he lived. He stilled wanted the hope that she gave to Grace but for now he might have to relinquished that dream and get back to reality. Eventually as he neared his mother's house he knew what he had to do.

Chapter 35

Monday came and so did the bus as Dawn ran out of the house to catch it before it left. She tried to catch her breath as she found her seat next to Rebecca.

"Late again." Rebecca said.

"Yes." Dawn replied annoyed.

"You know Dawn if you would get up earlier maybe you wouldn't be so late all the time."

"Well, I didn't know that you were keeping tabs on me now." Dawn answered back

"Sooooooory, I didn't mean to get on your bad side." Rebecca responded.

Dawn was slightly shocked at her response. Most of the time Rebecca was pretty laid back, maybe she wasn't having a good day either. After taking a minute to think about the whole situation Dawn thought it best to apologize.

"I'm sorry, Rebecca, it was just a bad way to start the day. I shouldn't have been mean to you."

"It's OK, I'm sorry too." Rebecca said as tears welled up in her eyes.

I became apparent that Rebecca was dealing with something far bigger than a small argument on the bus.

"Is everything alright?" Dawn asked sincerely.

"No, my parents just told me last night that they are getting a divorce." Rebecca whispered back.

"I'm sorry." Dawn told her as she gave her a hug.

Dawn wasn't sure what to say at this point but just sit there and listen. Dawn had been through a lot in the past few months but she realized that everyone has their own set of problems and that everyone needs a friend.

As they arrived at school Rebecca had calmed down and everyone exited the bus.

"Thanks." Rebecca told Dawn.

"No problem, any time." Dawn replied as their headed to their home rooms.

Dawn walked into the building and through the current of people as she headed for her locker. She looked to see Brandon and his goon standing at his locker talking. The once king of the school had faded into obscurity after the incident with Grace. Their eyes met as Dawn glanced over to him and he responded with an icy stare. She quickly turned her head to look at where she was going as she headed towards her locker. When she arrived and opened the locker she was shocked to see Brandon standing next to her.

"You better watch yourself Dawn; you don't know what that guy is capable of."

"His name is Max, for your information and he is nothing but a gentleman, but that is something that you know very little about." She responded with disdain.

"Whatever." He said as he head for home room shaking his head.

Dawn was a little concerned with what Max was capable of but there was no way that she would have told Brandon that. In fact no matter what Max did, she would never say anything detrimental about him to Brandon. She wanted Brando to realize that he gave up a lot when he crossed the line with her.

Dawn found it hard to concentrate and was thinking a lot about their date on Saturday. So far every time she and Max had been together it always ended in some sort of weird drama. Here she was again trying to decide on what to do with their relationship, on one hand she really thought he was her prince charming, on the other he very well could be the Devil. It was a quandary that she had to keep to herself; at this point she didn't need any more rumors floating through the school walls.

At lunch she went through the line, bought her lunch and headed for the loser table. Everyone realized that she wasn't really there with them again and that something was on her mind. They all sat there talking amongst themselves as if she wasn't even there. She sat there picking at her food as she pondered over Max and his delusions and what she should do. She was in such a trance that Bill almost initiated another food fight to bring her back to reality. His better judgment took over and he went back to reading his book. She sat there mumbling to herself on what to do next and what her options were oblivious that everyone was starting to stare at her.

"What?" She asked the crowd as she realized that they were staring.

"Welcome back." Bill said.

"Sorry, I was thinking about some things." She said embarrassed.

She tried to deflect everyone wondered about her by talking about random things and then the bell rang for lunch to end. They all stood up to enter the stampeded headed out of the cafeteria Bill waited for Dawn.

"Are you alright? You don't seem to be in reality anymore." He said

"Yes, I am fine, I just have to work out some things that all."

"OK, but remember I am here if you need a friend to talk to." He said caringly.

"Thanks, but I'm fine." She said as they headed for opposite parts of the school.

For the rest of the day Dawn resided in her own little world to the point that some people started to think that she was actually spaced out on drugs.

The day finally ended and everyone stampeded as usual to their bus. Dawn was so out of it that she almost missed her bus and had to walk home. She entered the bus and sat next to Rebecca.

"Dawn, are you high or something?" She asked thoughtfully.

"What?"

"Are you high on drugs or something? Have you been huffing something?" She asked again.

"No, of course not! Why are you starting such a rumor?"

"I'm not starting a rumor. Just everyone at school said that you were completely space out today."

"Well, maybe I wasn't paying attention most of the day, but it wasn't because I was on drugs; OK?"

"Alright, thinking about Max?"

"What?"

"Were you thinking about Max?"

"No, what would make you think that?"

"Brandon, he told me that you and Max have been going out quite a bit, that he even took you to some expensive restaurant."

"Rebecca, you really have to stop listening to Brandon, he's still mad about our break up. I've only been on a few dates with him."

Dawn didn't expound on where they went to dinner but she was wondering how Brandon knew where they went. For the rest of the trip home Rebecca and she exchanged in small talk until they arrived at her house. She entered the house finding her mother in the kitchen working on dinner.

"Hello, Sunshine." Her mother greeted her as she entered the house.

"Hi, Mom, how are you?"

"I'm good; did you have a good day?"

"Yes, but I have a lot of homework."

"Bummer man, well get ready for dinner, it's almost done."

Dawn got out the dishes and set the table and then her mother served up dinner. She had broken her trance and was back in the land of the living and the two of them talked about their day like they use to do when her father was alive. After dinner Dawn excused herself and headed upstairs to do her homework. It seemed that she had a little to do in every subject; it was like all the teachers got together to see if they could ruin her evening. She thought that there was no use complaining about and that she was just going to get it done. After a grueling twenty minutes of studying she decided that she needed a break from the monotony and turned on her computer. She usually clicked on YouTube and watched something funny but she wanted to know more about some things that Max had told her.

She entered, "Jack the Ripper" into the search engine and the screen was filled with hundreds of links to websites from historical to creepy. After reading the bland historical account she clicked on a site that actually had photos of the crime scenes. She was horrified after seeing some of the photos. The victims had been cut open and mutilated. It was so upsetting that she turned off the computer and tried to get back to her homework. But no matter what she couldn't get the images out of her head and the thought that Max was supposedly involved. All of this up and down stress of her relationship was truly taking its toll on her and she finally decided that she had to be proactive about where their relationship was headed.

She finally finished her homework, told her mother goodnight and got ready for bed. She got in bed and turned the light off and fell asleep. She fell into a deep sleep and started to dream. She was transported to 1800 London as she walked the streets. It seemed so real that she actually could taste and smell her surroundings. She could see the poverty all around her and feel the darkness that was falling with the sunset. She walked around like she knew where she was going, like she had been there before. The streets had tuned dark other than the occasion street lamp and the air was thick and dank with an awful stench. She walked around the corner to see a tall man in an over coat bent over the body of a woman on the street. He appeared to be cutting her with some sort of knife as blood started to pour out onto the ground. The man seemed startled at her presence and turned to look at her. He eyes met hers as she realized that the man was Max and he gave her a slight grin. She took a look at the woman and then back at him.

"No!" She screamed as she woke up.

"Dawn, are you OK?" Her mother asked as she came running.

"I'm alright, it was just a nightmare. I'm sorry."

"Are you sure?"

"Yes, I'm fine. Sorry I woke you."

She was exhausted but Dawn was too terrified to sleep at this point. She pulled the covers up over her head like she was three years old, afraid of the monster in the closet. She had nothing better to do so she decided that she would try and pray. She thought about what to pray about and as she started to relax and before she even realized, she had fallen asleep.

The morning came without another nightmare as she woke up late and had to hurry to get everything done before the bus came.

"Good morning, you gave me quite a scare last night." Her mother told her as she came down the steps and into the kitchen.

"I'm sorry it was just a nightmare."

Her mother left it at knowing that Dawn was very limited on time. Dawn as usual was in a whirlwind trying to get everything done. She was more focused this morning and had made her decision on what to do with Max. She finished getting ready headed outside and waited for the bus. Her mother watched out through the curtains making sure that she was safe. She might be an adult but she would always be her little girl to Mrs. Sinclair. The bus came and Dawn got on board and her mother went back to her daily routine.

To everyone's amazement at school Dawn was the back to being herself. She was focused and interacting with people. The loser table was happy to have her back as the table came back to life as she sat down.

"Glad to have you back." Bill told Dawn.

"I'm sorry there has just been a lot on my mind lately."

"It's alright; we're used to you being out in left field."

"What?" She responded slightly annoyed.

When she looked up and saw them all looking quite serous she started to laugh. Seeing that she was fine with what Bill said the rest of the table joined in.

Later that day after school Dawn decided to head to the library. She wanted to do some more research into Max's history. She was aware that most of the information she was looking for could be found on the internet but she didn't want her mother to suspect anything. She entered the library and headed for the reference terminal. She typed in things like the Polish uprising and Jack the Ripper. After finding a dozen titles she decided to find some books and start reading. She grabbed about six books and started over to a reading table trying to keep from dropping the tower of books she held.

"Can I help you with that, miss?" A young man asked.

"Thank you." She said as she handed him a book or two.

As they found a seat she took a good look at the man. Even before he had introduced himself she realized who he was.

"Hello, my name is Phillip." He said ever so politely.

A shiver of fear flowed through her like a lightning bolt that made her wince. She tried to act nonchalant but it was evident that she was jolted by his presence.

"Hello, thank you for your help, my name is Dawn." She said in the calmest manner she could.

"Quite a collection of books you have there." He said inquisitively.

"Just doing some research."

"I seemed to make you uncomfortable, are you alright?"

"I'm fine; it's just a little cold in here." She responded trying to keep her cool, even though she wanted to scream in terror and run home. From her experience with Max she tried not to look directly in his eyes and made sure that they weren't able to touch.

"I can see that you already know who I am."

"Yes, you are Max's brother, correct?"

"That is right. I also see that Max has had a chance to tell you about me, right"

She simply responded with a nod.

"I am sure that he told you about Jack? He always tells everyone that story. But did he tell you about Mary Rogers?"

"Yes, he told me all about it." She whispered back.

Max had never mentioned Mary Rogers but she wasn't going to tell Phillip that.

"I am not going to hurt you. I just wanted you to know that Max is not what he seems, Grace wasn't what she seemed. None of us are what we seem. If I were you I would distance my self from Max and Mrs. Smith, you might end up getting hurt." He said with a smile as he headed for the exit.

Dawn sat there numb to what just happened it would take her a minute for her body to catch up with her mind. Once the full weight of the encounter hit her she began to shake with fear. She stood up and left the books on the table as she headed for the door in a rush. She ran out the door and down the steps to find Brandon parked along the street. She was so terrified at what had just happened that she knocked on the window of his car. He reached over and rolled the window down.

"Brandon, can you give me a ride home?" She asked with a quivering voice.

"Sure, you're OK? You look pretty upset."

"I'm fine; can you just take me home?" She told him point blank.

"OK, OK, home we go." He said as he put the car in drive and headed to her house.

Even though she hadn't seen him for awhile nothing had changed when it came to his car. It still sounded like there marbles in the motor and a trailer of smoke still followed him were ever he went. It didn't take long for them to arrive and as they neared her driveway she told him to stop and she got out.

"Thanks a lot, I really appreciate it." She told him kindly.

"No problem, any time." He answered back as he left in a cloud of smoke.

"Was that Brandon?" Her mother asked as she entered the house.

"Yes, and I just realized that I left my books in his car." She responded in disgust.

"Why did Brandon bring you home, are you getting back with him?"

"No Mom, I went to the library and there was some creepy guy there that helped me get some books. I got scared and left. Brandon happened to be there so I asked him if he would give me a ride home."

"Are you alright, did the guy try something?" She asked concerned.

"No he didn't he just gave me the creeps."

"I understand that, I meet plenty of people like that in the hospital."

Her mother told her to sit down as she headed for the kitchen. She returned shortly with a bowl of ice cream.

"Thanks Mom, I needed this." She said sincerely.

"I know." Her mother responded as she gave her a kiss on the forehead.

After she ate her fill her mother had dinner ready, her mother tried to keep the conversation jovial and light and could gather that there was something about the confrontation that Dawn wasn't telling her. In fact Dawn behavior had become so erratic at times that her mother was worried that she might be experimenting with drugs. She still trusted Dawn and the fact that she hoped that she wouldn't do anything that would derail her future, but that didn't stop her from worrying about the things she might be doing behind her back.

They were both about done with dinner when there was a knock at the door. Her mother got up and went to the door. Dawn couldn't here what the two were saying but as her mother shut the door and headed to the kitchen she realized that it was Brandon and he had her books with him.

"Thank the Lord." Dawn said in relief.

"Thanks for getting the door; I still have a hard time talking to him."

"It's alright, but sooner or later you're going to have to forgive him."

"I did, I just don't want to be around him, that's all." She answered back as she headed for her bedroom.

"Have fun." Her mother said jokingly.

"Yeah, right." Dawn said sarcastically as she walked up the stairs.

Dawn did have some homework, but that wasn't even on her mind at the moment. She was more interested in finding out who Mary Rogers was. She entered her room closed the door, set down her books and turned on the computer. In the minutes that it took the computer to boot up she had time to think about her meeting. She pondered the question of how Phillip happened to know who she was and how did he know she would be at the library today. That brought the next question to mind that was why Brandon was parked outside the library.

Before she had too much to time delve into the matter the computer log on screen popped up and she signed in. The desktop appeared and she clicked on the Internet Browser icon and her search engine came up. She typed the name, "Mary Rogers" into the search bar. She was truly amazed at the amount of information that was produced when she hit the return key. They all said about the same thing, a pretty girl in her twenties was murdered and found in the floating the Hudson River in 1841. She was intrigued with the whole story and Max's supposed involvement in the whole thing. She was finally fed up with the whole mess that her relationship with the Smiths and Max had become. Her decision was made; all she had to do was talk to Max again. She knew her mother would be upset if she knew that she was making another date with him, but she had to find the truth, all she had to do now was wait to make the phone call. She knew that her mother was a creature of habit and before long she would be checking up on her and then taking her evening bath. Just like clockwork her mother knocked on the door to find Dawn studying hard, she said hi and told Dawn that she was going to take a bath. Dawn waited to she was sure that her mother was in the bathtub when she headed downstairs to get the cordless phone. She nervously headed back up the stairs and quietly keyed in Max's number.

"Hello, Max here."

"Max, this is Dawn, we need to talk."

"Yes, we do." He said back politely.

"When can we meet again?" He asked her first.

"What about this Friday?" She told him in a whisper.

"Iwill pick you up around 7:00 p.m., is that alright?"

"That will be fine, I will see you then." She answered and hung up the phone, she was so focused on keeping the call a secret that she forgot to say goodbye.

Max stood there with the phone to his ear as she hung up.

"Well, I guess that's that." He said as he hung up his.

"Who was that?" His mother asked.

"Just Dawn, she asked if we could get together and talk."

"I love Dawn, but you know what you have to do Max." She said concerned.

"Yeah, I know." He said in disappointment.

"I was hoping for a future here Max, but I know that dream isn't going to happen now, but we have to make the best of things." She said caringly.

"I will. I love you Mom."

"I love you too. I am going to bed." She said as she headed to her bedroom.

Chapter 36

Friday came and Dawn was late getting ready as usual. Max showed up early like he did for everything. Mrs. Sinclair let him in and showed him a seat in the living room. His over politeness was still a sticking point to Mrs. Sinclair; he was so polite she thought that he might be trying to hide something. She dealt with it went back to what she was doing as he sat on the sofa waiting for Dawn. Mrs. Sinclair yelled up to Dawn that Max had arrived and that she better hurry up. The distraction only slowed her down more but eventually she came down the steps, told her mother goodbye and they walked to his car. He opened the door for her as he always did; after she sat he closed it and got in on his side. He started the car and off they went. Mrs. Sinclair looked out the window watching them leave; she still had a strange feeling that there was something that Dawn wasn't telling her. She knew that she would have to confront Dawn here eventually but for now she was hoping that she could handle whatever situation she was in.

They headed to the restaurant and he asked the hostess for a corner both. After the waitress took their orders they sat there until Max broke the silence.

"Well, what is it you want to talk about?" He asked.

"Mary Rogers." She said bluntly.

He became visible moved by the name but didn't say anything.

"Did you hear me?" She asked.

"Yes, I heard you. I just haven't heard that name in a long time."

"Well, what can you tell me about her?" She demanded.

"Well, Mary was the pretty cigar girl of Manhattan. She was the most eligible woman at the time. She was funny and vibrant and a joy to be around. Every guy in town wanted to date her, and it seemed that she dated everyone."

"It that it?" She asked after he paused for a while.

"No, that's not it. I started dating her and I really felt like we had a connection, so much so that I wanted to ask her to marry me. But then I found out that she had been dating my brother Phillip for quite a long time. I felt betrayed and I was hurt. I told her that I would like to marry her but she would have to choose between Phillip and me. She laughed at me and told me that she would never marry me and that Phillip was the one she loved. I flew into a rage and strangled her with her own scarf and then threw her body in the Hudson River." He told her in a simple monotone voice.

"You act like she was nothing, like killing her was nothing." She said trying to stay calm.

"I am sorry it is the only way that I can live with the thing I have done. Most people only spend a lifetime full of regrets I am on my third. There isn't a day that doesn't go by that I don't see her face and her eyes as I squeezed the life out of her." He said as a tear fell from his eye.

She realized at this point that he seemed remorseful for what he did but that didn't remove his guilt.

"How did you know about Mary?"

"I met your brother the other day at the library. He knew who I was and made a point to introduce himself to me. He admitted that he was "Jack" but told me to ask you about Mary. I was so upset that I had my old boyfriend drive me home because I was afraid that he might attack me."

"Did he?"

"No, and that's the last that I saw of him."

"Good, I am sorry. I like you Dawn and would never want to see you or your mother hurt. That's why I have to tell you that my mother and I will be leaving Saratoga Springs for good."

"Really, why does your mother have to leave?"

"Leopold thinks that if she stays it will leave to many unanswered questions and he doesn't want any loose ends."

"So then what?"

"We both disappear into the pages of history and become a memory."

"That's really sad." Dawn said as she pondered the thought of being forgotten.

"It is the life we live."

"Wait, you spoke to Leopold?"

"Yes."

"Then did you figure out who killed Grace?"

"Yes."

"Well, what are you going to do?"

"There is nothing that I can do. What's done is done." He said without emotion.

"You act like Grace didn't matter."

"She mattered, she was my sister. She mattered a lot. There's nothing I can do, I am in no position to change what has happened."

"So did Phillip do it?"

"Yes, he did it to get back into the network. It was a show of loyalty to Leopold."

"And you're OK with the fact that he will get away with murder?"

"You have to see it from my perspective. Everyone in the "Network" has gotten away with murder. This one just happened to be my sister."

"You know Max I like you and I really hoped that our relationship would go to the next level."

"But." He interjected.

"But, the more I find out about you and your group of cohorts the more I become disgusted with the whole thing. I still haven't decided if this world you live in is real or you're all just a bunch of delusional crazy people."

"I understand." He said as he lowered his head in shame.

"There is one thing I want from you though." She told him forcefully.

"What is that?"

"I want you to come to church with me on Sunday. Maybe you can find the hope that Grace found. It made a difference for her, I am sure that it could do you a world of good."

"Don't worry, no one is going to burn you at the stake or impale you. This is not the middle ages. Grace was fine with it." She said after she saw him shudder when she told him about church.

It still took a minute or two for him to agree to go with her. They decided that he would meet them in the parking lot before church started and they would go in together. She decided to go in after the service started so Max wouldn't be overwhelmed by people welcoming a visitor.

After dinner Max become withdrawn and Dawn decided that it was time to go home, so Max took her there and walked her to the door as he always did. This time was different though, as she went to open the door he took her hand and pulled her close to him and kissed her on the lips. It was such a surprise to Dawn that it seemed like he picked her up off her feet. She was so completely filled with a rush of emotions that she got dizzy and almost fell down. He let go of her and she stepped off the cloud she was on and tried to retain her balance.

"Max." She said shocked.

"I'm sorry, I shouldn't have." He said like a scolded child.

"Maybe not, but I'm glad you did." She said with a smile from ear to ear as she reached for his hand.

He withdrew his hand and hugged her again instead but didn't kiss her again.

"I don't want to overdue it." He told her once he saw her disappointment.

"OK." She said as she said goodbye and he got into his car.

As she entered she found her mother sitting on the couch. Dawn's face was so bright that the house didn't need lights as she walked in and shut the door.

"Must have been a good date." Her mother jokingly said.

"The best." Dawn answered without even thinking.

"I take it he kissed you?" Her mother asked, trying to keep it secret that she was watching through the window.

"Is it that obvious?"

"Yes. There's just something about that first kiss."

Dawn was lost in the moment. Her mother could have told her the world was going to end in a minute and she wouldn't have cared. She was lost in a trance as she headed up to her bedroom.

"Goodnight, Sweetheart." Her mother said with a slight snicker.

"Goodnight, Mom." She said as she disappeared upstairs.

Chapter 37

Sunday came and so did the whirl wind, Dawn was trying to remain cool and collected but was so excited that she was going to show off her new boyfriend to the world. The kiss did away with any doubt she had about Max's intentions and fears of what he was. She hadn't had time to come to grips with the fact that the emotions she felt might have been planted there by him in the first place. Her mother was happy and annoyed at the same time. She found it comical that Dawn was so willing to go to church but annoyed that they were going to be late again. Her mother's anger was stemmed when Dawn explained that Max was kind of skittish about church and she wanted to get there a little late so he wouldn't be bombarded by all the inquisitive people.

They finally arrived at the church to find Max waiting standing by his car. Even her mother was taken back when she saw him dressed to the nines.

"Hello Mrs. Sinclair, how are you today?" He asked in his usual gentleman's dialogue.

"I am fine and you are looking very nice today." She responded politely.

Dawn was so star struck by his appearance that she stood there and stared not saying anything until her mother gave her a friendly nudge.

"Hello." She said with a school girl giggle.

"Let's go in, shall we?" Her mother said as she led the way.

Max was on edge and felt like a lamb led to the slaughter. He had no idea what to expect and all he knew about church is what he learned from those in the "Network".

"It's all going to be fine, don't worry." Dawn said trying to encourage him as she held his arm.

The church was larger than he thought and it seemed too filled with about two hundred people. He felt like they were all watching him as they entered and tried to find a seat in the back. He was noticeable out of place and looked like he wanted to scream in terror and run for the door. Mrs. Sinclair scanned the room and found them a seat. Even though Max thought the whole congregation was staring at him, most people were standing and singing songs and didn't even notice him coming in. Mrs. Sinclair was shocked to find that this was Max's first time in a church and he had do idea what was going on. She simply pointed to the front screen showing the words to the songs as they began to enter in.

The atmosphere of the service was so foreign to him that it might as well been on the moon. For most of his existence he had been surrounded by people lost in hopelessness and these people seemed to be in their own little bubble of joy.

Dawn noticed for the first time that Max was nervous and seemed like he had ants in his pants.

"Relax; this is supposed to be enjoyable." She whispered to him

The three of them seemed oblivious to the fact the Brandon was sitting two rows behind them on the other side of the sanctuary. He wasn't paying any attention to the service but he was watching the three of them as they stood there singing. He simply sat there watching ever so intently to Dawn and her new beau. After the song service ended the song leader instructed them to be seated and the choir sang a hymn. By this point Max and relaxed somewhat and was actually enjoying the myriad of voices from the choir loft. It was more than music to him; it was like water to a desert. His demeanor had changed and he seemed to be moved by the music as he became lost in this new found emotion. Dawn was lost in her distraction with Max and wouldn't have been able to tell anyone how the service was if they asked. She was still on cloud nine and had no intention of getting off anytime soon.

While most people listened intently Brandon sat there staring at his new found rival. He was more than a rival now, now he was a potential danger to the girl he once dated, and there was no way he was going to let him hurt her. Between watching Max, Brandon was watching the clock. He was pretty confident that they hadn't seen him and he wanted to keep it that way. So as the pastor ended his message he walked out the doors and headed to his car.

The message apparently touched Max as Dawn realized that tears were falling from his eyes. On realizing that Dawn was staring at him he became embarrassed and pulled out his handkerchief and wiped his eyes. She turned away quickly realizing her social gaffe. Without realizing that the service was over Max was bombarded with people welcoming him. Dawn noticed that he seemed to wince in pain with each hand that he shook. Finally the melee ended and the three headed to the parking lot.

"Are you alright?" Dawn asked him as they headed to the car.

"I'm fine, just a lot to absorb." He said politely.

"Would you like to go out for lunch?" He asked the two of them.

"No Thank You. You two have fun." Her mother told him as she got in her car and left.

"You too stuck up to say hi to me anymore?" Someone said as they were planning where to go.

"Oh, I'm sorry. This is Max, Max this is Bill." She said as she introduced the two of them.

"Nice to meet you, it's about time Dawn introduced me to the mystery man." He said with a smile.

"Likewise, would you like to go to lunch?" Max said politely inviting him to go with them.

"No, that's alright; I would be the third wheel, if you know what I mean." He said with a jovial attitude.

"Yes, I get it."

"Oh, one thing." Bill said as he was about to walk away.

"If you ever hurt her I will have to kill you." He said with all seriousness.

"Bill, what got into you?" Dawn said is shock.

"I just want him to know that you're my friend and I have your back."

"Thanks, but I will be alright." She said rolling her eyes at Max.

They decided to get fast food for lunch as the two of them put their seat belts on.

"Do you think you broke his heart by bringing me to church?"

"No, Bill and I are just friends, but we are good friends. We've known each other since we've been in grade school. He's always been there for me when I needed a friend. In fact he had eyes for Grace. They used to play chess together. The two of them seemed to click, I thought the two of them might have a future together but then she was gone."

"I hate to say this, but I'm not sure if she was capable of having a love relationship with a boy, you have to remember she might have looked sixteen but she was really ninety. It's one of the hardest things that we have to deal with."

"I bet." She responded.

They arrived at the restaurant and stood in line to order their food. The place was filled to the max with people just coming from church. Dawn didn't mention church and was waiting to see if Max was going to say something. She realized that he was uncomfortable and didn't want to make him feel any worse. They eventually got their food, found a seat and started to eat. Max didn't seem to want to talk much so they sat and ate pretty quickly. Max suggested they take a walk in the park after they were done and since it was a nice day so Dawn agreed and they headed there. After they arrived and he let her out of the car they started on the bike trail.

"You like hanging out at the park, don't you." She asked him.

"Yes, it is very relaxing."

"Max; why do you spend so much time alone, here at the park?" She asked concerned.

"Well, it's like this. Since I can read minds and feel other people's emotions, being in a crowd can be maddening. Imagine being in a mall and everyone is talking to you at the same time."

"That would be terrible." She interjected.

"It is, that's why most of us live a life of simple solitude. It keeps us from going crazy. That's why I told you before, this life is a curse. It's like being in a round house and never being able to leave. You get to walk around and around but the rooms never change."

For the first time since she had met Grace she realized the torment that Grace was in. No wonder she kept to herself and rarely interacted with people. It really touched Dawn's heart to think that there were people out there that were totally along in a world so filled with people.

"Max, if you have to leave, why did you kiss me the other night?"

"I guess I got caught up in the moment. I haven't felt like this is a long time."

"Do you regret it now?"

"No, but that doesn't change the fact that I will still have to leave. Leopold won't let me stay here."

"So Leopold dictates to you where you can live, love and be friends with?"

"Sometimes, remember we hide in plain sight, so if there is something that might draw attention to us he deals with it pretty quickly."

"So what would happen if you tell him no?"

"Most likely he'll kill me and possible anyone that I was in close contact with."

"You mean me?"

"Yes, that's why I have to leave. I am putting you in terrible danger."

Even before he was done talking he realized that they entered a more private area of the trail and took her in her arms and kissed her. Just like the other kiss, Dawn's head began to spin as he let her go from his embrace.

"Max, you have to stop doing that." She said in a slightly disheveled voice.

"What kiss you?"

"Know, catching me off guard. You have to give me some warning or something. Kissing you is like holding my breath for three minutes."

"I'm sorry; I forget that my emotions transfer at times."

She took a look around to see if they were alone and then she looked into his dark eyes. She hadn't looked into his eyes since before he kissed her and she wanted to see if they still affected her. To her amazement they seemed to hold a reflection in them for the first time. They were still dark but now there was something different about them. He smiled and stared back at her, but unlike before she didn't appear overwhelmed by his gaze.

"Ready?" He asked.

"Yes." She said.

He wrapped his hands in hers and the two stole another kiss with the trees being their only audience. Dawn seemingly walked on the clouds as they resumed their walk. Max was as happy as he had ever been but he knew in his heart that it would all be short lived. He was enjoying the moment but he was also aware that they were being watched, but at this point he didn't know by whom. After what seemed to be the fifth kiss he decided that they should stop for a while and enjoy the scenery. Hand in hand they walked on like young lovers until they came upon an empty bench and they sat down. They sat there looking at each other when Dawn broke the silence.

"What's wrong?" She asked seeing that he was thinking about something.

"Do you believe all that stuff that the preacher was saying today?"

"Yes I do, do you?"

"I am not sure. I'm not sure that God could forgive me for everything that I have done."

"That's the wonderful thing, Max, none of us are worthy of heaven, but God's grace makes a way even for the worst of us."

"Even for someone as evil as Leopold?"

"Yes, His grace made a way, even for Leopold. In fact in God's eyes we are all evil, we are all on the same playing field. There is no one that is better or worse."

It was apparent that Max wasn't to sure of this new found faith that he had encountered even though Dawn tried to reassure him that there was hope, even for a person like him.

"Dawn, you have to realize that I can't stay here. I got caught up in my emotions and lost my head. You've made me feel alive again, but staying here could lead to you getting hurt. Leopold is a heartless killer, and my brother is no better, in fact I think Phillip is on the verge of madness."

"Is that it, love me and leave me." She replied with hurt feelings.

"No, that was never my intention to love you and leave you. If this was a perfect world or a different time and place I think we could have a real future together. But for now a future with me is as dark as the midnight sky."

Dawn was filled with sadness and disgust. She wasn't sure if he really meant what he was saying or she was just another one of his conquests. That was the one problem that she had with Max, she couldn't figure out at times and if he was really telling her the truth.

"So that's it. You kiss me and then you tell me it's over. What kind of game are you playing with me?" She told him angrily.

"I am not playing a game. You've released something in me that's never been there and right now I don't want to see you get hurt. This is serious, these people have no conscience, do you think that any of them would even blink at the thought of killing you? Do you think Phillip even felt any sorrow as he sucked the life out of Grace? Do you think Leopold had a second thought about giving Phillip the order to kill her? They didn't and they wouldn't, because they are so far gone that they aren't human any more. They are the true vampire, leaching off of someone else."

"And you're not?" She asked sarcastically.

"I was headed in that direction, so was Grace, but meeting you changed our direction. You have to believe me. I am not lying to you. I lost my sister a short time ago; I don't want to lose you now."

"So what now, I just watch you ride away into the sunset like some old movie?" She said as the tears started to run down her face and she stood up to head to the car. He pulled the handkerchief from his pocket and went to wipe away her tears when Brandon made his presence known.

"Don't touch her you demon!" He shouted as he drove a knife into Max's throat and pushed him to the ground.

Dawn stood there frozen in terror at Brando pulled the knife out and grabbed her arm.

"What are you doing, let me go!" She screamed as he restrained her.

"Look at him, take a good look at him." He said as he made look at Max.

Max was still on the ground as blood spurted from his jugular vein. He was applying pressure with his hand to try and stop the bleeding as he attempted to get up. His eyes showed his pain as he winced and moan as he stood up.

"Just watch!" Brandon told her again as he held her even tighter.

Once Max stood up he removed his hand from his neck and to everyone's amazement the bleeding had stopped.

"Do you see Dawn, he's not human." He told her as Max stepped closer to the both of them.

"You stupid kid." Max said with his eyes glowing red like fire.

"You see Dawn, just like when he attacked my father."

Dawn was still to afraid to do anything. She was totally amazed at what had just happened but she was also terrified that Brandon could actually try and kill someone.

"Let her go." He told Brandon as he grabbed his shoulder and Brandon let Dawn go.

Max picked Brandon up by the front of his coat like he was a feather and stared into Brandon's eyes. Brandon became like a granite stature as Dawn stood frozen in fear.

218

Max held Brandon up with his right hand and then placed his left hand onto the side of Brandon's face. Dawn stared in amazement was Brandon's hair started to gray.

"Max, let him go!" She screamed as she came to her senses.

Max took a look at Dawn and then let Brandon's lifeless body hit the ground like a sack of potatoes.

"You killed him, you kill him!" Dawn screamed as she ran over to Brandon lying on the ground.

"I didn't kill him. It will all be like a bad dream to him. He'll be fine." He said in disgust.

Dawn felt a little better after she felt for a pulse and made sure the he was still breathing. Now that both Brandon and Max had calmed down, she was terrified. She wasn't sure what to do. She never thought Brandon could do such a thing, but now he appeared as crazy as Max and his family.

"You could have killed him." She scolded Max and he picked Brandon up and gently put him on the park bench.

"Well he was trying to kill me, or didn't you see him stab me?"

"I saw that, but he wasn't trying to kill you, he was trying to show me that you weren't human."

"What?"

"He knew that you were a vampire or something, he said that he recognized you that night when we went out to the movies. He called me and told me you weren't human and you were the one that attacked his father. Is that true, are you the one that attacked his father?"

"Yes, I was sitting her in the park and a man showed up. He was beating some woman and it was apparent that he was going to try and bury her. I couldn't stand back and watch so I interceded. Brandon showed up and kept me from killing him."

"But he died later."

"Yes, but I didn't kill him."

"How can I be sure? How can I be sure of anything anymore?" She asked him infuriated.

"What do we do with him?" She asked in a panic.

"He'll be fine, he's just asleep. When he wakes up it will just be a bad dream to him."

"We just can't leave him here." She contested.

"Dawn, we have to get out of here. There will be people coming down the trail soon." He said as he pointed to his blood stained coat.

Dawn then realized then that there would be a lot of people asking questions if Max didn't get out of there quickly.

"Do you promise that he will be alright?" She demanded.

"Yes, I promise, so let's go." He said impatiently.

The propped him up on the bench so he wouldn't fall onto the ground and tried to get back to Max's car without being noticed. The two of them headed off the trail and into the trees as some more people headed their way. No one really noticed Brandon sleeping there; he didn't seem out of place so most people just walked along. A few minutes later Max and Dawn made it to the car seemingly unseen and Brandon started to wake up. He was quite shocked waking up on the bench and not realizing where he was. It appeared that he only remembered coming to the park but he couldn't remember his altercation with Max, he stretched and then got up and found his car. Driving home he looked at his watch and realized that he couldn't account for a few hours of his time, but for now all he wanted to do is get back.

"Where have you been all day?" His mother asked him as he entered the trailer.

"I went to church this morning, is that alright?" He said with an attitude.

"Why didn't you ask me if I wanted to go, you know I wanted to start going?" She asked slightly hurt that her only son forgot about her.

"I'm sorry, it was a spur of the moment thing, I guess I went out for a drive and saw the church and figured what the heck, what could it hurt?"

"What church did you go to?"

"Christ the Redeemer."

"Isn't that where the Sinclair's go?" She asked intently.

"Yes."

"You and Dawn didn't get back together did you?"

"No."

"You aren't stalking her or something are you son?" She asked concerned.

"No, what makes you ask me something like that?"

"Well, you've been acting a little strange lately. You've been late for school, your grades are dropping again and there are times you are missing for hours on end. So tell me what is going on?" She demanded.

"Nothing is going on. I went for a drive, saw the church and decided to go. You would think that you would be happy, seeing that your hellion of a son was trying to better himself." He answered in a huff.

"Brandon, I love you, I just want to make sure you're not out drinking or taking drugs or something like that."

"Mom, don't worry, I will get my grades up, I will call if I am late, but I am not taking drugs or drinking. OK?"

"OK." She responded but still was worried about what he was up to.

"Well you went to church, but its three o'clock now, where have you been for the last three hours?"

"The park, I just went and enjoyed nature. I fell asleep on a bench and when I woke up I came home, that's all." He said as he headed to his bedroom.

"Just call from now on, so I don't have to worry."

"I will, I will." He said as he shut the door.

Dawn entered the house to find her mother watching TV.

"Did you have a nice afternoon?" Her mother asked.

"Yes, it was nice." Dawn answered with a slight quiver in her voice.

"Dawn are you alright?"

"Yes, why do you ask?"

"You just seem like you've seen a ghost. Your voice is shaky and you're trembling. What happened? Did you and Max break up?" She asked as any mother would.

"Mom, in order to break up we would have to be a couple, so no, we didn't break up. I am fine, don't worry, it was just a little cold outside." She answered trying to divert her mother's suspicion.

"If you say so." She said with a sarcastic tone.

Dawn was shocked to find that her mother could tell that something had happened simply by looking at her. It went back to the ability for her mother to seem to know everything about her. She wanted to tell her everything and what a mess Max and his whole family were, but after the incident at the park, she was aware that his crazy world was for real. Seeing Max's wound heal before her eyes was proof positive that Max was more than the average person and that she would have to take what he said at face value.

"Don't worry mom, nothing's going on." She said trying to be as convincing as she could be.

"I have some homework to do so I will be in my room." She told her mother as she headed for bedroom.

"Dinner will be ready at around five." She told Dawn.

"Thanks." She said even though there was no way she could even think about eating at the present time.

Her mother stayed on the couch but kept a close eye on Dawn as she headed up the stairs. She wanted to watch to see if there was any body language that would give some clue to what was bothering her. She didn't want to distrust Dawn but she was behaving strangely lately and wondered if Max was leading her down a path of drugs and alcohol. She whispered a prayer as Dawn disappeared to her room. This up and down rollercoaster ride that Dawn was on was affecting her mother far more than Dawn ever realized. For now though, all Mrs. Sinclair could do is hang on and pray.

Dawn entered her room grabbed her history book and sat at her desk. After she sat there for a minute she realized that she was still trembling after the day's events. She sat there trying to concentrate on getting her homework done, but she think about anything but the incident with Brandon and Max. She never thought Brandon was a violent person and even though Max said he didn't kill Grace, she now had her doubts. Her other question was how did Brandon know where the two of them were going to be, unless he was stalking Max or her. She wanted to call Brandon to make sure he got home and that he was OK, but doing could cause Brandon to question what really went on at the park. Max really didn't explain what Brandon would remember but Dawn didn't want to bring the incident back to the forefront of Brandon's mind, for now she would let sleeping dogs lie.

"What have gotten involved in" She said to herself.

Even though the deeper she got involved with Max the scarier things became, she still wanted to know more about the so called "Network" they all belonged to. She started her computer and put "Leopold Robespierre" into the search bar. To her amazement there seemed to be volumes of information about him. All of it pointed to a leader in the French Revolution that disappeared during the reign of terror and was presumed murdered amongst the countless others. Other than the name, she couldn't find anything even slightly related to an underground network. Apparently what measures they took to keep the organization secret had worked for all of these years.

Dinner finally arrived and she headed downstairs to eat. Her mother was sitting waiting patiently as she arrived, she said grace and then they began to eat. The whole day had stressed Dawn to the max and it showed in how hungry she was. She had totally forgotten her manners and was eating like a condemned woman when her mother interjected.

"Slow down." Her mother scolded her.

"I'm sorry, I was just really hungry."

"Well, even if you were starving you shouldn't be eating like a mad man."

"I'm sorry." Dawn said as she took notice and tried to eat in a normal fashion.

These tiny little incidents just added to the mistrust that was building between Dawn and her mother. Dawn did her best to hide her secret about Grace and Max but she wasn't doing a very good job at it. The two sat there in relative silence until they finished eating. Dawn wanted to put her mother's fears at bay so she stayed downstairs and the two watched television together. Whether Dawn realized it or not the secrets that she was keeping were slowly creating a rift between her and her mother.

Chapter 38

"Homicide, detective Jones speaking." The detective answered as he picked up the phone.

"Detective Jones, this is officer Mallory. I have an apparent suicide victim down her on the railroad tracks near Glenham Avenue."

"I'm sorry officer, you have the wrong department, this is homicide, and I don't do suicides."

"I understand that detective, but I thought you might want to be involved in this one, considering that I think it's your main suspect in that hit and run of that girl in the park." The officer interrupted.

"What, you're telling me that Brandon Phillips committed suicide?" The detective said in shock.

"That would appear so."

"OK, thanks, give me a minute to get there. I am on my way." The detective told the office as he hung up the phone and grabbed his coat.

He arrived around 10 minutes later just after the coroner was called. The officer in charge had stopped all railroad traffic to ensure the safety of the investigating team and was waiting for the medical examiner to arrive..

"What do we have here officer?" The detective asked.

"The body is pretty beaten up, but he did have a driver's license and a school id in his wallet and he was wearing a letterman jacket. He also had a note in his pocket." He replied handing over a plastic covered sheet of notebook paper.

"Forgive me for what I have done. I love you mom and tell Dawn that I am sorry." The detective read out loud as the medical examiner arrived.

"Pretty short and to the point don't you think doc?" He said after showing it to the medical examiner.

"You never know about a suicide, detective, no one knows what goes on in a person head."

"It looks like he's been dead for about 8 hours." The doctor told the detective as the medical examiners' technicians loaded the body onto the hearse.

"This looks pretty cut and dry detective. It wont take me long to do a positive id and run a cause of death."

"Thanks doc, I'll be waiting for your call." He told the medical examiner as he got back in his car.

The investigating officer sat in his car doing his paperwork, knowing that later that day he would have the job of telling Brandon's mother that her son was dead.

When Detective Jones arrived back at the station he was called into the captain's office.

"Sit down Jones." The captain instructed.

"I hear that the Phillips boy committed suicide on the train tracks this morning?"

"Well, the medical examiner is going to check his fingerprints to make a positive id but it does look like him."

"As soon as the M.E. makes a positive id I want you to close the Smith girl's hit and run case."

"But why, there was no evidence to link Brandon Phillips with the Smith girl's hit and run."

"Because, I just got off the phone with the D.A. and he wants the case closed and filed as Brandon Phillips being the main suspect and that he committed suicide from his apparent guilt."

"Captain, this isn't right. You're going blame the Phillip's boy when he has no way to defend himself for a crime that he most likely didn't commit." The detective said in a raised voice.

"Detective, unless you want to go back to traffic duty by the end of the day, you better calm down and file this report. Officially this case is closed. Do you understand me Detective?" He said with authority.

"Yes sir." He said sarcastically as he left his office.

"This isn't right. Something is going on here." The detective mumbled to himself.

"Thank you for your cooperation in this matter captain." The District Attorney said as he hung up the phone.

"Everything is taken care of Mr. Robespierre."

"I knew that we could come to a mutual agreement in this matter." Leopold said as he shook the district attorneys hand as he said his goodbyes and then walked out the door.

The district attorney had seen a lot of cases in his career but nothing like this. He also never felt as threatened with harm to himself or his family as he did now. He knew that implicating Brandon in Grace's murder was wrong but his family was worth more than Brandon's reputation. After he made sure that Leopold was gone he got in his car and headed home. On the phone he told his wife to pick up their daughter early from school and that he would meet them at home. She was in total shock when she arrived home with her daughter to find him at the door waiting with bags packed. After a quick argument ending with him telling her to trust him they got in his car and left town.

Chapter 39

The detective's phone rang and when he looked at the caller id he knew that it was the medical examiner's office.

"Hello, detective Jones, how may I help you?" He said politely.

"Detective Jones, this is the medical examiner, I have made a positive id of Brandon but if you could I would like to discuss some things with you."

"I will be there in a few minutes.'

He arrived to find the doctor over the corpse like he had seen so many times before.

"What do you have this time?" He asked inquisitively.

"Nothing much, officially Brandon Phillips committed suicide and death was caused by an impact with a train."

"That's the official statement, but." The detective interrupted.

"I just wanted to show you this. Brandon just had a physical at the start of school so all his records are up to date. He was in perfect health, low cholesterol, his blood pressure was good, no drugs or alcohol in his system. But the Brandon that I just examined had high cholesterol, his blood pressure was high, he had the starting of atherosclerosis along with the fact that his hair had started to gray. He also had a high concentration of epinephrine in his blood."

"So what are you trying to tell me, off the record of course?"

"What I am trying to say is that Brandon Phillip was showing the signs of advanced aging the same way that his father was."

"Couldn't that be genetic?"

"Maybe, but I don't think so. The other thing is the night of the hit and run a nurse at the emergency room told me that the Smith girl's skin looked like that of a hundred year old woman."

"Well, did you do an autopsy on her?"

"No, the cause of death was apparent so there was no need for an autopsy."

"So doc, what are you trying to tell me?"

"What I am trying to say is that I believe that all three of these deaths were caused by the same thing."

"Doctor, how could that be? Now you are really starting to sound a little off center."

"I don't know, but I do know that everyone of them showed the same signs of advanced aging when there shouldn't have been any."

The detective was intrigued at what the medical examiner was saying, if the doctor was right then his suspicion about the witness at the park might have been justified. The only problem was he simply seemed to have vanished and if anyone knew his whereabouts there weren't talking.

"Well, Doc, this case is closed, along with the hit and run."

"What how is that, do you find the culprit?"

"Between you and me no, but I was told this morning that the D.A. wanted the case closed and Brandon Phillips filed as the primary suspect."

"How can that be, I thought you weren't able to find anything to link Brandon to the Smith girl's death."

"We couldn't, so I don't know what is going on." He told the doctor in disgust.

"Something definitely is but I couldn't tell you, but I would say to watch your back."

"Thanks Doc, I'll see you around." He said as he left the examining room.

That morning Max was sitting on a bench in the park like he done so many other times. He was just enjoying the stillness of nature and sat there in solitude. Sitting there with his eyes closed he was just trying to drink in the sounds of his surroundings. It was quite a relaxing place to be and it would allow him to relinquish the thoughts in his head. Though the park was almost deserted he wasn't alone, someone was watching him, stalking him like a cat. The unknown figure moved silently through the trees and came closer and closer to Max until he was just about to touch him.

"Good morning, Phillip." Max said

"I never could sneak up on you, brother. How are you?"

"What do you want, haven't you done enough." He scoffed.

"Is that any way to treat you brother that you haven't seen in years?" Phillip responded coyly.

"You didn't have to kill the old man."

"Yes I did, you know he would have recovered. They all do."

"I guess I should say thank you. Phillip, I talked to Leopold, I know it was you who killed Grace."

"I know you are hurt, but I had a job to do and I did it, all I want now is the photo album, don't take it personally."

"I don't think the photo album exists, I think it was a ruse, I don't think it ever existed. I think she just wanted to die." Max said remorsefully."

"I understand why you killed her, but why did you kill Brandon?"

"Was that his name? I thought it was a perfect ending to a perfect mystery. They'll be talking about this for years. I didn't really mean to kill him that way though; it was such a waste of years. A strong young man like that would have added a good fifty years to my life."

"So why did you put him on the train tracks?"

"Well, I was walking down the street last night and he came out of nowhere and stabbed me in the chest. "Die, you demon." He told me. Apparently he thought that I was you, because you should have seen the terror on his face when he realized that he had just stabbed a stranger."

"So then what happened?"

"Well I was able to grab him with one hand and then I grabbed the knife with the other. "The stake was just to pin us to the ground, to kill us you have to cut off our heads." I told him as I pulled the knife out of my chest. You should have seen the terror in his eyes. In my anger I threw him up against a wall. He was apparently in a weaken condition and he died. I simply put a note in his pocket and placed his body on the train tracks. Leopold took care of the D.A. and as of this morning the Grace Smith hit and run case has been closed. I just wonder why a strong young man like that died so easily, is there something you're not telling me?" He said with a laugh.

"I think you already know, you've been watching me ever since I arrived."

"Max, you can't change who you are, once a man eater always a man eater, no matter how hard you try and suppress it, some day the heart of the lion is going to come out."

"Look Max it is time to go, get Destiny and get out of here. I am warning you as my brother. Don't put me in a position like Grace did." Phillip said sincerely.

"I understand." Max said as Phillip got up to leave.

"I am sure we will see each other more from now on." Phillip said with a smirk as he flashed the heart to Max.

"Phillip it will drive you mad, just like all the others."

"Maybe or maybe I am already mad." Phillip laughed.

"No doubt about that." Max responded.

"I will see you later, hopefully under better circumstances." Phillip said as he finally walked away.

Max watched Phillip disappear into the woods and he prepared to get up and leave.

Chapter 40

It didn't take long for news to spread once the medical examiner released a positive id of Brandon. Dawn's phone started to ring and Mrs. Sinclair answered it. Dawn didn't take notice and went back to doing her homework. A few minutes later Mrs. Sinclair was knocking on Dawn's bedroom door.

"Dawn, are you in there?" She said with a shaky voice.

"Of course mom, where else would I be?" She said sarcastically as she opened the door.

"Dawn, I want you to sit down."

"Mom, what's wrong." She said in a panic.

"Brandon Phillips committed suicide this morning."

"What? That can't be. Why would he do such a thing?" She said almost screaming.

"I don't know, but the pastor and a couple other women from church are going over there now to help Mrs. Phillips deal with all of this, would you want to come with me?"

"What, how could I go over there? This is all too crazy, first dad, then Grace and now Brandon." She said as she reached for her coat.

"Where are you going?" Her mother asked.

"To the park, I need some time to process all of this."

"Alright, but be home before it gets dark." Her mother said as compassionately as she could.

Dawn opened the door and headed to the park.

"Aren't you going to drive?"

"No, I need some fresh air." She said as she pulled her cell phone out of her pocket.

Mrs. Sinclair knew something was wrong and that Dawn knew more about everything that was going on then she would admit. She knew that she couldn't deny it any longer and needed to find out how Dawn was involved. She opened the telephone book and looked up the police department number.

"Saratoga Springs Police Department, how may I help you?" The receptionist answered.

"Hello, may I have the homicide department?" She asked

"Homicide, Detective Jones speaking, how may I help you?"

"Detective, my name is Mrs. Sinclair and I have a daughter Dawn, she and Brandon Phillips use to date."

"OK, what can I do for you?" He said intrigued.

"I am afraid that she might know more than she is telling me about Grace Smith death and Brandon's suicide."

"What makes you think that?" He asked more intrigued than ever.

"She has just been acting strange since Sunday and after she heard about Brandon's death she headed for the park."

"Why is that strange?"

"She was with Max Smith, Grace's brother, on Sunday at the park and I know he spends a lot of time there, I think she went there to talk to him."

"I'm sorry ma' am, but that isn't a lot to consider when it comes to a murder case. What do you want me to do?"

"I am afraid that Max Smith might have something to do with all of this and that my daughter might be in some sort of danger." She said frantically.

Max was heading to the parking lot when he saw Dawn walking towards him. He could tell that she was upset and had been crying as he walked closer to her.

"You killed him, you're a monster you killed him!" She screamed as she ran up to him and started beating on his chest.

"I didn't kill anyone, what are you talking about?" He said as he held her hands to keep her from hitting him.

"Brandon, they found his body on the train tracks this morning, they said that he committed suicide, but I know the truth, you killed him!"

"No, I did not kill him; I didn't see him after the park incident." He said.

"How do I know that, how do I know that anything that you tell me is the truth, you could plant the idea in my head, couldn't you, you could look into my eyes and make me forget anything, right?" She said with tears streaming down her face.

"Yes, I could, but you have to believe me, I didn't kill him and I am telling you the truth."

"But you know who did, right?"

"Yes, I know who did."

"But there is nothing you can do right? You're just a sheep in this "Network" of yours. You're just following orders, right?" She said demanding an answer.

"No! It's not like that. You don't understand. The "Network" is far more reaching than you can imagine. Leopold has pressured the district attorney into closing Grace's case and implicating Brandon."

"Maybe you didn't kill him, but your silence makes you just as guilty. These people are getting away with murder and you won't do anything!"

"What would you have me do? Go to the police? Tell the newspapers? I promise you that as soon as I would try something like that, I would end up dead just like Grace did."

"I am tired of all of this, life means nothing to you and your kind, I understand why you're called children of the devil."

Dawn's last statement cut Max to the heart and he became noticeable upset.

"Look, I am not a child of the devil; I am a human being just like you. I breath, I bleed and I feel." He said sternly.

Dawn could see that she had touched a nerve and was frightened at his demeanor and that his eyes had become red with fury. She started to walk backwards away from him when someone called out his name.

"Max Smith?" The detective called out showing the two of them his badge.

"Yes, that is me." He responded as he calmed down.

"Do you mind coming with me to answer some questions?"

"What is this about?" Dawn asked.

"It's about Brandon Phillips and his suicide. I need both of you to come down to the station. I would like to ask you some questions pertaining to the case."

"Are you arresting me?" Dawn asked in a panic.

"No, it's up to you. I would just like to fill in some time line gaps in the case."

"Alright." Dawn said after she looked at Max for his approval.

She was terrified at this point and wasn't going anywhere without Max. She might have been upset about Brandon but Max still made her feel safe.

"This shouldn't take long, so you both can ride in my car if you would like." The detective said politely.

The detective opened the door for Dawn and she got in while Max walked around the back and got in on the other side. The detective shut Dawn's door and walked around the front and opened the driver's door to get in.

"Detective Jones." Phillip called.

The detective turned around to find Phillip standing in front of him. He recognized Phillip from the sketch of the witness to the hit and run.

"You're John Villisca." He said as he placed his hand on his weapon.

"Do not come any closer." He demanded.

"What did I do officer?" Phillip responded as he took another step closer.

"I will shoot you where you stand if you come any closer." The detective said as he drew his weapon.

Dawn sat terrified in the back waiting to see what was going to happen. Max on the other hand stared at the confrontation and knew that it wasn't going to end well.

"Stay in the car, Mr. Smith." The detective instructed Max as he saw that the door was opening.

Max quickly shut and door and sat there in silence. The detective held Phillip at bay until he slightly turned to reach into the car and make a call to the station. Within a blink of an eye Phillip was standing with the gun pressed up against his chest.

"Wrong answer." Phillip said as the detective saw his face distort and his eyes turn fiery red.

The detectives training kicked in and within a heartbeat he had fired his weapon four times into Phillip's chest. Dawn started to scream as she watched Phillip fall backward to the ground. He appeared dead to the detective but Max knew better and it was just a ploy to get the detective closer to him. Without thinking Max opened the door and stood up.

"Get back into the car or I will drop you too!" The detective shouted.

"Max, get back in the car!" Dawn screamed.

Dawn thought to open her door and run but she still felt safer in the back seat.

The detective now had Max in his sights when he reached back for the radio to call in for an ambulance and backup.

"I wouldn't do that." Max interjected.

"Shut up sir and get back in the car."

As the detective grabbed the radio Phillip grabbed him and spun him around. Phillip had him by the collar and began to pick him up. The detective would have shot him again but one gaze into Phillips eyes and he dropped his weapon on the ground.

"Stop Phillip! What are you going to do, kill a cop?" Max yelled.

"I'm not going to kill him, but I will give him something to remember me by." Phillip said with a laugh as he brought up his other hand and began to cup his hands around the detectives head.

"You can't imagine how much that hurt, but you will know in just a minute." He said sternly.

"Make him stop!" Dawn yelled as she stood behind the car.

After hearing Dawn yell, the officer's body made a sickening thud as Phillip dropped him.

"What are we going to do with her, Max?" He asked in frustration.

"You're not going to do anything, I will handle it." Max responded.

"Max, I don't think you will. I don't think you can, so I will have to handle, like I had to handle everything else."

"Don't even think about it Phillip, I told you I will handle it and I will. Just get out of here, its over." Max said with authority.

"You think you are going to tell me what to do. I tell you what to do. I'm not the outcast anymore and I am not you're dog that you can kick around." He told Max.

Dawn wasn't sure what to do. If she ran, Phillip most likely would run her down. She could only hope that Max would protect her, but after their fight in the park, she wasn't so sure she could trust him anymore.

"Max, step aside, you're my brother and I don't want to hurt you. Go get Destiny and leave." He demanded.

"I can't Phillip. I won't let you do this."

"Or what, you're going to stop me, you sniveling little weakling."

"If I have to." Max said blocking Dawn from Phillip.

Phillip was right, he was much stronger than Max, but he couldn't concentrate very well anymore. Years of draining people left him with a thousand voices in his head, Max on the other hand could still pinpoint his concentration.

"You fool." Phillip muttered as he rushed Max and picked him up over his head like a rag doll and then pounding him onto the trunk of the car.

He grabbed him at his waist and spun Max around so his head hit the rear fender with a thud.

"Stop it!" Dawn screamed.

"Don't worry pretty girl, I won't kill him, but I am going to teach him a lesson." He told her as he continued to beat on Max.

The impact the Max made with the trunk made it open up. Dawn was terrified but she was sure that Phillip was going to kill Max and had to do something. She looked into the truck and pulled out a tire iron and tried to get close to Phillip while he was distracted. Max was doing his best to fight back but Phillip was just too strong and for now all Max could do was to take a beating.

"I will let you live long enough to see me drain every last ounce of life out of your pretty little girl friend." Phillip told Max as he lay there on the ground.

Dawn saw her opportunity so she reached back with all her might and struck Phillip in the head with the tire iron knocking him to the ground with Max. The blow didn't do much to hurt him and subsequently grabbed the iron from her when she tried to get a second blow in.

"You stupid little girl." He said to her as he threw her to the ground.

Knowing that Phillip intended on killing her she began to scream for help.

"Go ahead and scream, no one is going to hear you." He said fiendishly as he started to walk over to her.

She tried to get up, but she was in to much pain so she started to crawl away from him.

"Where are you going to go? You can't out run me." He said with a laugh.

As Phillip loomed closer to Dawn, Max had revived and stood up. He had time to allow his energy to recharge and he knew what he had to do. He ran to Phillip and put his hands around his head before Phillip had time to react Max released his total life force into Phillip while Dawn lay there watching it all like it was some sort of bad dream. Phillip's body couldn't contain the energy and with a scream a blue ball of light emanated out of him and then he exploded.

With his life force completely spent Max collapsed onto the pavement. Dawn was able to crawl over to him as she watched as his appearance started to change. The vibrant young man that she once knew started to age before her eyes. His hair started to turn gray and his face started to fill with wrinkles.

"Is he dead?" He asked in a whisper.

"Yes, he exploded." She told him as she put his head onto her lap.

He slid his hand into his pocket and pulled out his cell phone and attempted to make a call.

"Leopold, this is Max, I am at the park, and Phillip is dead. We need a clean up crew right now." He said in between breaths as his life slowly faded away.

"You have to get out of here." He told Dawn in a labored voice.

"I can't leave you, I can get help, I can save you." She said as tears flowed down her face.

"You already did, you lead me to the hope." He softly muttered.

With his last ounce of strength he reached up and touched her face for the last time.

"I love you, you have to leave or Leopold will kill you." He said as he breathed his last.

"I love you too Max." She softly whispered into his ear as she cautiously laid his head on the ground and got up. It broke her heart to leave him there but she had seen what kind of person Leopold was and knew that he would kill her if she stayed.

Epilogue

Mrs. Smith entered the lobby of Leopold's office.

"Hello Destiny, may I help you?" The receptionist asked.

Mrs. Smith was well known and well liked in the network. Even though she always seemed a little on the eccentric side, but when it came to their kind, being on the eccentric side was nothing new.

"I have an appointment to see Leopold." She replied.

"Yes, I will call to see if he is ready."

As the receptionist called she felt the photo album held tightly under her arm.

"You can go in now."

"Thanks." She said as she got up and headed for the door.

"Welcome, Destiny, how are you?" Leopold asked as he got up to meet her.

"I just came to give you this." She remarked as she handed him the photo album.

"Where in the world did you find it?" He asked energetically

"I had it all along; all you had to do is ask." She replied.

"You don't know what this means to me Destiny. You just don't know." He said as he reached out to give her a hug.

As he reached out to hold her Destiny reached her arm behind him and gave him a tight squeeze.

"I know, Leopold, I know." She said confidently.

Within a second of their embrace she pulled a knife out of her pocket and thrust it up under his rib cage and directly into his heart.

"For Grace." She whispered as she turned the knife once she drove it in as deep as it would go.

Leopold gave out a slight moan as his skin began to age. He began the throws of death as she held on to him twice as hard. He was trying with his last breath to break free but she was much stronger than he was. She never lost eye contact with him and looked into his cold dark eyes as he looked into hers, ablaze with rage.

She watched his face as his agony became evident and the aging process began. She knew that she would have to hold him long enough to ensure that he was dead as his face started to show his actual age. Within moments he breathed his last breath and his skin fell off his bones like dust as she let go of him and his bones fell to the floor and shattered like fine porcelain.

She looked down to make sure that he was all but gone and nothing remained but the dust of the "Heartless Demon". She calmly stooped over and picked up the knife from the pile of debris and headed for the table.

"Margaret, can you come in here." She said over the intercom.

A look of shock came over Margaret's face as she entered the room to see Destiny sitting in Leopold's chair and the pile of dust on the floor.

"Margaret."

"Yes, Ma'am?" She responded like a peasant to a queen.

"Leopold has retired and I have assumed his position." She told her matter of fact.

"Yes, Ma'am."

"Will you send out a memo telling the members of my new tenure?" She asked politely.

"Yes, Ma'am." She replied.

"Ma'am?" Margret asked.

"Yes."

"The king is dead, long live the queen." She said with joy in her heart.

Margaret had worked for Leopold for many years and had been witness to many of his schemes and murderous plans. She was happy to see him gone and wasn't about to shed a tear for him.

"Thank you Margaret, and oh, could you send someone up here to clean up this mess?" She asked.

"Of course Ma'am, I will get someone up here right away."

"Thank you."

Margaret left the room and shut the door behind her and left Destiny there by herself.

"I'm sorry Grace that I didn't save you." She whispered to herself.

After sitting there pondering her new position she stood up and went to the window.

"Look out world, because here I come."

The End